# BATMAN
## *FEAR ITSELF*

# BATMAN
## FEAR ITSELF

## MICHAEL REAVES & STEVEN-ELLIOT ALTMAN

### Batman created by Bob Kane

BALLANTINE BOOKS • NEW YORK

*Batman: Fear Itself* is a work of fiction. Names, places, and incidents either are products of the author's imagination or are used fictitiously.

A Del Rey Mass Market Original

Published in the United States by Del Rey Books, an imprint of The Random House Publishing Group, a division of Random House, Inc., New York.

ISBN 978-0-345-47943-3

Printed in the United States of America

www.delreybooks.com
www.dccomics.com
Keyword: DC Comics on AOL

OPM   9   8   7   6   5   4   3   2   1

This one is dedicated, with enormous appreciation,
to Maya Bohnhoff

*The only thing we have to fear is fear itself.*
—FRANKLIN DELANO ROOSEVELT

*The oldest and strongest emotion of mankind is fear. And the oldest and strongest kind of fear is fear of the unknown.*
—H. P. LOVECRAFT

*Terror is a most excellent emotion.*
—GREY BERWALD, *Gotham Citizen Magazine*

# ACKNOWLEDGMENTS

A tip of the tie-in writer's hat to my editors, Keith Clayton at Del Rey Books and Chris Cerasi at DC Comics; to John Nee; Steve Saffel; and to all the artists, writers, producers, et al., who made the Dark Knight what he is today.

# PROLOGUE

It was autumn in Gotham City.

This in itself was not surprising; the world turned on its axis, and the seasons changed, especially in this northeastern corner of the country. It was the last week in October, and the trees along Blake Boulevard were brilliant, every one of them, with scarlet, auburn, burgundy, and other rich colors. The air was still and crisp; every drawn breath promised winter. The sky was remarkably clear, the pale shade of a little boy's blanket that had been washed many times.

It was a remarkable day, thought Alfred Pennyworth, as he turned the Bentley left onto Churchward Street. He wondered if his passenger had noticed this. He had never asked him, *Are you aware of such things as fallen leaves, or the taste of a coming frost, or the crystalline quality of the sunlight? Do those things still touch you, stir you, make you long to linger on an autumn sidewalk or lie among the leaves, looking up into the pale blue vault?*

And why hadn't he asked? He was, after all, not a "normal" gentleman's gentleman, nor was his passenger a "normal" employer, nor did they have a "normal" employer–employee relationship. For one thing, a "normal" gentleman's gentleman did not drive Bentleys equipped with bulletproof shielding and police band scanners . . .

Even as the thought crossed Alfred's mind, the receiver crackled to life. This, too, was not surprising—the particular radio wavelength reserved for the constabulary was never quiet for long in Gotham City.

"*All units in Kubrick District . . . Code Two, Diamond Express Line . . . possible runaway train, say again, possible runaway train . . .*"

The voice from the darkened backseat was soft, but with steel underlying it. "Turn right on Hammett Street, Alfred. Stop in the middle of the block, over the manhole."

"As you wish, Master Bruce."

"And Alfred?"

"Yes, sir?"

"Step on it."

"Very good, sir."

The butler-*cum*-chauffeur pushed the gas pedal a fraction of an inch farther toward the floorboard, and the powerful engine responded immediately. He put on the turn signal and maneuvered the big machine around the corner onto the narrow, cobbled street. He did not have to glance in the rearview mirror to know what was transpiring in the backseat. Master Bruce had become quite adept in the last few years at quickly divesting himself of suits or evening wear and donning his "work clothes," even in the relatively cramped confines of the Bentley. In some other cities, phone booths were de rigueur, he'd heard.

What was amazing to Alfred was how sanguine he had become about the whole business.

He braked to a stop in the middle of the street, as requested. Traffic was light. Hammett was a residential thoroughfare, lined on both sides with brownstones and trees in small sidewalk plots of dirt, bound by wrought iron as if they might pull up their roots and attempt to escape. It was a one-way street, too narrow to allow traffic in both directions when cars were parked. Most of Gotham City's streets were like that, since most of them were well over two hundred years old. The equally aged brownstones were typical of city architecture; there was more than a hint of Gothic in Gotham.

"Please deliver Mr. Stack my regrets, Alfred, and reschedule our meeting. I'm sure you'll handle it with your usual diplomacy."

"Of course, sir. I look forward to the experience."

A horn honked impatiently behind them. Alfred looked in the left side mirror. A Lexus SUV sat on their rear bumper, its florid-faced driver glaring through the windshield. The vehicle's pristine finish testified to its unfamiliarity with off-road travel.

"Ten more seconds, Alfred."

The red-faced Lexus owner leaned on his horn. A woman wrapped in a paisley housecoat and walking a shih tzu glanced at the Bentley suspiciously. Alfred sighed, resigned.

He felt, more than heard, the egress plate in the automobile's floor slide open, then close a moment later. He sighed again, this time with relief, and accelerated. At the end of the block he turned left onto Hartsbred Drive, which, if memory correctly served, would take him to the Aparo Expressway.

The Lexus turned left as well. Its driver pulled up level with the Bentley, and the florid man made an obscene gesture at Alfred. He saw it from the corner of his eye, but did not give the lout the satisfaction of reacting. The other car roared on ahead.

*Sometimes, Master Bruce,* he thought, *I wonder why you bother.*

But he knew the answer to that.

# BATMAN
## FEAR ITSELF

1

*Trust the night.*

The sensei had told him that, not long after he had gone to Japan to study under the old man's tutelage. He'd no idea at the time—he still didn't—how Master Yoru had divined his intention, his purpose . . . his *Plan*. But somehow, he had. Bruce Wayne had known that from nearly the first day they'd met, in the peaceful dojo of lacquered wood and painted shoji, and he knew that the martial arts master had known he knew.

Eighty years old, at least, and nearly blind in one eye, judging by the cloud of cataract tissue that had spread across it. Yet he'd still been able to move like water between rocks, strike like iron against rice paper. No one in the dojo could touch him. Bruce doubted that anyone in the East could touch him.

He had learned much.

*Trust the night.*

The phrase always flickered like heat lightning through his mind as he entered the shadows. He quickly descended the rungs of rusted and verdigris-crusted iron, his cloak draping him. The tunnels were almost large enough to stand in upright; the storm drains and sewers that snaked below Gotham City rivaled those of Paris or Vienna in their size and complexity. They—and the rooftops—were by far the quickest and easiest way to get from one area of the city to another.

He moved swiftly along the relatively dry embankment. The sewer stench didn't bother him; he was used to it, plus he had daubed mentholated salve beneath his nostrils before leaving the car. It was a practice he had learned watching coroners and forensics investigators working over cadavers.

The darkness was nearly total, but his footing was sure, despite the occasional patches of slime and offal on the wet concrete. The wafer-thin white gallium arsenide plates that hid his eyes were Generation Five light amplifiers, developed, as was so much of his personal arsenal, by the R&D staff of Wayne Technologies. Their primary clients were the armed forces and private security firms. Their customer satisfaction quotient was high, largely because he field-tested most of the prototypes himself.

There were occasional cryptic combinations of numbers and letters stenciled on the curving walls, or at intersections; often these were nearly obliterated by decades of water and mold. They spoke, to those who could read them, of drainage levels, basin and sub-basin locations, outlet control junctions, and the like. They also gave directions. Following these, he turned left at a T-intersection, left again at a branching conduit. Eventually he was stopped by a rust-weakened iron grid, which one thrust of his booted heel easily reduced to chunky powder.

He was now in what the city infrastructure plans called the North Corridor Project. This had been originally intended as a linking commuter line, but had been abandoned in the late 1960s, when it was decided to put the Diamond Express Line in at a deeper level. The corridor now served as an emergency runoff drain during severe storms.

It would also, in this case, serve as an emergency access to the runaway train.

A small heads-up display blinked on just above his left eye plate, summoned by a subvocalized command. Along with a compass, temperature gauge, and air toxicity sampler, it gave him a digital time readout.

He had less than thirty seconds.

From one of his belt compartments he took a small quantity of plastic explosive and quickly molded it in a three-foot-wide circle in the center of the corridor's floor. The material was another WayneTech development—it had a TNT equivalence 20 percent higher than C4, and a brisance factor of thirty thousand feet per second. He moved back ten feet, shielded himself with his cloak, and triggered the built-in soft-circuit detonator.

The flash was dazzling, even with the Gen-5 polarizers. The audio circuitry in the cowl dampened the sound of the blast, and the shaped charge directed most of the concussion wave downward. Even so, it was not an experience he cared to repeat anytime soon.

Through the mist of aerosolized concrete and masonry he could see a ragged hole, its circumference punctuated by torn rebar. The eighteen-inch-thick floor of the drain was also, at this juncture, the ceiling of the Diamond Express tunnel.

Even as he stepped forward, he could feel the vibration beneath him begin to build, could see the faint light of the approaching train.

He would have only one shot at this.

He gathered the cloak around him, stepped forward, and dropped through the hole.

*Trust the night.*

For nearly five years now it had been his best ally; better than the R&D team, with their white lab coats and their computer modeling and their solemn expressions; certainly better than the GCPD, by turns brutal and blundering, with one of the lowest credibility ratings of any city in the country; even better than Alfred Pennyworth, esq., that irreplaceable and irrepressible butler who was also a certified field medic, a fair mechanic, a passable cook, and many more things, not the least of which was surrogate family and confidant without peer. It was the truth, pure and simple; he could not have done any of this without Alfred's help and support. He wasn't sure the butler would take that as a sterling character recommendation, but it was true nonetheless.

Yet even so, the darkness remained his first and foremost ally. It sheltered him, created and maintained the fear his enemies felt for him—even, in an odd way, nourished him. After all, he had lived with it for so long . . . ever since the age of eight.

Now, as he dropped through the hole, the darkness once again welcomed him. He landed lightly, one foot on either side of the third rail. The light was increasing steadily, as was the vibration. He leapt quickly to the narrow maintenance walkway that ran the length of the tunnel.

The roar of the wheels against the track grew louder. The cowl's circuitry automatically dampened anything over eighty-five dB but could do nothing about the bone-jarring vibration. The light filled the tunnel with stark, flowing chiaroscuro. He estimated the train's speed at better than sixty miles per hour. Faces in the windows flickered by, less than eighteen inches from him, a magic lantern of terror.

The timing had to be perfect; he wouldn't get a second chance.

The instant the last car shot past, he jumped.

His fingers locked around the rear guard railing; his feet found the plate. His cape snapped out to its full length behind him. The network of aramid polyfibers woven into his suit tightened in response to the sudden stress and kept his shoulders from being dislocated, although just barely. He pulled himself forward, fighting the momentum of the train. In situations like these, the cape was more a hindrance than a help, although it was light enough not to seriously impede him.

He tried the door but, not surprisingly, it was locked. He could see through the car's rear window that the interior was empty, save for an old couple huddled in one of the forward seats. He motioned to them, gesturing that they should let him in, but it was obvious that they were too frightened to move.

The train's momentum and sway made it impossible to try to cut or force the door open; the same applied to the reinforced window. He had to find another way to stop the hurtling juggernaut.

There was but one way, insane though it seemed. He had to reach the front of the train, and only one route was even remotely possible.

He reached up, seized the edge of the car's roof, and pulled himself up. Another moment and he was spread-eagled on the convex surface.

He kept himself flattened out as much as possible; there was less than two feet of clearance between the top of the car and the tunnel ceiling. Emergency light boxes mounted at regular intervals narrowed the gap even more.

He inched forward.

There were six cars; it felt like sixty. He crawled toward the lead car with agonizing slowness, acutely aware of the light boxes, piping, and other obstacles whizzing by so close overhead. Occasionally he glimpsed large, illuminated signs marking emergency exits flashing by. It seemed incredible to him that thrill-seeking teenagers would voluntarily seek out situations like this, yet he knew they did. "Subway surfing," they called it. A boy had been killed only last week on the Opal Line, his head crushed to a red ruin when he had misjudged the clearance.

He wondered why the system fail-safes had not automatically applied the emergency brakes when the routing computer first logged the runaway. He recalled that there had been a collision last year due to a switching mistake. The computer had applied the emergency brakes; the system had worked, insofar as programming went. Due to city budget cutbacks, however, the signal spacing and safety parameters—set back in 1907 when trains were slower, shorter, and lighter—had never been updated. The emergency brake system had not been able to stop the train in time, and thirty-six people had died. Perhaps something similar had gone awry this time.

Or perhaps there was another, more sinister reason for this.

While it was true that Occam's razor was best applied to situations like these, he had learned through bitter experience over the past several years that the simplest explanation was not always the right one in Gotham. This emergency might very well have been caused by operator carelessness, software failure, or a dozen other reasons that had nothing to do with terrorism or sabotage. In most cities that might well be the case. But this was

Gotham City, where the veneer of sanity was always stretched very thin.

He quickly went over the list of possible suspects as he wormed his way toward the front of the train. Harvey Dent? Unlikely; unless another train disaster had occurred or was likely to occur within the city limits very soon, this did not fit the former city attorney's insane "Rule of Two" modus operandi.

Cobblepot? Another thematic stretch; to the best of his admittedly limited knowledge there was nothing relating to birds going on down here.

Pamela Isley, Jervis Tetch, Victor Fries . . . again, all adhered fairly rigidly to the fixations and obsessions that had led the media to assign them their colorful nicknames. While it was true that it sometimes required deductive reasoning to find the connection, he had come, over the years, to develop a fairly good instinct as to who was behind what crimes. The fact that all the rogues who had come so far to mind were still incarcerated meant little; all had escaped before, and would no doubt do so again.

Also, with the occasional exception of Poison Ivy and Mr. Freeze, all were motivated by the same lure that had attracted criminals since time immemorial: easy money. Unless some sort of ransom had been demanded, sending a train on a runaway course didn't seem a very viable way to get rich quick.

But there was one whose madness was not restrained by avarice—or, it seemed, any other human desire. One who killed, tortured, and terrorized for the sheer, sick joy of the deeds themselves.

The Joker.

*If he's escaped again, then God help us all.*

There was no more time for speculation; he had reached

the lead car. He peered over the roof's lip, through the windshield into the engineer's compartment. The driver, a young woman, was slumped back and to one side in her chair, her knees drawn up to her chin, her hands nowhere near the controls. From this angle it was impossible to tell if she was alive or dead.

He contemplated the windshield. At this speed, penetrating it could have unforeseen circumstances, not the least of which was turning the forward compartment into a dead-end wind tunnel. He inched his way back to the accordion-pleated passage between the driver's compartment and the rest of the cars. He removed a bat-shaped blade from his belt—"Batarangs," the press had dubbed them—then reached down sideways as far as he could and slashed the tough, vulcanized material in roughly the shape of an X. He dropped his feet over the edge of the train's roof and kicked.

The stiff fabric gave, if grudgingly, and he was able to squeeze into the passage, his feet finding the metal pivot joint that formed its flexible floor. A glance back over his shoulder gave him a brief look at a woman's startled face. He ignored her, facing front and the door to the engineer's compartment. The door was locked, as regs demanded.

From another section of his belt came a tiny plastic vial, one of several different chemicals he carried with him. This one held concentrated hydrofluoric acid. He squeezed a thin stream onto the lock. The door made a popping sound as the airtight seal was breached. He stepped back long enough to let the Air-tech Type II filter in his mask detect the presence of dangerous gases.

There were none. He pulled the door open and let himself into the compartment.

He took in the situation at a glance. The driver wasn't

dead, as he had feared, but she was clearly not functional; she huddled against the wall in a fetal position, chin to chest, eyes tightly closed, moaning to herself. There would be no help forthcoming from her.

He glanced up and out the windshield. The train was beginning to ascend, nearing the terminus at Wayne Tower. He gave his full attention to the controls. They appeared simple enough: a large, knobbed lever mounted on a slanted dashboard. From a neutral center position, he knew, one moved the lever clockwise to increase speed and counterclockwise to brake. Right now, the lever was pushed to the right as far as possible. The train was running full-out.

He grabbed the lever in both hands, expecting resistance. Instead, to his surprise, it moved easily back, and the train began to slow in response. Within moments it had come to a stop.

He exhaled in relief. It seemed almost anticlimactic—but that was certainly something he could live with. He found the control that opened the doors. Faintly, he could hear the passengers in the cars behind him, chattering in mingled fear and relief as they disembarked.

He turned his attention to the driver. When he'd first entered the cab, he had fully expected to see her face frozen in that horrible rictus that was the physical evidence of the Joker's signature toxin. But she wasn't grinning or laughing. Instead she was rocking slightly back and forth, mumbling inaudibly. He leaned in closer to catch her words.

"In the tunnels . . . they only come out in the tunnels . . . they *feed* in the tunnels."

He waited, but she said nothing else, only repeated the same phrase over and over. Her dark skin was ashen. He put his hand on her forehead, gently peeled back an eyelid. The pupil was contracted. He passed his hand slowly before her eyes; the pupils did not react to the change in ambient light.

His augmented hearing picked up the sounds of several sets of approaching footsteps from the direction of the terminus. And something else . . .

He heard the audible gasp from the doorway behind him even as he turned. A tall, slender young woman stood in the adjoining passage, her oversized gray eyes wide. She ran a hand through short, spiky dark hair and said: "What happened?"

That question was followed by a stream of others: "Is she all right? Do you think she's high? How did you get in here? Was the train sabotaged?"

He cut the stream with a single question of his own: "Who are you?"

She blinked up at him, wonder and curiosity in her eyes, but no fear.

*Must be losing my touch,* he thought wryly.

"What? Me? Oh . . . uh . . . Magdala. Maggie, I mean—Tollyer."

"Why aren't you evacuating the train with everyone else?"

"I'm a . . . a journalist."

"You don't sound very certain of that."

"I . . ." She straightened, squared her shoulders. "I don't have to ask who you are."

And neither, he reflected, would the police, whose electric torches he could see swinging through the dim tunnel less than fifty feet from the nose of the train.

Without further comment he took the woman by the shoulders, moved her bodily aside, and slipped into the passage behind her. From there he lifted himself through the hole in the pleated cover, out onto the roof of the train, and thence to a maintenance catwalk in the shadowy roof of the terminal approach. There he crouched to watch.

Maggie Tollyer spent a couple of deep breaths wondering what had possessed her to brazen it out with Gotham's most ambiguous citizen. And that line about being a journalist—what was that? Her way of returning to the scene of the crime?

"Tunnels . . . ," murmured the driver, like a child caught in a nightmare. "They feed in the tunnels."

Maggie crouched beside the other woman. She felt her forehead—no fever, but there were beads of sweat there, though the compartment was relatively cool. Her pulse was rapid, her breathing shallow, her large, dark eyes—staring at nothing—glassy, pupils dilated.

Drugs? Allergic reaction? Forgotten meds?

The strap of a bright red backpack peeked out from beneath the driver's seat. Maggie wrestled it out and emptied it onto the floor. Lipstick—*a lovely shade of bronze,* she thought—sunscreen, hair pick, cell phone, classy little notepad with a ballpoint, plastic packet of tissues, sunglasses, tin of breath mints, wallet, checkbook, bottled water, plastic lunch pack with what looked like ravioli within, rolled-up Windbreaker, telescoping umbrella, and paperback novel. No medicine bottles presented themselves, and the breath mints, Maggie discovered when she opened the tin, really were breath mints.

The voices outside the train were growing steadily louder. She hurriedly replaced the contents of the bag, glancing at the book as she picked it up. It was the latest by the bestselling horror maven Grey Berwald, a fat novel with a lurid cover, titled *Fear Itself.* The driver was apparently about halfway through the thick volume; she'd inserted a deposit slip from her checkbook into the pages to mark her place.

Following some morbid impulse, Maggie opened the book to the marked page. Her gaze fell on the first paragraph, and she read without intention.

It was not a good place for anyone to be alone—not a navy SEAL, not a ninja, not even a hardened criminal. And for Ellen to be here—alone—was insane. She knew what these tunnels contained besides tracks, besides moss, besides rats. She'd known it when she entered, which was ample testimony to her desperation.

*They* were here.

*They* lived in the tunnels, lurking in the darkness, never fully seen, dimly glimpsed only on those occasions when something wandered into their realm. A flicker out of the corner of the eye, a scrabbling sound as much imagined as heard—and then, before you were sure if it was reality or imagination, the sharp teeth sinking into your flesh . . .

Ellen looked at the third rail and wondered how quickly it could kill her.

Maggie suppressed a deep chill. Tunnels—how creepy a coincidence was that? Her skin crawling, she started to return the book to the driver's backpack, then hesitated.

Maybe not a coincidence?

A sharp sound behind her woke her to the realization that the rescuers were making their way through the connecting corridor behind her. She jammed the paperback into her fanny pack and took up the other woman's icy hand.

"It's okay," she told her. "The paramedics are here. They'll help you."

The driver grasped the hand as if it were a lifeline. Her gaze, unfocused up till now, came fully and suddenly to life and met Maggie's. What Maggie saw there chilled her more than the words she'd just read—inarticulate, irrational, *suffocating* terror.

She rose quickly as the first paramedic stepped through the door.

He watched as the paramedics took the driver away. Watched her swiveling her neck to peer wildly back down the tracks that receded into the tunnel's gloom. Even when they fought to ease her onto a litter, she kept her eyes on the train's backtrail.

He watched the journalist, Maggie Tollyer, give a statement to the police, attuning his mask's ultrasensitive audio surveillance system to catch her half-truths.

She told the police about entering the compartment after the train had come to a stop. No, she didn't know who'd stopped it. Had to have been the driver, right? And she hadn't noticed if the fabric of the connecting corridor had been torn when she came forward.

She told them about her search of the driver's bag, looking for medication, she said. She hadn't found any. Nor had she found any sign of illegal drugs.

She didn't tell them she had met him in the driver's compartment. And she didn't mention the paperback novel she'd inexplicably lifted.

Odd.

He would have to do some checking up on Maggie Tollyer, alleged journalist.

2

The blog was going nowhere. After relating in some-what vague fashion her experience on the runaway sub-way train, Maggie's mind wandered, and her fingers slowed to a lazy, incoherent crawl on her laptop's key-board. Her gaze strayed to the paperback novel sitting atop her coffee table, while her mind toyed with the in-sane idea that there was a connection between the story in the book and the train driver's bizarre seizure.

After long moments of silent wrestling, during which she strove to drive her thoughts back to the subject at hand, her fingers wandered as well. Before she quite realized what she'd done, she found herself doing a Web search for "Grey Berwald."

Idle curiosity, she told herself.

She already knew who he was, of course. If you so much as poked your nose into a bookstore these days—whether brick and mortar, or silicon and pixels—you'd heard of Grey Berwald. If you didn't frequent book-stores, then you were still likely to see his name, face, and lurid titles and covers in magazines and newspapers, on billboards, and in the inevitable online pop-up ads.

Until very recently a casual observer might have concluded that bookstores were built merely to hawk

Berwald's wares and that his publisher, Chance Publications, had no other fiction authors in its stable.

Maggie's knowledge of the writer was entirely academic. She didn't read horror, and thought it ludicrous to set oneself up for the embarrassment of having to sleep with a night-light. She preferred nonfiction overall, but if her taste strayed occasionally to make-believe, she would pick up a mystery or historical. There was more than enough to be afraid of in Gotham City; she felt no need to exacerbate nascent paranoia.

Her lookup proved more than fruitful; there were *thousands* of links with information about Grey Berwald's life and career. He was active in fan conventions, did a plethora of book signings, and spoke at book clubs, writers' organizations, and schools. He was an alumnus of Gotham University, where he'd obtained a bachelor's degree in English but dropped out before he got his master's, saying he wanted to *do* things, not study them. He was panted after by his female fans; he was great with kids and dogs.

Maggie grimaced. *Be still my heart.*

A number of the hits linked to the website of the Horror Book Club, which, somewhat to Maggie's surprise, was not one vast advertisement for the Berwald literary dynasty. Running neck-and-neck with Berwald on the book club home page, not to mention various bestseller lists, was a writer named Todd McGraff, whose second novel, *Indigo Evil,* had been released by Normandy Publications within a month of Berwald's latest.

Of greatest interest was the official Grey Berwald site, which trumpeted the "much-heralded" release of his latest blockbuster, *Fear Itself.* She looked at a parade of book covers, from his first to his latest, noticing that, as his work grew more and more popular, the cover designs became progressively less about illustrating what lay within and more about simply advertising "another Grey Berwald book." It was an important watershed in a writer's career when he reached the point at which his name was featured at a size equal to or greater than the book's title. On Berwald's latest, his name took up 90 percent of the page; the title was ridiculously small in comparison.

The face that looked back at her from one of the sites was not a handsome one in the classical sense of the word. It was perhaps too square, with a nose that seemed an afterthought and eyes that looked too lazy, somehow, to belong to a writer of horror fiction—at least in Maggie's opinion. But something about those eyes suggested that this was a man who had never really grown up; that a child resided within, a child who still thrilled to scary stories told over toasted marshmallows.

She read one of his recent quotes:

Horror is about wanting to know what's behind the door and not wanting to know what's behind the door. As a *reader* I never want that door to open all the way, because I know I'll always be disappointed. As a *writer* I never want to open the door all the way, because I know I'll always disappoint. I want my readers to be afraid of the *door*—not what's behind it.

Maggie stood, stretched, and picked up the paperback of *Fear Itself* from the coffee table.

The deposit slip still stuck out of the top of it, marking the page the train driver had been reading. Somewhat to her surprise, Maggie realized she was reluctant to return to that page. To do so was to invite memory of the woman's vapid face and terrified eyes.

She looked at the cover and gave an involuntary shiver at the sight of it. She wasn't sure why. It was a murky depiction of a generic "dark place" with a figure silhouetted at the center in a bright and bilious green light. The figure—a woman's—was frozen in the act of turning to look over its shoulder. Berwald's name and the title were embossed in bas-relief over it. There was nothing particularly scary about it. In fact, what she found most disturbing about the book was the simple fact that she had taken it. She had lifted potential evidence from the scene of a crime.

Crime? Maggie frowned. Accident. The scene of an *accident*. Why had she thought crime?

It didn't matter really, did it? It was wrong to have taken the book. She knew it, had known it at the time—and yet here she stood with it in her hands.

Maggie opened the novel to the first page and read:

Charles Framington opened his morning paper and read the headline without fully grasping its significance at first.

ANOTHER BIZARRE DISAPPEARANCE PUZZLES LOCAL PO-LICE

Charles had swallowed a mouthful of coffee when his eyes leapt to the phrases "local artist" followed by the fragmentary question: "Kidnap, murder, or suicide?" He choked on the coffee and tried to focus on the page.

Not high art, she thought, but not bad. A few too many words in that last sentence. And he was guilty of a literary faux pas that always set her teeth on edge: having people's eyes following, falling, darting, or otherwise refusing to stay in their sockets like sensible organs.

*He probably should have died. Might've been better.*

The words were not on the page, but in her head. The

voice was hers, but distant, hovering on the brink of memory.

Maggie shook herself. She realized her breathing had turned shallow and rapid. She tried to read the words Berwald had written, but suddenly, in a vivid, hard-edged flash, she was holding a newspaper in trembling hands. The headline read: THEATRICAL HANGING: ACCIDENT OR ATTEMPTED SUICIDE?

Maggie's face and body flushed with sudden warmth; the same expectant warmth she had come to associate with live theater, where, sitting in the front row, she could feel the nap of the immense velvet curtain, soft and heavy against her face, as if it impressed itself into the air. She did not want the curtain to open.

"Damn!"

She dropped the book, jumping back as it hit the hardwood floor of her office alcove. Her arms were puckered with gooseflesh, and she rubbed at them, wondering how a writer she'd never before read could so thoroughly push her buttons.

After a moment she bent and picked up the book gingerly, then quickly put it in the top drawer of her desk, treating it almost as if it were alive and annoyed.

Was *that* what Grey Berwald was all about—finding his readers' traumatic hot buttons and pressing them? She wondered if he had any idea what his skill at that could do to an unstable psyche. She felt a renewed flush of heat, but this time it was a visceral anger that rushed up from what her New Age sister would have referred to as her "second chakra." She looked around. The office alcove was the same: walls lined with bookshelves, the small desk and swivel chair, the filing cabinets. All matching cherrywood, all illuminated by the roseate glow of the banker's desk lamp. A small electric space heater kept it comfortably warm; a cozy little space in a cozy little apartment, in an ancient high-rise. Nothing was different; nothing that she could see.

But things *felt* different. And even though she could see and feel that the heater was still working, Maggie perceived a chill, as if an icy finger were being run slowly up her spine.

She sat down at her desk. Her back was to the bookshelves; she could see the alcove's arched entrance. And even though she knew it was silly, it made her feel better.

Maggie looked down at her computer and began typing the blog again.

At some point during the past two hours, Alfred had placed a plate containing a Black Forest ham sandwich and a thermos mug of coffee next to his keyboard. Bruce noticed it when the smoky-maple taste and scent of ham intruded on his senses and he realized he was chewing.

He smiled and swallowed. "Thank you, Alfred. Is this lunch or dinner?"

Alfred, sitting at a second terminal at the other end of the long workbench, looked up and blinked owlishly through the lenses of his reading glasses. "You're entirely welcome, Master Bruce. And it's high tea."

Bruce glanced at the ongoing rendering of the photo he was digitally enhancing, and stretched. In the cavernous vault above his head, bats echoed his movement in their sleep.

"Anything?" he asked.

"It appears that Maggie Tollyer's claim to a journalistic background is no mere window dressing. Five years ago, she was a freelance reporter with seemingly endless bylines."

"And then?" Bruce watched the image on his screen—

the image of Maggie Tollyer kneeling in the cab of the subway train next to the semiconscious driver—grow increasingly sharp as the server array filled in pixels at an extremely high density. He had an entire series of digital images taken with the tiny Omni-light camera that Lucius Fox had so obligingly let him make off with, but this was the only one in which he might possibly be able to read something from the cover of the book she'd stolen.

"And then," Alfred said, "she won the Gotham Caliber Award for journalistic excellence and promptly vanished."

Bruce sat up, rocking his chair forward. "Vanished?"

"Journalistically speaking, yes. She seems to have ceased publishing her work in the print media."

"You made it sound as if she'd been kidnapped."

"Not kidnapped. She has a blog." He said the word as if it were closely related to *slug*.

"You have it in front of you?"

Alfred returned his gaze to the flat display. Colored lights danced across the lenses of his glasses. "Indeed."

Glancing once more at the rendering, Bruce got up and moved to look over Alfred's shoulder. The weblog—*Maggings,* by name—was well designed, with attractive if rather somber colors. There was no picture of Maggie Tollyer on it. Instead there were photos of people who figured in her running commentary, and some simple graphical images. Including, he noticed, a cartoon rendering of his alter ego with a link to a "Bat-Sightings" page. He'd have to check that out.

The heart of the site was the blog itself. Today's installment was a brief but acerbic piece on the subject of "Artistic Autism."

"Autism" is Latin for "self-ism." It's defined as a mental state in which the sufferer has difficulty communicating with others, and fantasy often dominates reality. The autistic personality has trouble relating to other people, and may indulge in socially inappropriate behavior because he simply can't put himself in the other person's shoes.

Ironically, the word "autistic" is one character off from "artistic," and in some cases the behavior of artists is but "one character" off as well.

Let's play "what if." What if an "artist" produced a work that triggered psychotic behavior in a borderline personality, which in turn produced catastrophic results? Who's culpable: the artist who produced the work, the venue in which the work appeared, or the consumer who absorbed the work? Or all of the above?

You could argue that the artist and the venue have no way of knowing the mental state of their consumers, and that, in the same way that a person allergic to peanuts shouldn't accept handouts from flight attendants, the mentally "allergic" shouldn't consume the artistic "peanut."

But what if the consumer doesn't realize she's allergic? Who's responsible if she finds out in a way that's both personally devastating and publicly dangerous?

Today I was party to a near disaster. Were it not for the appearance of a certain Dark Knight in shining Kevlar, I might not be alive to write this blog entry.

And now that my heart has stopped playing pinball in my chest, I'm wondering who would have been responsible if the disaster had not been averted. More later . . .

A time-and-date stamp indicated that Maggie Tollyer had posted the entry within the last fifteen minutes.

Bruce straightened, frowning, aware that Alfred was watching his face with interest. He ignored the look and, reaching over Alfred's shoulder, activated a Web tracing program named Bloodhound. Targeting the blog page, he sent the program off to sniff out activity from its source.

Alfred cleared his throat delicately. "May I assume you have some inkling of the context for this woman's ruminations?"

"Some. I'm pretty sure she's referring to the subway incident this afternoon."

Alfred's eyebrows rose. "Ah. Then you would be the 'Dark Knight in shining Kevlar'?"

"Presumably. But I don't see . . ." Bruce broke off and returned to his own computer, which had finished building its high-res rendering. The resolution was so precise, he could see that the journalist wore a sword-shaped earring with a blood-red garnet set in the hilt. Of the book cover, however, only one word was visible above Maggie Tollyer's shoulder.

"Grey."

"Excuse me, sir?"

"On the book cover. The word *Grey*—G-R-E-Y. Question is: is that part of the title or the author's first name?"

"Americans don't spell *grey* with an *e*," Alfred observed.

"So either it's a British release—maybe rare? Or . . ."

"Or the title is secondary to the writer's name. Grey Berwald, perhaps?"

*I should know this,* Bruce thought. "Right. Fantasy writer . . . ?"

"*Horror* writer, sir. You might want to take care not to make that mistake when you are introduced to him this weekend. I'm told that writers who specialize in particular genres can be sensitive about such things, although Mr. Berwald is apparently no longer concerned with such details. The publishing industry considers him one of a kind."

Now he remembered. "The Halloween party."

"Ah, you do remember. I'm relieved. It would be even more embarrassing if you failed to put in an appearance at your own costume ball."

"I remember the party, Alfred. I just don't remember everybody we invited."

"No reason you should, sir. You do have more . . . important . . . things on your plate, after all."

Bruce grimaced. Alfred Pennyworth was acutely aware of how abhorrent his employer found the Bruce Wayne half of his double life. Pretending to be a profligate wastrel who slept all day and indulged in high-profile debauchery at night, was, in its own way, more wearing than his role as solo vigilante. And more likely to kill him, he sometimes thought, by simply grinding away at his soul.

Alfred's computer chose that moment to bay like a bloodhound in full cry, startling the butler.

"I will never get used to that," he said. "I find it difficult to believe that Lucius Fox devised such . . ."

Bruce smiled. "I believe the word you're looking for is

*slapstick,* and Lucius didn't come up with it. An over-eager übergeek did."

"I beg pardon, sir; über—?"

"His name is Rosen. Jesse Rosen. He's the newest member of WayneTech's software group. I asked for a program that could backtrack activity on a website—postings, uploads, that sort of thing—and this is what I got."

He moved to the baying machine and shut down the alert, clicking the CLOSE button on the message box with its happily panting cartoon bloodhound. The program displayed a list of the online activity initiated by the computer that had most recently uploaded to the *Maggings* site.

Bruce followed one of the links, nodding in satisfaction. Ms. Tollyer was, it seemed, suddenly quite interested in the career of Grey Berwald. Curious, though, considering the contents of her blog. Was she really suggesting that a horror novel had been the cause of the near disaster in the subway tunnel?

"I'm going out, Alfred."

"Fine, sir. I'll bring the car around."

"No need—I'll be taking the 'company' car."

"Ah." Alfred checked his watch. "Sunset is in half an hour, sir. Why don't you finish your sandwich?"

Bruce nodded, picking up the sandwich and biting into it. As he was drinking his coffee, he became conscious of his almost Pavlovian obedience to Alfred's suggestion that he eat.

*Old habits die hard,* he thought.


*Batman.*

The Dark Knight, the Caped Crusader, the avenging

shadow that strikes fear into the hearts of Gotham City's criminal underworld.

*Batman.*

The sound of justice, falling from the sky on swift wings. An image of burning eyes in a shadowed, demonic silhouette, the pain of a gloved fist jackhammering against a jaw. Scalloped wings, spread across a night sky, departing as mysteriously as he came, leaving criminals unconscious or bound for the always tardy arrival of Gotham's Finest.

*Batman.*

He'd *hated* the name at first.

"Well, sir, what did you expect?" Alfred had asked the first time Bruce Wayne had opened the paper and stared in shock at the banner headline: MYSTERIOUS "BATMAN" FOILS ARMORED CAR ROBBERY! "If you slink about the city dressed up like a giant chiropteran, you're fortunate to be called something as relatively innocuous as that."

"You're saying it could have been worse?"

"A few sobriquets come to mind, which propriety forbids my mentioning," the butler had replied as he gathered up the breakfast dishes.

"You're enjoying this, aren't you?"

Alfred had not replied to that, save for a slight but unmistakable smile as he disappeared discreetly into the kitchen.

He had been right, of course. Bruce had never intended his grim alter ego to have a name; quite the contrary, in fact. A name, he had felt, would diminish the mystery, put a limiting label on the fear that was to be his first and best weapon. He had intended to be known to Gotham City's criminal element only as Retribution. But the media had named him the Batman—or, more informally, just Batman; the article seemed to attach itself to the noun haphazardly, sometimes within the same sentence—and so now Batman he was.

Similarly had the car become the Batmobile, the motorcycle the Batcycle, and so on. The local news channel had even instituted a "Batwatch" segment, reporting sightings both confirmed and unconfirmed. He felt sure that, if the press were to somehow become aware of the cavernous headquarters under Wayne Manor, it would be immediately (and ungrammatically) dubbed the Batcave. And now, of course, there was "Bat-Sightings"—his own little corner of Maggie Tollyer's blog.

He'd grown somewhat used to it; had even come to think of his costumed identity as Batman. And fortunately, it didn't seem to lessen the effect he was having on the criminal element. Likewise the kitsch peddled on street corners and in stores downtown—T-shirts, baseball caps, bumper stickers, and the like, all emblazoned with the sigil he'd chosen. He'd been dismayed at first, fearing that all his efforts would be reduced to parody, that he'd become merely an unwilling shill for the tourist trade.

But criminals apparently didn't buy kitsch, so it hadn't happened. And he wouldn't let it happen. He couldn't.

Because if he trusted the night, the night also trusted him.

"Don't turn on the light."

"Jesus!" Captain James Gordon took a reflexive step backward and collided with the doorjamb of his office. He fought to keep his breathing under control and peered into the darkened room, pushing at the bridge of his glasses, though they were about as far up his nose as they were likely to go. "I wish you wouldn't do that."

"Trust me." The voice was low, dark, and somehow warm and menacing at the same time—like the purr of a jungle cat. "I'm scarier in broad daylight."

He did trust his shadowy visitor, Gordon reflected, despite the frissons brought on by his sudden appearances and disappearances. Trusted him with good reason. Batman had come to Gotham's rescue several times, little though the general populace knew it. To James Gordon the strange, ethereal relationship was both a blessing and a curse.

"I believe you," he said now, looking at the pool of black on black from which the voice had come. "To what do I owe the pleasure?"

"The subway incident this afternoon."

"You were there."

"Was I?"

Gordon shrugged. "Call it a hunch."

"The driver—what's the prognosis?"

"She'll recover fully. Or so say the doctors. Doesn't seem to be any lasting trauma, anyway." He dared to slip farther into his office and sank into his desk chair, turning it so that he could see the shadow in the far corner.

"Diagnosis?"

"Sudden acute paranoia and a mild psychotic break brought on by . . ." He shrugged again. "They're not too clear on that. Though the words *anxiety* and *performance pressure* came up once or twice."

There was a textile slither as Batman moved restively. "No alcohol or drugs in her system?"

"None. Not even aspirin. Nor has our forensics team found anything in the train cab. We impounded it, by the way, in case you want to have a look."

"I do. Where's the driver now?"

"Sun Valley Hospice. I love the names they give those places. She's due for release day after tomorrow. Did you want to interview her?" He realized the absurdity of the words as they left his mouth. "I mean," he said, backpedaling, "there's a transcript of Sergeant Reynoso's official interview with her on the division server, but I can't upload it—"

"Thank you. No need. I can access it where it is."

This information wasn't surprising, and only marginally unsettling.

Gordon took off his glasses and rubbed the bridge of his nose. "I guess the long and short of it is that the doctors at this point haven't been able to tie Ms. Epcot's . . . seizure to any external factor."

"But?"

Gordon started to push his glasses up his nose, then realized he was still holding them. He put them back on. "But that's not very likely, is it? *Something* triggered that seizure. And Janet Epcot has no history of epilepsy, migraine, or mood disorder. Drinks socially, restricts her intake to wine, and doesn't smoke or do drugs. She's an apparently healthy thirty-two-year-old woman."

"Who had a sudden, inexplicable psychotic break." The shadow in the corner moved marginally to its right, not quite allowing the light from the outside corridor to reach it. "I read of a case once in which a man discovered he had a brain tumor when the strobing lights from his son's video game threw him into convulsions. You get a strobing effect in the subway coming up out of the underground."

Gordon nodded. "Yeah. The skylights in the roof of the terminal approach. But she's had an MRI—no tumor." He paused for a five-count, then said: "Are you thinking this might not have been an accident? What, then—an isolated act of terrorism?"

"If it *wasn't* an accident—if it was an attack of some sort—then it probably won't be isolated."

"I hope to God you're wrong."

"So do I. Time will tell. Meanwhile, we'll also need to run a name through the system."

"Sure. Whose?"

"Magdala or Maggie Tollyer. Journalist. Won the Caliber five years ago. I'd like to check if she's got a criminal record."

"She doesn't." He was pleased to have already done that bit of sleuthing. "We checked because we found her in the compartment with Ms. Epcot. She was clean."

"Any other impressions of Ms. Tollyer and the situation you found her in?"

"She was evasive. Why or about what, I don't know. Just a sense that she was . . . editing her answers as they came out. Of course, she *is* a journalist. They generally do that as a reflex. We did wonder if maybe she'd been in the cab longer than she said—"

"No. She came in after the train stopped."

"I see. Ah . . . would you happen to know anything about the big hole in the tunnel ceiling?"

"I know it doesn't have anything to do with the cause of the runaway. You were telling me about Ms. Tollyer . . ."

Gordon nodded. "She was apparently a bit of a crusader early in her career. The Caliber Award was for an exposé she did for some media magazine. Something about . . ." He tried to recall the exact context.

"The responsibility of artists for the consequences of their work?"

Gordon nodded. "Yeah, I guess that about covers it.

Why so interested? Or is that something you're not ready to share yet?"

"It's got more to do with certainty than readiness."

"Ah. Well, if you do become more certain—"

"You'll be the first to know."

The shadowy pool rippled with sudden upward movement, accompanied by the swish of fabric. Gordon felt more than saw the darkness that was Batman lift toward the ceiling to vanish. There was a tiny tick of metal on metal as the ventilator panel shifted back into place, and then the prickling sense of presence was gone.

"*Dios mio*, Captain, you just sittin' here in the dark?"

Gordon spun out of his chair so fast, he half expected to see himself still sitting there. What he saw was Sergeant Arturo Reynoso peering at him from the doorway.

"I . . . I think I fell asleep. Time to go home, I guess." He suited action to word and reached down to drag his coat from the back of his chair.

"Asleep? I thought you were on the phone. You talk in your sleep, Cap?"

"Ah . . . yeah. Stress, I think."

Reynoso grinned. "You and my wife. Although what she's got to be stressed about, I can't fathom."

"Art, your wife's a shrink. Her whole business is stress." Gordon slid into his coat and pulled a woolen scarf out of the pocket as he stepped into the hallway. It seemed bright after the twilight he'd left behind.

"Well, that's what I mean. She eats stress for breakfast. *Her* life oughta look pretty cushy by comparison."

Stress, Gordon thought, as he waved good night to Reynoso and the other detectives still on duty. Wasn't that essentially what doctors were suggesting had thrown a perfectly healthy young woman into a seizure?

\*       \*       \*

Batman returned to the cave through the labyrinthine network of sewers, storm drains, and other passageways that honeycombed the ground beneath the city. Many of these had been partially or wholly blocked by what had come to be known as the Great Gotham Quake that had, along with the subsequent fire, devastated the city decades ago and created the bizarre no-man's-land of Undertown. But more than enough subterranean passage remained to allow him relatively quick and easy access to most of the city, even at peak traffic times.

Traffic had been too congested to use the car, so it now rested in what appeared to be a ramshackle warehouse near the docks. After a mile's trek he reached a small kiosk disguised as a City Works station. The lock opened to his thumbprint. Inside was one of the off-road motorcycles he'd had designed for this environment.

There were only a few points of egress between the cave proper and the tunnels, and all had been camouflaged to prevent accidental discovery. In less than an hour he was back in the main cavern.

He activated the cowl's hands-free as he parked the bike.

"I'm back, Alfred."

The butler's voice, carried directly to his ear, was tinted with relief, or perhaps reproach. "Good to hear your voice, sir. Will you be taking dinner now? It is after seven."

"Down here, if you don't mind. I still have a little research to do."

"As you wish, Master Bruce. Will you be returning to the city later for your usual nightly perambulations?"

Bruce pulled the cowl back from his face as he reached the mainframe, and simultaneously keyed the speakerphone with his other hand. As he replied, he shifted his shoulders, wincing slightly. His suit was woven with fibers designed to tense against sudden shocks, supplementing his own muscles and tendons; still, there was no denying that grabbing a speeding train couldn't just be shrugged off. He'd had a hell of a time negotiating the roof of police headquarters tonight.

"Haven't decided yet, but I'm leaning toward actually sleeping tonight. I have a little surveillance job to do in the morning."

"Sleeping?" echoed Alfred. "Are you quite sure you recall how to do it?"

"Funny, Alfred. You should do stand-up."

He sat down before the big screen. The train operator had indeed been in the throes of some sort of psychotic episode; specifically, she'd been terrified. And the words she'd been repeating sounded like some kind of fear-induced hallucination: *They come out in the tunnels . . . they feed in the tunnels.*

Bruce leaned back in the chair and steepled his fingers beneath his chin. Since she had no history of mental illness, this might still be the first indication of a lurking chemical imbalance in her brain. It could have been something unique to the woman. A freak incident.

But as he knew from bitter experience, that wasn't the way to bet in this town.

3

Maggie overslept. Slept right through her alarm, as a matter of fact. Which meant she had to rush to make the morning visiting hours at Sun Valley Hospice.

It had been a weird night, she had to admit. She'd been filled with a sense of creeping unease, had imagined stealthy noises from the living room, the sound of riffling paper and keyboard patter from her office. Nor could she stop thinking about the novel in the top drawer of her desk. Several times she swore she heard the drawer opening, as if the book were trying to escape or whispering *Read me* from its hiding place.

She actually got up once and went into her office to look. She'd gone so far as to open the drawer, stare at the book, and reach for it. Then her inherent sense of dignity kicked in and she sheepishly closed the drawer again.

In the end she slept with the living room light on. She also checked her door locks and burglar alarm . . . twice.

So, sleep-deprived and a latte short of full wakefulness, Maggie headed off to Sun Valley in a most uncharitable mood, damning Grey Berwald for stirring up old ghosts. Ghosts that he couldn't possibly have known about, argued her inner Devil's Advocate voice . . . which she'd once credited with making her a good journalist.

*Shut up,* she told it now. *You're a damn nuisance.*

She produced an outdated press pass to gain entrance to Janet Epcot's room. The nurses didn't question her credentials, only the newsworthiness of Ms. Epcot's condition. Human interest, she told them, and a floor nurse walked her to the room, leaving her just outside the door.

Janet Epcot was sitting up in bed, reading a *Popular Science* magazine. It wasn't what Maggie would have expected from a pretty woman of her age. "Hi," she said brightly as the other woman looked up from her magazine. She flourished her pass. "Can I talk to you for a couple of minutes?"

The other woman hesitated, then shrugged. "Why not," she said, plopping the magazine onto the bed. "For sure those nurses are no damn fun."

It was harder to navigate in the daylight. There were fewer effective places to hide, even on an overcast day like today. He had occasionally arrived at one end of a block as Bruce Wayne, only to disappear into a building and reemerge elsewhere as Batman. He couldn't pull that trick off very often, he knew, without the risk of drawing unwelcome attention. Not everyone could be counted on to be unaware of what was going on around them, and Sun Valley Hospice offered no convenient cover. It was isolated, self-contained, and well guarded.

He entered the grounds on the roof of a laundry truck, moved from there to the ventilation shafts in the basement parking structure, and thence into the sanatorium itself. He was able to position himself in the crawl space above Janet Epcot's third-floor room before the

erstwhile journalist had made it past the opening pleas-
antries.

The insulated ceiling he hunkered above was no barrier to WayneTech gadgetry. The women's voices came
to him as clearly as if he were hiding under the bed.

"I'm feeling fine," said Janet Epcot, in answer to a
question from the alleged reporter. "Bored. But okay.
Tired of being scanned and prodded and needled, too.
But they're just trying to figure out what's wrong with
me. I'm glad about that."

"No luck, so far?" Tollyer asked.

"Nope. Oh, I've got low blood sugar, but that doesn't
account for . . . you know."

There was the sound of something sliding across the
tiles of the floor. He could imagine Maggie Tollyer
scooting a chair up to the side of Epcot's bed and making herself comfortable.

"Hasn't happened since?" she asked.

"I've been fine. Heck—better than fine. Whatever
they gave me to make me sleep last night worked like a
charm."

"Would you mind if I asked you a few questions
about what happened?"

"I got my answers pretty well down by now. Shoot."

This last was delivered in a wry tone of resignation.
Batman wondered how many times Ms. Epcot had had
to answer "a few questions" since yesterday afternoon.

"When did you first feel something was wrong?"

There was a long pause, then: "Like I told the cops
and the doctors, I'd felt a little hinky all day. Like someone was watching me or might slam a door behind me
or sneak up on me in the cab. Jitters, you know? One
cup of coffee too many at break, I figured. Then, as I

was bringing the train down from the El, getting ready to go into the underground again, I just freaked."

"Freaked?"

"Yeah. Scared witless. Minute I saw that tunnel mouth. I think I would've done anything not to have to go back underground."

"Claustrophobia?"

"Never before in my life, Ms. Tollyer."

"Maggie."

"Maggie. I mean, *never*. And I'm not afraid now. I think about going back to work . . ." There was a muted shift of fabric that might have been a shrug. "No problem."

"Why were you afraid of the tunnels suddenly?"

"Well . . ."

He could almost see the journalist leaning into the answer, feel her intensity as she waited for it the way a catcher waits for an off-speed pitch.

"This is gonna sound silly."

"I doubt it."

"I was reading this book—*Fear Itself* by Grey Berwald?"

"Yeah, I . . . uh . . . I have a copy at home."

The silent listener above allowed himself a slight, momentary smile.

"Well, there's a scene in it with these . . . things that live in tunnels. Awful things."

"What—giant rats?"

"Worse. Shapeless, nameless . . . *awful.* I don't usually read, y'know, horror stories," she said, her tone almost apologetic. "But Berwald . . . his stuff is interesting no matter how silly it gets. Anyway, I don't know, I just . . . I'd just read that chapter on my break and I guess it weirded me out. I saw the tracks go into that tunnel like a roller coaster to Hell, and my heart started pounding, and my head started spinning, and I just lost it, plain and simple."

Nothing plain and simple about it, he thought. A young, healthy woman, with no history of claustrophobia—and, he'd be willing to bet, no other phobias—suddenly developed full-blown paranoia after reading a scary story? Nonsense.

"Tell me about the book," Maggie was saying. "So you're not a horror fan?"

"Not really. But I'm a big Berwald fan. His last one—*Walk with Me*—was kind of disappointing, but I just had the feeling when I picked this one up that it was going to be good."

"And was it?"

"Good—and scary. I think I lost my copy, though. Fell out of my bag. Either that, or one of the cops was a Berwald junkie, too."

He heard not the least bit of contrition in Tollyer's laughter. "Interesting way to put it—'a Berwald junkie.' Why do you read him? Or maybe the question is: Why do you like to be scared?"

This time Janet Epcot laughed. " 'Cause it feels so good to be safe again, I guess. And . . ."

She paused long enough that Tollyer prompted her. "And?"

A subtle riffle of bedsheets. "And the scary stuff in the books makes the scary stuff in real life . . . easier."

"Does that mean you want to finish reading the book?"

"Well, I don't know about that. Maybe. Maybe not. I guess it depends on what the doctors tell me. If I've got some sort of . . . phobia or something, then maybe I'll have to stay away from Mr. Berwald for a while."

"But you don't want to."

"No. I'd really like to finish the book."

"But it scared you so badly, you nearly had a—"

"That wasn't the book," Janet protested. "How could that be the book? They'll find something, those doctors. You know how many old chemical dumps there are under Gotham. Probably just a leak from one of those or something in my coffee, or—"

"You're probably right. You know, I'll bet I can get you a new copy in the gift shop."

"Oh, you don't have to—"

The chair slid across the tiles again. "Consider it a gesture of thanks, for letting me talk to you."

"Hey, I'm just glad you didn't ask me the same old questions those policemen did. I thought I'd be saying that stuff in my sleep. 'No, Officer, I don't remember seeing anything strange. Yes, Officer, I guess I really thought something was gonna get me. No, Officer, I don't do drugs.' "

"Be right back," Maggie Tollyer said, and he heard the door open and close.

How could it be the book, indeed? He'd never heard of fiction inducing psychosis. Was there something to the idea of a toxic leak somewhere along the train route? Janet Epcot was right about the substrate beneath Gotham; it was riddled with the waste and wreckage of its citizens' ignorance and greed. Had it been an accident then? Or had something inimical made its way into her coffee?

He'd suggest those possibilities to Captain Gordon, he decided. But in the meantime there was another angle he wanted to explore.

True to her word, Maggie Tollyer brought a new paperback copy of *Fear Itself* back to Janet Epcot. He hadn't doubted that she would; it was, after all, a cheap way to expunge any feelings of guilt over having stolen the other woman's copy.

He waited long enough to be sure that Tollyer meant to ask no further questions, then slipped out the same way he'd entered.

There were several psychopaths who had terrified Gotham City in the past by specializing in head games and mind control. There was Jervis Tetch, the Mad Hatter, whose radiopathic circuit chips, when placed near a victim's head, gave him total control over that person. But the Hatter was obsessed with the works of Lewis Carroll, and nothing about this smacked of Wonderland or the Looking Glass world of Alice's dreams.

There was Dr. Hugo Strange, who had perfected a thought-scanning device to the point of being able to actually view his patients' innermost secrets. But Strange was now a drooling vegetable, giggling away in an Arkham cell, having had his own mind accidentally erased by one of his own devices.

And there was, of course, the grinning madman who called himself the Joker. Bruce felt his gut tighten in disgust and concern.

*He can't have escaped again. They've got him under the tightest security Arkham can muster. Besides,* he reminded himself, *it isn't his MO.* That woman had been about as far from laughing herself to death as she could get. She had been, in fact, on the verge of being *frightened* to death.

Frightened to death. That narrowed down the list pretty dramatically.

"Computer," he said. "Latest data on Doctor Jonathan Crane, aka Scarecrow."

"Collating data," replied the emotionless system voice. "Doctor Crane currently incarcerated in Arkham Asylum. Maximum security, twenty-four-hour surveillance, DNA identity check administered daily, food intake restricted to—"

"Enough." The computer had told him nothing he hadn't already known, but it was nonetheless reassuring to hear it again. Crane was being held under the same absolute conditions as was the Joker; in fact, they were the only two under such extreme constraints. And they were the only two whose modi operandi ran to chemical and very intimate warfare.

In addition to the measures the computer had mentioned, every bit of furniture in their cells was of formcast plastic, unbreakable, and totally inert to any form of chemical reaction. They wore paper coveralls, which were discarded daily in the presence of the guards, and flash-incinerated on the spot before new ones were issued in sterile packages. Even the air was carbon-scrubbed. There was no way so much as a molecule of anything unauthorized could make its way into or out of either criminal's cell without the entire Arkham staff hearing about it.

That didn't stop Batman from making Arkham his next stop.

The foreboding Gothic mansion now called Arkham Asylum was actually the second structure to bear that name, the original complex having been destroyed some years earlier in a conflagration that had sent its inmates on a shrieking, near-apocalyptic orgy of destruction in a city already known for its tribulations.

Gotham had purchased the Mersey Mansion and started a process of rebuilding and retrofitting that had resulted in the newer, but still infamous, asylum. Years later the work was not yet done, largely because of the difficulty of laying fiber-optic cables, sedation gas piping, and the like through solid concrete walls and floors. And of course, during all of this there was the constant need to keep watch on the asylum's inmates—each of whom gave new meaning to the word *unique.*

It was a daunting task. The guards, doctors, and occasional visiting city officials kept watch over the asylum population via closed-circuit cameras, patrols, and careful monitoring of mail, calls, and visitors. Some inmates required constant supervision, even after the ten o'clock lights-out rule, and were monitored by light-amplification viewers. Others needed special preemptive treatment to foil escape attempts. One of these was Pamela Isley, whose cell was regularly sprayed with herbicide to prevent rapid, wall-shattering plant growth. The temperature in Victor Fries's cell was precisely calibrated to be just cold enough for the hypothermic madman to survive, but warm enough to keep him in a state of lizard-like lassitude.

The rear wheel of Batman's motorcycle spewed gravel as he cleared the front gates of the asylum. A doctor, replete with white lab coat, was waiting on the front steps as the Dark Knight parked the bike and removed his helmet.

"You're the new administrator?"

"That's right, uh—Mr. Batman. I'm Doctor Fenton Avery."

"Just 'Batman' will do." Batman made his way toward the steps that led up to the forbidding structure, wondering briefly who would name a child "Fenton."

Dr. Avery followed. "This is an unscheduled visit," he commented. "If I'd known you were coming—"

"*I* didn't know I was coming until this morning."

"Then . . . ?"

"You're aware of the incident downtown with the runaway subway train?"

"Yes. It's been all over the news."

They stepped into the huge foyer. The décor was sparse: a few chairs and tables, the main desk with its anachronistic monitoring station, and the large portraits of Amadaeus and Jedediah Arkham, forever watching. The orderly behind the desk and the two guards present stared at Dr. Avery's cloaked companion. Avery, noticing this, led the way quickly up the stairs and into the main transverse corridor on the second floor.

He glanced at Batman, his eyes wary. "You're not thinking that had anything to do with one of *our* inmates?"

"I'm just trying to eliminate possibilities."

Avery stopped in the middle of the hallway and turned to face him. "But it was an accident, wasn't it? The woman had a seizure of some sort . . . Is that just a cover-up? Is there more—"

"There's no cover-up. But there are a number of odd . . . elements in the case. And a few unanswered questions."

Avery was nodding. "The driver's 'seizure,' of course. You're thinking, I assume, that it might have been caused by external factors."

"That's one theory."

"Another theory might be that the woman herself is the source of her own disturbance. Not all mental illnesses show up on an MRI or CAT scan. We've only to look at Jonathan Crane, or the Joker, or Harvey Dent to know that."

Warming to his topic as they walked down the hall,

Avery continued, "Dent's condition is so unusual that Commissioner Akins has been lobbying to have him transferred out to Blackgate." Avery looked disapproving as he added, "The commissioner has always felt that Dent does not fit the clinical definition of insanity, as required by the state for institutionalization. While it's true that Dent technically is not a textbook case of dissociative personality disorder—in fact, I think we're safe in labeling his psychosis sui generis—he still—"

"But he's still here, isn't he?"

Avery spent a split second looking like a floundering sea bass. "Still . . . well, of course, he's still here. The transfer is only talk—"

"And the Scarecrow?"

"Doctor Crane is in his cell, as he has been, day in and day out, since his incarceration."

"The Joker?"

"Of course. You're not suggesting—"

"Show me."

Avery gestured toward the staircase. "The control room is downstairs."

"I want to see them in their cells. I want to speak to them."

"But the monitors—"

"Can sometimes be fooled by the very clever. And both the Joker and Crane, insane as they are, are exceedingly clever."

"Which is why," Avery said, "we keep both men under *close* twenty-four-hour guard. We don't rely solely on technology with either of them."

"Wise of you." Batman made a slight *after-you* gesture with his cape, and Avery moved on toward the thick steel doors that formed the portal to what was supposed to be the most secure environment in penal history.

The serpentine corridors and hallways of Arkham Asylum were almost enough to confuse even Batman's sense of direction. Occasionally they passed isolated habitats, home to the strange and varied population. It was asylum policy to keep the inmates sequestered, as they seemed to exacerbate one another's "idiosyncrasies," as Avery put it.

Currently Arkham played host to six of those whom Alfred had once dubbed the "Rogues Gallery." The names they had taken for themselves were like a mélange from a child's book of fairy tales: Two-Face, the Riddler, Poison Ivy, the Mad Hatter, the Scarecrow . . .

And of course, the Joker.

Of all of them, he was easily the most dangerous. More cunning and convoluted than the Riddler, capable of inspiring more fear than the Scarecrow, and far better at mind games and control than the Mad Hatter. The twisted mind behind that perpetual grin was the single most evil thing Batman had ever known, purely because it was so cold, so clinically detached from the mayhem and agony it caused.

The Joker's true identity remained a mystery. All the others had documented names and biographies, lives they had led before becoming what they were now. He had even known some of them personally—Harvey Dent, for example, who had gone from DA to deadly at the flick of a criminal's wrist and a splash of acid.

Not so the Joker. No one knew where he came from, or how he had acquired that hideous dead-white skin and nightmarish rictus. Where there were no facts, however, there was plenty of speculation. The possibility existed that the mysterious underworld figure called the

Red Hood, who had supposedly plunged to his death, falling into one of the seething vats of the Gotham Chemical Works during an initial confrontation with Batman, *might* have survived. The toxic soup he'd fallen into was known to cause extreme depigmentation, among other things. But Batman knew that, even if he learned for certain that the Joker was the same man as the Red Hood, he would just be trading one cipher for another, since no one knew whose face had been beneath the crimson mantle that had been left floating on the vat's bubbling surface.

*And speak of the devil . . . literally,* he thought as Avery led him around a corner.

The Joker's cell was spartan, with only a metal cot, a chair, a table, and the ubiquitous sink-and-toilet combination. The furniture was welded to the floor. Everything was painted a stark, glaring white and exposed for inspection behind a three-inch-thick wall of transparent bulletproof aluminum.

No bars for the Joker, and no privacy, either. He received his food through a small sally port in the wall, the inner door of which could be opened only after the outer one was sealed. The food was always delivered by two armed guards. His eating utensils and plates were made from a special biodegradable plastic that disintegrated fifteen minutes after exposure to the air, and his food consisted mostly of purées and soups; nothing with bones or shells or anything that could possibly be made into a weapon.

The Joker had no books, no magazines, no TV—nothing with which to pass the time in his cell. He didn't seem to need anything, however; the Grand Guignol atrocities that played endlessly in the theater of his mind were apparently enough to occupy him. A young psychiatric intern had once made the mistake of asking the Joker about his dreams and fantasies. She'd committed suicide two days later.

Batman recalled once watching part of a twenty-four-hour tape of the madman sitting cross-legged in his cell, silently performing children's finger plays: *Where Is Thumbkin, The Eentsie-Weentsie Spider, Grandmother's Glasses* . . . over and over, for a full day and night.

As they approached his cell, the Joker was apparently deep in thought, balancing on one leg with the other foot poised akimbo against his knee. He waved in exaggerated good humor as Batman and Avery approached.

Harvey Dent had just become DA when the psychotic clown first made the news, unleashing a canister of his deadly "laughing gas" into a movie theater. The irony characteristic of his plots was evident from the start: the movie being shown had been a restored print of Paul Leni's 1928 silent classic, *The Man Who Laughs*. Conrad Veidt's makeup for the role of Gwynplaine was eerily similar to the Joker's disfigured face—as were the thirty-seven victims in the audience after the attack, all of whom had literally laughed themselves to death, their faces frozen in horrific hilarity.

Harvey had been appalled by the crime, Batman recalled. He'd vowed that, no matter what it took, he would bring this "Joker"—who had left that very playing card as a signature—to justice. Eight months later he'd fulfilled that promise, and the Joker had been incarcerated in Arkham—for five weeks.

The security of his cell had not been nearly as elaborate then; he'd broken out by pulling one of his own back teeth and wedging it in the door's lock when the guard was distracted. Each successive time he'd been returned to the asylum, the security had been heightened, until it was utterly escape-proof.

Or so everyone thought . . . until the Joker escaped again.

Harvey had launched an investigation into Arkham's staff, from the highest echelons down to the rank and file. The result had been the exposure of pervasive corruption and graft—no big surprise; this was, after all, Gotham City—and both the medical and administrative staffs had been almost completely replaced.

Oddly enough, despite all this, the Joker never once attempted any sort of revenge on the district attorney, even though Harvey had stated publicly many times that one of his top priorities was to get the Joker off the streets for good. The Joker, like the Scarecrow, apparently had only one target, one idée fixe: Batman. He had robbed banks, held public figures for ransom, looted valuable art collections, all to finance his obsession with bringing down his archenemy. Harvey Dent, one of the most powerful men in Gotham City's law enforcement department, was evidently not important enough to bother with.

The Joker had roamed the streets of Gotham one last time before his most recent incarceration, but this time he had not escaped. This time Harvey Dent's alter ego, Two-Face, had let him out.

*God help us,* Batman thought, *if they all start networking.*

"Well, if it isn't the Bat-man," the Joker purred, subtly emphasizing the second syllable. "And what brings you out on this possibly bright and sunny day?"

Avery turned to Batman. "As you can see, he's quite himself."

"Yes." To the Joker, Batman added: "Actually, it's

quite blustery and cold. A miserable day to be out-doors."

The Joker simpered, maintaining his stork stance. "Oh, well, then I guess I should be thankful I've got a roof over my head. A *padded* roof . . . but a roof nonetheless. We should all be grateful for the simple pleasures in life."

Batman glanced at Avery. "Scarecrow?"

"This way." The doctor moved off down the same corridor. Near the end, around a corner, was a cell of identical size to the Joker's, though not nearly so spartan. While it was still unrelieved white, this cell had one chief departure from the Joker's: along its walls, though not touching them, were bookshelves of transparent plastic filled, for the most part, with psychology reference books, history texts, and a smattering of fiction—mostly classics.

Dr. Jonathan Crane was sitting cross-legged on his cot, reading a thick tome with a worn cloth cover. He looked up as Batman and Avery approached the clear barrier at the front of the cell, his large, pale eyes exaggerated by the lenses of his wire-rimmed glasses. Though nowhere nearly as pallid as the Joker's, Crane's skin was still almost as colorless as the paper overalls he wore. It made his thick shock of dark hair look wildly out of place.

Batman was always taken aback by the extreme gentleness of Crane's personality when the Scarecrow alter ego was turned off. He was an unprepossessing man—a studious, quiet, exceedingly polite man, proper to the point of primness.

Which did not, of course, forgive in any fashion the atrocities his alter ego had committed. A former professor of psychiatry and biochemistry at Gotham University, Crane had been obsessed since a child with one thing: the evocation and study of fear, particularly phobic fear. While still in his early twenties, he had written a monograph on the subject that was considered the definitive analysis of the emotion.

His reclusive ways and slender physique gave an impression of frailty that was misleading; like many obsessive personalities, Crane had surprising stamina. He was also hyper mobile, or "double-jointed," and could dislocate his shoulders and hips with little or no apparent pain. Batman had seen Crane, in his Scarecrow persona, contort his supple frame into postures and positions that were startling to behold. Such poses, when used with his "fear gas" and hideous mask, were utterly terrifying to his victims.

"A visitor?" his soft voice inquired. "I wasn't expecting any visitors."

Batman stepped into a pool of light at the entrance to the cell. Crane's gaze flicked to him, but he spoke to Avery. "Doctor, that man with you—that . . . *thing* with you—isn't welcome here. He's upsetting the inmates. I can feel it. I can almost smell the epinephrine wafting in the air. It won't do to get them all riled up, you know. Even slight trauma can lead to bizarre behavior." He smiled, looking almost boyish. "Of course, there's no end to bizarre behavior around here, is there?"

"What are you reading, Doctor Crane?" Batman asked.

"*Doctor* Crane, is it? How very . . . courteous. You weren't nearly so courteous the last time you spoke to me."

"Neither, if I recall, were you."

"You must be confusing me with someone else. I am *always* courteous. I'm reading Poe, if you must know.

The Freudian psychoanalyst Marie Bonaparte has attributed all manner of sexual allegory to Poe's work, but I'm telling you, I don't see it." He frowned, dark brows drawing together over his sharp nose as he gazed down into the book. "I'd love to write a defense of Poe on the subject, since he's not alive to defend himself. If they'd only give me a pen, I'd do it. Her theories are sheer hokum. Sexual allegory, indeed. Poe would never descend to such base evocations. His intentions were far more elevating." He thrust his nose back between the covers, ignoring them.

Avery glanced at Batman. "Satisfied?"

Batman nodded, eyes still on the lanky figure behind the glass. "He seems quite happy."

"I daresay he is. He spends his days doing what he loves most—research." Avery turned and led his guest back the way they'd come.

They had just turned the corner into the main corridor when Batman heard from behind them Crane's soft, plaintive voice: "For the love of God, Montresor!"

4

His return from Arkham had precipitated some minor nagging on Alfred's part that he eat lunch before pursuing any further activities. And Alfred, already decked out in his chauffeur's uniform, was brooking no argument. Not that Bruce was prepared to give any. He had a strategy meeting at WayneTech that afternoon, besides which he wanted to have his engineering team probe into the possibility of a toxic leak in or around the subway tunnels.

He also wanted to pat Jesse Rosen on the back for programming above and beyond the call of duty. Bloodhound had been a rousing success.

The toxic leak theory was a long shot. After all, if it had been a generalized condition, wouldn't someone else on the train have reported similar symptoms? He made a mental note to talk to Captain Gordon about it as he changed clothes, then went downstairs to meet Alfred in the entrance hall.

"Very good, sir," Alfred told him, dusting nonexisting lint from his charcoal-gray silk suit and straightening his tie-less collar. "You look, perhaps, a bit less than well rested, but quite iconoclastic and 'hip.' "

Bruce rubbed his jaw. "Maybe I shouldn't have shaved."

"Quite all right, sir. I suppose even the most profligate might occasionally look kempt. Lunch first, I think."

"Of course."

Bruce let himself be ushered into the Bentley. He called police headquarters from the luxury of the backseat. The call was routed through dozens of trunk nodes around the world, rendering it untraceable.

"Gordon," he said when the switchboard picked up. "It's Masterson." This was a code word they'd adopted to let the captain know Batman was on the line. Gordon had concocted the name out of his own childhood fascination with the fictionalized Wild West lawman Bat Masterson.

"Question," he said when Gordon picked up. "Any of the crew or passengers aboard our runaway train report anything out of the ordinary?"

"No one. Half of them didn't even realize there was a problem. The rest noted that it seemed to be going much faster than usual for a terminal approach. What are you thinking?"

"Possible toxic leak somewhere along the route."

"Interviews with passengers and crew don't suggest that anyone besides the driver was affected, but I can certainly look into getting some Hazmat teams down there."

"Do that. You might also contact WayneTech— they're always working on new toys. Some might be helpful. I'll do some checking at my end, as well. Do you know where Janet Epcot got her coffee yesterday?"

"Checked that, too. The French Press—a little bistro over on Fiftieth. We tracked down a number of other patrons. Nothing unusual so far. I've sent some of their water to the lab, though. Just in case."

"They use tap water?"

"Bottled. Gotham Springs. And yes, we're checking that out, as well."

"I'd like to analyze some samples of the water—and any other ingredients they were using yesterday—myself. I'm not doubting either the diligence or the expertise of your people, Captain," he added when Gordon made a noise of protest. "But I suspect I have access to more advanced equipment. Can you arrange to leave samples somewhere in your office?"

Gordon's voice lowered. "Top file drawer of the cabinet under the ventilation shaft?"

"Perfect."

He told the captain of his visit to Arkham—a purely precautionary visit, he added, when the detective exclaimed in dismay.

"Everything seems as it should be. Walls unbreached and doors sensibly locked."

"Dear God, I should hope so," Gordon said. "If I thought this had anything to do with one of that bunch . . ."

"Apparently not."

Bruce rang off then, sitting back to enjoy the ride into Gotham. Which meant that he let his mind wander back through the last two days, turning over ideas, picking up theories and shaking them to see if anything fell out. He came back a number of times to Maggie Tollyer. At his first opportunity, he decided, he'd pay her a visit. Or rather, his more imposing alter ego would.

"Top of the Tower, sir?" Alfred asked from the driver's seat. "That will put you half a block from WayneTech."

"Sounds fine. I can pretend I'm there for the simple

pleasure of curling my lip at those not invited to my Halloween party."

"I don't believe I've ever seen you curl your lip, sir. It sounds most daunting."

"Indeed, Alfred, it's nearly as lethal as gazing upon Medusa."

Grey Berwald hailed from Austin, Texas, and had just enough of that country-boy charm—if, indeed, one found country boys charming—to nicely balance his artistic conceits. He was single, never married; wasn't romantically linked with anyone of note; and was a bit of a recluse.

He was also, as far as Maggie was concerned, a piece of work.

*Terror is a most excellent emotion,* he'd said. Then visited hospitals bringing gifts for kids who had met with real horrors. (What was it Janet Epcot had said: Fictional horrors made real horrors easier?)

*Chaos is at the heart of all true horror,* he'd written. Then endowed a library whose bountiful stacks were the essence of order.

He had myriad fan sites—run, Maggie was certain, by a bevy of young and middle-aged women with aspirations of having their cherished manuscripts read by their literary hero. One of the sites had so many obviously candid photographs on it that she wondered if Mr. Berwald had acquired a stalker.

She grinned: the unintended consequences of celebrity?

As she scanned his many carefully transcribed interviews, she found one that actually touched on the subject of artistic accountability. She read an excerpt from it with great interest.

**Q:** Your books contain a substantial amount of violent content. Do you believe your writing has contributed to violence on the part of your readers?

**A:** That's quite a question! It sort of cuts right to the core of the ongoing debate, doesn't it? Does the availability of a gun make some people want to use the gun? I'll be honest with you—in some cases, it probably does. How often? Enough to make me not want to be part of that problem. I'd like to think that if one of my books was ever implicated in something like that, I'd withdraw it from publication. Without regret.

*Right,* she thought. *Thereby costing you and your publisher millions.*

She was about to surf to a different website when her eyes caught on a photo of Berwald shaking hands with another handsome and roguish society buck: Bruce Wayne. The two men were apparently at a movie debut—red carpet underfoot, crowds of onlookers in the background, marquee lights forming a bright border. Both seemed to be in transit on opposite sides of a black velvet cordon.

*Rumor has it,* the caption enthused, *that Grey will be among Bruce's guests at his annual Halloween bash. Oh, if I could only find the right costume—the Invisible Woman, perhaps.*

Maggie sat back in her office chair, gazing thoughtfully at the ceiling. She recalled a day when her press pass was "the right costume." Not likely to be the case at one of Bruce Wayne's exclusive soirées.

The Invisible Woman, eh?

She smiled.

*      *      *

Bruce nodded at Nick, the aged yet eternally cheerful security guard, as he walked past the reception counter at WayneTech.

A good man, he thought.

It warmed him to remember that Nick had been working here since before he was born. It gave him a sense of continuity, a connection, however tenuous, to the days when his parents were alive. He hadn't come to these offices, or those of WayneTech's parent company, Wayne Enterprises, very much as a child, for the simple reason that his father hadn't been there much. Thomas Wayne had largely left the operation of the "family business" to the board of directors, and particularly to his chief technical officer, Lucius Fox, whom he trusted completely. Delegating the tasks of management had given him the time to pursue the profession that had called to him since his own childhood: medicine.

The senior Wayne's determination to follow his inner calling, despite the lure of a more glamorous life as a multimillionaire businessman, had been a great factor in Bruce's resolve to stay on the path he'd chosen for himself, no matter the odds or consequences.

At times he wondered, of course, if it was indeed the right path. He questioned whether it made greater sense to be more hands-on in the decisions and policies of WE and its subsidiaries. After all, he could, theoretically at least, make more difference in the world for the greater good as a full-time philanthropist than as a masked vigilante. The various crime-fighting devices that he'd developed through WayneTech and WayneMed alone would vastly improve the effectiveness of law enforcement. In fact, some of them already had.

Every time he pondered retirement, however, he came to the same conclusion: Batman was his calling, his raison d'être . . . his duty. He wasn't sure how or why he was so certain of this—he only knew that it was so.

His alter ego had been born initially out of a need for vengeance, spawned from a child's impotent desire to do *something,* to find an obsession that would see him through the endless night. But he'd come to terms with that. He'd avenged the brutal and senseless murder of his parents a hundred times over; he no longer awakened, wide-eyed and trembling, from the nightmare of the falling pearls.

And yet he still could not hang up the cape and cowl. For if Batman was his raison d'être, it was also his bête noire, seeming at times to own him—as if the cowl were the real face, and Bruce Wayne the disguise. He often entertained the image of himself at eighty—if indeed he lived that long—hobbling through dark alleys with the help of—what else?—a Bat-cane. There was a small voice from within that, every so often, whispered at him to put the persona aside, but he didn't—couldn't—listen.

For a time he'd told himself that because he'd so painstakingly set up the infrastructure of his obsession—had spent hundreds of millions, carefully filtered through offshore accounts and fictional corporations, to create a subterranean base of operations with a forensics lab, computer database, land, air, and sea vehicles, and GPS capability that rivaled that of most governments—he couldn't simply let it all lie fallow.

But he'd soon realized he was fooling himself. For whatever reason, he was hardwired to be hands-on in the guerrilla war on crime fought every night in Gotham City's gritty streets. He was a tactician and a strategist, it was true, but he was also a frontline fighter. He had to put his life on the line to feel that he was doing any good. And he was content that it was so.

"You okay, Mr. Wayne?"

Nick was looking at him with an expression that was two parts amusement, one part concern. Bruce realized he was standing in the middle of the lobby, wool-gathering. People, many of whom he recognized as his employees, were going to and fro and shooting him be-mused glances as they passed him.

He smiled and nodded at the security guard. "Just lost in my own head for a moment, Nick."

Nick grinned back. "You too young to be havin' se-nior moments, Mr. Wayne. Wait till you as old as me. I have entire senior *days*." He laughed, and Bruce chuck-led as he turned back toward the bank of elevators.

Loyalty like Nick's was hard to find these days. The sea of changes that a man sails over the years rarely de-posits him on the same shores for very long. He'd have to take a moment to review Nick's salary, Bruce decided, to make sure his loyalty was being properly rewarded.

Nick had already called for the elevator, and as the doors slid open Bruce stepped in, giving Nick a final smile.

The elevator rose smoothly toward the executive floors. Bruce glanced up at the escape hatch out of habit, considering the shaft, the pulleys and counterbalance in play as they functioned. How many corporation own-ers, especially those largely in absentia, thoroughly knew the layout of their buildings' labyrinth of ventilation shafts, service conduits, and elevator shafts? Probably not too many . . .

He had an envelope under his arm that detailed the afternoon's agenda, but it remained unopened—no time to review it, as so often was the case. Bruce knew that he could maneuver the meeting just as easily as if he were familiar with the docket by paying careful attention to what the division heads had to say. He thought of it as "surfing the moment."

And of course, eventually he would defer to the recommendations of Lucius Fox. Lucius, in his fiduciary capacity, would know every word, every chart, and the dollar amount corresponding to everything in the report. So Bruce didn't need to.

Since he'd begun his dual masquerade, Bruce's appearances in the boardroom had been reduced largely to a formality. He was a figurehead—he knew it, Lucius knew it, and the division heads surely suspected it, if they weren't already certain. Only Lucius had even an inkling of the true reason, of course—as far as everyone else was concerned, Bruce Wayne was simply a wastrel, a dilettante who cared nothing about the family enterprise as long as it kept him well supplied with blondes, brunettes, and redheads. Business went on as usual, and there were always papers that continued to require his signature. So he would occasionally put in an appearance and sign them. As for what Lucius knew or did not know, it was simply never discussed.

Lucius was waiting, as he often was, with a somber smile and an outstretched hand to meet him as the elevator doors opened. Bruce shook the proffered palm and wondered idly if it was Nick or the receptionist whose job it was to call and announce that the boss was on his way up.

"Afternoon, Bruce," Lucius said. "Rough night? You look tired. Wine, women, or song?"

Bruce smiled his playboy smile at Lucius. "All three," he said in answer to Lucius's question, and nodded at the employees moving past them in the elevator core. The concealing lie was easily given. "In the wrong combinations, I'm afraid."

The older man looked at him as if reading between some invisible lines, then shook his head. The gesture was one of rueful amusement. "You must have quite a nightlife, Bruce."

Bruce smiled. "What's on the agenda for today?"

He got the rundown as they made their way to the tasteful art deco opulence of the WayneTech boardroom. Nothing out of order, nothing pressing, nothing unpleasant.

"Lucius," Bruce said as they were about to enter the room. "After the meeting, I'd like to have a word with you about a special project."

Lucius turned and gave him another searching look. "I'm fresh out of high-tech toys, Bruce."

Bruce shook his head. "More in the nature of analysis, actually. WayneTech has been asked to give the GCPD a hand with something." He made a negligent *whatever* gesture. "It all sounds entirely too serious for me." Lucius's salt-and-pepper eyebrows rose elegantly, but he said nothing.

"I'd also like to thank Jesse Rosen for that little software job he did for me back in August. Works like a charm."

"Sorting your little black book by hair color?"

Bruce laughed and slapped Lucius on the shoulder. "How well you know me." He turned and preceded the older man into the room.

The board meeting was uneventful but not entirely tedious, though Bruce took pains to pretend that it was. Afterward he accompanied Lucius Fox down to the underground level where WayneTech's extensive laboratories were located.

In addition to his fiduciary duties, Lucius maintained a working knowledge of the other WayneTech divisions. They visited the computer lab first, where a crack technical team created the programming modules and interfaces that were the engines and steering mechanisms for many of WE's products.

Jesse Rosen was a small, slender young man with a shock of curly black hair, large amber eyes that missed nothing, and a beak-like nose. His mannerisms were bird-like, as well, quick and nervous. He greeted Bruce with perhaps just a bit of awe—albeit less than at the Wayne heir's first visit—but shook his hand with no sign of timidity.

"So you used it?" Jesse asked, seemingly torn between eagerness and wariness. "Can I ask what for?"

Bruce smiled. "Nothing illegal. I sometimes get curious about who posts to certain websites. Sometimes I see . . . ideas . . . I like; ideas that bear watching." He shrugged artlessly.

"And it worked—you were able to trace the posts?"

"Yes."

Lucius cleared his throat. "In that case, we might want to incorporate the Bloodhound program into our commercial law enforcement package, see if the GCPD want to beta-test it as part of the police arsenal."

Jesse looked at him. "Sure. I mean, if you think it might be useful to them."

"Thank you." Lucius turned to Bruce then and said, "On a possibly related matter, I got a call from Captain Gordon this morning. He was interested in what tech we might have that'll help him solve this subway incident. He indicated that there are some anomalies in the situation. So he wants to be able to sweep the subway tunnels for things that don't belong there."

Bruce made a point of barely stifling a yawn. "Of course, Lucius. Whatever you think is best. We're always happy to help the authorities."

Jesse looked interested.

"Things that don't belong there? Like . . . what? Like giant armadillos or something?"

Giant armadillos? Bruce could see a momentary bewildered look cross his business manager's face and was sure it matched the one on his own. "I believe it's more like chemicals," Lucius said.

Jesse blinked and his face pinked. "Oh . . . uh . . . okay. No-brainer. You put Ultra-Sniffers on the trains."

Bruce didn't have to fake ignorance his time. "Ultra . . . ?"

Lucius said, "Jesse is talking about a new generation of detection devices we've been readying for production. Rather like the Air-tech filter we developed for . . . that client you brought us. Only this is a bit more . . ."

"Brawny," said Jesse. "And proactive. It's got an effective range of five hundred feet."

"How—?"

"Full-spectrum analysis," said Lucius, "of the type NASA uses to tell what stars are made of."

Jesse nodded. "Yeah. Very cool."

"That would take care of anything widely dispersed," Lucius said. "There's also the possibility that the driver might have been targeted in some way."

Jesse frowned. "Hard to do in that environment. Unless something was introduced directly into the driver's compartment." He snapped his fingers. "Subsonics," he said.

Both Lucius and Bruce turned to look at him. He

shrugged. "You know, frequencies below the range of human hearing—"

"I'm sure Mr. Wayne knows what subsonics are, Jesse. What are you proposing?"

"Someone might have aimed a sonic charge at her. Screwed her nerves up real good. Same principle as the low, creepy sounds they build into movie soundtracks these days. The monster appears and they crank up the boom box. *Dah-dunt, dah-dunt, dah-dunt, dah-dunt...*" He trailed off. "That was from *Jaws*," he added.

"You could target someone with something like that?" Bruce asked.

"Sure. Why not? You could also do it with light, but somebody'd probably notice."

Bruce realized he was showing a little too much interest in Jesse's tech talk. He shrugged and turned to Lucius. "Whatever you think is best, Lucius," he said again. He made a show of checking his watch. "I'm due on the links."

Lucius nodded. "I'll inform Captain Gordon about those Sniffers for the subway engines."

"Great!" Jesse said. "I can put together a demo of how it works if you want."

"That might be helpful," Lucius mused. "How soon can you—?"

"How soon do you want it?"

"How soon can I get it?"

"Tomorrow night?"

"That's Saturday," Bruce reminded him. "You don't need to do this on your own time."

"Hell, I *want* to do it. Sounds like fun. Besides, the cops need this sort of information, right? They need to know if subsonics are a possibility. I'll even bring the stuff out to your house if you'd like, Mr. Wayne."

Bruce recognized the ulterior motive in the gleam of the younger man's eyes—Jesse wanted a peek inside the famous Wayne Manor. "That'd be fine. I've got a costume ball going on that night, but come on over anyway. Lucius will be there, and it might not be a bad idea to invite Captain Gordon, too. Stay for the party if you want. Costume optional."

Jesse grinned. "Tell you what—I'll come as a computer geek. Complete with laptop."

5

*The best-laid plans of bats,* he thought, *suffer similar vicissitudes as those of mice and men.* He'd had every intention of paying Maggie Tollyer a visit that evening, but reality, Alfred, and, most of all, the D Street Dawgs had had other plans.

His late afternoon was entirely taken up in acquainting himself with the guest list for the costume ball. If he was to play the part of a dilettante, then he really ought to study his lines, Alfred had informed him.

"One cannot, Master Bruce, be a socialite without knowing the social *set.* Especially, in your case, the available young women, and their inestimable families."

Bruce had bitten his tongue. Available young women, indeed. Available they might be, but with few exceptions their blatant availability—for someone with his bank balance—was their only redeeming quality. If he were to take it into his head to genuinely seek out female company, the last place he'd search would be one of his own stupendously lavish (and boring) parties.

"I suppose," he'd told Alfred, "it wouldn't do for me to go around peeking under masks and asking, 'Who the hell are you?' "

"No, sir. It wouldn't do at all," Alfred had said, but his lips had twitched when he'd said it.

With his guests memorized, Bruce found himself with just enough time to grab a quick meal before becoming Batman for an evening's foray. Weather dictated the use of the so-called Batmobile, and he drove into the city with every intention of putting the fear of the Bat into Maggie Tollyer, in an attempt to determine if she had played more than a bystander's role in the train incident. There was always the chance, he figured, that her speedy arrival in the driver's compartment had not been coincidental, or had been motivated by something other than curiosity.

But alas, the D Street Dawgs had intervened.

He was negotiating an intersection in a particularly seamy area of Gotham when a Molotov cocktail exploded across the gleaming black hood of the car. At first he'd thought it was meant for him, but it took him only a moment to realize he'd intercepted a salvo in a turf war between a couple of street gangs. The firebomb had been the doing of the Dawgs who, until recently, had been the undisputed lords of this squalid realm. They were now under assault by a rival gang calling themselves Los Muertos and whose apparent designs on D Street were striking at the heart of Dawg territory and forcing those who lived to rename their gang.

The Molotov cocktail was swiftly answered with a series of machine-gun volleys and a larger firebomb. The hatred of the rival street fighters was such that even the sight of the Batmobile didn't inspire more than a momentary slowing of hostilities. Batman was about to radio the police and move on when he saw a couple of terrified youngsters huddled in the lee of a Dumpster about thirty feet up a cross alley.

Without hesitation he drove past the alley and pulled

the Batmobile up to the ruined curb. He slid out of the car into the shadows of the alley and climbed up a twisted fire stair.

The boys didn't see him until he was literally on top of them. He reached down and grabbed each one by the shoulder.

"Bad seats," he murmured. "You should get your money back."

The boys—he guessed they were eleven or twelve—stared up at him with terror-filled eyes. He wasn't sure whether to be glad or dismayed that he was obviously scarier than a couple of vicious and overarmed street gangs. Then the boys' mouths opened and they shrieked in perfect unison.

He dragged them back into the shadows—the screams still soaring from their throats like twin sirens—wishing fervently they'd run out of air. He hauled them toward the Batmobile, deciding it would be safer to simply take them to the precinct house and have the duty sergeant contact their parents.

But in his brief absence the Batmobile had become the centerpiece of a weird standoff, and it was clear he wasn't going to get anywhere near it without some seriously kick-ass tactics.

He glanced into the enveloping shadows. To his immediate right was the gaping maw of what appeared to be a broad, shallow staircase. Fitful moonlight, along with neon and trash-barrel flames, illuminated steps that descended into darkness and seemed to end in a brick wall. A peculiar architectural detail; he could only assume it was a relic of the quake, and knew there was every chance it connected with the gritty shadow realm below known as Undertown—those several city blocks of inner-city real estate that landfill liquefaction had dropped, more or less intact, below the surrounding streets during the temblor. It had been deemed cheaper and more practical to simply pave over the sunken structures and leave them languishing in the dark than attempt to recover them.

The stairs might make a decent bolt-hole for the two noncombatants, should that become necessary, though he hoped it wouldn't. There were other dangers in the darkness.

He brought his attention back to the unfolding situation. To the left, near the rear of the Batmobile, hunched a rank of Dawgs, identifiable by the thick choke chains and studded dog collars they affected. Other than that bit of sartorial flair, there was a lot of black leather, denim, and calculatedly stiff and scruffy hair. There were also a lot of guns, chains, clubs, and unidentifiable weaponry that was probably homemade. One Dawg even sported a Civil War–era saber.

To the right, just beyond the nose of the car, ranged the rival gang. Los Muertos had, if not superior firepower, at least a much better look. They were, to a man, tall, ramrod-straight, and spare, dressed entirely in black, affecting long, paneled coats that seemed to float as they moved. But it was their faces that were most striking. They were an almost luminous white, in which eyes and mouths looked like slashes of primordial darkness. Very effective, Batman thought.

His two young charges, taking this all in, offered immediate and shrill commentary. Heads swiveled toward them.

"Son of a bitch!" said one of the Dawgs. "He's got Dar and Carlos!"

No time for this, Batman thought. "Go," he said to both gangs, his voice low but pitched to carry.

A couple of Los Muertos twitched; a couple of Dawgs raised their weapons. None looked particularly anxious to get within reach of the apparition, whose amorphous black cloak melded seamlessly with the dark alley shadows. Then one of the Dawgs hefted his rifle—a sawed-off affair with a small dog's skull affixed over the forward sight—and took a step forward.

Batman shoved the two boys down the phantom staircase and leapt straight up.

The drive back from the city was blessedly uneventful. He took one of six routes, picked at random by the car's uplink to the server array back in the cave. The car also had radar sensitive enough to pick up a hummingbird in flight at a thousand yards; if it detected anything that remotely resembled a following vehicle, or some other kind of suspicious action, he would turn around and either return to the city or take another road entirely, one that led out of town. He could not take the slightest risk of anyone finding the secret entrance to his underground headquarters.

He turned off the road, as he'd done so many times before, and drove the half mile to the ravine. A forced-air blower, mounted in the car's trunk, activated automatically, erasing the tire tracks with powerful gusts.

As he approached the ravine, Batman smiled slightly as he thought of all the times Alfred had accused him of paranoia. He didn't deny it. Given the life he led, paranoia wasn't a curse, it was a benison.

The huge slab of reinforced polyurethane faux-rock, camouflaged to look like a section of the cliff face, lowered, triggered by a remote command. Without slowing, the Batmobile crossed the bridge and plunged into the underground depths of the hills to the north of Gotham City.

The narrow road followed the contours of the cave, twisting and turning. At times, crevasses of unknown depths opened on one side or the other. He'd never put up guardrails along those stretches. He didn't want to become complacent, even in his own sanctum.

At last he brought the car to a stop in the center of the huge turntable. As he stepped out, he saw that Alfred was there to meet him, with the customary bottle of liniment.

"A productive night out, I trust, Master Bruce?"

"Not terribly, though I did stop a turf battle between Los Muertos and the D Street Dawgs." He pulled the cowl back from his head as they climbed the stairs to the main level. Damp, cool air fanned his cheeks, but did little to resuscitate his flagging energy.

Alfred, who had raised an eyebrow at his report, now said, "The D Street Dawgs? And you were unhappy with your appellation."

Bruce gave his butler a wry glance as they entered the elevator. There were two modes of egress to the cave: a hidden lift that was disguised as a large grandfather clock in the hallway, and the stairs concealed behind the library's sliding bookcase. Usually he took the stairs. Tonight, however, though he would never admit it to Alfred, he was a bit tired. It was nearly 4 AM, after all, and stopping the throw-down between the two gangs had been . . . challenging. A number of bullets had come uncomfortably close. The polyfibers woven into his suit and cloak had protected him—that, and the fact that he'd never stood still long enough to present a target. Still, he had to admit he'd had an uncomfortable frisson at times.

"And Ms. Tollyer?" Alfred asked. "She was the *intended* target of your reconnaissance, was she not?"

"I never made it to her place."

Alfred looked mystified. "You spent the entire evening—the entire *night*, I should say—in a gangland rumble?"

Bruce felt a moment of absurd defensiveness, as if Alfred was rebuking him. "Well, there were over two dozen of them, and I did have to return some youthful wannabes to their oblivious parents, so yes, pretty much the whole night."

"I see," Alfred said as the elevator stopped and disgorged them into the entrance hall. The butler said nothing more, but Bruce still felt slightly discomfited. Amazing, he thought, how the man who was nominally his servant could still, after all these years, make him feel defensive with no more than a raised eyebrow.

"I found another entrance to Undertown," he added.

"Delightful. Will it be of use, do you think?"

Bruce shrugged. "Only if I'm going to make a habit of shadow dancing with Los Muertos."

"Perish the thought," said Alfred, expressionlessly. Then: "A bite to eat before bed, Master Bruce? Something to replenish the inner bat?"

"No thanks, Alfred."

"As you wish, sir."

Bruce started up the stairs to the master suite.

"And sir?"

He turned to glance back down at Alfred.

"You *do* intend to sleep now, do you not?"

He chuckled at the poorly disguised concern. "Yes, Alfred. The Halloween party will require me being up rather late tomorrow—I mean, tonight."

"Very astute of you, sir. I shall take pains to see that you are not disturbed."

"You realize, don't you, that this could be categorized as 'risky behavior'?"

Bruce glanced up from the sword belt he was cinching about his waist and into the full-length mirror he stood before. Alfred was stationed behind him, a black cape lined with red silk draped over one arm.

"More risky than breaking up a gang war?"

"It gives a rather large number of people occasion to see Bruce Wayne in a black half mask and a cape."

"Yes, and a poufy-sleeved shirt and gaucho hat. Not part of my usual attire. Besides," he added, straightening the open collar of the shirt, "it's not a half mask, it's a domino."

"I don't imagine," said Alfred, "that the average partygoer would remark on the difference."

Bruce lifted the cape from Alfred's arm and swung it about his shoulders. "No. No more than they would make a connection between Batman and Zorro."

Alfred looked at him critically. "It's the eyes that give you away, sir. They aren't always hidden by those light-sensitive plates you fancy."

"I seriously doubt that anyone who's had an opportunity to gaze deeply into Batman's eyes is going to be present this evening."

"As you say, sir." Alfred turned and moved to the door of the bedroom, pulling on his white gloves. He paused with his hand on the knob. "Your young friend, Mr. Rosen. How will he be recognizable?"

"He said he'll be dressed as a geek."

"A . . . you mean a *Greek,* sir?"

"No, Alfred, I mean a geek."

"A *circus* geek?" Alfred looked repulsed.

"No, a computer geek. In fact, he'll be carrying a computer."

"Ah. Very good, sir. And, may I say, you look quite dashing."

Five minutes later Bruce started for the entrance hall. He was resisting the urge to swagger; there was something about the Zorro costume that was swagger-inducing. Odd, really. It was just a mask and a cape, after all; not so different from the cowl and cloak he wore nearly every night. And yet his "work clothes" inspired no desire to swagger.

*Must be the sleeves,* he thought.

From the second-floor landing he could see his guests arriving. There were at least three Marie Antoinettes— one with a sloppy necklace of surgical sutures around her neck, an original if somewhat bizarre touch. There was a plethora of pirates, space aliens, and magicians. A couple of Gotham's media personalities had come as their onstage personae. And there was even, he realized with a frown, a Joker. He raised an eyebrow as a pair of Catwomen—tall and short—entered arm in arm. They were followed immediately by Jesse Rosen.

*He wasn't kidding about coming as a geek,* Bruce thought. Jesse had exaggerated his habitual dress a bit; his black pants were belted high on his slender waist, and his socks were a pair of blinding-white bands between his trouser cuffs and black penny loafers. His shirt was an excruciating shade of mustard yellow, which clashed with a mangled green tie. He'd greased back his longish hair, exchanged his wire-rimmed glasses for horn-rims, and clutched a battered computer bag under one arm. Bruce heard him introduce himself to Alfred as "Poindexter." The butler shot his employer a look as he handed the programmer's jacket to the coat check.

Near the end of the stream of arrivals was a costume Bruce didn't recognize. It consisted of formfitting pants, shirt, and knee-length cutaway suit coat, all of unrelieved opalescent gray that rippled with phantom colors as the wearer moved beneath the lights of the entry hall. The half mask, which completely covered the top of his head, was of the same shade of twilight, as were gloves and matching shoes. Bruce couldn't see the face, but the shape beneath the somber clothing was male, not female.

He was overcome by the niggling sensation that he should recognize the character. He studied him a moment longer, then shrugged. Perhaps Alfred was right; maybe there was such a thing as being too paranoid, even for Batman. He slipped back into the shadows of the upper hall and went down to the ballroom via the kitchen to mingle anonymously with his guests.

The band was playing themes from well-known horror films, and food and drink were flowing freely, when Alfred appeared at Bruce's side to inform him that all guests were accounted for.

There was something about the tilt of his butler's graying eyebrows that made Bruce ask, "Anything wrong, Alfred?"

"I believe we may have a gate crasher, sir. Andrei's guest count is one off from my tally."

"Jesse?"

Alfred shook his head. "No. Andrei was instructed to count him as an invited guest."

Bruce nodded, his mind's eye immediately picturing the mystery guest in the gray costume.

"Of course," Alfred added, "this *is* the social event of the season and all that, so perhaps we should be surprised that there's only one 'Banquo's ghost' in attendance."

Bruce smiled. "Perhaps even slightly insulted?"

Alfred gave him another of those looks. "I doubt it's necessary to go that far." He checked his watch. "It's time for the official welcome, sir."

Alfred vanished into the milling celebrants, leaving Bruce to make his way to the bandstand. With the musicians momentarily stilled, he welcomed and toasted his guests, then called for a little drumroll to herald the unmasking. He took quick stock of his trick-or-treaters as they doffed their headgear, then turned to survey one another. One of the Catwomen was a debutante he'd once dated, named Serafina Orloff; he didn't see the second one anywhere on the floor. And the man dressed all in gray was none other than Grey Berwald.

Of course—he was supposed to be "Mr. Nightfall," the shadowy protagonist of his breakout novel of over ten years ago. Even Bruce, not the most inveterate reader of popular fiction, had read it—and enjoyed it.

He bade everyone "Happy Halloween," refastened his domino, and stepped from the bandstand to the dance floor, making a beeline for the long refreshment table where he could see Jesse Rosen juggling his computer satchel and a plate of food.

*       *       *

"Beware of Geeks bearing gifts."

Jesse opened the laptop and set it down on the reading table, turning it so that Bruce, Lucius, and Captain Gordon—the latter dressed as a Confederate soldier, that being the only costume he could get on short notice, he'd claimed—could see the screen. They had adjourned to the library, where they would ostensibly have more privacy. Faint sounds from the party intruded occasionally.

"What you're looking at," Jesse continued, shoving the horn-rims up the bridge of his nose, "is a schematic I drew up for—"

"A long-range subsonic transmission device," Lucius murmured, his eyes scanning the intricate rendering.

"I was gonna say *a sonic cannon,* but yeah—what you said will do." Jesse shoved his pants down around his natural waistline, banishing the white socks from sight. Then he fished his regular glasses out of his shirt pocket, swapped them with the horn-rims, and finally dragged off the tie, stuffing it into the front pocket of the computer satchel. "Much better. Now, look . . ." He tapped the computer screen. "Here's the transmission range and intensity. Not bad, if I do say so myself."

Gordon shook his head. "But the broadcast area is too broad. Could it be narrowed for greater accuracy?"

"How narrow?"

"Roughly the area of an underground train cab. Three, four feet. Otherwise—"

Jesse nodded. "Yeah, otherwise more people would have gotten caught in the blast, and you said they hadn't been. Okay, but that's going to increase the power requirements. This thing is already six feet long and two feet in diameter, with a generator the size of a microwave oven—"

"In other words, a cannon," Lucius concluded. "But to focus the sound wave—"

"Would require a longer barrel and a more powerful generator."

"Which would be difficult to conceal in a subway tunnel."

"It would have to be a straight, unimpeded shot, too. Any solid surfaces between the cannon and its target would absorb and disperse the sound wave."

Bruce sat on the edge of the table, remembering to look slightly bored. "If I'm understanding this correctly, it's a dead end."

Jesse looked discomfited. "Sorry."

"Not your fault," Lucius said. "It was a good suggestion. In fact, it's probably something WayneTech should look into. Might offer SWAT and search-and-rescue teams a viable alternative to explosives."

"It's an area worth exploring," Gordon agreed. He and Lucius returned to the party, still discussing the possible law enforcement applications of the sonic cannon. Jesse, however, remained behind. He closed the lid of the laptop, his eyes fixed on Bruce's face. It was a look eloquent with bemusement.

"What?" Bruce asked. "Is my mask crooked?"

"You're not what I expected, Mr. Wayne. I mean, Mr. Fox said you were a—" He stopped, color suffusing his neck and cheeks.

"A what?"

"A smart guy with a lot of hidden talents, was the way he put it. I thought he was just being politic, but—"

Bruce laughed. "Hidden talents? Are you sure he didn't say *wasted* talents?"

"Look, I didn't mean—"

"My ego's not that fragile, Jesse. I know Lucius would like me to take more of an interest in WayneTech. But if I had to attend every board meeting, I'd go out of my mind. It's not my thing."

"Whatever you say, Mr. Wayne."

"Bruce." He stuck out his hand.

Jesse shook it and grinned. "Does this mean I can stay for the party?"

"Please do."

Bruce ushered the programmer to the library door and pointed him down the hall toward the ballroom. A moment later he followed.

The next order of business would be a casual chat with Grey Berwald.

Bruce stood in the broad archway and surveyed the room, looking for Mr. Nightfall. He spotted Berwald—the costume's very drabness made it stand out—just stepping out onto the long marble terrace that over-looked the gardens behind the house. Catwoman was with him.

Serafina Orloff? That was a surprise. Among the many things she "simply could not abide"—and which she'd adumbrated over the course of a mind-numbing two-hour dinner date—was "trashy genre novels." She read award-winning mainstream books only—or claimed to.

He hesitated a moment, then stepped down into the ballroom and started across it to the long row of French doors that gave out onto the terrace. Halfway across the room he heard Serafina's distinctive laugh . . . from the dance floor.

Bruce turned. Serafina was in the arms of an American Revolutionary War soldier, for whom she was nearly a match in height. The *other* Catwoman was with Berwald, he realized. A much more petite Catwoman.

And one, he now suspected, who was not on his guest list.

6

He got sucked into two conversations—one with the mayor—and dodged several more before at last slipping out onto the pale, moonlit marble of the terrace. The air was so crisp, it seemed to crackle as it brushed the exposed flesh of his cheeks, chin, and neck. The voices it carried came to him from along the balustrade to the far right, not quite overwhelmed by the music and chaotic hubbub from within.

"Honey," said a man's voice in a soft Texas drawl, "you don't have to read the book if you don't want to. Not everybody likes to be scared."

To which Catwoman responded: "But some people *do* like to be scared, and *shouldn't* be. Just like some people like peanuts but shouldn't eat them."

Bruce recognized the voice immediately. It belonged to the woman he'd met back on the train. The journalist and blogger, Maggie Tollyer.

Mr. Nightfall chuckled at her statement. "Are you suggesting that some folks are allergic to my books? Now, that's a rare thought!"

"Not allergic. Sensitive. Aren't you, as a writer, responsible in some measure for the way readers react? I read an interview—"

"As a writer," Berwald said, with a bit more steel and a lot less drawl in his voice, "I'm responsible to my craft. My responsibility is to make it the best it can be. Since I write horror, that means making it as scary as it can be. That's all there is, pussycat."

"How scary is too scary, Mr. Berwald?"

"I set limits. I don't resort to graphic gore or glorify violence, if that's what you're on about. But I don't suppose you've actually read any of my work. People like you rarely do."

" 'People like me'? As it happens, I *have* read some of your work. And yeah, it was scary. But why no gore? Why draw the line there? Scary is as scary does, isn't it? Does it make a difference whether it's graphic gore or— or sheer terror that sends someone over the edge?"

Berwald took a step back from the journalist. "What the hell are you talking about, over the edge?"

"Something happened Thursday, Mr. Berwald. In the subway—"

"I saw it in the paper. What does that have to do with me?"

Bruce crossed the patio in three long strides, carefully placing himself so that Maggie was trapped between him and the balustrade. "Grey Berwald—Bruce Wayne." He shook hands with the distracted writer, peripherally aware that the petite Catwoman had shrunk against the railing, her head swiveling as she looked vainly for an avenue of escape.

He stilled her with an iron grip on her shoulder. "This particular villain isn't on my guest list. I hope you'll accept my apologies for her behavior."

Berwald glared for another moment, then relaxed. He made an expansive gesture. "No apology necessary, Bruce. I've gotten used to having people corner me at parties and read me the riot act for one thing or another. Goes with the territory, I guess. Fans sometimes get a little rambunctious."

"I'm *not* a fan," Catwoman growled.

"That's pretty clear," murmured Berwald.

"You're not a guest, either," said Bruce. "How about telling us who you are?" He knew already, of course, but since Bruce Wayne had never crossed paths with her, it wouldn't do to reveal that.

She glared. "I'm Maggie Tollyer. I'm a journalist. I wanted to speak to Mr. Berwald about—" She broke off as her gaze met Bruce's, bringing his earlier words to Alfred home to roost for him: *I seriously doubt that anyone who's had an opportunity to gaze deeply into Batman's eyes . . .*

Bruce spun her about, took her elbow, and marched her toward the French doors, dragging the Zorro hat and domino from his head as they neared the brightly lit ballroom.

"If you want to speak to Mr. Berwald about *anything*," he told her, "you should set up an interview through his publicist. You do realize it's illegal to crash a private party in order to harass a guest. Not to mention damn rude. I really ought to call the police."

"Go ahead," she replied as he guided her through the doors and across the ballroom toward the archway that gave access to the library wing. "Then I could have you charged with assault." She pulled free of his grasp. "Which I will, if you touch me again."

"If you'd like, Alfred can make the call right now. Then I'll have *you* charged with trespassing and invasion of privacy, and we'll see whose pockets are deeper."

She glared at him with such anger that he was momentarily grateful she wasn't the actual Catwoman, with real claws sheathed in those gloves. She clenched and unclenched her fists. "You win," she said through her teeth. "I'll go quietly."

"That's better." Apparently he'd acted quickly enough to prevent any comparisons between Batman's masked face and his to rise in her mind. Inwardly, he breathed a sigh of relief.

They continued toward the library and were a mere yard from the archway when Serafina Orloff's voice sliced through his concentration.

"Bruce! I think you've got the wrong kitty cat. *I'm* right here." She stepped directly into their path, completely ignoring Maggie. "Why'd you take off your mask? I was hoping to dance with Zorro."

"Oh, don't mind me—" Maggie started to say, edging to one side.

"Sorry, Sera." He blocked Maggie's attempted escape and gestured her toward the library's entrance.

"I want that dance, Zorro," Serafina said, pouting.

Bruce shook his head. "Right now, I've got a devil to dance with."

Maggie stood in the center of the imposing library, watching as Bruce Wayne dropped his black hat and mask on one of several massive mahogany reading tables. He raked a hand through his hair and perched casually on the corner of the table, crossing his arms in a pose that reminded her of nothing so much as a young, pre-tenure college professor she'd had. On Professor Howard, the pose had been a blatant attempt to look simultaneously scholarly and suave. On Bruce Wayne, it was something else again.

"I'm waiting," he said.

"For?"

He kept his gaze on her. Gray—were they gray eyes? Or hazel?

"For you to steal the silver. Come on, Ms. Tollyer, what the hell did you think you were doing out there? Crashing my party, badgering a celebrity guest? You came in with Serafina Orloff. Do you even know her?"

Maggie sweated a little beneath her vinyl mask. "I caught the Serafina part. Would that be the shipping Orloffs or the automaker Orloffs?"

"Both. And neither. Serafina gets seasick and doesn't drive. You met her at the door," he accused.

"Yeah, I did. She thought it was a hoot that I was wearing the same costume. I was going to use my press pass, but I didn't have to. I got in on her invite."

"So you could vilify Grey Berwald."

"So I could find out—" *So I could find out what?* she wondered. If he'd somehow spiked his novels with psycho-trauma?

"I'm listening."

"So I could gauge his sense of social responsibility."

Bruce Wayne shook his head, causing a lock of dark hair to fall across one eye. "Lame."

Her face felt hot, her hands cold. She reached up, unzipped the cat cowl, and pulled it off, knowing from the twitch of his lips that her hair was standing up in straight spikes, no doubt making her look like a hedgehog decked out in patent leather. She resisted the urge to smooth it.

"Not as lame as his bit about his 'responsibility to his craft' and 'setting limits.' He's obviously quite proud of himself for not spilling a bunch of blood and guts in his books."

Wayne shrugged. "Shouldn't he be? You pretty much demanded limits. He has limits. Where's the problem?"

She shook her head. "It's not good enough."

"Who are you to say?"

"Someone who . . . someone who knows the effects of *not* considering the audience."

He stood, uncrossing his arms, and stepped away from the table, making her acutely aware of how tall he was.

"I caught some of what you said to him. Something about sending someone over the edge. Were you talking about the train driver in that accident the other day?"

He'd surprised her. Her intelligence on Bruce Wayne had led her to suppose that he read only the society and entertainment pages and couldn't care less about what happened in the real world to the "little people."

She glanced toward the closed library door. "Look, are you going to call the cops or not?"

Wayne said nothing. He just looked at her.

The silence grew long and sweaty. No one knew about the novel but her. If she said anything now . . .

"Either call the police or let me go," she told him. "I'm fine with either. But I have to wonder what your guests would think if a team of Gotham's Finest suddenly showed up at your front door."

"Oh, I think I can trust the GCPD to be discreet. Alfred would just let them in through the back. No one would even know they were here. Anyone who did see them would think they were in costume."

Maggie shrugged with far more aplomb than she felt. "Fine. So call 'em. I'll just curl up on the ottoman over there and take a catnap."

He smiled lopsidedly, giving her a long, speculative

look, then put an elegant hand down to finger the detailing on the corner of the reading table. "I could've sworn cats were nocturnal. As are hedgehogs, I believe."

She felt her face burn again and wished she'd left the mask on. She reached reflexively toward her hair, then stopped herself. "You son of a bitch. What's the matter, if a woman doesn't fall all over you, you have to insult her?"

"I wasn't insulting you. I *like* hedgehogs. Prickles and all." His eyes widened. "Oh, you thought I meant your hair! No, Ms. Tollyer, I was referring to your—"

Whatever he was referring to was left unsaid when the library door swung inward to reveal a handsome white-haired gentleman in butler's regalia.

"You rang, sir?"

Maggie stifled laughter, feeling like she'd somehow fallen into an episode of *Upstairs, Downstairs*. Was he real, she wondered, or was he a security guard in costume?

"Alfred, if you would kindly see that Ms. Tollyer receives her coat and whatever else she needs to get home." He turned his gray-hazel eyes to her. "A cab? A car? I have several."

"I drove."

"Then make sure she retrieves her car and gets pointed the right way on the road back to Gotham."

"As you wish, Master Bruce."

Bruce Wayne scooped up his hat and mask but did not put them on. He clicked his booted heels together and bowed from the waist. "Ms. Tollyer, it's been an experience."

"It certainly has," she agreed, and swept out of the room on the butler's heels.

She was standing in the entry hall, waiting for her coat and bag and wondering if she should try to slink back into the party or simply go home and call it a failed evening, when Grey Berwald appeared from the direction of the ballroom.

He was bareheaded, the reflected light from the improbable chandelier above the entry riding the waves of his blond hair. He stood on the opposite edge of a magnificent Persian carpet that must have used up at least three generations of rug weavers. He was turning his headgear in his hands.

"Why do you dislike me so much?" he asked. "What'd I do?"

"I . . . I don't dislike you, Mr. Berwald. I just—"

He took a step onto the carpet. "You just think I'm— what? Prostituting my art? Lacking in scruples? A bad writer?"

"You're a very good writer, as it happens. Maybe that makes you even more . . ." She'd been going to say *dangerous,* but it sounded so melodramatic.

"Somehow that didn't sound like a compliment." He was smiling. Charming. To a woman who'd just attacked his artistic ethics.

"Look, Mr. Berwald, if you're afraid I'm going to write a scathing review of your last novel, or a nasty op-ed piece about your artistic scruples, you can stop worrying. I wouldn't. I don't do exposés. I don't name names. Those are *my* limits."

He took another step toward her. "Call me Grey. And I'm not worried that you'll write me up, Maggie-the-Cat. I just don't want to have someone hatin' me and me not knowin' why."

She stared at a him for a full five-count before it

struck her—the soft almost smile, the way his Texas accent deepened as he spoke. She laughed. "You can stop oozing country-boy charm, honey. It rolls right off the cat's back."

"I'm not trying to charm you," he protested, then glanced off to one side. "Well, okay, maybe just a little bit. Fact is, you made me stop and think. Most people don't find thinking as edifying as they do frightening, but I'm not most people. I'm not worried about you writing a flame piece on me. That's the truth."

Alfred the butler stepped back into the entry with her coat just then, pausing to look askance at her.

She kept her eyes on Berwald. "Just so happens that Tennessee Williams is one of my favorite playwrights. What is it Maggie-the-Cat says? 'Truth, truth—everybody keeps hollerin' about the truth. Well, the truth is as dirty as lies.'" She accepted Alfred's help with her coat, then let him escort her out to the veranda, where the valet was waiting with her aging Beemer.

It was close to 1 AM when he finally slipped into the Batmobile and made his way back into Gotham. Inevitably, there had still been a few guests wandering the halls. When he'd left, Alfred and his inimitable staff had been in the process of tracking them down and seeing them away in their limos, or packing them off to guest rooms to sleep off the festivities.

He mulled over his conversation with Grey Berwald as he drove. It hadn't been much of a conversation. Or at least not a particularly enlightening one when it came to Maggie Tollyer. Whatever her deepest reason for attempting to pinion Berwald and subject him to her views on art and social consciousness, she'd been no more forthcoming about it with the author than she had with Bruce Wayne.

No surprise, really. After all, the item that connected Berwald to the narrowly averted train wreck had never been entered into evidence by the police, and Maggie Tollyer apparently wasn't ready to admit to anyone that she had taken the book from Janet Epcot's backpack. Nor, as Bruce Wayne, could he have accused her of having done it.

But as Batman—well, that was a different kettle of fish, as Alfred was occasionally wont to say.

"An interesting woman," Grey Berwald had mused as the two men had shared a glass of Merlot in Bruce's private study.

"Perhaps, if you tend toward masochism. I don't; do you?"

Berwald had laughed. "Maybe I do, at that. Or maybe I just occasionally like to be reminded to stay humble."

Lack of humility had not been among the writer's apparent failings, Bruce Wayne had had to admit. Celebrity seemed not to have made him proud, and his gently self-deprecatory humor was engaging. By the end of the evening, the two men were as comfortable as old friends, which, considering the sort of life Bruce had led, was novel, to say the least.

They'd parted company with tentative plans for a pre-lunch game of racquetball early the next week. Grey had gone home in his Mercedes SL, and Batman had gone on the prowl.

Maggie Tollyer lived in an ancient high-rise that had somehow survived the Quake, though just barely. The building was fifteen stories tall and looked as if it might soon require crutches. The penthouse floor, which was topped with a garden and a small greenhouse, seemed to lean toward the street, as if eavesdropping on its neighbors.

Bruce Wayne had driven past it anonymously in daylight the day before, getting the lay of the land. Now in the dead of night, with no place to safely stash the Batmobile nearby, he'd been forced to leave the vehicle in an underground bolt-hole and surreptitiously navigate the subterranean passages on the fringes of Undertown to the one building in Gotham that would grant him a literal bat's-eye view of the city—Saint Peregrine's Cathedral. It was from that soaring, moldering edifice that he now looked down upon Maggie Tollyer's apartment building some blocks away, contemplating the best avenue of approach.

Maggie lived in a front corner apartment on the tenth floor, which would be easily accessible from the rooftop. The roof was empty, his night-vision lenses informed him. Not surprising, at this late hour.

He carefully inspected the buildings between here and there and drew up a mental map. Then he activated his newest WayneTech "toy"—dubbed a traction gun by Lucius Fox and shortened to T-gun by Jesse Rosen, in part because of its unique shape. A simple name for such a marvel of compact engineering and technology.

A pressurized reservoir, no larger than a deck of cards, held a biomimetic liquid polymer based on silk proteins. Combined with the trigger, it fit comfortably and securely into his gloved hand. When triggered, the polymer shot from a spinneret port in a thin monofilament line, solidifying on contact with the air. The end would adhere to practically any solid substance, and the thin line was capable of supporting twice his weight.

It was infinitely more portable and versatile than the

jump lines and collapsible grappling hooks he'd used at the start of his career, and certainly made getting around lofty downtown areas easier. Combined with the poly-fibers of his suit, which were designed to lock up in response to torque and shear forces, and his years of gymnastics training, the T-gun enabled Batman to swing from rooftop to rooftop almost as fast as he could run a level course—certainly faster than he could drive even through the near-empty streets of a sleeping Gotham.

He stood on the head of a massive stone gargoyle that jutted from one of Saint Peregrine's crumbling towers. The surface was slick, worn smooth by centuries of rain and covered with a sooty patina of air pollution, but he balanced upon it as easily as a mountain goat might. He lifted the traction gun, fired it. The line, nearly invisible in the gloomy dusk, struck and anchored itself to a cornice on the building across the street.

He jumped.

These acrobatics were always calculated risks—or leaps of faith. Even with his suit mitigating the stress, a slight error in judgment could leave him with two painfully dislocated shoulders—if he was lucky. Unlucky meant winding up a bat-shaped blot on the pavement.

It might happen sometime—but not this time. This time he swung in a graceful arc that would have put a trapeze artist to shame. His caped silhouette passed over the street, but there was no one below to mark it. He dropped to land on a wide ledge that wrapped around the target building. He jettisoned the first line—a tiny burst of concentrated acid from the spinneret port did the trick—turned, and fired again. And leapt again to swing to a new location. He'd contemplated using two of the new devices so that he could brachiate from arm to arm; it would have increased his speed considerably.

But the higher risk of injury wasn't worth the travel time saved.

He came to rest, at last, on the roof of Maggie Tollyer's building. The layout of the apartment, gleaned from a building floor plan housed in the doddering mainframe of the Gotham Department of Housing and Development, was still fresh in his mind. The two windows below belonged to the kitchen and bathroom, and both looked out onto a narrow alley. The bathroom window was dark; the kitchen's formed a rectangle of mellow light.

Batman triggered the traction gun, dropping a line straight down to the parapet, then stepped over the edge of the roof.

It always amazed her, Maggie thought, how alike men were. Take, for example, the expression on a man's face when his surefire disarmament routine didn't work with the woman he'd targeted. The child-like bewilderment, the crooked smile, the sudden need for the hands to be doing something—diving into pockets, ringing the butler, twisting a defenseless Halloween mask. She'd seen it tonight in host and guest: matching expressions of bemused disbelief that this obnoxious woman refused to be won over by charm and good looks, be they urbane or artless.

She curled her legs around the rungs of her stool and closed her eyes, letting the steam from the mug of hot apple cider caress her face. The scent of cinnamon and clove made its way up her nose and coerced her shoulders into relaxing.

*Wish I'd had a camera. I'd immortalize Bruce Wayne and Berwald on my website.*

"Too late for that," she murmured, "they're immortal already. Legends in their own minds."

"Do you often engage in conversation with hot beverages?"

She froze, her heart going from zero to sixty in one beat. *That voice.* She opened her eyes, hands no longer feeling the heat of the cider in the mug.

He stood just at the other end of her kitchen island—no more than four feet away, arms crossed over his armored chest, dark, looming, terrifying. The blank white panels that had covered his eyes when she first saw him on the train were gone now, and gunmetal eyes looked out at her from the black frame of his cowl. A wave of heat coursed from the top of her head to the soles of her feet.

"Wow," she said. "Batman in my very own kitchen. I feel like I should jump up and ask for your autograph, but I don't have any Bat-memorabilia for you to sign."

One corner of his mouth twitched. "Glib" was all he said.

She kept her gaze on his, though her body was shaking so hard she knew he surely must feel it through the intervening wood and tile of the island. She made herself take a sip of the cider, then set the cup on the island, struggling not to slosh. "Want some?"

"No, thanks. What I really want . . ." He took a sudden step around the edge of the island and closed the distance between them to a mere arm's length. His cape billowed behind him, making it seem to Maggie that he swelled to fill the entire kitchen, leaving no room for her.

She lost it. Yelping, she shoved herself away from the island. The stool tilted crazily and she went down.

He caught her before she hit the floor and let her down gently onto her back before straightening again to his full height. The cape settled around him, around her, forming silken walls. She could do nothing but stare up at him—which he no doubt intended, she thought, bristling.

He waited a beat—for the sheer threat of his presence to register, she figured—then said: "As I was saying, what I really want is the item you removed from the subway train Wednesday afternoon."

*No, he couldn't have seen that. He'd have to have X-ray vision to have seen that.* She felt suddenly naked.

"Yes, I saw you," he said, seeming to answer her private thoughts. "Don't even think of lying to me, Ms. Tollyer. You have a book, which you took from the driver's bag. The police have a name for that—removing evidence from the scene of a crime."

Maggie darted a glance around the kitchen floor, noticing that it needed to be mopped. *Oh, heaven forfend that Batman should think you're a slovenly housekeeper,* she berated herself. To her intimidating guest, she said: "Well, I sure as hell can't get it for you lying down here on the floor. Are you going to let me up?"

"I'm not holding you down." He moved back a mere inch, raising his arms slightly so that the cape lifted away from her body.

Of course he hadn't been holding her down. What in God's name had made her think he had? Maggie scrambled to her feet, turning to face him. He still loomed over her, even after she'd regained her footing.

*He looms well,* she thought crazily. "It's in here." She turned to lead him to her office.

"Don't try to run."

She hesitated. "I'm not stupid, Mr. Bat."

"Batman will do fine."

With her back to him, she couldn't see his face, but she thought there was the tiniest bit of—not warmth, but a lessening of his guard, perhaps?

She entered her office alcove, running her gaze quickly over the two overstuffed bookcases. She'd give him something random, just to get him—

Wait. He knew that she'd taken the book in the first place, which meant it was just as possible that he might know what book it was. And what if the book really *was* evidence?

She was in the alcove now, standing in front of the shelves. She knew without turning to look that he was blocking the archway behind her.

"Does this really bear on the case?" she asked.

"It may."

"Are the police . . . do the police know about it?"

There was the slightest hesitation before the dark voice said, "No."

"Well, then why do you think it has anything to do with a runaway subway train?"

"Because you do."

She turned to him then, trying to read the shrouded face. But he was backlit; his features were in complete darkness. She reached over and flicked on her desk lamp. The steely eyes followed the movement but did not blink even once at the sudden light.

"How do you know that?" She barely got the words out. Her mind was racing.

"I do a lot of my work online. So do you." He stepped into the room, making it feel suddenly the size of a dovecote. "You take the book; you develop a sudden, seemingly insatiable interest in its author." Again, a calculated pause. "You crash a high-profile Halloween party and verbally assault said author. Do I need to remind you how the conversation went? I have it memorized."

"How . . . ?"

"Trade secrets," he said. "Let's just say that when the cream of Gotham society gathers, it draws my attention."

"W-why?"

"Because it also draws the attention of others." One black-gloved hand reached out, palm up. "The book, please."

Whatever imagined lessening of severity might have been in his tone before was gone now. That voice could give someone's ears frostbite.

She turned away from the bookshelf and opened the drawer of her desk, hesitating only slightly before lifting the paperback and holding it out to him. He took it, and she wiped her sweaty palms on her plaid flannel pajama bottoms.

"The book just . . . creeps me out." She'd given up questioning the compulsion to explain herself to him. "Maybe just mental associations with almost being in a train wreck, maybe because it's a genuinely scary book— I don't know. I just don't like . . . touching it."

"Then you've read it."

"I started to. But like I said, it gave me the willies. Check out the dog-eared page. That's what the train driver read just before she . . . had her little episode."

He opened it, scanning the marked page. With his gaze momentarily not on her, the strength seemed to leave Maggie's legs as if she'd been hamstrung. She sat down heavily in her desk chair, quaking again. The last time she'd felt like this, she'd just had a near collision on the freeway.

*Or, dear God, like the moment* . . . She had a sudden searing memory of a newspaper headline.

"Are you all right?"

She looked up, startled to see that he had come fully into the room and was again standing right over her. She began to rise, then thought better of it. She wasn't sure her legs would support her right now.

"I'm fine. Do you . . . see what I mean?"

"This is what Janet Epcot was mumbling about?" He looked at her as if he could read some kind of strange aura she was giving off. "It's not a particularly frightening passage, in itself."

"Well, sure, it's not going to scare *you*. But it scared the crap out of *me*." She rubbed bare arms suddenly clad in gooseflesh. "It wasn't even that part so much. It was the opening paragraphs, where the protagonist begins to suspect that his subconscious thoughts are . . . are taking on a life of their own."

He dropped his gaze again to flip back through the book to the first page. He read it quickly.

"A man opens a newspaper to a story about a suicide—you found that frightening."

She shrugged. "Takes all kinds, I guess. The point is: I *did* find it frightening. It dug up . . ."

"Old ghosts?"

She shrugged again and looked away. She felt—what? Embarrassment at allowing herself to be manipulated by a professional horrormeister like Grey Berwald?

That wasn't fair. She couldn't imagine anything that would scare this creature of the night standing in her office. Suddenly angry, Maggie turned back to him.

"Are you a robot?"

There was no one there to answer.

In the brief moment that she'd taken her eyes off him, Batman had disappeared—taking the book with him.

*Good riddance,* Maggie thought. Still shivering, she shuffled back into the kitchen, where the open window's curtains were blowing slightly in the chill breeze from outside. She closed it, knowing that, even with the radiators going, she wouldn't be warm again for the rest of the night.

7

Dead of night.

There was a reason they called it that, thought Ulysses S. Cutter as he made his way through the interstices of Gotham City. At this hour, Gotham seemed dead—heartbeat stilled, breathing stopped. Even Undertown seemed to die a little, to shrink in on itself, its byways becoming almost exclusively the province of those who fed on death. Urban maggots carrying out their small desecrations in the body of the great city.

Cutter liked to think he was different. He wasn't, first of all, about his own selfish business this night. He was on a mission.

He liked the word *mission*. It had a poetic ring about it. And his mission did not involve theft, or rape, or murder, as so many others down here did. It involved only *enlightenment*. That was another word he liked. It was one his employer used often to describe his own mission.

It was to further the cause of enlightenment that Cutter traveled up from his Undertown digs to the maze of passages that underlay Saint Peregrine's Cathedral. He planned to surface in the crypt, where two loosened uprights in a wrought-iron fence would allow his spare six-foot-two frame to fold itself between the bars. He'd come this way before, many times.

He was approaching the last intersection, across from which a short flight of steps would take him up onto sacred ground, when a frisson of cold static raced up his spine. He paused just short of the intersection, held his breath, listened.

Most people's senses would not have picked up on the Other's approach. Cutter's senses, however, were not those of most people. He sensed, more than heard, the movement coming toward the junction from his right. The step was light, quick, certain; not like the usual denizens of the deep, who tended to shuffle. And overlaying the rhythmic tread was a soft susurration, as of fabric being dragged lightly across the facing of the stone walls.

Cutter carried no light—he didn't need one—so he pulled his long black greatcoat about his lean body, covering the lighter-hued material of his shirt and jeans and protecting the precious cargo he carried in the many small pockets that lined the coat. That, along with pulling his slouch hat down over his face, was the only movement he allowed himself. He didn't try to hunker against the wall or to shuffle backward to the previous turning. He simply waited as the Other moved out into the intersection and then, to his utter dismay, turned and started lightly up the steps into the crypt.

The form that was silhouetted momentarily in the wan blue-gray of filtered moonlight was like something out of a child's nightmare—one of the cathedral's great gargoyles come to hideous life. It was nebulous, its outer edges rippling black on black. And as it reached the top of the stairs, it blotted every last bit of light from the passage below.

Cutter held his breath as long as he could, then let it out silently as dim light returned.

*Damn.* He would not be able to use this egress now. How could he, when that demonic *Thing* might still be up there, waiting? Cutter had chosen Saint Peregrine's because it was relatively close to his destination. Now he would have to carry his cargo out of the underground a different way.

Cursing silently, Cutter used his anger to keep himself focused as he retraced his steps to the last intersection and turned uptown, to where the topside territory of the D Street Dawgs intersected that of Los Muertos. He knew a portal there, the doorway to a machine shop he'd owned a lifetime ago, before the Quake. Lamentably, it was farther from the university than this one, and perhaps not much safer.

But it wasn't like he had a choice.

Scurrying along beneath the streets, now several blocks from the crypt and its mysterious visitor, Cutter let go of his focused anger and relaxed to a stop in the stippled light from a sewer grate. He gazed up at the dripping ceiling of the tunnel and exhaled, his breath a stream of mist in the damp chill air.

"Sonofabitch!" he yelled. "*Sonofabitch!* SONOFA-BITCH!" He didn't care if anyone above heard him. He struck the walls with his open palm, once, twice, three times; stomped his right foot in syncopation, raising sodden cloudlets of dust. Then he clutched the front of his coat and moved forward again, faster now.

He had a mission to perform. He wouldn't complete it tonight, certainly, but he must set it in place. And he must not fail his savior.

\*          \*          \*

"A horror novel, sir?" Alfred looked at the fat volume as if it might do something objectionable on the spotless workbench.

"*The* horror novel, Alfred. The one Maggie Tollyer stole from the train driver's backpack. I . . . retrieved it from her this morning."

"You intend to analyze it, Master Bruce?"

Batman pulled off his cowl and took a deep breath of cave air. He realized, not for the first time, that he found the subterranean scent of damp earth and stone soothing. He exhaled and said, "I intend to read it first. Or at least portions of it."

He opened the novel to the dog-eared page and read the taut description of the tunnel creatures. Good writing, he thought. Tight, visceral, but nothing particularly shocking.

"Shall I activate the equipment, sir?" Alfred asked quietly.

Bruce looked up at him with a wry grimace. "If you can tell me which equipment to activate. A grammar checker and a Fog index might be more appropriate here than an electrospectrograph."

"Sir?"

"I have no idea where to start." He let Alfred lift the cape from his shoulders, then sat down at the workstation to tug off his gloves. "Maybe I'm jaded. Years of attending crime scenes and autopsies and reading police reports will do that to you, I guess."

"Perhaps," suggested Alfred, holding out a hand for the gloves, "you need an objective audience to read the passages? Someone who does not attend autopsies on a regular basis."

"Are you volunteering, Alfred?" Bruce handed over

the gloves and picked up the novel, turning to the dog-eared page.

She felt their presence as she stepped out into the main tunnel. A shiver in the dank air, a sudden heaviness in the mist . . . then she *smelled* them—a cold, sodden smell with an undercurrent of something acrid. She tried to think, tried to sense where they were. Ahead? To the left? To the right?

The movement, when it came, was directly behind her, as if the earth itself had shrugged or spasmed. She spun, caught her foot, and fell. Looking up into utter darkness, she thought the tunnel had come to life . . .

*Darkness. Damp, clinging, suffocating darkness all around him. An even darker hole before him—a passage straight through the core of the earth, to Hell. The sound of myriad wings—then an explosion of a thousand tiny bodies, sharp-toothed and slash-clawed. Eyes like tiny beads of shining black jet. He was bathed in them, drowning in them, in the sound and touch of their wings, deceptively soft on his skin, their rugose faces flickering before him. The endless echoing of their shrieking, like a stylus being dragged across vinyl . . .*

"Master Bruce?"
There was a sharp edge to Alfred's voice. It cut through the sudden, vivid, chilling memory of the day he had discovered this place—and perhaps discovered himself as well. He laid the book flat on the workbench and stood, looking down at the palms of his hands. They were naked, as for the briefest moment, his psyche had

been. "The electrospectrograph will do just fine for a start," he said, keeping his voice level. "I'll want to . . . to analyze the paper, too, and the ink. Full chem battery."

"What was it?" Alfred asked.

Bruce grimaced. "A blast from the past."

"What can I do?"

"Help me out of this gear. Decontaminate it. All of it. And me. I'll go take a shower."

"Our night is not over, is it, sir?"

"Not even close."

They looked at each other. "Coffee," they said in unison.

Late. He was running very late. The detour through the machine-shop portal had proved dicier than he'd anticipated—the territory belonged entirely to Los Muertos now, which wasn't good. They were far more observant than the Dawgs had been, less interested in the sort of payoffs someone like Cutter could command, and more sophisticated in the means they used to deal with trespassers. He'd been forced to spend much precious time hunkered at the bottom of the stairwell, waiting for clear passage. After that he'd had to hurry, which always worried him. Haste was dangerous. It made a person sloppy. He couldn't afford to be sloppy.

Luck was with him, however, as he departed Los Muertos land. Someone had chained a bicycle outside an all-night convenience store and hadn't pushed the lock in all the way. It wouldn't have mattered much if they had; Cutter knew how to liberate locked things, with a dexterity that bordered on prestidigitation. But the oversight did save him time, and some of the fear of discovery.

It was perfect, he thought, as he glided at last onto the university campus. There were literally hundreds of bicycles here, some parked neatly with their front wheels slotted through concrete or metal stands, others chained to fences, stair rails, even small trees.

He paused between two darkened dormitories to consider the layout of the campus, his mind providing a 3-D map that he tilted so that he could mentally "see" the building he was seeking. Having an eidetic memory didn't quite make up for his legion problems and failings, but it helped.

He pedaled across the quad, beneath the nodding heads of century oaks, and set the bike in a stand before the Carl Sagan Research Library. He scanned the front of the building for lights. Other than the pair of Gothic lanterns that flanked the broad entry, he could see none.

His right arm threw a sudden, violent salute at the sleeping building even as he used his left to pull together the lapels of his coat. He stomped his left foot several times in the soft grass, literally biting his tongue. There had been a time when he would have tried to grab the errant arm, to still it.

He knew better than that now.

Clutching the front of his coat, Cutter scurried into the layered darkness along the building's broad left flank. There was a small loading dock at the rear of the library, and it was there that he went. It was an old mechanism with no fancy mechanical or electronic devices to guard it—after all, who would steal fat volumes of fact and theory?

He vaguely remembered his brief tenure in college. Those musty tomes were hardly any sane person's idea of a good read. They were archaeological artifacts; one studied them, scribbled slender notes, prayed to absorb enough to pass a test, and left them in situ.

It was Gotham University's captive audience of reluctant students that his employer had chosen to be the first recipients—or nearly so—of his beneficence in the form of the vials secreted in Cutter's coat.

"Learning, Ulysses," he'd said, "indeed, enlightenment itself, is a matter of absorption. Your mission is to deliver to those poor benighted souls the ability to absorb knowledge."

"What sort of knowledge?" he'd asked, wishing he might absorb some himself, if only to counteract the effects of the alcohol and cocaine he'd imbibed for so long—the alcohol to numb him; the cocaine to bring him back, however briefly, to quaking awareness; then alcohol again, to hide himself from being aware.

He'd heard the smile in his mentor's voice as the latter said, "Why, the best kind of knowledge, Ulysses. The forbidden kind."

No one had called Cutter "Ulysses" since his father, that iron patriarch who refused to acknowledge pet names or the softer feelings that went with them. He'd always called his wife Elizabeth, never Beth or Elly or El as friends and family did. Never dear or honey as a husband might.

His mother, Cutter recalled, had always called him Uly. He liked Uly, and he had liked finding another woman who called him that. So much so that he'd married her.

He shook himself, concentrating on the task at hand, on the lifting of the pleated door of the loading dock. That part of his life was long over. There was nothing left of that Ulysses S. Cutter but a missing person report filed by his in-laws.

This was his life now.

His manipulation of the door's belt chain resulted in a gap just wide enough for him to roll beneath. He removed his coat, pushed it through the gap, then followed.

Inside, the loading area was in complete darkness. Cutter got out his flashlight and flicked it on, aiming it at the floor. Then he picked his way into the library, past derelict shelving units and boxes of books that were either coming or going.

There was a maintenance closet in the hallway leading to the main reading room. It was this place he chose to divest himself of his cargo. Beneath a rough workbench were several loose floorboards. He had made sure they were loose on his first visit several nights earlier. Beneath them was a metal banker's box. Within that was an air compressor with a football-sized tank and a short hose. He'd stashed both these items earlier, as well.

Now, spreading his coat carefully on the floor, Cutter knelt and added to the box the little vials of tempered glass that lined it. Each one was about the size of one of those hard-shelled eyeglass cases that were currently all the rage. And each sloshed delicately as he set them in place.

His employer had assured him that the tempered glass could withstand quite a bit of rough handling, but he didn't want to take a chance. He'd gotten so much wrong in life; it was important that he get this right— that he not disappoint the man who had given him a third chance after he had so thoroughly blown the last two.

He held the last vial, fingering its smooth surface as he checked the glowing dial of his watch. Nearly dawn. Damn! If only he'd started on his mission earlier. If only he hadn't been so shortsighted and cocky as to assume he'd be able to use the cathedral egress again.

Perhaps he should try to do some of the work this morning. He could certainly treat some of the books and leave enough time for the liquid agent to dry before the library opened. He laid the vial on his coat and reached down into his cache for the compressor. He had just lifted it free when his arms went into a sudden, wild flapping movement as if they would lift him bodily to the ceiling. The compressor dropped, falling directly onto the unprotected vial.

Even before the episode ended, Cutter could see a tiny liquid stain on the coat's soiled white lining. It was no bigger than his pinkie nail, but it meant the vial had been breached. He snatched up the little bottle, righting it. The glass itself hadn't broken—he could see that when he held it up to his light—but the lid had been dislodged and dented.

Swearing under his breath—intentionally this time— Cutter freed the lid and quickly poured the Liquid Enlightenment into the compressor tank. Then he recapped the little flask and stuffed it into an outer pocket of his coat. Moving as swiftly as he dared, he secreted the stash and returned the floorboards to their places. He gathered up his coat, rolling it into a tight ball, and made his way back out the way he had come.

It was all he could do not to put his head down on the workbench and give over to unconsciousness. But the chemical analysis of the partially dismembered paperback was nearly complete. Between them, he and Alfred had drunk enough coffee to wake the dead, and now he felt as if his skin were trying to shrug itself free of the muscles beneath.

He rubbed his arms and focused on the computer display. "Nothing in the ink," he said.

"But the readings on the paper seem anomalous," Alfred observed. "Trace amounts of—"

Bruce sat bolt-upright, his mind suddenly clearing as the last of the results scrolled onto the screen. "Of course," he said. "The binding glue."

He and Alfred both bent to the display, eyes trailing through the list of recognized chemical components.

"Alkaloids, piperidines, phenylethylamine . . . unknown, unknown, unknown . . . ketamine," Bruce murmured.

"A virtual stew," Alfred observed.

"A familiar stew. Except for the unknowns." Bruce reached for the mouse and called up the medical report on Janet Epcot. Yes, she'd had elevated adrenaline, serotonin, and endorphin levels, but here there had been more unknowns, as well. There had been nothing in her stomach, her lungs, or her blood . . .

He snatched up what was left of the book, his hand still swathed in a surgical glove. He held the torn novel as if to read it, gripped between thumb and fingers—his thumb pressing the pages open, his fingers wrapped around the spine.

"It's transferred by touch," he murmured.

"Which explains why you did not initially react to it." Alfred punctuated the sentence with a yawn.

"And which raises several questions. Is it just this book . . ." Bruce turned the volume so that Alfred could see the torn, gold foil label on the flyleaf.

Alfred blanched. "Or are there others?"

Bruce ran his gloved thumb over the label: GOTHAM BOOK EMPORIUM. "Who's done this, Alfred? And why?"

"If I might suggest, Master Bruce," said Alfred. "To

answer but one of those questions might well imply answers to the others."

Cutter brought the bicycle all the way into Los Muertos' barrio. The sun was near rising, and the streets had taken on the smoky, silver gleam of predawn. He hurried, pedaling for all he was worth, praying that he would make the sanctuary of the seemingly dead-end stairwell before the sun rose. It did not occur to him that there might be any of the gang members still about at this hour.

And so he was literally bowled over when a black-and-white stick figure stepped out of nowhere and grabbed his handlebars. The bike twisted, and Cutter sailed off to skid painfully on the gritty asphalt. He came to rest against a wall, between a couple of cardboard boxes, the coat still clutched against his body.

The Muerto was on him in a heartbeat, painted face leering. He grasped Cutter's shoulder with one hand and thrust a knife at him with the other. Cutter did the only thing he could think of—he shoved the coat upward into the guy's face.

It was futile, of course; the Muerto merely tore the coat away from him and started to cast it aside. He stopped, though, feeling the weight of the vial.

"What's that, mole? Liquid courage?" He laughed.

"Liq-liquid E-e-nlightenment."

"Right." He draped the coat over his shoulder, reached into the pocket with his free hand, and drew out the vial. He shook it, eliciting the weakest of splashes. The blackened lips made a moue of feigned disappointment. "You didn't leave me any. That's not very polite."

The Muerto stuck one booted foot in the center of Cutter's stomach and pinned him to the ground as he worked the lid. It came off suddenly, and he uttered a violent curse. Cutter saw a bright bead of red swell from the tip of one finger before the guy stuck it in his mouth.

The Muerto sucked the wound for a moment, then dropped the coat and the vial and leaned over Cutter, his eyes wild, the knife trembling in his hand.

"Before I gut you," he stage-whispered, "tell me your name. I'll add it to my shrine and say prayers for your pathetic soul."

"C-c-cutter," he stuttered. "I'm C-cutter."

The Muerto stilled. His face, if possible, paled further. "Cutter? Like a butcher? I-I knew a guy named Butcher. Because he *was*. He made me—made me . . ."

Cutter was never to hear what the "guy named Butcher"—or who *was* a butcher—had made the gangster do. The Muerto went suddenly mad, dropping his knife and staggering backward with his hands over his face, rubbing at his eyes, at his cheeks. White and black blurred to the gray of the surrounding mist and stone.

*"Butcher!"* he shrieked and ran off down the alley.

Cutter did not stop to ponder the gift of life. He simply accepted it, scrambled to his feet, gathered up the coat and vial, and staggered back to his portal, obscenities jerking from his throat into the warming air.

8

He left a message for Captain Gordon, revealing the existence of the novel and outlining the results of his analysis of the book's binding. He called Arkham but was forced to leave a message there as well, requesting that Scarecrow's cell be checked for anomalies, and telling Dr. Avery to expect him first thing in the morning. Which, he realized, was not that far off.

He had told Alfred to pack it in at 4 AM, but didn't fall into bed himself until two hours later, when the sun was taking its tentative first peek over the treetops. He had long ago trained himself to awaken, if necessary, after just one complete round of polyphasic sleep, which he usually completed in less than two hours. He could go for a week or more on just two hours every twenty-four, but eventually the lack of sleep would catch up with him, and when it hit, it hit hard. Alfred was used to him sleeping the clock around or more, and fielded the inevitable phone calls, mail pouches, e-mails, and other intrusions that were as much a part of Bruce Wayne's life as the endless martial arts kata and weapons training were of Batman's.

The redoubtable servant was gone when he woke—having driven into Gotham to be present when the doors of the Book Emporium opened. He was to purchase all existing copies of Berwald's novel and bring them back for analysis. He was also to purchase several other volumes of horror fiction as well as books published by Chance Publications in a variety of genres. He had left a covered tray for Bruce—eggs Benedict and coffee, still hot.

Showered and more or less awake, Bruce called James Gordon again at the GCPD.

"I got the message," Gordon told him the moment he recognized Batman's voice. "Neurotoxins. You suspect Jonathan Crane had a hand in this?"

"It's his MO."

He could almost hear Gordon shaking his head, see him pushing his glasses farther up his nose. "I called Arkham immediately when I got in this morning. Crane was in his cell. They'd gotten your message, as well, and had already rousted him out and checked the walls, the floors, everything. He's there, and he hasn't had a visitor—besides you—for the better part of a year."

"But he has had them?"

"One, two maybe. Do you want me to—"

"I'll check that myself. In the meantime, I'll upload my chemical analysis of the novel to the police database."

There was the merest hesitation on Gordon's end of the line. "About that," he said tentatively. "You knew about the novel—"

"It came into my possession early this morning. I felt it would be most expedient to analyze it myself."

The captain sighed audibly. "Well, you're right on that count. I wish I could say you weren't. Okay, but this Tollyer woman—what part does she play in this? Could she have actually placed the contaminated book in Ms. Epcot's pack? . . . No, wait. Scratch that. Epcot mentioned the missing book to her nurse at Sun Valley. And she duly reported it to the investigating officers."

"Then you knew about it already."

"Yeah. Only I didn't remember that I knew about it. It didn't seem relevant. A missing paperback? We figured it just got misplaced or lost in all the hubbub." He drew a deep breath. "I'm glad you were at the scene. We'd be nowhere if you hadn't been."

Bruce sat for a moment after he rang off, wondering where, in fact, they were now. The MO was definitely that of the Scarecrow, but the Scarecrow was in his cell at Arkham. He'd had no access to a laboratory since he'd been incarcerated over a year ago. And though it was by no means certain that the police had gotten all of his equipment and stores, it was certain that Jonathan Crane had had no contact with them . . . physically.

How, then?

He left a message instructing Alfred to randomly select books to analyze from among his purchases. Then he donned his alter ego and paid a visit to Arkham.

Cutter lay in the ruined basement of his former machine shop for some time, quivering on the gritty floor, his left leg jackhammering the dank air. His heart beat so fast, he feared it might trip over itself, and his lungs seemed unable to take in enough oxygen.

He knew how narrowly he had averted a painful and messy death, but that was not the sole reason for his quaking. It was the look of abject terror on the face of the Muerto . . . *after* he had tasted the contents of the vial. Cutter clenched his fingers and felt the hard outline of the bottle through the layers of wool wrapped about it.

When his leg had ceased its wild spasming, he heaved

himself to his feet and stumbled to the far western corner of the half-collapsed room. There a jumble of bricks
hid a narrow slot from which steam rose in wan, semi-
transparent banners. He slipped behind the debris,
knelt, and let himself into the slot.

He slid a good nine or ten feet over the flat, sandy surface of broken masonry, and was reassured when his
feet touched down on solid ground. He moved swiftly
now, at a shambling run, making for the place where he
kept his lodgings and guarded his employer's precious
effects.

He had to cross through the heart of Undertown to
get there: a welter of narrow, winding streets, many
of them cobbled or bricked, with horse posts on the
curbs. The streets were buckled and cracked, of course,
and the old brownstones and Victorian town houses
that lined them tilted and staggered crazily, like images
in a fun-house mirror. But many were surprisingly intact.
A few places actually had light and power, filched from
Gotham P&E. Undertown was largely deserted, but the
downtrodden and the disenfranchised had made parts of
it their home, and even opened a few businesses down
here.

Though he meant to avoid it, he found himself drawn
from the filthy, steaming, damp byways into the comforting, noisy gloom of Blackie's Tavern, where he made
his way to the bar. The coat balled up in his lap, he
begged a cup of hot apple cider from Blackie himself,
eyes transfixed by the spastic flare of neon, which painted
the albino bartender's paper-white skin in a rainbow of
colors.

When the lights flashed blue, reminding him forcibly
of the man in the alley, Cutter pulled his gaze away.
What had terrified the Muerto so? Was there some prop-

erty of enlightenment so potent as to have that effect? Did it, perhaps, expose past sins?

He shivered anew at the thought, sipping his cider and hunching lower over the coat. His employer had specified that the potion was to be dispersed on the books in the school library and thus taken in through the skin. Was it possible that the Muerto had merely overdosed, and that an overdose of even something as beneficial as knowledge could inspire fear?

This caused him to reexamine his feelings about the inoculation he'd been required to give himself before he took on the University Project. He had felt almost slighted when he'd received the instructions. Why couldn't *he* have enlightenment? Why did *he* have to suffer with a brain so full of drug-induced holes that he must make and follow daily lists in order to function? Yes, he was improving—every clearheaded day was another step toward potentially putting his life back together— but why would his benefactor not let him experience a less painful path to knowledge?

Now, having seen the effects of the concentrated potion, Cutter wasn't sure he shouldn't be grateful. If it had been he who'd gotten that blast of "brain-food" . . .

"What's the matter with you, man?" Blackie asked.

Cutter looked up at the tall albino and realized that his hands, wrapped around the hot mug, were shaking. He licked his lips. "Almost got whacked by one of Los Muertos."

"Yeah? How'd you get away?"

"Don't know."

"Whaddaya mean 'don't know'? How d'you not know?"

"Sun came up," Cutter said, trying to be nonchalant. "Maybe it fried him or something."

Blackie shook his head. "That's vampires, Cutter. You gotta get your monsters straight."

Cutter smiled wanly and finished his cider. "Yeah. Yeah, I gotta get my monsters straight."

He got up, slapped a handful of change on the bar, and left the dark, cozy sanctuary. The roadway overhead was beginning to fill with traffic, growing steadily to a muffled rumble, as he made his way home.

"His cell is clean. Not a sensor out of place, not so much as a hairline crack in the paint. And he has been in that cell under tight surveillance day in and day out, twenty-four hours a day, for over two years." Seated behind his oversized mahogany desk, Dr. Avery looked sleepy, disgruntled, and put upon as he went over the morning's activities—again. "The police have already asked me all this."

Batman ignored the comment. "He never leaves the cell for any reason?"

"Well, he left this morning because the police demanded his cell be searched."

"And his visitation log?"

Avery turned the display of his computer around so his imposing visitor could see it. "I already read these entries to Captain Gordon of the Gotham PD."

There were only three visits logged, all early in Jonathan Crane's incarceration. Two of them were from his therapist—who now met with him by telephone—and the third was by a journalist, though not Maggie Tollyer. Batman recognized the name as belonging to one of the *Gotham Gazette*'s senior reporters. He recalled the article that had been the result of that visit. It had centered on him, rather than Scarecrow, and carried the unfortunate headline of BAT BUSTS.

"This is it? These are all the visitors he's had?"

Avery gave him an arch look and turned the display back. "If these are the only ones logged, these are the only ones he's had."

*Dead end.* Unless . . .

"Might Doctor MacMillan have arranged for a . . . private visit? A visit that didn't get logged?" Roderick MacMillan, the doctor who had assumed the role of administrator after Crane's own brief and disastrous tenure, had been known to make inadvisable decisions where his notorious inmates were concerned; had been known, in fact, to treat them as if they were his private collection of oddities rather than wards of the state.

Avery's brow puckered and his lips opened to protest. They closed again, pursing into a shape reminiscent of a prune. "It is possible that Doctor MacMillan himself might have brought someone to see Doctor Crane. He was . . . fond of making our inmates accessible to academics."

"Academics?"

"Behavioral psychologists and neurologists for the most part. Mostly they observed. They never interacted directly with the inmates—they were never allowed in the same room—so they were not logged as scrupulously."

"And did Doctor Crane receive such an observer?"

"I really can't say. If he did, only Doctor MacMillan could have said."

"While you searched Crane's cell this morning, where did you hold him?"

"An interview room on the same level. Just down the hall, in fact."

"Show me."

The interview room was cell-like and spartan: stainless steel and white enamel. The sole piece of furniture was a molded, transparent Plexiglas chair. There was not even a table beneath which something could be hidden. And there was a surveillance camera in every corner. At the front of the room was a panel of bulletproof glass that gave onto a second room, which hosted visitors. It was every bit as naked as this one. Avery was correct—the inmates never interacted directly with anyone but prison staff.

Though his expression remained as stolid as ever, inwardly Batman seethed with frustration. The smug tone in Avery's voice didn't help any as he said, "Satisfied?"

"No," Batman told him. "Which means I'll be back."

He turned and strode down the hall, his cape swirling behind him like a Rorschach inkblot against the white walls of Arkham Asylum.

9

"And how are you coming with your homework, Ulysses?"

"Oh, very well, sir. Just a little behind. I ran into some trouble with a street gang last night. I didn't have time to treat the books, but everything is in place for tonight."

"Tsk. Homework late again, Ulysses? This may affect your grade."

"I-I-I . . ."

"Three 'I's in a row? That's quite an ego you've got there."

Cutter laughed, licked his lips, cleared his throat. He appreciated his employer's deft use of humor to defuse his tension. "That's pretty funny. Me with an ego. I'm going back tonight to administer the treatment," he said, making his voice as confident as he could.

"Very good. I'll consider giving you full marks if the quality of the work is high. I expect it will be; you've yet to disappoint."

Cutter nearly wept at the words. Someone he had failed to disappoint! That sort of failure he would accept gladly.

"You will turn your paper in the moment you've completed it, yes?"

"Oh, yes. Of course. Immediately, if not sooner." He laughed weakly.

"Well, then . . . are there any questions before we move on?"

"Well, sir, um . . . yes. That is, I . . ."

"Well, speak up, Ulysses. What is it?"

"If a person . . . got a concentrated dose of the formula, what might happen?" There, he'd asked.

A long moment ticked by before his employer said, softly, "That's a very interesting question. There can be such a thing as too much information. I certainly would never ask you to put every bit of data you had at your command into your work."

Cutter sighed and worked his way back through the vagaries of the peculiar code his employer insisted upon using. "I didn't intend to, sir. But, the stuff is in liquid form, which means it's pretty diluted when I spray it, and I just wondered—you know—what would happen if someone were to get some in their mouth, for example?"

There was a quavering hiss from the other end of the connection that might have been a gasp of horror or a laugh. Cutter couldn't tell.

"I should think the student who turned in *that* paper would get at least a D. Really, it's a dead issue. Now, I think you've got plenty of information for your papers. They must be completed and turned in to me by Wednesday of this week. Is that clear?"

"Yes, sir. Very clear, sir."

"Class dismissed."

*D is for Dead,* thought Cutter as the connection fell silent. He shook his head, trying to wrap his mind around the idea that knowledge was something you could OD on.

He left the computer room and went back out into the main laboratory, his gaze moving unwillingly to the "clean room" where the formula was prepped and stored. It was a stand-alone booth, twenty feet on a side, made of bulletproof impermeable transparent aluminum three inches thick. It had an air lock, and even he, immune though he was to the effects of Liquid Enlightenment, had to wear a Hazmat suit to enter it, lest he carry some residue out on his clothing. He had stowed the damaged vial there and consigned the coat to the decontamination chamber in the corner.

Tonight. Tonight he would complete his assignment. He would be careful to do it just right so that the formula would be spread evenly on the books. So that no one would overdose on knowledge.

Until then, he would sleep. He checked the security system, making certain that the dedicated computer was on and running the holographic security program that caused anyone peeking through the building's filthy windows to see nothing but a rat-infested and empty warehouse.

Cutter was rather fond of the holographic rats. He liked that they never seemed to do the same thing twice. Something referred to as an AI algorithm ensured that— an artificial intelligence algorithm. That big, fancy phrase simply meant, in this case, that the program didn't repeat itself. The movements of Cutter's holographic pets were infinite in their diversity.

He'd studied the code that made them cavort and play and forage for virtual food. He had learned to find meaning in the strings of strange "words." It was just a different language—like gang-speak.

Cutter watched the rats for a moment, then went to bed. Behind him, the computer's big LCD monitor went to its screensaver, obscuring the WayneTech logo on the AI program's opening screen.

"Bingo, sir." Alfred stood at the top of the staircase that led up from the garage floor. Despite the uncharacteristic colloquialism, he sounded quite grim.

"Bingo?" Bruce pulled off the cowl, raked his fingers through his hair, and squinted up at the butler's backlit figure.

"As you say, sir. I have now tested twenty-two books. Every volume of *Fear Itself* contains the same chemical compound as the first. I chose them at random from among the ones I took from the shelf and from among those still packed in an unopened box."

"A box from the distribution center?"

"Indeed. Freshly so, in fact. And before you ask, yes, I did get an address and a phone number for the distributor. They will be open at nine tomorrow morning, according to their answering machine."

"And the other books?"

"None of the other books published by Chance contained the toxin, though all came from the same distributor. I also took the liberty of visiting my favorite independent bookstore and purchased a couple of copies of *Fear* there, as well."

"And?"

"The toxins were also present in those books."

Bruce nodded, still frozen in the act of mounting the steps.

"Do you intend to come up, Master Bruce, or will you be going out again directly?"

"Coming up."

He took the steps two at a time, handed off the cowl

to Alfred, and sat down at his computer console to check the results of the chemical tests.

"Same compound; same amounts," he murmured. "If these books are coming from the distributor like this . . ."

"The implications are staggering, sir."

They were. While it was true that Grey Berwald's last two novels had not been the raging successes of the preceding ones, they still sold in the thousands in a market like Gotham City and possibly even millions nationwide. If all of them had been contaminated, well . . . *staggering* was hardly the word. More like *cataclysmic,* he thought grimly.

"The manager of the Book Emporium told me they'd sold five thousand copies of the book in the first two weeks of release," Alfred said quietly.

"We need to get this information to the police; they'll have to involve the FBI. This goes beyond Gotham. That distributor is shipping books across the country."

He tugged at his lower lip, thinking. It was indeed the Scarecrow's MO, but Crane was out of the picture. Was Grey Berwald directly involved? Having met the man, spoken to him—having been so *comfortable* with him— it was hard to believe him a criminal mastermind, but stranger things had happened, and stranger criminals had victimized Gotham City.

He pictured the author in his Halloween costume— dusky gray from head to foot. Was he facing a new archvillain in Mr. Nightfall?

"I think Batman needs to pay a visit to Grey Berwald. In the meantime . . ." He reached for the phone to bring James Gordon up to date, then changed his mind. A face-to-mask meeting was best for information this critical.

Alfred handed him the cowl as he rose. "Sir, this book has been on the stands for a little over a month. If this toxin is so widespread, why haven't we seen more incidents like the one in the subway?"

"Who's to say we haven't, and simply didn't recognize them? We connected the runaway to the book because of Maggie Tollyer. If she hadn't intervened, I doubt the Gotham PD would have been suspicious of an innocent-looking little paperback." He picked up the original book, clad now in a ziplock bag. "Have a box of the books sent to Captain Gordon so he can get them to the crime lab. Have the other delivered to Lucius Fox with a note from the GCPD; I'll forge Gordon's signature. He should do whatever he can to isolate the unknown elements in that compound and get started on an antidote and a vaccine."

"At once, sir. Do you have a preference for the pickup point I give the courier for the police delivery?"

"The one closest to headquarters. And I need Lucius to get R and D on this as soon as possible. After you've set up the deliveries, take a suit of my clothes with you and wait in the alley between Ott and Derocher."

"Of course, sir. I always enjoy parking alone on a disreputable backstreet in an expensive town car."

Batman turned in a swirl of black, and took, once again, to the road.

Captain James Gordon gazed at the torn paperback in its well-sealed plastic bag and felt dread. "And you suspect these were treated at the distribution point?"

Across from him, under the eave of a stairwell cupola atop police headquarters, Batman was a blue-black specter in the soft, gray mist that cloaked the upper sto-

ries of the building. His cape eddied like liquid darkness
about his still form, dancing with the chill breeze. As
always, Gordon's gaze was drawn, unwillingly, to his
eyes—cold as steel, colorless as the underbelly of a
storm cloud.

"Yes. And if that's the case, those books are being
shipped to hundreds, maybe thousands of destinations."

Gordon shivered. "So we'll have to involve the FBI.
Do you still suspect the Scarecrow?"

"At this point I don't see how it could be Crane."

"Someone new?" God, now *that* was a depressing
thought.

"Possibly."

Something in Batman's voice brought Gordon into
tight focus on the cowled, enigmatic face. "You have
some idea who?"

"Nothing concrete. But I have every intention of pursuing the lead."

"You think it's the writer, don't you? Berwald. You
said it was just his books."

"Just this particular book, in fact."

The title of which, James Gordon had to admit,
would in and of itself point to Dr. Jonathan Crane—
were he not sitting serenely in Arkham, slowly working
his way through his large collection of fact and fiction.

Except . . .

"Doesn't seem big enough for the Scarecrow, does it?
I mean, it's not resulting in rampant death and destruction."

"No, but the potential is there. The more people who
read this book . . ."

Gordon nodded. "The first thing to do is get them off
the shelves. Immediately. And carefully. And we'll need

to get the formula out to hospitals, emergency rooms, and the coroner so they can recognize victims."

"I'll have someone working on an antidote by midday."

Gordon's gaze had drifted back to the cover of the paperback, with Berwald's name taking up over half the space. "We've had an upsurge in attempted suicides over the last month. I checked after you called this morning. More than the usual number of single-car accidents and DUIs, too. When someone claims they swerved to avoid a Sasquatch, you don't usually suspect they've been gassed."

"Not gassed. The infection is topical; it enters the body through the pores."

"Heaven help anyone who licks their fingers when they page through a book."

"Doctor Gant?"

Medical Examiner Mortimer Gant glanced up from his computer screen to the door of his office, where his most junior assistant, Steve Callan, stood with a case file tucked under his arm.

Gant raised his graying eyebrows, which Callan apparently took as an invitation to enter.

"Have I got one for you," the younger man said, waving the bright red file folder. "Member of Los Muertos was brought into Gotham General early this morning by . . . well, they said they were next of kin, though I've got my doubts. They claim he was murdered by magic."

"Magic? Really. What caliber?"

"That's the funny thing. Not a mark on him. Just started acting wacky, then *pffft*!" He made a popping gesture with his fingertips.

Gant leaned back in his chair. "Symptoms?"

Callan flipped open the file. "First the kid's scared spitless. Gabbling about a butcher. Then he seems to calm down—gets almost cheerful. They think he's over it, whatever it was. Not long after that, he suddenly starts to act like he's on speed: jerky, exaggerated reflexes, twitches, can't sit still, then staggering around like he's drunk."

Gant shrugged. "And that surprises anyone?"

"But they didn't see him take anything. And they'd been watching. His blood gases were WNL. Then somebody checked his temp again, and all of a sudden the guy's spiking a high fever. They'd started talking hospital when he just keeled over. He died in the ER."

Gant closed his eyes. Euphoria, followed by hypoesthesia, hyperreflexia, muscle spasms, restlessness, syncope, pyrexia. It sounded almost like . . .

"Did whoever brought him in make any further comment about his mental state?"

Callan consulted the file again. "Confused about where he was. Seemed to be having flashbacks to his childhood. Terror, then euphoria, then hypomania."

"Mental confusion and violent mood swings," Gant murmured, "followed by loss of consciousness and death."

"You've seen this before?"

Gant nodded. "But the symptoms describe two different conditions: serotonin syndrome and neuroleptic malignant syndrome. Every case I've seen of either has been the result of an overdose or toxic buildup of prescription drugs—antidepressants or antipsychotics. Was this guy on SSRIs or MAOIs?"

"They asked about drug use in the ER, including prescriptions. According to his 'family' members, he smoked

ot, did Ecstasy occasionally—a social druggie. There
as no mention of prescription drugs."

"Which doesn't necessarily mean he didn't take them.
ooks to me as if the kid got into someone else's medica-
on. You know how those gangs are. He probably
pped off some homeless guys and thought it might be
an to pop all the pretty little pills he found on them.
Vhy does his clan think it was magic?"

"Story is, this kid was—how'd they put it?—involved
a a 'disagreement' with this character they call 'Twitch'—
hich probably means he was beating the crap out
f him. They said he got right in this Twitch guy's face,
yeball-to-eyeball, and they figure Twitch does some sort
f hocus-pocus, 'cause the next thing anybody knows,
he kid's freaking out, and this guy never even touched
im."

"And this other guy—Twitch?"

"Ran off. Disappeared. They figured he was from . . .
*Un-der-town.*" Callan said the last word in an over-the-
op creepy voice. While the gangs of Gotham patrolled
ts perimeters, they tended to view Undertown itself
vith suspicion, if not outright fear. Undertown was run
y gangs of a completely different color from Los Muer-
os.

"So . . ." Callan looked expectant. "You want to do
his one yourself?"

"No. Take it to Doctor Marshall. I've got more im-
ortant things to do."

Callan shrugged and left Gant alone in his office. The
nedical examiner was less than five minutes into his
more important things" when a message came down to
he morgue from Captain Gordon that radically affected
is priorities.

*    *    *

By eleven that morning, she had left three messages o
his private line asking for an interview for her blog-
God knew how she'd gotten the number. Grey wasn
sure whether he admired Maggie Tollyer's tenacity an
inventiveness or was irked at her sheer audacity.

The phone rang again exactly forty-five minutes aft
the first call, half an hour after the second, and fiftee
minutes after the third. Okay, he admitted, he admire
her, was intrigued and bemused by her . . . maybe just
little bit afraid of her.

And he wanted to know what she'd meant by her tal
of driving people over the edge and the allusion t
Thursday's subway incident.

He picked up the phone on the third ring. "Gre
Berwald."

She was apparently so stunned to have gotten the ma
himself, she was momentarily speechless. He smile
wryly. *Bet* that *doesn't happen often.*

"This is . . . Wait a minute. Are you. . . ? You'r
not."

Grey chuckled. "Hello, Wait-a-minute. And I'r
pretty sure I am."

There was a chuff of exasperation on the line befor
she said, "You answer your own phone?"

"Only when I'm pretty sure I know who I'm going t
be talking to."

"You knew it was me." She sounded skeptical.

"Well, you called forty-five minutes ago, then fiftee
minutes after that, then fifteen minutes after *that.*
thought the chances of it being someone else were prett
slim. And there's also the fact that I have caller ID
How'd you get my private number?"

"A journalist never reveals her sources."

"That hoary old chestnut. Look, Ms. Tollyer, I just gotta know: were you planning on calling me every fifteen minutes for the rest of the day?"

Her laugh was low-pitched and warm—didn't go with the spiky hair or the prickly exterior. "Just for another hour or two. So, Mr. Berwald, is this where you tell me once and for all to take a hike or you'll sic the cops on me for stalking?"

"This is where I ask if one o'clock today would be good for an interview and if you'd like to do it over lunch." He grinned into the silence on the other end of the line. "That's twice I've gotcha, Ms. Tollyer. I thought hard-nosed reporters didn't flummox easily."

"Flummox?" she repeated. "What sort of word is that?"

"Verb. Mid-nineteenth-century English. From the dialectic *flummock,* meaning 'to confuse.' "

"Oh, and I thought it was a noun descriptive of my ox-like stubbornness. Lunch is perfect. Where?"

They met at Conway's, a restaurant downtown, on the twelfth floor of the Grande Hotel. Ostentatious enough to impress, but not enough to overwhelm, it was a cozy, dark blend of earth tones and wood. The décor was somewhere between deco and North Mediterranean, but with not a curlicue of rococo in sight. Grey felt relaxed here, and he knew instinctively that in his encounter with Maggie Tollyer, it would be best to remain relaxed.

They ordered drinks—an eggnog latte for her and a malt liquor for him—and settled into desultory conversation: What did she think of Wayne Manor and the master thereof?

Arrogant, takes himself damn seriously.

Not attractive?

Oh, well, if you found *that* sort of guy attractive . . .
"Why?" she asked. "What was your impression of
him?"

"I liked him. But then, I suppose I'm the wrong gen-
der to have alarms go off when a guy with that much
money and clout smiles at me."

"You were there long enough to *like* him?" Maggie
asked.

"I was there long enough for two glasses of Merlot
and an appreciation of sassy journalists in catsuits."

Her cheeks pinked. "You talked about me?"

"For all of five minutes, then we talked about sports,
beer, fishin'—you know, guy stuff."

She glanced up at him sharply. "Go ahead. Have a
laugh at my expense."

"Darlin'," he said, raising his glass in a toast, "my
laughin' ain't costin' you a thing. So now, why don't you
just whip out that little notebook or PDA or laptop or
whatever it is you're hiding in your bag and shoot."

"How do you know it's not a .357 Magnum I'm 'hiding' in my bag?"

"You're too petite for a .357. Besides, the pen is
mightier than the sword—or the handgun, as the case
may be."

To his surprise, her lips pressed into a straight line and
the color drained from her face. What had he said to get
*that* reaction?

She covered the awkward moment by digging through
her bag for a tiny digital recorder.

Grey whistled. "That's even smaller than mine. How
many megs of memory?"

"Enough to—" She cut off as the waiter came back to
take their lunch order.

The break in the sudden and inexplicable tension had

given her time to chill out just a bit. When the waiter had gone, leaving behind a basket of hot breads, she was smiling at him wryly.

She placed the recorder in the center of the table between them and said, "Interview with author Grey Berwald. November first. Mr. Berwald—"

"Grey."

She waggled her head in a way that said, *Yeah, that was inevitable.* "Grey, I've heard you expound on why you write horror: dealing with demons, facing fears, escaping from reality—"

"*Running* from reality."

"What?"

"You had a nice alliterative streak going there. I hated to see you break it up."

He saw her hackles go up. Now, why had he done that? Did he want to keep her alienated?

"The point is: I've heard—or seen—where you address that subject. Ultimately, though, doesn't it come down to exercising control over the emotions of your readers? Isn't that the big rush in writing horror?"

"Every writer aims to engage the emotions or minds of his readers. Not just horror novelists. Dostoevsky had the same goal. So did Melville. Otherwise, why bother to write at all?"

"But in horror fiction, it's more than that, isn't it? Engaging is fine for a history text or a political polemic, but don't you need—don't you aim for—control? Don't you want the ability to chill their blood, make them jump at shadows?"

*Okay, I'll bite.* "I suppose so."

"Do you think a good horror writer can do that—control the emotions of his reader?"

She seemed focused with an intensity that was entirely

out of proportion to the question. Maybe it was time to put aside the aw-shucks attitude and get serious; he couldn't afford for anything, even if it was just an ineptly phrased response to a question, to go wrong now. Berwald leaned back, steepled his fingers for the scholarly touch, and said, "To the extent that the reader is willing to suspend his disbelief and allow it to happen, yes."

"Should you? Should you exercise that type of control?"

"Again, only if the reader is willing to allow it."

"What if she's *not*? What if what you've written catches her by surprise and sucks her in to the point that she can't disengage?"

He took a deep breath. "I don't believe for a moment that can happen. At least not to anyone who's playing with a full deck."

"But it *did* happen," Ms. Tollyer said. "Thursday. On a speeding subway train."

He shook his head. Careful, he cautioned himself. Here there definitely be dragons. "I have no idea what you're talking about."

"Yes you do. You said you'd read about it in the paper. The subway driver was reading your book *Fear Itself*." She leaned forward, lowering her voice. She seemed less of a newshound now, and more an inquisitor putting the Question to some hapless heretic. "Something in the pages of that book, something in the words *you* used, evoked such sheer terror in that woman that she became paralyzed. Unable to think clearly enough to do her job. If Ba—" She paused a beat, obviously becoming aware of her own intensity. "If circumstances had been different, that train might have entered the terminus at eighty miles per hour, causing untold devastation and loss of life. All because you succeeded only too well in attaining your objective."

He looked hard into her face, searched her eyes, and wondered how she could be so certain. What could she possibly know? Or imagine she knew?

He forced himself to sit back in the private, high-backed booth. Forced his fingers to pluck a piece of bread from the basket and gently pull it apart. "This your 'peanut' argument, again, Maggie-the-Cat?"

"Just Maggie will be fine. And yes, I guess it is. You know there's a segment of the population that is . . . unstable—"

"Was this woman unstable? The paper didn't say she was. This morning's paper said she'd been treated and released. Clean bill of health. Big mystery."

"Then the peanut analogy is even more apropos." Maggie put her elbows on the table and leaned toward him earnestly, seeming to ignore her own recording device. "We're not talking about a raving lunatic here, Grey. We're talking about an essentially normal woman who happens to love Grey Berwald fiction. Because she loves it, it's a given that it . . . I don't know . . . inspires some sort of deep, satisfying emotion in her. This time it was too much for her system to take."

He swallowed a piece of bread. Even the butter didn't keep it from sticking in his throat. He took a sip of water. "And that's my fault?"

She shrugged. "Who else's would it be?"

He studied her for a moment, then asked, "Did you know that this restaurant has a smoking room?"

"What?"

"A dining room where patrons can smoke. Air locks. Filtration systems. The works. They sit in there and pollute the air and eat food they can't taste and are happy as smoked clams, if you'll pardon the—"

"Okay, I see where you're going with this." Maggie waved fingertips in airy dismissal. "But they're in that room by mutual consent. They know the risks, and still choose to—"

This time it was he who interrupted. "Exactly. They *choose*. Even in the face of overwhelming evidence that smoking poisons you and everyone around you, they just keep on puffing. They choose—hell, they *want* to be in that room.

"And so do my readers. They've all agreed to lock themselves in a dark room with me, and anything I choose to bring in with me." He added a tiny, self-effacing chuckle. "Unlike smokers, my readers know everything will come out okay in the last chapter."

Maggie, at this point, looked more like a sphinx than a cat. "So if horror kills, that's okay?"

"Horror doesn't kill, Maggie. It tingles. It gives the reader a delicious scare. Yeah, maybe it even makes her turn on the light, or check the locks on her doors—"

She blushed violently and lowered her gaze.

"Gotcha," he said softly, almost under his breath. "Maybe my stories do all of that. But they can't hold someone captive, Maggie. They can't put the fear in your head, it's got to be there to begin with, waiting to be . . ."

"Awakened?"

"Exposed." He leaned forward and gave her "the daggers," as his last ex-girlfriend used to call it; he liked to think of it as his steely-eyed look. "Is that what this— this *crusade* is all about? I poked some old haunts out of hiding? I scared you, and you hate being scared?"

She hesitated, then reached over and turned off the

recorder. "It did more than scare me. It . . . it *disturbed* me. It reached into a deep, dark, private place and . . ." She shook her head. "Maybe because I really *do* hate being scared, I just put the book down. *But Janet Epcot didn't.* She *liked* being scared. I know because I interviewed her and she told me as much. She didn't put the book down because she didn't *want* to. And a few minutes later, when something in life imitated art . . ."

"What?" he prompted, not really wanting her to finish the sentence, but needing her to.

"I don't know. Maybe in that moment, something in her head awakened—or was exposed, if you prefer. And it pushed her over the edge."

He took another sip of water, pulled his hand away from the chunk of bread he'd shredded, and tried to think of a halfway intelligent response. *Maybe some people's demons are less manageable than others,* he thought. What came out, as the waiter appeared with steaming plates, was: "Here's our lunch."

"I've seen this before." Lucius Fox looked up from the chemical analysis of the new fear toxin into his employer's face. "Or something very much like it." He nodded toward the box now sitting in the lab's clean room. "In those books. Absorbed into the binding glue."

Bruce shook his head. "Fear toxin in a horror novel— who'd think up something like that?"

"Any breakouts at Arkham lately?" asked Jesse Rosen. His gaze was on the toxin's still-incomplete specifications.

"Not a one," Lucius said. He looked thoughtful. "We did synthesize an antidote to the last neurotoxin Scarecrow tried to use. I wonder if this is one of his." He looked at the box again. "Or maybe a copycat."

"Or apprentice," Jesse suggested.

"We'll know a lot more once we find out whether the existing antidote works on this."

"What a city," Bruce said. He moved restlessly around the WayneTech chem lab, looking at, but not touching, the various test tubes, beakers, retorts, and other glassware. "Sometimes I wonder why I stay here. The South of France is so much nicer this time of year."

Lucius pointedly ignored him. He asked Jesse, "Those Ultra-Sniffers we discussed the last time we talked—how many of those do you have on hand?"

"Five—the original prototype and four production models."

"Do they work?"

"Oh, they work just fine, if you can give them a solid profile to start from."

Bruce asked, "Then they can be—what's the word—calibrated to detect this stuff?"

Both Jesse and Lucius looked at him in mild surprise. Bruce shrugged. "Hey, I'm not completely oblivious to all this. Alfred and I are both readers. One of us could pick up a book and become infected, too."

"The Sniffers can be calibrated to detect just about anything," Jesse replied. "Problem is, the profile's got holes in it, so we'll only be able to approximate."

"Meaning?" Lucius asked.

"Meaning it might find other stuff as well."

Lucius turned to give the younger man an over-the-glasses look of sheer incredulity. "How many different shades of neurotoxin do you expect to find on the street?"

"Oh, yeah, right. Pretty unlikely, huh? Well, we'll be

working at tying down this formula anyway. Most likely we'll have to do that to create an effective antidote or vaccine. I don't suppose you could get some for us in its pure form?"

"Jesse," said Lucius, "if we had access to it in pure form, we wouldn't be having this discussion, would we?"

Jesse ran a hand over his hair, sending it into even further disarray. "Oh, yeah, right."

Lucius smiled. "We'll leave you to it, then." He started toward the door, with Bruce following. Lucius paused and added, "If you do crack this and you can't get in touch with me, call Captain Gordon. Likewise if you can get those Sniffers to detect the toxin. That would make the captain's job much easier, I'd think."

"Right," Jesse answered in an abstracted tone. He was already immersed in research, the alphanumerics on the laptop's screen reflected in his glasses.

The pure form, Bruce thought as he took the elevator back down to the lobby. How could he acquire some of the toxin in its pure form? He stared absently at the art deco frosted-glass fan that displayed the floor numbers— an anachronism in this modern building. Maybe what he needed Lucius to create was a truth serum that really worked. He'd cheerfully dose everybody who was even tangentially connected to this case and squeeze the truth out of them drop by drop. Everyone from Jonathan Crane to Dr. Avery to Grey Berwald to Maggie Tollyer.

He stepped out of the elevator on the ground floor and looked up to where Alfred awaited him in the Bentley.

*Well, speak of the devil.*

Even as he approached the front doors, the journalist

was moving slowly past them on the sidewalk, her attention deep in her shoulder bag.

He stepped through the doors in front of her and let her run into him.

She squeaked and glanced up. "I'm so— Oh, it's you."

"That's a hell of a greeting from someone who so recently presumed on my largesse."

"I'll presume on your brand-new Guccis if you don't get out of my way, Mr. Wayne. You do not intimidate me."

"I wasn't trying to intimidate you. But I *was* trying to run into you."

She stopped digging in her purse and looked him right in the eye. "Really. Why?"

"I wanted to ask you . . . a favor."

"I don't believe this."

"Have we met? I'm the guy who *didn't* turn you over to the police. I let you slap your mouse around for a few minutes before I took him away from you. So I figure you owe me."

"Okay. I owe you. Just exactly *what* do I owe you?"

"Dinner tonight. My place."

She stared at him as if he'd opened a door at thirty thousand feet and said *Jump*.

"You didn't get to taste Alfred's seafood linguine with lobster sauce. That's a worse crime than crashing my party. It was a pretty boring party, anyway. You didn't miss much by leaving early." He leaned down, putting his lips almost to her ear. "You were the most fun I had all night."

She closed her mouth. "I have a date tonight."

He straightened. "Give me a name. Who is it? I'll buy him off."

"Grey Berwald."

Would wonders never cease? The very man he intended to visit! The momentary tingle of adrenaline was followed by the sobering thought that if Mr. Nightfall were responsible for the toxic reading material, this woman's life could be in danger.

He laughed and snapped his fingers. "Damn! Can't buy him off, he's almost as rich as I am. Oh well—Monday night, then."

"Oh, darn. Washing my hair." She tried to step around him.

He blocked her. "Tuesday."

"Book club."

"Wednesday."

"Drying my hair."

"Alfred's linguine. Ask anyone. It's to die for."

"It really is very good, miss." Alfred had materialized on the sidewalk next to them as silently as a ghost. "I have a Cordon Bleu certification." He smiled, and seemingly against her will she smiled back.

Sometimes Alfred amazed him. Bruce pressed his sudden and unexpected advantage. "I wanted to ask you, too, about your blog. Your essays on artistic responsibility are extremely thought provoking. You write with such conviction."

Her gaze moved from Alfred's face to his, eloquent with surprise. Present a journalist with an anomaly, and, more often than not, she'll bite.

He put a hand lightly on her shoulder. "Wait, I know. Saturday. A trip to Six Flags Over Gotham and a picnic lunch. You're a roller-coaster fan—am I right?"

She nodded, her lips flirting with a smile. "How'd you guess?"

"Oh, I never guess. I deduce."

"Like Sherlock Holmes?"

"Something like that."

"It's a little chilly for theme parks and picnics, isn't it?"

He shrugged. "Okay, Orlando, Florida, then. There's lots of roller coasters there. Beaches for picnics."

"What about Alfred's linguine?"

"Monday night for linguine, Saturday for roller coasters?"

She glanced sideways at Alfred. "Uh . . . fine. We can meet—"

"Give Alfred your address. I'll pick you up."

She reached into her bag for a card. "Give *Alfred* my address? Does he keep your little black book for you?"

"That, and so much more," Bruce said, meeting the butler's expressionless gaze over Maggie's head.

He was in the car on his way back to Wayne Manor when his special cell phone rang. It was Captain Gordon, sounding—if it were possible—even more grim than he had during their rooftop meeting earlier.

"I just spoke to the medical examiner," Gordon told him. "He performed an autopsy on a member of Los Muertos. Are you familiar with the gang?"

"More than I'd like to be."

"Kid died of a hyperserotonergic condition."

Bruce sat straight up in the backseat. "Serotonin syndrome?"

"That's the term Gant used. You've heard of it?"

"Yes. Usually, it occurs because of a bad mixture of drugs prescribed for various mood disorders."

"Well, this kid wasn't on prescription drugs, yet somehow he got a double whammy of the stuff. Gant initially suspected he'd wolfed down a cocktail of stolen medication, but there was nothing in his stomach. Not even residue." Gordon let out a long sigh. "Looks like we've got our first confirmed fatality."

Which, given the mere trace amounts of neurotoxin found on the books, would indicate the victim had come in contact with a seriously more potent form. How? Where? Gotham's gangs weren't famous for their literacy.

"Give me everything you've got on this—the circumstances of the boy's death, witnesses, everything. That includes whatever you've got in electronic form." He had already slid back the concealing plate over the limo's built-in computer console in anticipation of the download.

"I've got men down in the 'hood already, but they're not having much luck. Even in a case like this, it's hard to get those gangs to talk to the authorities. They're more inclined to want to take things into their own hands."

"Don't waste the effort. They'll talk to me."

## 10

Grey Berwald lived in a large, two-story Gothic Revival
in the new gated community of Blackthorne. It was sub-
stantially more than a house and somewhat less than a
mansion. Roughly E-shaped, its automatic gates opened
onto a cobbled drive that swept in a graceful arc to the
front door in the short crosspiece of the E.

The house itself was of warm, golden stone topped in
green tile. The grounds were lush with evergreen foliage
and deciduous trees in a riot of fall color.

Sitting in the drive, where she'd parked her old
Beemer next to a dove-gray Mercedes, Maggie could
just make out some topiaries off toward the north wing
of the house. Odd-looking shapes that she didn't recognize. Her brain tried to make a giraffe out of the tallest
one, but it refused to be categorized as such. A bron-
tosaurus, maybe?

She'd insisted on driving to Berwald's house and
leaving her car there. She had no intention of being at
his mercy when it came to leave-taking. She knew from
experience that there were few things worse than having to ask a guy you'd just gut-punched to drive you
home. Experience, limited though it was, had taught
her that wealthy, good-looking men could be arrogant
as hell, and prone to making assumptions about how

far their wealth and good looks would take them on a date.

She got out of her car and closed the door. She started to lock it, then realized how silly that was under the circumstances. When she turned back to the house, Grey Berwald was already moving toward her along the cobbled drive.

Seeing him, Maggie heaved a sigh of relief. She didn't often get to dine at the Top of the Tower—in fact, she'd only been there once, and that had been in high school—and she was afraid she might have underdressed for the occasion in a mid-calf-length green knit dress and simple suede ankle boots. But Berwald's suit, though elegant, was also understated.

And he wore a string tie. The last place she'd seen a string tie had been on an old photograph of Mark Twain.

"Welcome," he said, "to Nightfall Manor."

She smiled tentatively and held out her hand. He didn't shake it; he bowed over it and raised it to his lips.

Maggie shook off the shiver of . . . whatever-the-hell-it-was that evoked and said, "Well, wouldn't your momma be proud of you?"

He looked up and met her eyes without relinquishing her hand. "I sure hope so. God help me if she's not. You ready for dinner?"

Maggie raised her eyebrows. "What? No tour of the homestead?"

He seemed vaguely embarrassed. "I . . . ah . . . thought I'd save that until after dinner. Chef Franco's making a special dessert. He's got a Cordon Bleu certificate, and damn proud of it."

"Funny," Maggie said. "Bruce Wayne's butler also has a Cordon Bleu, or so he says."

Grey tucked her hand through his arm and led her around to the passenger's side of the Mercedes. "Yeah? You had occasion to talk to Bruce, did you?"

"I quite literally bumped into him this afternoon in front of WayneTech, on my way back from lunch." She started to mention that he'd asked her out, but thought better of it. That seemed a very shallow thing to do, as if she were trying to set these two society bucks off against each other.

*Pinch me,* she thought as she settled into the solid comfort of the Mercedes's passenger's seat. *I've been asked out by two of Gotham's most eligible bachelors in one day. Wouldn't my mother be proud?*

She smiled and shook her head. It was a turn of events that owed nothing to her feminine charms. It was her big mouth these guys were concerned about.

"What?" her companion asked, seeing the smile.

"Just trying to decide if this is our first date, or our second," she told him.

"First," he said emphatically. "Lunch today wasn't a date. It was an interrogation."

"It wasn't that bad."

"I didn't say it was bad. Just that it wasn't a date. *This* is a date." He glanced at her meaningfully.

She groaned. "Are you going to make me promise not to talk shop?"

"Not promise. Just try. I understand that your work is your passion." His gaze was disconcertingly direct. "I *really* understand, Maggie. So if the subject comes up . . ." He shrugged. "But try to leave it till dessert, okay?"

She smiled, genuinely this time. "Okay."

\*     \*     \*

". . . so then *I* said, 'This is an experimental proto-type, you complete moron. It's worth more than your entire *career.*' I mean, honestly, these rent-a-cops figure they can just order *anyone* around. No matter who you are. And that nasty old woman, sitting there, lurking for my parking spot like a—like a *vulture.*"

Serafina paused in her monologue long enough to give Bruce Wayne a sideways look. "What's the matter? The other cat still got your tongue?"

Bruce darted a glance at the elevator readout—seven floors to go—then turned to look at her. "I just didn't have anything constructive to offer." *And no opportunity to say it if I did.*

"But don't you agree? I mean, these private security guards can be incredibly high-handed."

"That depends on your definition of *high-handed,* I suppose. You were, after all, parked in a handicapped zone. And there was a handicapped person waiting to use it."

"Jayce was carrying half a dozen parcels!"

He smiled at her protest. "And how many were you carrying?"

"Me? Why would I carry any?"

"So that Jayce wouldn't have to carry all of them and you wouldn't have been tempted to park in a handi-capped zone. Here's our floor."

He took her elbow and guided her out into the sump-tuous foyer of the Top of the Tower, his attention already on the room beyond the maître d's station.

They were crossing the dining area to his permanently reserved table on the upper level when he saw his targets seated by a window.

He caught the maître d's attention. "Alphonse, I see

someone I know. Why don't you take Ms. Orloff to my table while I go say hi."

Serafina turned to follow his gaze. She made no attempt to hide her displeasure when she saw Maggie Tollyer. "Actually, I think I'll go say hi, too."

Bruce grimaced, then led her to Maggie and Grey's table. He had every intention of speaking first, but Serafina beat him to the punch.

"Well," she said in a gusty, overloud soprano, "imagine running into you here? Does the maître d' know you're using this table, or did you crash the restaurant?"

Maggie and Grey looked up in unison from their menus, clearly startled.

"I'm sorry," Grey started to say, then saw Bruce. Smiling, he rose to shake hands. "We still on for racquetball tomorrow?"

"Definitely. Serafina Orloff," said Bruce, "I'd like you to meet Grey Berwald. You may have heard of him; he writes books."

Serafina was suddenly all smiles. "Charmed!" She held out her hand; he shook it politely. "What sort of books?"

"Horror novels," he said. Seeming to enjoy the minute contortion of her face, he added, "I just *love* to scare people."

"Actually, I've heard of you," Serafina said. "Didn't I read that Todd McGraff just surpassed you for the largest advance ever for a *genre* novel?"

Grey's face went momentarily blank. "You may have read something like that, yeah."

"He writes suspense, though, doesn't he? I *like* suspense."

Bruce exchanged rueful glances with Grey, then edged Serafina a bit to one side so he could speak to Maggie.

"Well, Ms. Tollyer, I see you got what you were after at my party the other night."

"I guess I did," Maggie replied tartly.

"You really shouldn't indulge this woman, Grey. She's what Alfred would call a hoyden."

The writer merely laughed. "I suppose she is, but I've always had a soft spot in my heart for hoydens." He winked at Maggie, who smiled uncertainly in return.

"Later." Bruce was already moving away. He prodded Serafina Orloff ahead of him, carefully adjusting the volume of the miniaturized audio receiver embedded in the left temple piece of the glasses he'd affected this evening. Before he and Serafina reached their table, he was eavesdropping on the conversation between journalist and novelist, relayed from the tiny microphone he'd affixed to the sleeve of Grey Berwald's suit coat. He'd be able to monitor both Serafina's chatter and the far more interesting conversation below simultaneously. He was recording that dialogue, as well, in case he missed something.

"Bruce Wayne's dance card fills up quickly, doesn't it?" Maggie observed.

"What do you mean?" Grey asked.

"When I saw him this afternoon, he asked me out to dinner tonight. It didn't take him long to find a stand-in."

"Me-ow," said Grey blandly.

Bruce smiled, wondering what Serafina would think if she knew she was playing second fiddle to the other cat.

Cutter was nervous. And for a variety of reasons, not the least of which was that his fear of coming face-to-face with the Unknown Menace of Saint Peregrine's had forced him to use the alley egress in what was now solidly within Los Muertos territory. That fear had nearly cost him his life.

He was thankful that his hands were free this time and he wasn't freighted down with his employer's goods. The weight now tugging at his pocket was that of a handgun he'd acquired from Blackie. It was a Glock 17 that had once belonged to a policeman; Cutter didn't want to know what had happened to the previous owner or how he had been separated from his weapon. He'd simply bought the gun, loaded it, and prayed he wouldn't be called upon to use it. Cutter didn't like guns. Until this evening he'd never even held one in his hand.

The Glock's weight was oppressive as he made his way up through the machine shop and out into the alley. He was nearly clear of Los Muertos' territory when he heard a chilling medley of sounds up ahead, between him and the open street. A low, discordant moaning seemed to cascade off the alley walls, punctuated by the clash of metal on metal and the sound of many pairs of feet dragging across the grimy cobbles.

Cutter froze, listening, peering into the intersection ahead where the ground mist had now begun to eddy. His right arm chose this moment to flap wildly against his side. Terrified of being discovered, he scuttled backward and ducked behind a stack of decaying orange crates. Hunkered there, clutching his long coat about him like a cocoon, he peered between the slats and watched as a horrific parade passed him by.

There were about thirty of them, all dressed in unrelieved black, their kohl-rimmed eyes like open wounds in moon-white faces. The pair in front carried between them a banner with something written on it in chaotic letters. Behind them, some carried candles, others small placards, each containing a photograph.

Cutter squinted. The face in the photograph was also white with black-rimmed eyes. He thought of the youth who'd confronted him in the alley the night before, but shoved the thought aside.

*Coincidence,* he told himself. *They all look alike. Could've been anyone.*

They moved by, never ceasing their rhythmic moaning, their feet shuffling through the alley's debris.

*Zombies,* Cutter thought. *Zombies on parade.* He put a hand over his mouth to stifle a horrified giggle.

The funeral procession had almost faded from sight when his left leg shot straight out, toppling him. He fell against the orange crates and sent them tumbling into the alley. He didn't wait to see if anyone heard or cared. He was off, running.

When he had gone four blocks and found himself on a busy street full of shops and restaurants, he slowed his pace, shoved his hands into his pockets, and made a bee-line for Gotham University, his fingers tentatively exploring the grip of the Glock.

By the time the waiters had cleared their dinner plates, Bruce Wayne was impressed, if frustrated, with Maggie Tollyer's restraint. Her dinner conversation with Grey Berwald had strayed nowhere near the subject of artistic responsibility, or overly potent prose, or potential disasters.

They discussed writing for the most part, and the only moment of real interest came when Grey asked Maggie why she'd left such a promising and high-profile career in journalism to pursue a quieter lifestyle.

A long moment of hesitation was followed by: "It just

didn't suit me. I think a good reporter stays in the background. I ended up in the limelight. Not where I wanted to be."

A lie, Bruce's BS-meter told him. Or at least a fib. He doubted it related to the doctored books, but filed it for future reference anyway.

"Now that, I just don't understand," Grey admitted. "I want people to see what I'm doing—like it, buy it, beg for more. I don't want to hide my light under a bushel." He chuckled. "I'm just a feedback junkie, I guess."

Serafina had already ordered her dessert when Bruce realized the other couple were rising to leave. He pulled back his sleeve to look at his watch, tapping a tiny button that caused his cell phone to ring.

"Excuse me," he said, unpocketing the phone.

Serafina's carefully tweezed brows rose. *Must you?* they seemed to say.

He gave her a rueful grin and spoke into the phone. "Bruce Wayne."

Of course, there was absolutely no one on the other end. The faint vocal buzz that Sera no doubt heard was a pre-recorded performance by Alfred.

"I'm a little busy, right now, Alfred . . . Well, yes, a date . . . He, who? Oh, damn—I forgot all about that. Well, that's inconvenient." He looked up at Serafina and rolled his eyes. "Yes . . . yes. I understand. I'll be right there. Thanks, Alfred."

He pocketed the cell phone and rose. "I had a late business meeting scheduled with . . . someone. A prospective WayneTech client. Can I get you to forgo dessert?"

She folded her arms across her breasts. "No. You can't. You can either sit right there and watch me eat, or you can leave me sitting here, in which case your name will be mud in the Orloff household. *And* in the weekly society columns. I'll make sure of it."

"Well, since you put it that way, I'll have Alphonse get you a cab when you're ready to leave. Enjoy your dessert." He pushed his chair up to the table, blew her a kiss, and strode off, leaving her openmouthed and alone in the still-crowded restaurant.

He felt the many pairs of eyes trained on him as he made his way across the dining room, and knew he had just solidified Bruce Wayne's image as a complete and utter cad. *Oh, well . . .*

Cutter had stopped quaking long before he reached the college campus. The long walk in the chill night air had calmed him significantly. His only moment of pause came when he realized that the library was open extra late this evening.

Notwithstanding there were students among the stacks, there was no one in the loading area, and he was able to conceal himself in the maintenance room without being seen. Forty-five minutes later, the library closed; fifteen minutes after that, Cutter came out of hiding carrying the air compressor, from which he'd removed the tank. His coat was loaded with vials.

He let himself into the main room of the library. It was illuminated only by the three green EXIT signs—not enough light for him to navigate by. He slipped on the night-vision goggles he'd acquired some weeks ago at a handsome price. Like the gun, these had come through Blackie, and he had not asked after their provenance. Certainly his employer didn't care—no more than he cared how much they had cost. Richer than Croesus, his shadowy mentor.

Cutter fit a vial into the air compressor's loading

chamber and twisted it into place. The bottle's neck slid into the collar and sealed with a *click,* even as a sharp flange within the collar assembly perforated the metal lid. A small green LED lit up on the compressor, indicating that it was ready for use.

Cutter hefted the nozzle and approached the first shelf full of books.

"Impressive," Maggie said, and meant it. She leaned back into the comfort of the wingback chair, its microfiber upholstery soft and warm beneath her fingertips. The fireplace before which she sat was huge—the mantel must have been ten feet tall, she reckoned, and seemed to lean out into the parlor, dwarfing the room's two inhabitants. The boars' heads mounted atop it only added to the surreal sensation the room produced.

Across from her, in a matching chair, Grey Berwald poured coffee from a silver pot into Blue Onion Flower cups arrayed on a low coffee table whose ball-and-claw feet would have looked at home on a Great Dane. He looked up at her as he set her cup and a dessert plate containing Chef Franco's caramel flan in front of her.

"Me or my house?"

"Your fireplace, actually. I can't seem to shake the impression that I've seen it somewhere before."

"You ever see an old Universal film called *Son of Frankenstein*?"

She sipped her coffee. "Basil Rathbone and Bela Lugosi, right? And Karloff, of course."

Grey nodded. "Very good. Lugosi played Ygor, the crazy old shepherd. One of his best roles." He relaxed, sitting back to look up at the huge hearth with a fond gaze. "This is designed ˙after the fireplaces from the

Frankenstein castle. There's a matching one upstairs in my bedroom."

She didn't tell him, of course, that the only reason she'd known the cast members was that she'd done research on classic horror films earlier today, having read about his love of the black-and-white monsters that had stalked the Universal back lot.

"Yeah?" she said, in response to his last statement. "You ever wake up in the middle of the night thinking it's trying to eat you? It has that lean and hungry look."

He laughed. "Actually, I find it . . . comforting. Eat up. I want to show you something."

"Dare I hope it's something in your library?"

Truthfully, that had been the most impressive part of the ground-floor tour Grey had taken her on while Chef Franco prepared their dessert. She could have spent a happy year or two in that vast room, poring over the thousands of volumes that lined the floor-to-ceiling bookshelves. Grey Berwald was every bit as much a bibliophile as she, but he had the money to indulge his passion.

He raised his eyebrows in exaggerated dismay. "Ms. Tollyer, I'm disappointed. I thought it was me you found wildly attractive and now I discover it's a simple case of library envy."

"Yeah, well, *my* library consists of a single double-wide shelf in my office that's groaning under the weight of my so-called research library. Mostly secondhand volumes."

"A lot of mine are third- and fourth-hand."

She made a face at him. "Oh, yes, my thrift-store edition of *Macbeth* is so much better than a hand-copied, leather-bound volume of Shakespeare's original. I mean, after all, it's newer."

He laughed. "Sorry to disappoint, but my surprise is not in the library. What I want to show you is in a different part of the house."

She glanced at him sharply, trying to read his face. "Not your etchings, I hope."

"Nope. Nor my matching fireplace. I want you to see my inspiration rooms."

"Your what?"

He nodded at her flan. "Eat up. But not so fast you don't remark on the excellence of Chef Franco's creation. He's very sensitive."

Batman abandoned his window-ledge perch as soon as Berwald and Maggie left the parlor. He moved so that he could see where they were headed through the wide doorway. Berwald was still wearing his suit coat, so he could at least hear their conversation.

As he watched, figuring his next move would be up and over the rooftop, the writer led Maggie across the entry. But instead of going up to the second floor, he stopped in the foyer, facing the inside wall of the curving grand staircase. He reached up to touch a wrought-iron wall sconce. There was a soft hum and a *click,* and then a section of the staircase wall pivoted open, as if on a turntable.

"You're kidding," said Maggie.

"Nope. I'm just a sucker for secret passages and stuff like that."

The two disappeared through the doorway, leaving Batman to listen to their footsteps and consider his options. There weren't many.

*Okay. Inside it is.*

He dropped down before the French doors of the solarium at the back of the house. In a matter of seconds, he had rerouted the electronic path of the burglar alarm and let himself in.

As he reached the top of what proved to be a hidden flight of spiral stairs, he heard Maggie gasp through the pickup mike. When she spoke, her voice came out in a breathless murmur.

"Oh, my *God*. What *is* all this?" She sounded uneasy.

Batman slipped into the darkness of the stairwell, vaulted over the ornate railing, and let himself down to the basement floor via a supporting beam.

"C'mon, Maggie. Don't tell me you don't recognize it."

"It's a—a chamber of horrors."

"Yep," Berwald agreed cheerfully.

Batman crouched on the flagstones beneath the staircase and peered out between the risers. The room that stretched down the length of the house was a gallery of life-like mannequins engaged in a variety of horrific activities. Headsmen wielded gigantic axes; a guillotine hung suspended in midchop; Jeanne d'Arc looked heavenward from her stake. At the far end of the hall a mannequin dressed as a ringmaster stood before a circus wagon that advertised MR. DARK'S PANDEMONIUM CARNIVAL.

Maggie moved farther out into the long chamber, rubbing her arms as if she were cold, though the air here was as thoroughly heated as that upstairs. "*This* is where you get your ideas? Childhood nightmares you've imprisoned in your basement?"

"Imprisoned," he repeated, following her. "I've never thought of it that way. I suppose you're right. I lock 'em up down here, and then let 'em out when I need a classic scare."

"And yet," said Maggie, turning to look at the writer, "this isn't what you write about. You write about . . ."

"Weird stuff?"

"Not to put too fine a point on it, yeah." She nodded to her right. "What's behind the doors? Or do I not want to know that?"

"Ah, those are my *special* rooms."

"Special?" She stared at him. "*Special*? Like this wax museum is *ordinary*?"

Berwald chuckled. He crossed to the door Maggie had indicated—the first one on their right—and opened it. "Come on, Maggie. It's perfectly safe. It just looks scary."

She hesitated, then moved to poke her head through the door. "It's a . . . a dungeon?"

"A wine cellar."

"With a cell?"

"You've never read Edgar Allan Poe?"

She snapped her fingers. " 'The Cask of Amontillado.' "

"Ding!" said Berwald. "Tell the young lady what she's won."

"A one-way ticket upstairs?" asked Maggie, sounding hopeful.

"Seriously? You don't want to see more?"

Maggie stepped back out into the main gallery. "There's more?" She sounded stunned.

Berwald spread his arms wide and moved down the room ahead of her, turning slowly. "I've got 'The Pit and the Pendulum,' Frankenstein's laboratory, Carfax Abbey, the Mummy's Tomb, even the Gill-Man's grotto in the Black Lagoon." He grinned. "Can you tell I'm a sucker for the old monster movies?"

She followed him, shaking her head. "You're just a big kid, aren't you? Who are you, really? Peter Pan or—"

She stopped in midstride, staring at something that Batman couldn't see from the alcove behind the staircase.

Curious, he slipped sideways into a pool of shadow and thence to a doorway on the left side of the gallery. From this new vantage point, it was clear that what seemed to have stolen Maggie Tollyer's breath was a large metal trunk suspended from a chain over a real tank of water that bubbled and seethed as if invisible sea monsters roiled it. The trunk had a grille set into one side, and laced through the close-set bars were a man's fingers—or, rather, a mannequin's fingers.

Maggie pressed her hands to her mouth and took a step backward, jumping as she came into contact with her host.

His hands went to her shoulders. "Maggie? What's the matter? He's not real, you know. None of this stuff is real."

"Sinistra," she whispered. "It is, isn't it? It's Sinistra."

"That rip-off artist? This is Harry Houdini. Good grief, Maggie, don't tell me that loser actually *scared* you with all his Hollywood FX crap."

"Scared me?" Her voice sounded as if it were coming down a long-distance connection. "Yeah, he scared me. But not for the reasons you'd think." She suddenly sounded very tired. "Can we go back upstairs, please?"

"Uh, sure thing." There was concern in Berwald's voice. "How about another cup of coffee? Warm the blood."

They turned back toward the spiral stair and ascended to the first floor, their footfalls sending metallic echoes down the length of the gallery.

The sound of the door closing above was accompanied below by the shutting down of the basement's main overhead fixtures. In the atmospheric illumination of

Grey Berwald's chamber of horrors, the displays took on an even more sinister aspect.

Batman waited until he stood in complete silence before he moved soundlessly down the hall. Curious, he opened the door to the "Cask of Amontillado" room. There were two mannequins here. Montresor knelt, his back to the door, troweling mortar onto a brick by the light of his oil lamp. Before him, at the back of the room, the lethal alcove was about five bricks short of completion. Through the small gap, high up in the new wall, stared a pair of realistic and starkly terrified eyes.

He could hear the ghostly echo of Crane's voice, in the halls of Arkham: *For the love of God, Montresor!*

"Is it anger?"

The sound of Maggie Tollyer's voice in his ear jarred Batman out of the fictional world Grey Berwald had created in his basement.

"Is what anger?"

He glided to the staircase, then moved lightly up it, his soft-soled boots making no sound on the metal treads.

"Is that what drives you to scare people? You keep the things that scared you when you were a child so you can turn the fear outward as an adult? Is that it?"

Grey's laughter didn't sound particularly mirthful. "What's that—Pop Psych One-oh-One? I'm not an angry person, Maggie."

"Fear and rage are about a hairbreadth apart, Grey. It's all part of our flight-or-fight response. Something scares us, we get a surge of adrenaline, and we puff ourselves up and fight back. Are you fighting back?"

"Fighting what? Fighting how?"

"I don't know what. But how—with an escalation of terror, maybe? You're damn good at what you do, Grey.

I'd have to be brain dead not to admit that. In fact, you're *too* good."

A coffee cup clattered against another ceramic surface. "What the hell are you talking about, Maggie? You keep making these—these insinuations, but you never just come out and *say* whatever it is you really want to say."

The door beneath the stair rotated on silent gimbals, admitting Batman to the two-story entry. Closing the door, he slipped toward the back of the hall, into the darkness of a short passage that gave into the solarium. From this vantage point, he could just see Maggie and Berwald framed in the parlor's wide doorway, both leaning forward in their chairs as if they were ready to pounce at each other. The flames leaping in the fireplace seemed to fill the space between them, providing an appropriate metaphor for the moment.

"All right," said Maggie, setting her own cup down on the table. "Here it is. The driver of that runaway train was reading your new novel, *Fear Itself*."

There was a moment's hesitation before Berwald asked, "So?"

"So, she read a passage about monsters living in tunnels just before she drove that train. When she saw the mouth of the tunnel-approach to the terminal, it was as if her synapses overloaded. She shut down. When I . . . came across her in the cab of her train, she was muttering about the tunnels. About how 'they feed in the tunnels.' She was repeating something right out of your book."

Berwald sat back in his chair; Batman could no longer see his face. "You . . . you're not serious."

"Yes, dammit. I'm serious. I interviewed her. She described what she experienced when she saw that tunnel—

a tunnel she's been navigating for years without qualm—sheer, unreasoning terror."

There was no response from the writer, and after a moment Maggie went on. "I read—or rather, I *tried* to read—the beginning of the book. I didn't get very far past the first paragraph. The headline."

"The headline?"

"About the—the suicide." She drew a long, shaky breath. "You're too damn good at what you do, Grey. If fate hadn't intervened, that train would have—"

"Look, I didn't mean for—" He broke off and stood, suddenly, as if the wingback had bit him. He faced the fireplace, leaning into the looming surround. "I mean, I'd never do anything to hurt anybody. Not intentionally."

Maggie stood then, too. "I'd better go. I'm sorry. I guess I broke my promise."

"You didn't promise me anything."

"No, but I promised myself." She moved toward the door, then paused. "I didn't mean to hurt anybody, either."

Batman was gone before she reached the foyer, slipping along the back of the house and away through the topiary gardens. Ducking beneath the nodding head of a skillfully trimmed Loch Ness Monster, he returned swiftly to where the Batmobile awaited him beneath a drooping forsythia just beyond the gates of Blackthorne.

He had just started the engine when he heard a soft murmur of sound through his earpiece. It was Grey Berwald, back in his house, talking, Batman felt sure, to no one; no one, save perhaps his own private ghosts.

"Oh, God," he said. Just that. "Oh, God."

\*       \*       \*

Cutter felt badly about stealing. It ate at him when he had to steal. But he'd needed the bike tonight, at least as much as its collegiate owner did. He'd promised his employer a report as soon as he'd completed his task. He'd be waiting. Cutter's shadowy mentor was a patient man, but he had already waited an extra day to hear that his orders had been carried out. Cutter didn't want to exhaust that patience. He had a feeling that whatever was at the other end of it wasn't pleasant.

So Cutter hurried, pedaling as fast as his legs would go. He headed for Saint Peregrine's first, but ended up just skirting the massive building. He couldn't make himself go into the now suspect crypt. The Unknown Demon might be there.

He went back the way he'd come, diving into Los Muertos' grim domain two blocks from the derelict machine shop. He left the bicycle at the mouth of the alley and slipped into the mist. A colorless man in a dunnish coat, he all but blended in with his faded and filthy surroundings.

The short flight of steps in its arched recess was within sight when they loomed out of the fog—a line of white-faced men, like skeletal pandas in long black coats.

Cutter knew he was going to die.

Batman would have thought himself lucky to have located one of the ghostly gang members, but to have encountered an entire posse was beyond reasonable expectation. They had a particularly purposeful look about them as they slunk through the fog-bound alleys off Graham Street. None of them so much as looked up into the moonlight that wafted down to street level, filtered through vapor and fitful neon. So none of them saw the dark, graceful shape that seemed to flow through both moonlight and mist.

He went on alert as they began to spread out around a narrow intersection, hiding themselves in the gloom. Alighting on a fire escape that trembled beneath his feet, Batman saw their prey enter the crossroads, saw the trap close behind him before he recognized it as such.

The snared man stopped and turned, seeming to be less looking for an avenue of escape than acknowledging his fate. He was tall, and too thin for his height, but not malnourished in appearance as many denizens of the ghettos were. His hair was collar length and disheveled, but his clothes, which actually fit him, were unusually well kept.

One of Los Muertos stepped forward, a long, serrated blade clutched in one hand. "You killed El Pájaro," he told the man at the center of the circle. "And before we kill you, we want to know how you did it. We want to understand your magic."

Batman leaned out over the alley, intent on the scene below. So this was Twitch, the man supposed to have the Touch of Death. What was it he really had? And had he gotten it from Grey Berwald?

Batman watched Los Muertos as they circled, performing the ritual dance of the mongoose about the deadly cobra. Although, to all appearances, their quarry was about as deadly as a garter snake.

They'd asked about magic, seemingly dead serious. Batman had the feeling they were ambivalent about their desire for an answer, though. And that would determine how quickly he'd have to act.

"I d-didn't do anything," Twitch stammered. "Honest. Your buddy was in my f-face. He had a knife. I was just s-scared. I didn't d-do anything."

"That's not what El Ratón says," said the leader, and every blacked eye turned to a small, mouse-like kid with long, pale dreadlocks who stood at the perimeter of the group.

"He made a sign at him," the boy said, licking his lips. "El Pájaro stole his bottle so he hexed him. I saw it. He made the Bird's finger bleed, then he made him crazy. I think he poisoned his blood."

Twitch's right hand slid to his coat pocket, pressing whatever it contained against his thigh. The hand shook.

"Look, Fantasma," the boy said, "he's still protecting it—his bottle. Stupid old wino."

Twitch's feet suddenly stamped uncontrollably at the ground, like a flamenco dancer warming up for a performance. "I'm not a-a w-wino! It wasn't liquor, it was—it was—*Enlightenment*!" The word popped out of his mouth as if pressurized. He followed it with a string of obscenities.

Around him, Los Muertos flinched, stared, then quickly regrouped.

El Fantasma, the Ghost, stepped forward again, tapping his wicked blade against the palm of his hand. Fear warred with fury in his eyes, as if somewhere deep in his primal soul a voice whispered that it was taboo to harm the insane.

The voice went unheeded. The Ghost took a swift step toward his prey, swinging the blade above his head. Twitch reached into the pocket of his coat and pulled out a gun.

Above them, a shadow momentarily eclipsed the moon as it fell.

·

## 11

Even though she told herself she wouldn't, she kept replaying the last moments of their conversation again as she lay in bed.

It was weird, she thought—Grey's reaction to her pressing him, to her retelling of Janet Epcot's story. She'd expected him to shoot back, to ask her what the hell she expected him to do. She'd asked herself that same question repeatedly throughout the evening, even as she snapped at him like a provoked pit bull.

Shame swept through her. *God, you'd think I'd know better by now.*

The worst thing was, she wanted to like Grey Berwald—hell, she *did* like him. He was intelligent, graceful, witty. Even as the accusations had been propelled out of her mouth, she'd wanted to apologize for them.

But she hadn't. Instead, he'd almost apologized to her.

*I didn't mean for*— For what? He didn't mean for his vivid prose to disturb people? To scare them literally senseless?

Maggie rolled over and looked at the wall. It was no more sleep inspiring than the ceiling. Something, her reporter-sense told her, was out of kilter. Something about the book itself. Her own reaction to it only reinforced the idea. *I mean, really,* she thought, *what's so scary about a guy picking up a newspaper?*

Oh, yes, of course, the headline sparked memories. But the proper reaction to that might have been a deep twinge of guilt, a moment of self-flagellation, not abject, mouth-breathing terror.

She thought about the passage. Even now it gave her a bit of a shake, but it was a faint, remembered queasiness, as if the effects of the book were . . . what—wearing off?

She wondered about the book now, wondered what, if anything, Batman had discovered about it. Wondered how she could find out.

*Gordon.* The name came to her as sleep finally began to toy with her senses. Detective Captain Gordon was the Keeper of the Bat-Signal. Maybe he'd know what was really going on.

At last she slept, and thankfully, she did not remember her dreams.


Batman stepped from the fire escape, arms outstretched, the wings of his cape extended to catch the air. He activated a signature electrical charge, and the memory molecules in the fabric responded, forming a rigid configuration in the shape of a modified parafoil. He dropped straight down into the alley in a billow of black, coming to rest behind the hapless Twitch, who looked over his shoulder, screamed, and crumpled to his knees.

The scream triggered chaos. Los Muertos were in sudden and furious motion, some fleeing, others brandishing weapons against their new adversary. El Fantasma was first to attack, swinging his lethal short sword as if it were a reaper's scythe.

Batman stepped over Twitch's huddled form and swept an arm upward to deflect the blow. In a single fluid movement, he caught the jagged edge of El Fantasma's blade in the protective serrations along the length of his glove and ripped it from his grasp. It spun away to clatter against the cobbles.

The rest of them were on him like a pack of wolves, in a group effort that kept those armed with guns on the sidelines, denied a clear shot. They raged against his resilient armor as he delivered a series of blows to the centerline of the Ghost's body. The lanky youth tried to return the punches, but was barely able to get his hands up before he reeled and toppled.

Batman turned to the next two adversaries, taking them down in the swift sweep of one stiffened rib of his cloak. He turned again, struck again, with knees and elbows this time. His fighting style was eclectic, utilizing elements of Wing Chun, Silat, Keysi, and other tight, close techniques. He had also studied the Fenómeno style of the toreadors and matadors in Spain, and adapted the swirling movements of the capote to distract and confuse foes with his cape.

Weapons clattered to the broken alley floor; growls and cries of frustration and rage flew to the eaves. A few more fled from the fringes of the pack, while others picked up the fallen weapons and attacked again.

After a few minutes Los Muertos pulled back, not in full retreat, but to regroup at a slight distance. Batman moved with them, spinning into the longer-range movements of Biu Jee, Hapkido, and Savate, his arms and legs becoming flails that caught and toppled the retreating enemy.

He heard the report of a handgun, felt the slicing impact of a bullet grazing the armor over his left shoulder.

He dropped to a half crouch and spun, feeding electrical current again to his cape. It stiffened into a vast wing, becoming at once a shield and a weapon. More shots were fired. He kept moving; the aramid fiber weave would protect him against a ricochet or an off-center impact, but a dead-on shot could still penetrate.

Amid the chaotic ricochet of bullets and the shouts and cries of his adversaries, Batman realized that the man called Twitch was no longer at the center of the action.

Pivoting, he raked the periphery of the intersection with his night-filtered gaze. There! He spotted his quarry slipping across the open alley to the left. Odd. Why wouldn't he simply flee *down* the alley and away from danger? Unless . . .

He saw the ruined stairwell just as his target darted for it, disappearing behind a low retaining wall. He straightened out of his rotation, gratified to see more of Los Muertos fleeing. Rising to his full height, he advanced on El Fantasma, who was stirring groggily. The little one, El Ratón—the Mouse—had crawled to his leader's side in an attempt to help him rise.

Perfect. Just who he wanted to talk to.

He stopped at the gang leader's feet, peripherally aware of his cohort eddying in the shadows, watching. He deactivated the night lenses so the two could see his eyes.

"Who was the man?" he asked, pitching his voice so that it grated even on his own ears. His eyes, though, were on the little Mouse, who stared up at him as if he'd never seen anything so utterly terrifying in his short life. And probably he hadn't, for on closer inspection Batman doubted the boy was more than nine or ten years old.

As tempting as it was to soften his manner, he did not. Instead he took another step forward, towering over the two on the ground. He lifted his arms away from his body so that the great blue-black wings unfurled and rippled on the inconstant, prowling wind.

"*Who was the man?*"

"Twitch," said the boy, his voice breathless with fright. "We call him Twitch."

Batman was aware of stealthy movement behind him and turned his head very slightly. "Tell them to stand down," he said, then turned his eyes to El Fantasma, locking his gaze. "*Tell them.*"

"Do as he says!" the Ghost snarled, not daring to break eye contact.

The furtive movement stopped. Batman lowered his arms. "You said he killed your friend."

"Hexed him," said the boy.

The Ghost wiped blood from his lower lip with the back of one pale hand. "Poisoned him. Poisoned his blood."

The Mouse nodded. "He made El Pájaro cut his finger, then drink his own poisoned blood. It made him wack out."

"And where does this wizard live?"

Both cast glances over their shoulders toward the ruined stairwell. "Down below," said the Mouse.

"Where, down below?"

"We don't go there. There are demons."

*Ironic.* "Like me?"

The kid shook his head, making his dreadlocks quiver. "No. None like you. More like . . . like real men."

El Fantasma had been watching with veiled expression, his pale eyes like chips of diamond on black velvet.

"You know who they are," he said shrewdly. "You fight them."

"You think Twitch is one of them?"

The older kid let out a bark of laughter. "Twitch? He's no demon. Just somebody's gofer. He scares easy and he does funny stuff when he's scared." He sat up straighter, squaring his narrow shoulders and meeting Batman's gaze, though it made him sweat. "That's all the Bird was doing when Twitch got him. Just trying to scare him into a little show. He didn't have no reason to kill him. None at all."

*Somebody's gofer.* Whose? Berwald's?

Instinct told him he wouldn't find that out here. Palming his traction gun, he raised an arm to point at the eaves directly over the stairwell. The pair of Los Muertos cringed in unison as he fired a line of monofilament at the eaves. He glimpsed the stark terror on their faces as he soared over them and into the darkness behind them.

There was no one in the wrecked shop beneath street level, nor had he expected there would be. He made a quick circuit of the room, spying at last a jagged pile of bricks and splintered planking in the far corner.

The access was tight; it would have been even if he hadn't been clad in the protective armor. His quarry was smaller, thinner. He worked his way down to solid ground and found himself stooping in a low-ceilinged vault formed by the crumbled substructure of the building above. This, in turn, led to a vantage point from which he viewed a cityscape that still gave him pause, no matter how many times he saw it.

Below the streets and alleys of Gotham, beneath the solid floors of department stores and restaurants, of churches and schools, of private homes, was another

Gotham. A city of perpetual twilight, where the only light filtered down through airborne grit from rents and grates in the upper layers, or spat from inconstant electrical or gas lighting, or billowed from burning trash cans. A city where people moved in a dark parody of their neighbors on the surface. They worked and played, slept and ate, but mostly they fought—tooth and nail, knife and gun, for survival.

Undertown was a place where crime did more than flourish; it was the Way of Things—the Tao of Hell. And it was, above all, a good place to disappear—providing you could stay alive long enough to take advantage of its labyrinthine streets.

It looked, for the most part, like a distorted mirror reflection of its surface counterpart. Due to the mass sinking of three or four city blocks, the pavement was cracked and buckled, the buildings—brownstones, Victorians, and other styles of a previous time—leaning against one another like row houses in an old black-and-white cartoon. Over the years, the buildings and streets had been slowly excavated from the liquefied mud and landfill detritus. Little could be done about the mephitic stench, however, save to keep fires burning in trash cans and open pits. The rebuilding on top had resulted in a few tenements, a park and pavilion, all of which had promptly fallen into disrepair and were now fought over in vicious turf wars by various gangs.

Batman considered the possibilities. None was good; all were time consuming. But they were possibilities only he could follow up on. The GCPD did not have much presence in Undertown, and when it did, its operatives were usually on the wrong side of the law.

He moved away from the narrow tunnel, slipping from shadow to shadow, toward another egress outside of Los Muertos territory. His thoughts returned, reluctantly, to the part Grey Berwald might play in all of this. As much at odds as it seemed with his own experience of the writer, Grey's reaction to Maggie Tollyer's pointed remarks had not been that of an innocent man in the face of unwarranted accusations.

But neither was it the reaction of an inveterate criminal. He had seemed . . . subdued, ashamed. Ashamed of what?

12

"Where is she now?"

Captain James Gordon gestured over Batman's shoulder toward the brick housing of GCPD headquarters' rooftop exit. "In my office, mainlining coffee. Woman looks as if she hasn't slept in a week."

Batman knew that beneath his mask he looked similarly worn. Another reason it was better Gordon didn't see his face. "And she wants . . . ?"

"You. Or to be more precise, she wants to know what happened to the book you—uh—confiscated."

"Did she say why?"

"Will you talk to her?"

"I'm not sure it would advance the investigation—"

"She won't talk to me," Gordon said, "and she claims to have new information."

"Do you believe her?"

"What other reason could she possibly have—"

"Captain, she's a journalist. A journalist who barged into what might have been a crime scene and removed evidence. A journalist who crashed a high-profile Halloween party at Wayne Manor in pursuit of an interview. A journalist who has a 'Sightings' page dedicated to me on her website." He didn't mention that she had also finagled a date with a celebrity bachelor in pursuit of a personal crusade.

"A journalist who has reason to believe she's just stumbled onto a connection between the book and the train incident."

The female voice came from Batman's extreme right. He turned to see Maggie Tollyer looking up at him from the open door of the stairwell.

"Don't you ever just stay where you're put?" he asked.

"What kind of journalist would I be if I did that?"

He didn't take the bait. "You think you know something."

She nodded, stepping out onto the roof and closing the thick metal door behind her. "I . . . spoke with Grey Berwald last night. I pressed him about the book—about the effects the book had on the train driver and on me. He reacted strangely. Guiltily. As if he had something to apologize for. I thought that was odd, and it started me wondering about the book. If words alone can have that sort of effect . . ." She looked from Batman to Captain Gordon. "They *can't*, can they?"

The two men exchanged glances over her head, then Gordon said, "Ms. Tollyer, in an ongoing police investigation—"

"This isn't about a story," she said. "This is about me. I need to know about that book. I *handled* that book. I had it in my apartment—in my *hands*." She spread her fingers, palms up, and turned her gaze to Batman. "Am I nuts or is there something else going on here besides artistic license?"

Batman bit back an observation about her sanity that

Bruce Wayne would have delivered and said, "The books have been treated with some sort of neurotoxin. I doubt you're in any danger from the small exposure you had."

"Neurotoxin?" She wrapped her arms around herself and shivered. "Do you think Grey . . . *Grey* did this? But why?"

"I can't answer that," Batman said, "and I mean *can't*," he added when her mouth opened in protest. "Not *won't*. I don't *know* if Grey Berwald has done anything, let alone why."

"But he—"

"Obviously, he said something that you *interpreted* as an admission of guilt or responsibility. It may have also been simple defensiveness. You did imply that his work has had near-tragic repercussions."

Maggie subsided.

"No motive," murmured Gordon, "no opportunity, no means. Where do we go next?"

"Undertown again," Batman said. "Or at least I do. I have a lead on the character Los Muertos call Twitch. Lives below. He's the only connection we've got to the pure toxin."

Maggie stared at him. "Twitch?"

"Not his real name. I think he has Tourette's syndrome."

"And he figures in this—how?"

"Ms. Tollyer," said Gordon, "I think it's time you left. We're grateful for your observations—" He was already moving toward her, gesturing at the stairway.

She stepped quickly to one side, away from both men. "Let me help. There's got to be something I can do to help."

"You've done enough already," said Batman.

She turned on him. "Look, I know I shouldn't have taken that book. I can't even begin to explain the urge. I've never done anything like that before. Maybe it was the—the neurotoxin, maybe it was sheer stupidity—I don't know. But I do know that it's partly my fault you didn't have the book to examine earlier. If I can help . . ."

Batman grimaced inwardly. If Maggie Tollyer hadn't purloined Berwald's novel, would they have ever made the connection? He suspected they owed her a debt of gratitude. And perhaps that was enough reason to keep her in the game.

"What did you have in mind?" He ignored Gordon's startled glance.

"Well, you wanted to do some sleuthing in Undertown." She gestured at him. "Pardon me for saying so, but you don't exactly leave a small footprint. I mean, I'm sure you do when you *try,* but you can't track down a contact without talking to people, and if *you* talk to people, you're going to scare the bejeezus out of them."

"You have an alternative suggestion?"

She shrugged. "You need to find this Twitch guy. Give me what you know and I'll go down and ask around."

Captain Gordon shook his head vehemently. "That's ridiculous! You're a civilian—"

"I'm an investigative reporter."

"With a death wish?"

"With a . . . a purpose. A desire to help. To do something positive."

"We're talking about Undertown."

"Where I've often gone in pursuit of stories. I'm not afraid."

"You should be," Gordon said. "The place is one subway stop from Hell."

"Then send an armed guard. As long as he—or she—doesn't look like an armed guard—"

"Out of the question."

Batman, watching the verbal rally from his fog-bound shadow in the lee of the roof house, said, "I think you should consider it, Captain."

Gordon gawped at him. "What?"

"She's right about being able to do a more efficient job of tracking Twitch. I'd have to keep such a low profile that it could take more time than we've got. Time in which this toxin could surface again the way it did yesterday." He felt the weight of Maggie's gaze on his face, heard her unasked questions.

"It's already surfaced again." Gordon was obviously disturbed . . . and reluctant to say more.

Batman gestured for him to continue.

He did, with a glance at Maggie. "This information is not to be shared. Is that clear?"

She nodded, solemn.

"Twenty minutes ago there was a twelve-car pileup at the eastbound entrance to the Stuyvesant Tunnel on Cobb Boulevard. A cab braked suddenly at the entry to the tunnel. It spun out and hit several other cars. One confirmed death, at least nine injured, several critically. The cabbie—he was the fatality—had a copy of Berwald's novel in the vehicle. I sent it to the lab. I'm pretty sure I know what they'll find. Accidents like that are probably happening even as we stand here trying to figure out how to stop them." He paused, letting out a long breath. "I think it's time we picked up Berwald."

"For what?" Batman asked.

Gordon jammed his glasses up the bridge of his nose so violently, he left two red ruts. "His books are loaded with the neurotoxin, for God's sake! *Only* his books!"

"So far. Do you think that's enough grounds to arrest him? Most authors don't have anything to do with the distribution of their books, Captain. That's handled by the publisher. If it weren't for the reaction Maggie witnessed, it would be more reasonable to assume that someone at the publishing house or distributor did this. Or that some unknown party doctored the books in an effort to sabotage Berwald's career."

Gordon groaned. "You mean a competing author might have done it? Tell me you're not suggesting that."

"I said *if*, Captain. We have no conclusive evidence. Any number of people could have doctored those books for any number of reasons."

"We could pick him up as a material witness."

"Before you do that, I'd recommend you make sure it's only *his* books that have been treated. I believe you have the means to do that now."

Gordon nodded. "We deployed some specialized equipment we got from WayneTech this morning."

"I don't think it's time to pick Mr. Berwald up just yet," Batman said. "But I think it may be time that he finds out there's a problem with his books."

"You want me to contact him directly or go through his publisher?"

"Through his publisher. Getting it secondhand should make him feel a little more out of control of the situation, a little more uneasy. And if he really is feeling guilty about something"—he glanced aside at Maggie—"he may be inclined to react emotionally instead of rationally. Also, if someone at Chance Publications is behind this, you'll be sending them a message, as well."

He turned toward the rear of the roof, glancing at Maggie as he moved. She looked miserable. "Set Ms. Tollyer up with everything we know about our contact in Undertown. And a discreet bodyguard."

He leapt up onto the parapet and paused, looking back at the police captain and the journalist. "Be careful," he said, and stepped over the edge of the roof.

Cutter had showered. His hair was combed, his clothing far more upscale than anything he'd have affected in Undertown, where it would have drawn the wrong kind of attention. His long coat folded neatly in the cargo basket of his stolen and camouflaged bicycle, he entered the Sagan Library at Gotham U looking quite professorial.

Catching sight of himself in the glass of the entry, he was surprised, as always, at how well he cleaned up. He looked . . . distinguished—that was the word—in a brown tweed suit coat with gray suede patches at the elbows. His father had had a coat like this. It had smelled of cherry pipe tobacco and Old Spice. He had loved that smell. It was a safe smell, a comfortable smell. *His* tweed suit coat reeked of cedar from being packed away and infrequently used. Not unpleasant, but not as rich as the perfume of memory.

Standing in the quiet of the library, Cutter could almost believe he belonged in this environment among these students and educators. Except, of course, for the raw fear eating away at his gut. He'd been sent here on a mission, once again. This time his employer had instructed him to observe.

"Congratulations, Ulysses," his mentor had told him during their last communication late the night before.

"You've turned in your assignment in a most timely manner. But it's not complete until you've observed the results as advanced by your hypothesis."

"My hypothesis, sir?"

"Indeed. You need to take your conclusions into the laboratory and try them. Prove them. You must study your subjects and note their reaction to the . . . material."

Cutter had a sinking sensation. He had really hoped to be done with this. "Wouldn't you rather observe for yourself, sir?"

"Observe for myself? Oh, I shall. In due time. But at present, this is your province, don't you think? You do want a passing grade?"

"Oh, yes, sir. I do." Cutter took a deep breath. "What exactly am I looking for?"

"What are you looking for? Excitement, Ulysses. Agitation. Trepidation. Expansive, excellent emotions."

Cutter hesitated, then asked, "No one gets hurt, right?"

"What an odd question. What's the harm in a little excitement? That's the problem with institutions of higher learning these days, Ulysses. They are boring places, stagnant, devoid of passion. We are bringing excitement back to education."

"But you will come see for yourself, won't you?" He hesitated, then asked, "You did get the—ah—the item I left for you?"

"Rest assured, I will join you soon enough. Which should answer your second question. In fact, I hope to put your delightful gift to use very soon."

Cutter had almost swooned with relief. He'd been half afraid that his careful work had gone unnoticed— or had been noticed by the wrong parties.

Soon, his employer had said. Soon, he would join Cutter to complete the experiment.

Now Cutter glanced around the library. There were very few students here this early in the day. Later this afternoon, as more and more students sought research materials for their morning class work, the pace would pick up. He could only hope his employer would have joined him by then—he felt out of his depth, notwithstanding his mentor's hearty reassurances.

Focusing on the task at hand, Cutter slipped into the stacks to gather a pile of books, then seated himself at a table where he opened a random volume and a yellow legal pad and prepared to take notes.

*Hard-ass.* That's how Maggie Tollyer would have described her look as she strode—insofar as a woman of her stature could stride—down the steamy avenues of Undertown. The buckled asphalt beneath her knee-high black boots glittered with flecks of shattered glass that crunched beneath her soles. It looked almost like a dusting of snow in the wan light.

She was clad head-to-toe in black leather. In fact, every visible article of clothing she wore was black leather: beret, camisole, jacket, pants, boots. Her companion, a tall, sturdy policewoman named Judy Wheelock, was similarly clad and carried a motorcycle helmet (also black) under one arm. There was a microphone concealed in that, but the policewoman's firearm was worn in plain sight on her left hip. Judy—or "Jude," as she was to be called—did not stride. She swaggered.

Maggie had refused to wear a gun, but she was damn glad her escort carried one.

As they moved deeper into the section of Undertown

that underlay D Street, Maggie cataloged what she knew of their quarry. He had Tourette's; he was tall and thin with longish hair, but well kept for a denizen of the Deep; his clothes were clean and well mended. He had been involved in at least two altercations with Los Muertos, and might've spoken to someone about it. And since he had entered the underground from the sub-structure of a ruined machine shop, that was where Maggie and her companion would begin their search.

"La-a-dies!" A male voice bounced off the brick and mortar and concrete slab that tightly surrounded the two women as they drew near the cut through which Twitch purportedly entered Undertown.

Maggie and Jude stopped and turned, locating the source of the voice in a gaudily painted and carved door-way diagonal to the target entry.

The man was slender and of indeterminate age, dressed in what looked like a Chinese lounging outfit of bright peacock green. The clothes suited his classically beautiful Eurasian features and long, gleaming mane of jet hair, which he tossed, as if aware of Maggie's ap-praisal.

"You girls are pretty hot stuff for down here."

Maggie glanced at Jude. "And I heard this part of Undertown was lacking in class."

"Not anymore," the guy said. "Not with you here. You looking for work? 'Cause if you are, I got it for you, right here."

He gestured with his head, back through the ornate doorway, and Maggie realized that there were dragons carved into the posts and lintel. Dragons that were en-gaged in activities of a decidedly erotic nature.

*Ah,* that *kind of work.* "Sorry," she said. "We're looking, but not for . . . employment. For a guy."

"Buyers, not sellers, huh? I got guys. Lots of guys. Every size, every shape, every color."

Maggie shared another look with Jude, then sauntered over to where the picture-pretty pimp stood. "What's your name, hon?" she asked him.

"Wang. You want a guy? Maybe me?" He shot her a smoldering glance from beneath thick black lashes.

"S'criminal for a guy to have lashes like that," muttered Jude. "Ditto on the hair."

Maggie stifled a chuckle. "Look, Wang, you're real pretty and all, but Jude and I, we're on a job, see? For Fawcett. You know Fawcett?" She named a crime boss she knew held a decent chunk of real estate on Gotham's East Side, near the wharf.

"I know of him. Who doesn't?" Wang seemed suddenly aloof.

*Good.* Maggie continued to weave her tale. "Well, Mr. Fawcett is looking for a guy. They call him 'Twitch' upstairs. He's a runner. Usually pretty competent. Pretty trustworthy. Until his last gig. Then he got stupid. Tried to rip off the boss."

Wang pursed his shapely, full lips and whistled. "Bad idea."

"No kidding. Rumor has it that Twitch disappeared in this lovely neighborhood. Maybe you've seen him. Tall, skinny dude, longish hair, wears pretty nice duds for downside. Has a kind of nervous tic—can't control his body sometimes, or his mouth. He maybe shouts when there's nobody around to shout at, that sort of thing."

"Nut case, huh? No wonder he screwed up."

"You seen someone like that?"

"Maybe." He straightened and gave the two women

an appraising once-over. "WIIFW, ladies. What's In It For Wang?"

Maggie smiled. "What does Wang want?"

"A quick bounce with you two would be kinda fun."

Jude rolled her eyes, but Maggie deepened her smile and ran a long, fake fingernail down Wang's cheek. "Sorry, baby, Jude 'n' me's on the clock. Will this do?" She reached two fingers into the top of her black leather cami and pulled out a hundred-dollar bill.

He took it, tucked it into the front of his pants, and then nodded up the street. "I seen a guy like that in Blackie's place sometimes. Never talked to him, but I seen him sitting at the bar, sucking up cider. I seen him do that tic thing, too."

"Blackie's, huh?" Maggie flicked a glance up the street.

"Right there on the corner. You should talk to Blackie if he's in there. He's the big albino."

"Blackie's an albino?"

Wang leaned into Maggie's space, sending a wave of exotic perfume before him. "It's called irony, sweet cheeks. You sure you two won't take a break and join me?" He was stroking one of his painted dragons.

Maggie patted his cheek. "Maybe later. If we find this guy, I suppose we'll be looking to celebrate."

His grin was wanton. "I'm good at celebrating."

"I'll just bet he is," murmured Officer Wheelock as she and Maggie made their way up the street to Blackie's. Maggie was surprised to see a genuine smile curling the other woman's lips.

Inside, Blackie's was like the inside of a chimney—sooty brick, smoke, flickering red light from half a dozen neon beer signs, and close, stifling warmth. Maggie ignored all of this and moved directly to the bar, her eyes primed to find the inappropriately named Blackie. He wasn't in evidence.

"What you girls want?" asked the stringy-haired zombie behind the bar. His eyes were bloodshot, and his nose was running.

"A chat with Blackie."

"He's in back. Eating breakfast. Chat with me instead."

"We need information about someone who comes in here now and again."

The zombie shook his head. "Uh-uh. Blackie'd have my gnarlies on a plate if he thought I was passing out intel on his regulars."

"She didn't ask you to pass out intel, moron," said Jude. "She asked to talk to Blackie."

The guy started to turn away, when Maggie added, "We're here on behalf of Mr. Fawcett."

He turned back, visibly uneasy. "All the way from Quay-side? What the hell for?"

"That's for Blackie to know and you . . . not."

"Get Blackie, mop-head," said Jude Wheelock from over Maggie's shoulder. Her holster creaked as she rested one formidable hand on the butt of her Glock. "Now, if you don't mind."

He got Blackie, who was none too pleased with the interruption of his breakfast. He towered behind the bar, glaring balefully down at the two women through bunny-pink eyes.

*One hell of a bunny,* Maggie thought.

Blackie cut immediately to the chase. "Fawcett sent you two?"

"You know a guy named Twitch?" Maggie asked.

"Nope. That it? Can I finish my breakfast now?"

"Funny. Twitch is what Los Muertos call him. He may go by Butcher or something like that."

Blackie shook his head.

"Tall, skinny goofball with a lot of nervous tics and twitches. Swears out loud for no apparent reason. Starts dancing or waving or—"

"Tourette's syndrome," said Blackie. "Yeah, I know a guy with Tourette's. What do you want with him?"

Maggie read the suspicion in Blackie's eyes. Instinct provided her with dead certainty that this guy would protect his mark, not give him up. Which meant there were two ways to get to him: intimidation or . . .

"This guy we're looking for did a job for Fawcett. Running for him through Los Muertos territory. Almost got himself killed trying to bring Fawcett's stuff through. Mr. Fawcett was impressed. Wants to give the guy a bounty—maybe hire him again. Problem is, the guy they connected through is dead and Fawcett only knows the runner as Twitch."

Blackie's pale eyes studied Maggie, then moved up over her shoulder to her companion. Jude's holster creaked again.

"Running for Fawcett, huh? When did this happen?"

"Sometime this past weekend."

Blackie nodded, as if something had just fallen into place. "Yeah, I saw him. Last night, I think it was. Scared out of his wits. Okay. This is legit, right? You're not gunnin' for him or anything?"

"Do we look like gunslingers?" Jude asked.

Maggie could almost hear her gaze collide with Blackie's over her head.

"Actually," Blackie said, smiling, and showing a row of gold teeth, "you look like my kind of woman."

"Imagine how flattered I am."

"You two can connect romantically later," said Maggie. "Where's Twitch?"

"His name's Cutter," said Blackie. "He's got a place two blocks south, under Serling Court."

13

Grey Berwald had won any number of celebrity racquet-ball tournaments, but the man who faced Bruce Wayne that afternoon at his private club played as if he'd picked up the racquet today for the first time. Or as if his body was on earth while his mind was on Mars. And while that might have been the case, figuratively speaking, Bruce was willing to bet Grey was not so much distracted by Maggie Tollyer's female charms as with the dialogue he'd had with her the night before.

Bruce had beaten him four games out of five when Grey finally threw in the towel.

"You okay?" he asked the writer as they lounged against the wall of the court and swigged bottled water.

"Didn't sleep well," Grey said.

"Publishing woes or romantic ones?"

Grey grimaced. "A little of both, I guess."

"Last book's doing okay, isn't it?"

"Oh, yeah. It's—um—it's doing great. Sales figures are through the roof." His upper lip curled. "Todd McGraff, eat your heart out."

Bruce knew it was the truth. He'd checked. Tens of thousands of copies had sold nationwide, and book-stores were already restocking—some for the third time.

The press reviews had been no less ecstatic than the reader reviews online. "A towering terror," raved *Book-list*, while Emma Hawkins in *The New York Times* claimed reading it was "the scariest experience I've ever had."

"By the way," Bruce said, "I'm really sorry about those catty remarks Serafina made last night. She's . . . well, she's a piece of work, is what she is."

"So why do you go out with her?"

Bruce looked down at his water bottle, feigning hesitation. "You want to know the truth?"

Grey nodded. "Yeah. Curious me. I figure a guy like you could get any woman he wanted. Why that one?"

"Because she was available on short notice. And because any woman I wanted was out with you last night."

Grey's eyes widened, then he chuckled and shook his head. "You got the hots for Maggie-the-Cat, too, huh?"

"Something like that. She's . . . different."

"Yeah," he murmured. "Different." The writer had suddenly gone deep into his own head. Bruce could see it in his eyes' sudden lack of focus.

Bruce nudged him with his elbow. "What'd she do to you, Grey? Put Love Potion Number Nine in her perfume? Chemical warfare—that hardly seems sporting."

Grey's gaze flicked to his face, then away. "Yeah, hardly."

Bruce rolled to his feet. "One more game? You look like you need to sweat out some more toxins."

Grey pulled himself upright. "No. I'm pretty sure I don't have any more game in me. I'm gonna go shower down."

Bruce put a restraining hand on the other man's arm

and met his eyes with a look that was 100 percent solemn. "Look, I don't know what's eating at you, but whatever it is . . . I'd like to help. Is this about Maggie? Do you want me to back off?"

He was shaking his head. "No. Not about Maggie. Not directly anyway, she just . . ." He glanced at the door that led from the court to Bruce Wayne's private dressing room. "I gotta think about this, Bruce."

Bruce didn't press the issue as the two men showered and dressed. He found himself waiting for the inevitable phone call, hoping it would come sooner than later. It did.

Grey was just gathering up his effects and shoving them into his gym bag when his cell phone rang. He picked it up on the second ring, said "Hello," then listened as the female caller went into a loud ramble.

Bruce continued his own packing up, keeping his eyes on the writer's face.

Grey said very little. He asked only, "What are they doing with the books?"

By the end of the call his face was ashen and the expression in his eyes reminded Bruce of the man in the alley—alone, with several kinds of death on every side. As if he were living inside one of his own novels.

Grey ended the call and stood staring at the phone.

Bruce moved to stand next to him. "You look like your best friend just died. What the hell happened?"

"Nothing." He shoved the phone into his jean pocket.

"That was not nothing, Grey. Come on. I know we're new acquaintances and all that, but I already consider you a friend. Let me help."

He shook his head. "You can't help. No one can help. I . . . I gotta get out of this on my own."

Bruce took another step in, lowering his voice, even

though they were alone. "Out of what? Good God, what's wrong?"

Grey looked up at him, briefly, just grazing his face. "What your girlfriend said about Todd McGraff out-earning me? It was true. And it was also an understatement. My novel before *Fear* didn't do so well. In fact, it did so poorly that I had to cancel a book tour about halfway through. It earned out—just barely—but the publishing industry these days isn't so much about publishing as it is about industry. My publisher said that if this newest novel didn't do better—a *lot* better—they'd pull back on PR for the next one and cut the advance as well."

"That seems . . . counterintuitive. Wouldn't they want to put *more* PR into the next one?"

His smile was ironic. "Only if you think like a writer. Fact is, I lost it on that last book. Some things were going on in my life that I couldn't seem to control, and I didn't perform well. And when I sat down to write *Fear Itself,* I found myself with a real bad case of the yips. Performance anxiety. I wanted to make sure that *Fear* did well, but I didn't trust my talent or my craft anymore. I was terrified it wouldn't be a good book. And I *needed* it to be a good book." His tone, his expression seemed to plead for understanding.

He paused and Bruce said, "It *is* a good book, Grey." He wasn't lying; he'd actually read the whole thing, with gloves on, and had to admit the writing was vivid, deep, and satisfying.

The compliment seemed lost on the writer. After a moment's silence, he said, "That was my editor at Chance. The Gotham police are confiscating every copy of *Fear Itself* in the city. They've also issued a recall to purchasers and shut down the East Coast distributor. The

FBI was on their way up to the publisher's office when my editor called." He looked up and met Bruce's eyes, his own bleak. "God, Bruce, they think the *publisher* did something to the books."

"What?" Bruce asked.

In the profound silence following the question, his own phone rang. Not the Bruce Wayne number, but the other one. Swearing silently to himself, he took the call, responding in monosyllables as Captain Gordon relayed the results of Maggie Tollyer's fact-finding mission.

When he was done, the moment was gone, and so was Grey Berwald.

Bruce was driving his Jaguar X-class today. He raced to the car, dialing Gordon back as he went. He was behind the wheel when the captain finally picked up. He quickly synopsized what Berwald had told him, reciting it as an overheard conversation between the two millionaires in the supposed privacy of Wayne's health club.

"It wasn't clear whether he was upset because you pulled the books, because they were doctored, or because the publisher was under suspicion. Maybe a bit of all three. Wayne didn't press the issue—probably didn't want to get too involved."

"That's not exactly a confession. And where in God's name does someone connected to a publishing house get that kind of biotech?"

"That's what I'm hoping to find out in Undertown. Put Berwald and his publishing connections—"

"Under surveillance." Gordon finished the sentence with him. "That was going to be my next move in any event."

The yellow pad remained empty for a very long time. Long enough to make Cutter sweat beneath his tweed jacket and wonder what the hell had gone wrong. Then, as more students poured into the library, and more books were pulled from the shelves, he began to see something.

Or rather, hear it.

It was the soft sound of tapping that first caught his attention. He glanced over to see a kid at the next table bouncing his pencil eraser on the tabletop as if it were a drumstick. He didn't take a note just then, but a moment later, when the kid's knee started bouncing in syncopation, he sat up straighter and surveyed the room.

There was a lot of pencil bouncing going on out there. Also hair twirling, foot jiggling, and page riffling. Cutter bent to his legal pad and began to write.

At the table next to his, the pencil bouncer, a lanky, bearded youth, leapt to his feet and gathered up his books. "Dude," he said to the trio of students at the table with him. "I gotta get out of here. See you guys later."

He was gone in a flash of angst that Cutter felt as static along the bridge of his nose.

He was casting about for more reactions when a young woman plopped a stack of books down on his table and threw herself into the chair opposite him.

"Hi," she said, giving him a gamine grin.

His heart fluttered in his chest. She was nothing like the daughter he had left behind in a suburb of Gotham, yet she reminded him of Becky so strongly that he nearly spoke her name. Instead he merely returned the smile.

The girl settled in behind her books, opening a laptop to one side. She pattered at the keyboard while Cutter continued to record his observations about the growing sense of unease in the big room. She flipped open one of her library books and propped it up on its fellows.

Then she did something that made Cutter's blood run cold: she licked her index finger and turned a page.

His hands jerked toward the book in a reflexive urge to knock it away from her. But he couldn't do that. He could only sit in horrified silence and watch her repeat the innocent action: *lick, flip, lick, flip.*

Beneath the table, his left leg stiffened, his foot shooting straight out from his body. He stood abruptly, knocking his own stack of books askew.

The girl was looking at him.

"Cramp," he said, then stifled a sick moan as he gathered up his notepad and fled.

Maggie Tollyer stood outside the Gotham PD and barely felt the chill November wind tugging at her clothing, seeking access. The black leather repelled the wind well enough, but Maggie still felt cold to the bone.

The lair she and Officer Wheelock had discovered at the end of their sleuthing had been enough to frighten her in a way that Grey Berwald's chemically enhanced novel had not. They hadn't gained access, but they'd toured the perimeter of the building, peeking through windows.

They'd seen nothing but a gigantic rat condo until they used the support pillars of a loading dock to gain access to a ledge high up that ran across the back side of the building.

Officer Wheelock did it because she was a pro. Maggie did it because she was curious . . . and pretty certain Batman would disapprove.

They'd clambered onto the ledge and inched along it until they found themselves peering down through a grimy window into the cavernous interior of the warehouse. The view from here was different somehow, and patently strange. Maggie could still see the rats waddling along the walls, stopping to chat in the middle of the dusty floor, wiggling their little rodent noses at each other. And she could see the pile of shattered crates that had obscured their view of the back wall from the front windows.

But both rats and crates seemed insubstantial somehow, filmy, rippling, as if she were looking at them in a fun-house mirror.

"That's not right," Jude had said and actually rubbed her eyes before bending to the window again. "I can see through that rat. See him—the big one down there by the crates?"

Maggie had seen him . . . and through him.

"Either those are ghost rats," Jude said, "or someone here's playing with holograms."

The only reason either of them could think of for someone to go to those lengths was to hide something.

Maggie felt a sudden, urgent need to know if that someone was Grey Berwald.

She pulled out her cell phone and called Bruce Wayne's house. She got the ubiquitous Alfred.

"Master Bruce is playing racquetball in town today," he told her. "Would you like his cell phone number?"

Of course—the lunch date with Grey. She almost changed her mind about what she meant to do. The two men seemed to have really hit it off. Maybe Bruce Wayne knew something . . .

God, no. How could she keep a frivolous date with a dyed-in-the-wool playboy when Grey might be implicated in a crime?

"No, that's all right," she said. "Just give him a message for me. Tell him I have to cancel our date tonight. Something's come up."

There was a distinct hesitation on the other end of the

line, then the butler said, "Are you sure you shouldn't be speaking directly to Master Bruce about this, Ms. Tollyer?"

"Yeah. I am pretty sure." She hung up and stuffed her phone into the pocket of her leather jacket, already moving toward where she'd parked her aging Beemer. It occurred to her that she'd just been offered the private cell phone number of one of the world's most sought-after bachelors, and had turned it down. The realization was worth nothing more than a momentary faint, ironic smile.

What if Grey *was* responsible for the toxic books? What did that mean? Was he some sort of insane criminal mastermind like many of the denizens of Arkham? The thought of him there—the thought of him *belonging* there—made her sick to her stomach.

No, that couldn't be it. There had to be another explanation. She tried to remember what she'd read about multiple personality disorder. Was that possible? Were there two polar opposite personalities inside the one seemingly gentle man: Grey Berwald, country boy and famous writer, and Mr. Nightfall, horror junkie and homicidal control freak? Was that what enabled him to write what he did—to live in that brick-and-board memorial to the horrific and the insane? To unleash a potentially deadly terror on the innocent people who read his books?

Surely that took more than just a splitting of the personality—that took a patently twisted and unwholesome mind. A sociopathic mind.

Maggie reached her car, slid into the driver's seat, and tried to call Grey, but though she left several messages in rapid succession on his office line, he didn't pick up. She tried his residential number next, this time getting his housekeeper.

"He's not in, Ms. Tollyer," the woman told her, "and hasn't been for most of the day."

"Do you expect him back this evening?"

"Well, I see that Chef has a menu penciled in for tonight, so I assume Mr. Berwald will be here. Would you like to leave a message?"

"Yes, please. Tell him Maggie called and would like to see him tonight, to—finish the conversation we were having. He'll understand."

Maybe. And maybe he wouldn't *want* to finish the conversation. She couldn't help but remember the desolate look on his face when she'd left last night.

"I didn't mean to hurt anybody," he'd said.

*We never do, do we?*


The scrapbook was covered with dust. No surprise— it had been sitting on the top shelf of her bookcase for the better part of five years. Maggie dusted it off, wondering, even as she did so, what had changed. Why was she pulling her past out of mothballs now?

She sat in her office chair with the scrapbook on her lap, closed. It was a cautionary tale, she decided. A warning to herself: *Don't get involved with this. Leave well enough alone.*

But she was already involved. Up to her ears. And she'd already pushed "the Button"—already said the words of accusation. She had pointed at Grey Berwald and assigned him guilt. It almost didn't matter that he actually might *be* guilty, and that, to a degree, she was still having trouble accepting the idea. She knew from experience that even the most seemingly callous individ-

ual could be hiding a sense of shame, and Grey Berwald—
his strange, mad house aside—seemed not at all callous.

Maggie opened the scrapbook. On the very first page
was a photograph of her receiving the Caliber Award for
investigative journalism. It was accompanied by newspaper articles praising her "shark-sharp instincts" and
"rare courage." There were several pages like this, each
showing the fruits of her labors—speeches she'd given, a
letter from a major publisher proposing a book deal,
photo ops with various members of mental health and
law enforcement organizations.

The fourth through seventh pages were taken up by
the award-winning piece itself, serialized for publication: "My Brother's Keeper" by Magdala Tollyer.

She flipped quickly past it to get to the archives. These
pages were a study in the evolution of an article. They
began with the seed story—the catalyst that had sent
Maggie Tollyer off on her crusade.

Shivering, she unfolded the brief column.

## TWO DIE IN UNINTENTIONAL SUICIDE

Sioux City, Iowa—The bodies of two eleven-year-old
boys were found Thursday morning in a pond on property
owned by the family of one of the victims. The boys,
identified as Brad O'Connell and Jeremy Tanner, were discovered inside a large steamer trunk that was partially
submerged in the pond. Investigating officers, reconstruct-
ing the events of the previous afternoon, determined that
the trunk had been suspended by a rope from a tree limb,
plunging into the pond when the limb broke.

According to County Coroner L. E. Shipley, both boys
drowned, indicating they were alive while in the trunk.
Friends of the two victims claimed they were trying to re-

create a magic trick performed by professional "extreme escape" artist Sinistra.

"This is not the first incident of this type," police spokeswoman Candace Murray said of the drowning. "There have been at least two other cases of death or bodily injury stemming from kids' attempts to emulate routines from Sinistra's magic act. These boys were unfortunate in that they chose to perform their stunt without an audience."

Sinistra, whose legal name is Benjamin Lieberman, could not be reached for comment, but his legal representative released a statement denying that the popular magician bears any liability in the deaths of the two boys.

"Our client is a professional escape artist," stated attorney Henry Drew. "He issues the standard disclaimers before and after every performance warning amateurs not to attempt to replicate his stunts. If people choose not to heed those disclaimers, our client is powerless to stop them."

Funeral services for the two boys will be held Saturday at the Cedars Memorial Park.

It was not, Maggie had confirmed, the first incident of its type. The same scrapbook page contained several more such columns, clipped from the back pages of various local, regional, and national newspapers.

She had been stunned, saddened, outraged, galvanized. And, galvanized, she had run each thread to ground, interviewed survivors and witnesses, grilled law enforcement personnel, consoled grieving families . . . and written.

And finally, she had interviewed the man, himself, Benjamin Lieberman—aka Sinistra. He had agreed to the interview because she had presented herself as a reporter from the *Gotham Gazette,* which was true, and an entertainment correspondent, which was a lie. And she'd pretended at first to be a bit of a fan—also a lie.

The lies didn't bother her, Maggie reflected, nearly so much as the truth—or rather, the consequences of pursuing it.

Her transcripts from that interview were moldering in a safe-deposit box somewhere in the basement of Gotham Mutual Savings and Loan, but she recalled one comment in particular that had stuck in her mind and set her course.

"How can I be responsible for what these kids do?" Lieberman had asked her, voice perplexed, dark eyes troubled—or at least she'd read that into his expression, because she'd *wanted* him to be troubled.

" 'Am I my brother's keeper?' " she'd murmured, and Lieberman had nodded his studiously chaotic head of hair.

"Precisely," he'd said. "I mean really, am I the keeper of every half-wit who ever parked himself in front of the TV? You can't expect me to limit myself because some dim bulb out there doesn't know the meaning of the word *amateur* or thinks it doesn't apply to him."

She'd been so repelled by the response that she'd found it difficult to continue the interview. But she had continued. And then she'd gone home and written "My Brother's Keeper."

She had turned, automatically, to the last page. Taped to the inside of the cardboard back cover was an envelope. She opened it, removed the newspaper clipping within, and spread it out on the scrapbook.

### THEATRICAL HANGING: ACCIDENT OR ATTEMPTED SUICIDE?

Las Vegas, Nevada—Mr. Benjamin Lieberman, better known as "extreme escape" artist Sinistra, was rushed to the ER at Saint Canice Hospital late last night after an apparent suicide attempt.

Emergency units responding to a 911 call by Mr. Lieberman's fiancée, Aurora Quinn, found the performer suffering the effects of a fall from his third-floor bedroom window after a failed attempt to hang himself from the casement.

Ms. Quinn told investigators she came to Mr. Lieberman's home because she was concerned about a phone call he'd placed to her earlier in the evening.

"He sounded despondent, morose," said Ms. Quinn. "Which is so unlike Ben. I got worried and drove over to see if he was all right. He wasn't."

The article went on to relate how Aurora Quinn, finding the house locked, had gone around to the rear to enter through the back door, for which she had a key. That was when she had seen her fiancé dangling from a third-floor window by his neck, twitching like a hooked fish.

She'd gone in, raced up the stairs, and tried to pull him back inside, but she was a small woman, a terrified woman, and had been unable to do so. Desperate, she'd cut the silk sash tied to the window treatment, dropping her fiancé two and a half floors to the rear patio.

Maggie didn't need to read that part, because she'd memorized it. Worse, she'd reenacted it countless times in her head, putting herself in Aurora's shoes as she witnessed the hanging, the fall, the slow spread of blood from his broken skull.

He'd gone from the ER into surgery for injuries related to the fall, and thence to the ICU, where he'd spent a week before being transferred to the ward. He was now in a comfortable care facility somewhere in the hills outside Las Vegas. A place, Maggie imagined, not unlike the one in which Janet Epcot had found herself . . . but only for a few days.

Benjamin "Sinistra" Lieberman was in his Las Vegas haven on a life sentence, little more than a drooling vegetable. And Maggie Tollyer had put him there.

Two months, Maggie thought. That's how long it had taken for her career to rise and fall. From the heady apex of the Caliber Award ceremony, to the deep chasm that had opened beneath her feet the morning she'd opened her paper to read this.

She smoothed the article beneath her fingertips, then reached over to snatch a couple of pieces of tape from the dispenser on her desk. Her hands did not shake as she taped the article into place on the last page of the scrapbook.

14

Cutter was whimpering by the time he finally got back into Undertown. In his despair over what might befall the girl in the library—he'd started to think of her as "Becky"—the possibly haunted crypt and passages beneath Saint Peregrine's held no terror for him. At least none greater than what he now felt.

He saw other denizens of Undertown as he traversed the subterranean passages, but no black-clad demons. He dropped into Undertown three blocks from the warehouse and ran the remaining distance, fetching up behind the building like flotsam. He slipped beneath the loading dock and unlocked his well-hidden entrance, scooting through into the cavernous interior.

Ignoring his pet holograms, he made a beeline for the computer room, hoping against hope that he could catch his employer before he left for the university, could share his fears for the students, could beg an antidote.

But even though he pinged the receiver several times, sending his special ident-code, there was no answer.

He sat at the keyboard for a long moment, desperately trying to think. Perhaps he should have stayed where he was, waiting for his employer to arrive. Perhaps he should return there now.

He stood, backed away from the desk. There were still at least two vials of the antidote left in the clean room. He could take them, return to the college campus, try to find the girl . . .

What if he was too late? What if she was already experiencing an overdose of Enlightenment? What if—

Cutter took a final step back and met a solid barrier where no solid barrier should have been.

"Mr. Cutter, I presume?"

He spun and found himself facing the demon—again. He let out an ear-piercing shriek and collapsed toward the floor. He never got there; the creature swept him back to his feet and pinned him against a wall.

"Who were you trying to contact?" it growled.

"Nobody. N-nobody answered."

"Trying, I said. Who?"

"M-my boss. Just my boss."

The demon gestured at the warehouse beyond the computer room with his cowled head. "The one who put this place together?"

Cutter nodded. "He . . . I can't reach him." He heard the desperation in his own voice, felt it in the sweat that covered his forehead and crept beneath his chambray shirt.

He had recognized the demon by now. It was the one the denizens of Undertown referred to in whispers, the one they called "Batman." The recognition in no way mitigated his fear, however. It was still a demon facing him; the only difference was it now had a name.

"What do you do for your boss, Mr. Cutter?" Batman asked. "What *have* you done for him?"

"It was nothing. It was—it was just an experiment. Help—help the kids learn better, he said. He didn't tell

me it would hur-hur-*hurt* them. But they—she—Becky—
B-Becky *licked her fingers.*"

He felt himself dissolving, felt tears pressing for
release. He would never forgive himself if anything
happened to the girl in the library. Never. He already
had one death on his tab.

The significance of what Cutter said struck Batman
like the kick of a mule. El Pájaro had licked his fingers,
the Mouse said.

"The pure toxin?" he asked, shaking Cutter.

"No. Never that. Oh, no. Th-th-the spray. I sprayed
it. On the books."

"Where? What books?" He expected to hear that the
East Coast distributor for Chance Publications had been
the target. The police knew that and had temporarily
shut down the operation; if it were the only source of
doctored reading material . . .

"At the college. The library. To help them learn. But
they—*she* licked her fingers!" Cutter finished the sentence in a tortured whisper.

Batman stepped back, maintaining a one-handed grip
on Cutter's shoulder. "Gotham University? You sprayed
the library books at Gotham U?"

Cutter nodded. "To help them learn. Liquid Enlightenment, he said."

*He really believes it,* Batman thought. " 'He'—your
boss?"

Again the frantic nod.

"Who? Who do you work for?"

Cutter shook his head. "I don't know. H-he never
gave me a name."

"Where is he?"

"I don't know. He's not answering."

Batman slanted a glance at the computer, then twisted his captive around and sat him forcibly at the desk. "Try again to reach him. Do it!"

The smaller man trembled like a soaked dog. When he spoke, his voice sounded desolate and sick. "It's not . . . it's not Liquid Enlightenment, is it?"

"No, it's not Liquid Enlightenment. It's liquid fear." Batman activated the hands-free in his cowl.

James Gordon was standing in the middle of a crowded book warehouse, wearing an air filter and latex gloves, when his pager went off in a unique pattern of pulses, letting him know he had an urgent phone call.

He stepped to a quiet corner and opened the connection. "Gordon."

"Masterson," said the harsh voice on the other end. "We've got a situation, Captain."

A situation, indeed. Captain James Gordon listened in increasing horror as Batman outlined what was happening at Gotham University.

He would always love institutions of higher learning, notwithstanding the fact that they did not seem to love him. Most especially did he love libraries—places where books were present in abundance and where, therefore, a thirst for knowledge and understanding was to be slaked.

It made perfect sense that he should try his experiment here at his own alma mater, where he had spent his time well, if not always happily, and where he had a captive audience.

He arrived at the library incognito, of course. His picture had been in the local media often enough that his concern at being recognized was legitimate. He wore a red wig, a beard and mustache of the same color, and nondescript clothes—jeans, turtleneck sweater, denim jacket, sneakers, glasses; his own mother wouldn't have recognized him.

He felt the undercurrent of energy as he approached the library's entrance. It washed from the students exiting the building like the bow wake of a Gotham ferry. He was sensitive to such energies—one had to be in his line of work—and these were . . . not quite what he expected.

He moved up the steps at the front of the building, between its two guardian griffins, catching fragmentary snatches of conversation as he passed.

". . . worst case of the yips I've ever . . ."

". . . go to the gym, don't you think?"

"Gym? Hell, I'd rather grab a beer."

"If I don't get a latte in the next five minutes . . ."

A girl ran past him, rubbing her arms. "Brrrrr," she said. Just "Brrrrr."

Bemused, he stepped through the doors into the huge room. He was greeted by a buzz of activity and sound. A hundred conversations were taking place all about him; he could almost visualize a forest of cartoon-strip exclamation points.

"This is just too weird," said one young man as he and his study buddies gathered up their scattered books. "I usually fall asleep when I come in here. Now I feel like takin' about ten laps around the track."

"Track's closed," said another kid. "Basketball?"

Everyone at the table responded affirmatively and they left, dumping their books unceremoniously on the nearest cart.

He paused in the center of the main reading area, revolving slowly and taking in the total scene. There were still students trying to study (and looking supremely disgruntled), but for the most part what he saw was a mass exodus, fueled by palpable frenetic energy.

This wasn't at all what he'd expected, especially not after the initial trial with the novels. And this batch of the formula was at least as strong as that one had been. Had his underling made a mistake in its preparation, or perhaps simply failed to saturate the books?

Neither of those possibilities had much merit. A computer program determined the ratios of neurotoxins, both mundane and exotic. Ulysses Cutter had only to mount the vials in the carousel that rotated beneath the fill valve. But for that, the entire operation was automatic. And he had already successfully treated an entire warehouse full of books. It hardly seemed likely that Ulysses, despite his patchy gray matter, had forgotten how to do his job. Ulysses was like an automaton in that way, a creature of small and abiding habits. It was how he kept his Tourette's under control, along with his taste for drugs and alcohol.

Which left only one option: when he had reset the parameters for the formula for treating the library's diverse collection of tomes, he himself must have miscalculated.

The very thought made him chuckle out loud. What was it these kids said of such ideas? *As if.* He'd expected the varied binding glues to alter the properties of absorption, but he'd accounted for that. He was positive of it.

What, then?

He had moved to stand between two enormous mahogany shelving units, staring up at the volumes they contained, when he heard the sirens. His first impulse was to flee, but then he realized that his disguise made that unnecessary.

Hearing squeals of distress from near the main entrance of the library, he peered through the shelves. Uniformed police officers entered through the great main doors, already ordering people out of the building. Outside, a police broadcast system bleated, *"This is the Gotham City police. Please evacuate the library building immediately. This is the Gotham City police. Please . . ."*

He snatched a thick book from the shelf immediately in front of him, tucked it against his chest, and stepped out from behind the shelves into the reading room.

An officer spotted him and waved him toward the doors. "This way, please. This isn't a safe place to be right now. And—uh—leave the book."

"Yes, Officer, of course." He dropped the book onto the nearest table and moved toward the doors. "What . . . what's happened?"

"Sorry, I'm not at liberty to say. We need to evacuate the building."

He nodded acquiescently and fled with the dozens of other people being herded out onto the plaza in front of the library. The sight of all those police cruisers and ambulances stopped him momentarily, forcing sour bile up into his throat.

*Calm,* he told himself. *Breathe. They don't know you. No one knows you. You're a mere shadow. No one notices a shadow.*

He fell into step with a handful of students who were making their way across the quad. He had to find Ulysses—and then he had to think through what had gone wrong.

"What's the situation?"

Captain Gordon glanced up into the eaves of the Gotham University library loading dock. Batman saw his eyes widen as they found him there, half hidden by a support beam.

"I don't know." Gordon laughed, joylessly. "Hell, what I don't know would fill this damn building."

"What *do* you know?"

The detective glanced around warily. "Is there someplace close by we can talk safely? I've still got guys in there." He gestured with his head back into the main library building.

Batman rose, pulling farther into the shadows. "Walk out the back exit. Turn left and keep walking until you reach the sports complex. It's about a city block. Go down the eastern access to the baseball stadium." He turned and leapt lightly up toward a third-floor skylight.

"Oh, great," he heard Gordon mutter behind him. "Another tunnel."

It was a dark tunnel, too. Through night lenses Batman saw Gordon silhouetted against the theatrically silver light of suddenly looming clouds, watched as he started cautiously down the ramp into the bowels of the stadium, a hand on his sidearm.

"Here," he said, when the detective had drawn close enough that he must have been able to hear the soft ticking of cooling metal in the Batmobile's massive chassis.

Gordon stopped with a gasp. "I'm not so young a man," he said, "that I couldn't die of heart failure one of these times."

"Your heart is stronger than you think, Jim. Echoes here. Let's go inside."

They stood in the mouth of the access tunnel behind home plate. The roof there was cut away to reveal the sky, which was looking ever more forbidding. Gusts of autumn wind scudded across the infield, raising little puffs of dirt. Batman could smell the grass, still hanging on to its fragrance even as it lost its color in the gray afternoon. The ballpark was empty; the Batmobile stood sentry behind them, silent, but not inert. If anyone came within a hundred yards of them, it would know.

"Talk to me," he told Gordon. "Tell me what you have."

"Positive on the presence of the toxin. Sniffer picked it up the minute they brought it into the library. Whoever did this sprayed every shelf in there. And there was a stronger residual signature in a maintenance closet in the loading dock. So we searched, and found an air compressor in a toolbox beneath a loose floorboard." He shook his head. "How cliché is that? Anyway, the stuff must've all been used, because there were no samples left over."

"Not a problem. We've got plenty of the pure stuff to test."

Gordon stood away from the wall he'd been leaning against. "The warehouse in Undertown?"

"Yes. And I found our friend Twitch. But go on. What happened here?"

"Nothing. Well, not nothing, exactly, but not what we were afraid of. The place is lousy with toxin, but the most severe reaction seems to be a couple of kids who broke out in nervous hives. They felt the effects, but it just made them . . . twitchy. Edgy. Most of them reacted by wanting to exercise or get a drink or take a hot bath. Weird."

"You're keeping tabs on them, of course."

"You bet. Every student who was on campus this afternoon has been issued a list of symptoms to watch for and a twenty-four-hour emergency number to call if any of them manifest. How about you? Did you bring Twitch in?"

"His name's Ulysses S. Cutter."

Gordon snorted. "Parents can be cruel."

"He's got a history and, I'm willing to bet, a case file with social services. Ex-user. Swears he's clean now."

"Tourette's?"

"Classic symptoms. According to what I got out of him before you called, he was rehabbed by a nameless, faceless guy he knows only as his employer. Doesn't know where he is. Only knows that suddenly, he can't reach him. He was supposed to join Cutter to survey the results of his work, but didn't show."

"Where's Cutter now?"

"At the warehouse. I figured," Batman said when Gordon looked ready to jump out of his skin, "that since we still don't know who we're dealing with, it might be better to give Cutter's boss a safe place to call home. I'm willing to bet he'll go there eventually."

"Yeah, and his gofer will let him know you called."

"I don't think so. Our friend Ulysses was pretty upset by the time I got to him. What happened to the kid from Los Muertos seems to have hit him hard. While he was in the library, waiting for his boss to show, he saw one of the kids lick her fingers to page through a book."

Gordon's face seemed suddenly paler, even in the half-light of the human-made crevasse.

"He was between a rock and a hard place; he chose the rock. I told him if he really wanted to help that girl, if he was really sorry about that kid in the alley, he'd just play along."

"That's it? Just play along?"

"I left him something—a means of contacting me if his boss shows up."

Gordon started to reach for his glasses, then stopped,

instead buttoning his suit coat over his service revolver. "And you think he'll really do that?"

"I'm hoping he'll really do that. Anything significant at the publisher?"

Gordon nodded. "Only in the negative. We checked the shipping department at their printer. The books leaving there are clean. The treatment happened sometime after they left the printer's hands, which leaves either in transit or in the distributor's warehouse. I'll put my money on the distributor's warehouse. Each box of books we sampled had several very tiny apertures in various places. As if someone had inserted a relatively small, thin object through the cardboard."

"Such as the nozzle of an air compressor."

"Yeah, such as that. The books nearest these apertures were most thoroughly saturated. So I figure, we're not looking for a contact inside the publisher. I mean, first, you'd think they'd do it in-house. And second, how likely is it they'd want to sabotage their own star writer?"

"Not very, but then maybe that wasn't the point of the exercise. And we might still be dealing with someone with the publisher who's clever enough to know that if the books left there tainted—"

"It'd be the first place we'd strip-search." Gordon nodded, glancing back down the tunnel toward the Batmobile. "I've been away long enough. Better get back. Unless there's something else . . ."

"Not as yet. I have some follow-up I need to do on another angle. By then, I expect I will have heard from Cutter."

"And if not?"

"Then I'll pay him another visit to find out why."

15

He stopped at the bank before he made his way to Under-town, disguise intact. He liked being in disguise. People didn't recognize him, didn't stare at him. Anonymity had its upside.

Cutter had done his job well and thoroughly. There were ample funds in the account he chose to access from the ATM, and he withdrew enough to purchase more clothing and a meal. Then he went into the bank to a teller's window and withdrew enough cash from a sec-ond account, opened under a different name, to pur-chase a vehicle. Lastly, he accessed a safe-deposit box and retrieved a key card Cutter had left for him that would open the warehouse.

He purchased a well-used van—less chance of draw-ing notice, he figured—and drove it to a parking struc-ture on the corner of Beaumont and Matheson. Once inside, he headed for the sublevels. There had been five before the Quake. Now the second was the lowest level open to street traffic from above. The third level was a sort of no-man's-land, barricaded at both ends. The bar-ricades only looked solid; one part, over the course of the last year, had been breached, then disguised with a faux-wall that was actually a portal as large as a garage door. He guided the van carefully through it and continued downward until he emerged from the structure into the eternal twilight of Undertown.

He drove from one side of the subterranean slum to the other. It was a circuitous route that took nearly thirty minutes to navigate, due to the preponderance of broken and blocked streets. It also wasn't the safest of drives; twice he found his way blocked by hijackers who demanded he give up his vehicle. Both times they were routed by sprays of the pure toxin from nozzles mounted on the van's front and rear bumpers. The tactic was most effective; he hadn't even had to don his mask to add to it.

Three blocks north and two blocks west from the garage, he came at last to the sagging gates at the rear entrance of the warehouse. He parked the van next to the loading dock and let himself in through Cutter's secret entrance.

Just inside, he paused to watch the holographic rats play about the walls. The security system was apparently working well.

"I-is t-that you, sir?"

He glanced up to see Cutter staring at him from the low catwalk that ran along the front of the warehouse offices.

He smiled. "Ulysses! Good to see you. You've done a splendid job here." He gestured around the cavernous room as he crossed to the catwalk. "But we need to do a bit of strategizing. Our plans have changed somewhat."

"Oh . . . uh . . . what happened at the university? Did I screw something up?" He tugged at his sweater; the gesture began looping and turned into a frenzied tic.

"You did fine, Ulysses. It was my formula that was off, I think. And now I just have to figure out why." He watched his accomplice worry his sweater for a moment, then observed, "You seem unusually twitchy, even for you, Ulysses. Is something wrong?"

"Oh, no, sir. I was just worried about the college gig, you know, and . . . well . . . when I couldn't get in touch with you earlier, I was . . . worried."

"So you said." He patted Cutter on the shoulder. "Good of you to be concerned, but as you can see, I have reached our sanctuary unmolested."

Cutter nodded and dropped his gaze to the toes of his shoes. "Yeah. Great. So . . . where do we start?"

"With a change of venue. We're going to move our base of operations to a loftier locale."

"Yes, I've received your messages." Dr. Fenton Avery sounded as if a particularly sour lemon had left his mouth permanently puckered.

Sitting at his computer in the Batcave, Batman had a momentary vision of suspending the good doctor by his heels over the ramparts of Arkham. "Doctor Avery, I need to know—"

"*Yes,* Crane is still in his cell, and driving his guards up the wall."

"That wasn't the question, Doctor Avery."

"Well, then what *is* the question?"

"It's about his undocumented visitor."

Avery sighed volubly. "I've told you, he wasn't un-documented. He was merely *privately* documented."

" 'He'? Then you know who it was."

Avery hesitated, then said, "I'm not at liberty—"

"There's been at least one death related to the neuro-toxin that caused the train runaway last week, Doctor. Neurotoxins are rather a specialty of Crane's. If he's not responsible, he might have some idea who his competition is. Or his visitor might."

"That's quite a long shot, isn't it?"

"Long shots sometimes pay big dividends, Doctor. We need that information."

"Would that be a royal *we*?"

"No. I was referring to myself and the Gotham Police Department . . . Homicide Division."

"Yes, of course." Avery sounded minimally contrite. He bounced back quickly: "But I imagine if the police really wanted the information, they would subpoena our records."

"The case hasn't reached the point at which subpoenas are usually issued. I'd assumed you'd want to cooperate with the police investigation. If not . . ."

"I'll think about it. Is that all? I have work—"

"Tell me what Crane has been doing that's spooked his guards."

"Reading the most boring trash you can imagine . . . out loud. Loudly."

*Curious.* "Textbooks?"

"Fiction. Allegedly. But exceptionally tedious."

*Not Crane's usual reading material.* "No Freudian analyses of the works of Edgar Allan Poe?"

"Oh, that, too, but he never reads that aloud . . . thank God."

"You'll get back to me." It wasn't a request.

"Yes."

Somehow, though the answer came out in the affirmative, Batman had the distinct impression that the translated subtext was *Not on your life, you obnoxious flying rodent.* He said, "I'll call you back later today. I'm sure you'll have an answer for me then." Avery could take that as an endorsement of his powers of persuasion or as a threat. Batman didn't particularly care which.

\*       \*       \*

They loaded the van with a variety of items, including all existing vials of the toxin and the vaccine/antidote, some of the more portable devices from the clean room, and two of the three computers. The third was linked into the security system and had to be left behind, to perpetuate the illusion of an empty warehouse.

All the while, Cutter thought about the visit from Batman and wondered what the hell he should do.

*Play along,* the Bat-demon had said. That was a broad territory that blurred around the edges. How far along? Should he go with his employer? Should he try to stay here and await Batman's return?

He stood in the office, watching his employer make a last check for essentials and wondering what sort of excuse he could trump up for asking to be left behind. He could think of nothing, and turned his mind instead to some way he could leave behind a message that only Batman would get. His anxious gaze fell on the lone computer in the office. He sat down at the keyboard.

"Ulysses! What are you doing?"

Cutter nearly knocked the keyboard from the desk. Caught up in his work, he hadn't heard the other man come up the stairs onto the catwalk. Now he spun about in his chair, and found him standing in the office doorway.

"J-just checking the security system, sir. I saw a couple of glitches in it yesterday and I thought that if we were going to be gone for a while . . ."

His mentor nodded, looking pleased. "Good thinking, Ulysses. Very good thinking. I do want to maintain our lovely little bolt-hole. But hurry now—the van is loaded and it will be dark soon. I hope to relocate under cover of nightfall." He chuckled privately, as if at a joke Cutter couldn't share.

"Yes, sir." Cutter turned back to the computer and checked his work. It wasn't quite complete. But that, he realized as he reinitialized the holographic grid, might even be for the best.

Last of all, he sought out the transponder Batman had left him, which he had tucked beneath the computer keyboard.

He knew a moment of cold panic when he slipped his hand beneath the left edge of the keyboard and felt nothing but empty desktop, but the tiny device had merely gotten shifted toward the center. He activated it, slid it back beneath the keyboard, and went out to the waiting van.

He was surprised to find his employer sitting in the passenger's seat.

"Take the wheel, Ulysses. I'll navigate."

Cutter nodded and slid in behind the wheel. The engine was already running, none too quietly.

"Where to, sir?" he asked.

"To the house of the damned."

"Arkham?" The very name made him quiver. To Cutter, Arkham was a near miss, a dark, looming might-have-been. He hated the place.

His passenger laughed. "No, not Arkham. A place with a much better research library."

Cutter swallowed his alarm and disengaged the parking brake.

It was 6:30 PM when Maggie parked her Beemer next to the silver Mercedes. It was barely evening, but the car was already covered with a sparkling coat of hoarfrost. The house was dark but for the front parlor in which she and Grey had taken their coffee and dessert—was it only the night before? He hadn't even put on a porch light.

Maggie closed the door of her car quietly, not sure why she should be so cautious, and crossed the dark cobbles of the turnaround to the even deeper shadows beneath the portico over the front door. She used the huge knocker first—a replica, he'd told her proudly, of the satyr knocker that adorned the entry of Count Zaroff's castle in *The Most Dangerous Game*. When that brought no response, she plied the doorbell. It tolled like Big Ben; she could hear it even out here where the wind was beginning to whip about the trees and whistle through the eaves. *Good God,* she thought in Grey's direction, *get over yourself.*

"Who is it?" The voice fell from a speaker set into the wall beside the door.

Assuming the small grille next to it hid a microphone, Maggie spoke toward it. "It's Maggie."

The hesitation was so long, she thought he'd just left her standing there. She rapped the knocker twice, sharply. "Grey! I need to talk to you."

"I'm still here. I was just . . . surprised. I figured I'd never see you again after last night."

"Yeah, well . . . I've got a lot in common with the proverbial bad penny. I just keep turning up."

She heard bolts disengaging, and then the door opened. He stood just inside, looking disreputable in jeans and a faded sweatshirt, his face unshaven, his hair sticking up at odd angles as if an entire herd of cows had licked it.

"You look like hell," she told him.

"You don't."

She stepped through into the hall. "Give the servants the night off?"

"Except for Natalie and Franco, I don't have servants. And they live in the carriage house."

"The carriage house?"

He smiled wanly. "Okay, so it's never been a real carriage house. Hey, what do you want? This is only a scale model of a real Georgian mansion."

"That's okay. I live in a scale model of a real apartment." She grimaced. "That was uncalled for, wasn't it?"

His eyes were cold. "Probably. I did earn the money it took to buy all this, you know. Not everyone tosses away a promising career on a whim."

He turned and stalked down the hall toward the library. Maggie followed, torn between anger and contrition.

"What do you know about my promising career?" she asked, trailing him into the room.

He fell into an overstuffed chair near the fireplace, gesturing at the computer sitting atop the huge mahogany desk that dominated the north corner of the room. "I know you had one. And that you dropped out, as you said, because you didn't like the limelight. Now, let's assume for a moment that I could comprehend that—which I couldn't, up until today. How could you give up real journalism? Was it a martyr complex?"

Maggie flushed. "No."

"Well, whatever the hell it was, I don't see that it gives you the right to pronounce judgment on me or anyone else. I only ever wanted to engage people, entertain them. I *do* entertain them, dammit."

"The problem," Maggie said, moving to sit nearby on a love seat, "is that you've done more than that. Haven't you? You did something to your last book."

He paled. "What do you know about . . . who have you been talking to?"

"I helped the police uncover some evidence. I discovered the first tainted copy of the book. So I know what they found on the ones in the Gotham distribution center."

"They've impounded them," he said. "You're responsible for that—is that what you're saying?"

She felt a tickle of fear beneath her breastbone, searched his eyes for rage or insanity or God-knew-what. "I guess I am, in a way. They would've discovered it sooner or later anyway. I just happened to be in the right place at the right time and . . . ended up with a contaminated copy."

He tilted his head back against the chair and closed his eyes, chuckling softly. "The right place . . ."

Maggie leaned forward, gently touching his knee with the tips of her fingers. "Listen to me, Grey. I don't know what part you played in this, and I believed you when you said you didn't mean to hurt anyone. But responsibility goes beyond mere intention. You said I gave up my career on a whim. It wasn't a whim. I gave up my spot in the public eye because my work was directly responsible for condemning another human being to a life sentence in a sanatorium."

He opened his eyes to look at her. "What?"

"That magician I profiled—exposed—in the public press. He tried to commit suicide and failed. Now he's brain-damaged and locked quietly away where he can't hurt himself again. That happened because I put my interests—my passions—ahead of my sense of accountability. Funny thing is, it happened because I thought *he* was guilty of irresponsibility. That's why I went after him in the first place. His extreme escape routines were so beguiling, kids tried to emulate them—and some of them died or were horribly injured. He didn't seem to care. He didn't want to assume any responsibility."

Grey was looking at her with an expression of horrid fascination on his face. "Karma."

"Karma?"

"You know: 'As ye sow, so shall ye reap'? 'What goes around comes around'?"

"I know what karma is," she said. "But I don't see—"

"Maybe your magician friend got what he deserved, Maggie. Ever consider that? Maybe you were supposed to happen to him. To warn him. And when he didn't heed the warning, you became the instrument of karma."

She must have gone pale in the fireplace's ruddy light, because he sat up and leaned forward. "You didn't pull the trigger, Maggie."

"He tried to hang himself," she said in a small voice.

"Fine, then you didn't tighten the noose. He could have stopped doing enticing, dangerous stunts. He could've set up a foundation for the families of his unintentional victims. But he didn't. He had a choice." He broke off to stare into the flames that danced in the fireplace. "I have a choice . . ."

Maggie's blood ran cold. "You wouldn't—"

He gave her his attention then, smiling wryly. "No, Maggie. I'm not the self-immolation type. I'm surprised that you are."

"This isn't about me, Grey."

"Isn't it? I'd say it's very much about you." He rose and nodded toward the door. "I have a lot of thinking to do, Maggie. Mostly about how I'm going to salvage my situation."

She stood, reluctantly. "I'd like to help . . ."

"I think you've done plenty."

Which was, she recalled, almost exactly what Batman had said to her earlier. "Please, Grey. Don't shut me out. I've been through reinventing myself. Maybe I really can help."

He reached a hand out to touch her shoulder. "And maybe you already have."

He saw her to the door, turning on the lights along the front of the house and the drive. "I'll call you," he said. And at her look, he added, "I mean it. Wouldn't say it otherwise."

She moved away from him reluctantly, aware that he stood in the open doorway, watching. She was halfway to her car when she heard him laugh softly and murmur a single word: "Karma."

16

The best thing that could be said for Undertown, Batman thought, was that, being a world with a lid, it only
rained or snowed in spots. It always amazed him to
rediscover the peculiar rhythm of life here. There was
literally neither day nor night; the place neither slept
soundly nor fully wakened. It simply lurched along, like
Frankenstein's cobbled-together monster.

He shook off the sense of somnambulism Undertown
evoked and peered through the window he'd chosen as
an access to Cutter's warehouse, noting that the holographic security system was still in operation.

The glass cutter he pulled from his utility belt was
based on laser technology and absolutely silent. The
pane of glass adhered to the palm of his glove, held there
by a mild electrical dispersion current. He removed it
and set it aside, then slipped soundlessly into the shadows far above the warehouse floor.

The place was quiet and still, the only real movement
caused by air currents that breathed through narrow
chinks in the fabric of the building. But the proof it was
abandoned, at least temporarily, came when he made his
way across the floor to the office. All but one of the
desks were bare and empty, and the lone computer on
the last desk was the one that ran the holographic pro-

gram. The transponder he'd left with Cutter was tucked under the keyboard.

Had Cutter left willingly, or simply been taken away?

He pressed the space bar on the computer keyboard, turning off the screensaver. The screen beneath it was full of code, which Batman recognized as being a high-level subset of C++. He knew enough about programming to understand that the careful code controlled the actions of the "creatures" in the holographic display. According to the time-and-date stamp, the last page or so had been edited only hours earlier.

Grabbing the mouse, he put the program in debug mode, then moved the cursor to the beginning of the altered code and hit the ENTER key to run it.

He turned to look from the office window then, carefully scanning each of the moving elements in the room. Rats gamboled, scurried, cleaned themselves, hunted for invisible scraps of food. Except for one, a peculiarly colored rat that was a shade somewhere between magenta and rose. This rat climbed. It climbed straight up the rear wall of the room, as if its rodent feet had come equipped with suction cups. When it reached the window through which Batman had entered the building, it faded to transparency, then disappeared, only to reappear at the bottom of the wall to repeat its unlikely journey.

Was this Cutter's way of telling him they'd gone aboveground? He had to assume so.

He was on his way back to the Batmobile when he reached Captain Gordon on the hands-free. "They've left the warehouse," he told him. "Cutter and his boss. I'm pretty sure they've gone up into Gotham proper. Send a CSI team down; maybe they can pick up some tread castings from the area around the loading dock. I took a look myself. Looks like the last vehicle back there was a van or a one-ton pickup. Wide wheelbase, extra-wide treads—worn."

"Any chance of tracking it to the surface?"

"Even with filtered lenses, I lost it at the first intersection."

"Too bad." He could visualize Gordon pushing at the bridge of his glasses. "All right. I'll send the CSI team down and put out an APB on Cutter. We don't know what his boss looks like, but we can certainly ID *him.*"

He'd reached the Batmobile and slid into the driver's seat. "Good. I'm on my way—"

"Wait!" Gordon said sharply. "Hold for just a minute. I've got Fenton Avery on the other line."

He was gone only a moment before reestablishing the link with Batman. His voice was grim. "You'd better get out to Arkham. The Scarecrow's escaped."

"When?"

"That's a good question. Avery's not sure."


"We first realized something was wrong when he stopped eating." In his agitation, Fenton Avery had dropped his arch attitude.

"Stopped eating?" Batman followed the psychologist through the corridors of the asylum. Behind him were Captain Gordon and two forensics technicians from the GCPD.

Avery nodded as he palmed the security scanner at the entrance to the "extreme measures" wing. "The guards would slide the food in; he wouldn't so much as look at it. He read, he strolled the perimeters of his cell, he slept. But he didn't touch his food. When he'd missed lunch and dinner, I came down to talk to him."

"And he was gone?" Gordon asked.

"No. Not gone. Not exactly. Later—this morning—I returned, determined to force-feed him if necessary, and . . ." He hesitated, his jaw working as if he intended to chew the words and swallow them rather than say them aloud.

They had emerged from the dimly lit corridor into the wider antechamber that gave onto Crane's cell. Avery stopped abruptly before the transparent barrier and gestured. "See for yourself."

Batman was brought up short by the unexpected sight of Jonathan Crane perusing the volumes on his clear plastic bookshelf.

Captain Gordon cleared his throat. "Doctor Avery . . ."

"Watch." Avery moved closer to the barrier and said, "Doctor Crane?"

Crane glanced over from the bookshelf and asked, "What is it?"

"You haven't eaten your dinner."

Crane shrugged. "I'm not interested," he said, picked out a volume, and returned to his cot.

"Doctor Crane," Avery repeated. "You must eat."

Crane looked up, his expression bemused and perhaps slightly annoyed. "What?"

"I said: you must eat."

"I'm not interested."

Batman felt his gut tighten. "Crane!"

This time Jonathan Crane didn't look up, but merely said, "What is it?"

"Look at me."

"Leave me alone." Crane turned his shoulder to his watchers.

"Doctor Crane," said Avery.

This time there was no response.

*Damn.* Batman moved to stand in front of the nearly invisible door. "Open it," he told one of the guards.

Without even looking to Avery for permission, the man activated the security scanner, which, during his shift, was keyed to his unique palm print and that of his partner.

Batman stepped into the cell, the others on his heels, and strode to stand directly in front of the bed.

Crane continued to read his book.

"Crane," said Batman.

The prisoner raised his head and looked up toward the front of the cell, away from the men who confronted him face-on. "What is it?" he said, the sound of his voice coming from . . .

Batman reached down *through* Crane's shoulder and turned down the cot's neatly folded top sheet. The tiny lozenge-shaped speaker lay just beneath the thin material.

"The projection devices," said Avery, "are up there." He nodded toward the bookshelf.

Holograms and a high-tech audio system. Just like the setup at the warehouse. "How?" Batman asked. "How did he get them in here?"

Avery's face was ashen. "I can't imagine. I must assume he somehow acquired them . . . when we last removed him from his cell."

"When was that?" Gordon asked.

"Yesterday. There was, if you'll recall, some concern about his having contact with the outside. We removed him from the cell—at your request, I might add—and checked it for . . . well, for devices of exactly this sort. There were none at that time."

"And while he was out of the cell, you housed him in the interview room in the cross corridor," Batman said.

Avery nodded. "Yes. The room I showed you when you were here."

"I'd like to look at it again."

"Certainly."

Batman and Gordon left the forensics team in the cell to find and dismantle the holographic system while they followed the doctor to the interview room.

Gordon examined the clear, monoform chair while Batman surveyed the room, using several of his filtering lenses. Other than a vast array of fingerprints—all of which would have to be picked up and checked against existing records—he saw nothing. The only place to hide anything in here would be . . .

He took the chair from Gordon and used it to gain access to one corner-mounted security camera. Nothing.

"The guards would have noticed if he'd climbed up to the cameras, Batman," said Avery with a touch of his usual asperity.

Batman turned to look at him. "Do you still have the security video from his visit to the room?"

Avery nodded. "Do you wish to see it?"

Batman merely looked at him.

"Of course. The video records are stored on the server. We can access them from the guard station outside Crane's cell."

"What are we looking for?" Gordon asked Batman as they returned to the guards' anteroom.

"I'll know when I see it." At least he hoped that would be the case.

It took Avery several minutes to access the records they wanted. He started the playback from the moment the guard unlocked the interview room's thick, metal door and ushered Crane in. For the next half hour, the ex-psychologist paced the room, sat in the chair seemingly meditating, and hummed softly to himself. He went nowhere near the cameras. Then the guard returned and opened the door once more.

Crane rose and moved to the door, using his manacled hands to open it a bit wider so he could slip past the guard.

"Stop playback," said Batman.

Avery did as asked, then looked to his imposing guest.

"Back it up five seconds and run it forward in slow motion."

Avery complied. Crane approached the door, reached out, and grasped it in both hands. Then he slid his hands quickly down to the level of the lock mechanism and handle.

"Can we get a different camera angle on that?" Batman asked.

"Well, yes—the camera at the front of the room, the one you checked earlier. Let's see . . ." Avery moused to a camera selection menu, found the one he wanted, and ran the same time sequence as captured by that camera.

They watched as Crane grasped the door, pulled it open several inches wider, then ran his manacled hands down to the lock.

"There!" Gordon said. "He did something to the lock plate."

*He certainly did,* Batman thought, watching Crane's long, delicate fingers slowly caress the stainless-steel mechanism. But what?

"Should I stop it?" Avery asked.

Batman shook his head. "No. Keep going."

Crane's body obscured their view of the door for a moment; then they could see it again, gaining a clear view of the lock plate as the guard pulled the door closed.

Avery gasped.

Gordon cursed softly.

Batman was already on his way back to the interview room.

When the other men joined him, he was on his knees at the door, peering into the neat quarter-inch hole in the lock plate left by a missing screw. He pulled a long, thin pick from the small kit on his belt and inserted it into the hole. It was roughly two and a half inches deep and wide enough to have hidden an object as big around as the tiny microphone Crane had tucked into his bedding.

Behind Batman, a guard hovered anxiously, shaking his head. He looked up when Avery and Gordon approached, and said, "I'm sorry, Doctor. I never noticed it. None of us did. In fact, we had this lock repaired over a month ago. It wouldn't have occurred to us that there'd be something *wrong* with it—"

"Repaired," Batman repeated, straightening. "Why repaired?"

"It wasn't locking properly. You remember, Doctor Avery. We had to bring in that specialist from Wayne-Tech."

"What specialist?"

Avery shot Batman a dark look. "Well, really, do you expect me to remember the name of a repair technician?"

"No, but I expect you to have it on record. When did the door begin to malfunction?" he asked the guard.

"Sometime in early August. It'll be in the reports. We ran diagnostics, found the problem was a faulty electromagnetic connection in the locking mechanism, and brought in a tech to fix it. Standard procedure."

"Can you think of anything that happened in early August that might have caused the malfunction?"

The guard frowned. "Happened? What could have happened? How do you mess up something like that?"

"Good question. I could suggest a few things—an electrical charge—"

Avery was shaking his head. "Impossible. We don't let anyone bring any sort of electronic devices in here. Not prisoners, not visitors . . ."

Batman turned suddenly to look down at the smaller man, who took a step back against the wall. "Not even 'privately documented' ones?"

Avery reddened. "Not even those."

"Doctor," said Batman quietly, "I'm going to ask you a question to which a non-answer would probably be viewed by Captain Gordon as obstruction of justice. Did Jonathan Crane receive his 'privately documented visitor' in that time frame?"

Avery hesitated for only a moment, glancing obliquely at Captain Gordon, whose expression could not have been less comforting.

"Yes," said Avery tersely. "But I'll tell you right now, I don't know who the visitor was. Yes, it was a man," he added quickly as Batman moved restively. "A young man, one of those infernal journalists who's always poking about sensational stories. I know that he interviewed Doctor Crane at some length."

"In that room?" asked Gordon, jerking a thumb back over his shoulder.

"Yes, in that room. At least, Crane was seated in that room. The interviewer would have been in the adjoining chamber, speaking through the transparent barrier."

"Your choice, Doctor," Gordon said. "You can hand over the records pertaining to that interview today, or I'll subpoena them first thing in the morning." He turned to Batman. "The question remains: how long has our friend been on the loose?"

Batman considered that. "When was the last time he read out loud?"

"What?" Avery shook his head. "I fail to see—"

"When?"

"Yesterday evening. We assumed he'd finished that deadly boring novel and returned to his research. After all, he'd been reading the damn thing for . . ." He broke off, his gaze moving between Batman and the detective. "What are you thinking?"

"That he was using reading as a cover for contact with his accomplice in Undertown."

Gordon nodded. "Cutter."

Avery made an exasperated noise. "But that's impossible! We checked that cell for devices. The holographic system was not in place during that time. Clearly, he retrieved it from . . . from its hiding place in this door yesterday and set it up, I assume, as he pretended to peruse his bookshelf."

"I'm beginning to think there's very little strictly 'impossible' where Jonathan Crane is concerned," Gordon murmured.

"But—" Avery's further protest was interrupted by one of the forensics techs, who appeared in the corridor beyond them, a thick book tucked under his left arm.

"What'd you find, Templeton?"

The tech held out his right hand. A pair of short, gray plastic tubes lay in the palm.

Gordon took them, displaying them to the other men. "Looks as if these would have fit quite nicely into the screw hole. Here, you can even see where the two thread together. Crane could've popped 'em out of there in a split second."

"The holographic projectors were right where Doctor Avery thought they were," Templeton explained. "Hidden atop volumes at each end of the bookshelf. Not perfect triangulation, but sufficient to create the isolated image we saw. We also found this . . ." He held out the volume he'd tucked under his arm, opening it to a bookmarked page.

Batman took it, fingering the bookmark. It was a length of metallic thread with a plastic disk at one end. The disk was about an eighth of an inch thick and had a field of tiny holes arranged in a star pattern on one side—decorative as well as functional. He glanced up at the tech, who nodded.

"Microphone. And it's part of a really nifty little broadcast system. Check out the front cover of the book."

He did, and saw nothing at first, then realized that, given the volume's age, the silver leaf etched into the front cover was unusually bright.

He turned to Avery. "Was this the book Crane was reading aloud from?"

He read the answer in the doctor's eyes.

"How did it get into his cell?"

Avery cleared his throat. "It . . . it was a gift, I had thought, from Doctor MacMillan, before he—"

"*MacMillan* gave it to him?" asked Gordon.

Avery had begun to sweat. "Well, I actually *gave* it to him. At Doctor MacMillan's request. He merely said it was a gift . . . from someone."

"Let me guess," said Batman. "Sometime in early August."

Dr. Fenton Avery looked as if he might pass out.

17

It had been no surprise to either James Gordon or Batman that the book from which Jonathan Crane had ostensibly been reading aloud had nothing to do with a college professor; only Dr. Avery seemed particularly shell-shocked at the revelation.

Gordon had had every one of Crane's guards interviewed to see if there was rhyme or reason to the oral recitation. A pattern had quickly emerged. Crane only ever "read" the dialogue of a nameless professor giving classroom instruction to his students.

The only student name he ever uttered was "Ulysses."

They'd already uncovered Ulysses S. Cutter's checkered career of petty complaints—DUI, possession of crack cocaine, shoplifting. Also on record, his frequent and seemingly failed attempts at kicking his various habits: he'd been enrolled in every halfway house and detox program in Gotham City and had dropped out of every one. Then he'd disappeared from the rolls of the city's small-time criminals, apparently to go "south" into Undertown.

And now he'd resurfaced, as the Scarecrow's right-hand man.

Cutter had done much for Jonathan Crane: keeping his laboratory in working condition, mindlessly carrying out his instructions for potentially deadly experiments, bringing him the means of escape. Was he also the "academic" whom Dr. Roderick MacMillan had allowed an unscheduled visit? From Batman's description of the man, James Gordon had trouble imagining him capable of such a masquerade, but more unlikely things had happened.

The records on the repair of the faulty door lock cited a technician named Brian Hatchett, who was nowhere on WayneTech's employee roster, but who matched Ulysses Cutter's description. Still unclear was how Crane had actually escaped, but Gordon suspected it had been when Avery had first entered his cell to discuss his lack of appetite.

What was clear was that Cutter and Crane had been acquainted before Crane's last incarceration and had become quite good at working together, even separated by the walls of Arkham Asylum and the layered asphalt of Undertown.

"Addiction," Batman said thoughtfully. "Maybe that's the glue that binds Cutter to Crane. I saw evidence of his Tourette's, but there was no indication in his behavior or appearance to suggest recent drug use. Maybe Crane's been able to keep him clean."

Captain Gordon glanced over at him from where he sat in the passenger's seat of the Batmobile, still parked in the lee of Arkham's Gothic bulk. "Powerful glue, if that's the case," he observed. "You thinking that maybe Crane whipped him up some kind of cure cocktail?"

"Don't know. I do know that I didn't sense in him any fear of Crane. He was disturbed by what his boss was doing with the toxin, but didn't seem to be afraid of the man himself."

"Then he doesn't know him as well as we do."

Batman nodded, silent.

"You . . . you okay?" A weird question to be asking a man he'd personally seen reduce multiple armed foes to quivering blobs of fear.

"Tired."

"You?"

"I don't run on batteries, Jim."

"Of course not. Sorry." It was late, and Gordon had to admit a certain amount of exhaustion himself. "I guess even you have to sleep. In the meantime, I've got teams stationed at the college and the warehouse."

"Leave a team at Arkham. He knows this place like the back of his hand, and he has attempted to use it as a base of operations before."

Batman hit a switch on the dashboard, and the gull-winged passenger's-side door glided upward on silent hydraulic lifts.

Gordon accepted the invitation to leave with a mixture of relief and anxiety. Being in Batman's overwhelming presence was always a bit unnerving, but less so than having to step back out into a city in which the Scarecrow was at large.

Grey Berwald could not have said what drew him down to the basement. A sense of the maudlin, he supposed. Surely his career with Chance Publications was over, unless his agent and editor could convince them to reprint the thousands of novels the police and FBI had impounded. The book had been doing well, after all. Before . . .

But would it do well a second time around, unaided by dubious biochemistry?

He well knew that negative publicity of this sort was a two-edged sword. It would inspire fear in some; they would never touch another Grey Berwald novel for fear of being, quite literally, intoxicated. It would entice others to purchase a book they might otherwise have never noticed, either because they craved the notorious the way most people craved chocolate, or because they merely wanted to know what all the hubbub was about.

The thought of having to rebuild his career from scratch left him with a sick, hollow feeling—an exhausting dread that made him want only to crawl into bed, pull the covers over his head, and sleep until it was all over.

But he couldn't do that. In fact, he'd be lucky to sleep at all. And so he found himself in the place where inspiration was born—his own personal little House of Horrors.

He smiled grimly as he stepped from the last tread of the downward spiral stair: Grey Berwald on walkabout, exploring his inner landscape through unwholesome metaphor.

He took the walk slowly, starting on the southern side of the long chamber—the wax works, Jeanne d'Arc, Tick-Tock, all the way down to Mr. Dark's carnival wagon. He opened each room as he passed by, stood in each doorway, praying to feel that tingle of recognition, that upsurge of creativity, like an ocean swell building to a crest.

But it refused to come. Even Mr. Dark himself, even reciting Bradbury's fluid, savory, lyric prose, did nothing to soothe or enlighten.

He avoided looking at the suspended Houdini in his iron box; it reminded him, too forcefully, of Maggie Tollyer. But he stood before the display for a long moment, battling himself. If his career was gone—and he had to face the possibility that it might be—perhaps

Maggie meant what she'd said about helping him rein-vent himself . . . were there anything left to reinvent.

The one thing he *must* do was to try to put a stop to the poisoning of his books.

In the end he gave the escape artist's effigy the merest of glances as he moved to the last room. His favorite—the "Amontillado" dungeon.

He stepped into this one, rather than merely standing in the doorway. But the sight of the nearly completed brickwork did not inspire in him an appreciation of Poe's genius as it usually did. There was no answering desire to write, to lay out labyrinthine pathways that beckoned the reader to scenes of ghastly fascination. In-stead, he felt a horrid empathy with the man behind the wall, as if he, too, were watching light and air diminish, brick by karmic brick.

It took him a moment to realize that he couldn't *see* the man behind the wall. Puzzled, he moved forward to peer into the pitch-dark aperture. No light penetrated the gloom exposed by those several not-yet-placed bricks. The Fortunato mannequin was nowhere in sight.

Had rats knocked the dummy over? The prospect of having the wall demolished to fix Fortunato wasn't a pleasant one, but he was almost grateful for the distrac-tion presented by a problem of simple logistics.

He was turning away when a cold breeze oozed from the chink in Montresor's wall to brush his cheek. He gri-maced. Worse than rats. The recent rains must have under-mined the foundation of the house, causing masonry to crumble.

The cosmic irony of this was not lost on Grey Ber-wald: Nightfall Manor was well and truly crumbling on every conceivable level. He made a mental note to call a contractor first thing in the morning, and climbed to the first floor. He went to the kitchen for some hot milk, which he laced liberally with honey, nutmeg, and rum. Then, sipping that concoction, he went to the library to fetch a book he desperately hoped would prove sleep inducing.

He had the book in his hand when he realized he'd left the fire roaring in the library fireplace.

Except that he *hadn't* left the fire roaring in the library fireplace.

In the moment that he eddied there in the middle of the Persian carpet, a single pair of hands began a slow, rhythmic applause. Someone was sitting in one of the overstuffed reading chairs. Someone with tremendously long, spindly legs, one of which was draped negligently over one arm of the chair.

Grey took a step toward the hearth. Then another. The third step brought him face-to-face with a man he had met but once, and had hoped never to see again.

Large, liquid gray eyes gazed up at him out of a face so pale as to redefine the term *alabaster skin*. The wide, almost lipless mouth parted in a brilliant smile.

"Bravo, Master Berwald," the Scarecrow said. "Tell me, where *do* you get your ideas?"

18

Bruce Wayne woke of his own accord, glimpsed the clock, and growled in exasperation. He'd set an alarm for 6 AM and it was now 8, which indicated outside interference.

"Alfred!"

The butler appeared in the open doorway of his bedroom suite with stunning suddenness, as if he'd been standing in the corridor waiting.

Impossible, Bruce supposed, since he was holding an obviously hot breakfast tray in gloved hands.

"You turned off the alarm," Bruce accused.

"You required sleep . . . sir."

Bruce sat up, pulling the covers aside, and nodding toward the table that sat in the ample bay window of the suite. "Did I forget to mention that the Scarecrow has escaped from Arkham?"

Alfred moved to set the breakfast tray on the table. "No, sir, you did not. Nor did you forget to mention that the police have mounted a rather significant manhunt, to which I assume your fully functioning wits would be a great asset."

Bruce stared at Alfred for several seconds before bursting into laughter. The butler merely raised one silver brow and left the suite with exaggerated decorum.

"Point taken," Bruce murmured. He settled himself over breakfast, reflecting that he was giving Alfred far too many superior moments lately.

He had eaten everything on the plate and was sipping his coffee and mentally laying out the elements of the case when Alfred patched through a call for "Masterson." Bruce grimaced, reflecting that, one of these days, he was going to pick up a call for Batman while in Bruce Wayne's pajamas and forget which of the two he was supposed to be.

"Yes, Captain," he said now, pitching his voice to Batman's low growl.

"New quandary," Gordon said, not wasting any time. "The analyses have come back on the toxin we found at Gotham U and in what little was left at the Undertown lab. Both are, without doubt, the same stuff that was sprayed on Berwald's books. In fact, the concentration on the library books is actually greater than that on the novels we've tested."

*Odd.* "And yet it failed to cause even as strong a reaction."

"Thought you'd find that noteworthy."

"You're sure about the analysis of the book bindings?"

"The geek squad we got from WayneTech did the analysis. They seemed pretty damn sure."

"Is the lead geek named Jesse Rosen?"

"Yeah."

"Then you can be pretty damn sure, too."

"Uh-huh," Gordon said, "but what does that mean? If it's the same stuff, why didn't it have the same effect?

Hell, it should've had a *stronger* kick, given the concentration."

"Figuring that out is at the top of my to-do list, Captain."

"And running the Scarecrow to ground is at the top of mine."

Batman and Captain Gordon rang off, leaving Bruce Wayne to contemplate the possibilities. At the end of that contemplation, which took him through showering and dressing, he called Maggie Tollyer.

"I was just about to call you. I mean, literally. I was just picking up the phone. I . . . felt badly about canceling our date . . ." Not strictly true. Maggie felt badly about not taking an opportunity to probe Wayne about his new friendship with Grey Berwald.

"Yeah, I felt bad about that, too. Thought I'd give you another chance."

*God, the colossal ego of the man!* "I'm relieved. I didn't want to miss out on Alfred's linguine after all that buildup."

He laughed pleasantly. "Well, that's what I meant. I'd hate to see you cheat yourself out of a five-star meal. Of course, that means you have to put up with me for the evening."

Maggie revised her opinion of Bruce Wayne yet again. He seemed oddly willing to laugh at himself. "You're a strange man, Bruce. You don't seem to take anything seriously, not even yourself. Most egomaniacs I've encountered take themselves *very* seriously."

"Really? Wow. I guess I'm not doing this right, then. Maybe you can give me some pointers over dinner."

"What—help you increase your annoyance factor? I don't think so."

He laughed again. "I'll pick you up at six, then. Unless," he added, "you'd like to hop over to Six Flags for a roller-coaster ride first."

"The park is closed evenings at this time of year—with good reason."

"You just need to bundle up. I'm sure I can arrange for it to be open."

"I'll just bet you can. Dinner's fine, thanks."

"Wimp."

"Macho show-off."

After they'd hung up, Maggie sat and contemplated the evening's task. She was an old hand at getting people to talk about themselves. Tonight, the challenge was going to be getting a man whose favorite subject was probably himself to talk about someone else.

"You don't look well rested, Grey—may I call you Grey?"

Grey Berwald gazed blearily at the man sitting across from him at the table in his sunny breakfast room. The day was a bright if brief respite from the autumn storms, but the light and relative warmth failed to cheer.

"I'm not. I didn't sleep well last night . . . Doctor." Carefully tacking on his unsettling guest's favorite term of address, he glanced aside at the "Doctor's" peculiar sidekick, who was in the process of bringing a pot of coffee to the breakfast table.

"How . . . how did you manage to . . ."

"Escape?" Dr. Crane asked cheerfully. "Since you played an instrumental role in that happy eventuality, I should tell the tale, I suppose. Thanks to that—er—*delightful* volume you brought me, I was able to remain in touch with Ulysses. He, in turn, provided me the means to pull the wool over the eyes of my captors—

holographic wool, that is. My ersatz self and I showed a marked disinterest in food, and when Dr. Avery inevitably entered my cell to lecture on the necessity of eating, I was able to exit while everyone's attention was on the other me. Needless to say, the first thing I did, after changing my clothing—and thank you for that, Ulysses; it was right where you said it would be—was eat." He patted his nearly concave stomach.

Grey shook his head, finding it hard to imagine anyone escaping from Arkham, even with the help of artful misdirection. His own visit there had convinced him that he need never fear what had, in fact, happened. "But how? Escape, I mean. And how did you get into my house?"

Crane executed a full-body shrug that made him look as if his bones were made of rubber. "Have you ever owned a parrot, Grey?"

"A parrot? Yeah, when I was a kid. A sun conure. Why?"

"Did you ever have occasion to watch your little pet escape from his cage?"

He had, and remembered vividly how the bird seemed to deflate in order to squeeze through a tiny space between the cage's bars. The image of Crane performing such a feat . . . He blanched, hoping he'd never have occasion to see the man do it.

Crane, watching his expression, smiled. "If Fortunato had had such a happy turn of genes, Montresor would never have been able to hold him. Escape was simple; gaining entry here was simple. What was difficult was arranging for the distraction that would allow escape."

Grey nodded, watching Ulysses Cutter refill his half-empty coffee cup. "Thank you," he mumbled automatically. Glancing at the doctor's unlikely gofer, he met his

eyes, surprising a look that surely mirrored his own—
resignation with a touch of panic.

He sipped at the coffee and dared a bite or two of the
croissant that Chef Franco had made earlier this morning. He'd come into the kitchen, himself, as Franco was
taking them from the oven to cool. He'd almost sent the
chef to call the police, had desperately contemplated passing him a note telling of the Scarecrow's presence.

But he'd done neither. He'd merely smiled, praised the
baked goods, and dismissed Franco until suppertime,
saying that he'd fend for himself for lunch. He'd given
Franco's wife, Natalie, the day off, too. If his chef
thought his employer's behavior odd, he hadn't let on.

"So now you're here," Grey said. "Where do you
plan to go next?"

Crane raised an astonishingly long index finger. "Ah,
but I can't leave here until I've accomplished my mission."

*Oh, God.* "And that is . . . ?"

"To resolve a quandary." Elbows on the table, he
propped his chin atop steepled fingers. "I think you can
help."

"How?"

"As you know, I have been conducting experiments
with—" He glanced obliquely at Ulysses. "—certain
neural performance enhancers."

"Yes."

"The treating of your books was an unqualified
success—"

Grey stiffened. "People died. They weren't supposed
to die." He saw Ulysses, from the corner of his eye,
struggle not to drop his own coffee cup.

Crane shrugged, smiling. "You got what you wanted
out of the experiment, Grey. And more. And I got what

I wanted." He paused for a moment, expression vague, as if pondering that success, then snapped back to focus and continued: "But oddly, when I repeated the experiment in a different context, it failed utterly."

Grey could only watch his guest's—*captor's?*—face, aware of Ulysses Cutter leaning into the conversation as if his life depended upon catching every word.

"Applied to your novel, the formula performed perfectly. The subjects were deliciously terrified and unable to set aside the source of their terror. Applied to the various volumes in the Sagan Library at Gotham University, no such result was achieved. My subjects became hyperactive, nervous, short-tempered, but not terrified, notwithstanding the dosage was higher."

Grey felt as if the floor beneath his feet had shifted sideways. "You . . . treated the books in the Sagan Library? That's . . . that's thousands of books, hundreds of students."

"But it didn't work," blurted Ulysses, then blanched as Crane's gaze shifted to him. He swallowed a mouthful of hot coffee too quickly and choked.

"Ulysses is quite right," Crane said, unperturbed. "It didn't work. And I spent most of last night trying to determine why. I eliminated the possibility of an error in my formula. My lab equipment—which fits delightfully into your Frankenstein exhibit, by the way—is in perfect running order; the delivery device operated as planned. What, I asked myself, was the difference? And I could come up with only one answer."

He reached into the pocket of his obviously new tweed jacket and pulled out the untreated copy of *Fear Itself* that he'd taken from Grey's bookshelf last night. He laid it, faceup, on the table.

Grey stared at it. "My book."

"Your book. I finished reading it last night. And my opinion of your skills has risen considerably." He shook his head. "My dear friend, you have contrived to push every fear button in the human psyche. I am agog. I am amazed. I am, truly, your biggest fan." He bowed forward over the table as if in homage.

*Then get the hell out of my house!* Grey thought. Aloud he said, "I don't understand what you're saying, Doctor. My book is why your experiment at the college failed?"

"Your book—your dark and liquid prose—is why *Fear Itself* succeeded. My formula was merely a 'goose,' as they say. Experiments will have to confirm it, of course, but I suspect that without your terror-inspiring prose, my new toxin is next to useless. Isn't that fascinating?"

*Fascinating,* Grey thought, *is not the word I'd use.* Then he caught the implications of what Crane had just said: *Experiments will have to confirm it . . .*

He met Ulysses's eyes again on that emotional thunderclap and was convinced the other man was drowning in the same icy dread.

## 19

"You're sure you want to go along?" Lucius Fox gave his employer a sideways glance as they rode the elevator up to WayneTech's R&D suites. "I thought you found this sort of thing boring."

Bruce grinned. "Probably too much coffee this morning. Besides, Grey's a friend of mine, and, like I mentioned the other day, I've been known to read a book from time to time. I don't fancy getting contaminated by some fear potion. Or a love potion, for that matter . . ."

They stepped from the elevator into the broad corridor that fronted the various labs, and made their way to Jesse's. Someone, Bruce noticed as they entered, had tacked a sign to the wall outside the lab's sliding doors: MAVEN HAVEN, it read.

Lucius, catching Bruce's raised eyebrows, misinterpreted the look. "Sorry about the tacks in the wall covering. Jesse and his boys sometimes get carried away."

"I don't care about a couple of little holes in the vinyl, Lucius. Hell, they can draw a bull's-eye on the wall and call it an archery range if they want. But *Maven Haven*?"

"That's what our friends over in the Gotham PD have started calling it. Jesse thought it should be official. And don't tell him," he added sotto voce as they approached Jesse's workbench, "about the archery range."

"What archery range?" Jesse asked, looking up from his work.

"Just thinking about putting one in up at the house," Bruce said. His gaze was on the bizarre-looking object currently in the clutches of the workbench's soldering frame. "What—?"

"If you really want to know, I can tell you," Jesse said. "But be warned: there's math involved."

Bruce raised his hands in mock surrender. He caught a glimpse of the look that passed between Lucius and Jesse: *The boss wants to be "involved" again, God help us.* Good, he thought. It was exactly the attitude he wanted them to have.

Lucius said to Jesse, "Captain Gordon was asking about the analysis you did for the GCPD. He mentioned that we're dealing with the same toxin in every case."

Jesse nodded. "Yeah. Same ratio of ingredients, anyway. Different concentration. There's a higher dose of the stuff on the books at the college than on the Berwald novel."

Bruce looked at Lucius. "I thought you said the victims at the college didn't react very strongly to it."

Jesse's nod became an exaggerated bobbing of his shaggy head. He answered before Lucius could. "Yeah. And we did some tests with lab rats here, as well as some computer modeling. Results don't make sense. The rats didn't show any fear response at all, but you could've powered the city for a week on the energy output from their exercise wheels." He grinned. "Great new renewable energy source."

Bruce looked again to Lucius. "Why?"

"We don't know. Mitigating factors . . . missing elements . . . possibly elements canceling each other out at higher concentrations."

"Nothing's missing," Jesse said. "Everything that was present on Berwald's book is present on the textbooks from the college library. Cancellation?" He shrugged. "Maybe, but cancellation isn't predicted by the computer models. According to the computer models, our rats should have exhibited paranoid behavior at the very least, and psychotic breaks at the top end of the spectrum. And we've filled in all the gaps in the profile," he added. "So we're not dealing with unknown factors anymore."

"Differences in the delivery method?" Bruce suggested.

Jesse shrugged. "Books."

"But different *kinds* of books. All of the novels were paperbacks—as close to identical as possible, right?" He looked at Lucius, who nodded. "Same binding glue, same paper, same ink. But over at the Sagan . . ."

Lucius was still nodding. "Different types of paper, different binding glues, different cover stock."

"Contamination," breathed Jesse, looking at Bruce as if he'd just sprouted antennae.

"Just a guess," Bruce said, grinning at Jesse's open-mouthed stare. Lucius was also looking at him in slight surprise. "Anything else?" he added, looking at his watch. "Something planned for tonight," he added, by way of explanation.

"The Sniffers," said Lucius to Jesse. "Gordon says you sent him three more this morning."

"Yeah, and the police have teams assigned to making continual sweeps of the city—commercial areas, for the most part."

Bruce said, "It sounds like you guys have the situation

in hand. I'd better—" He stopped, his attention captured once more by the object Jesse had been working on. "Is there a way to explain this without the math?"

The younger man caught the direction of his gaze and grinned. "Real *Star Wars*, huh? Looks like a ray gun, doesn't it?"

It did look like a ray gun, Bruce thought. The kind that, in the hands of Han Solo or Flash Gordon, would spit out neat little rings of green or red light with a high, quavering whine. The fat metal barrel was about six inches long and mounted on a rubberized grip.

"So what is it?"

Jesse's grin broadened. "Say hello to the WayneTech Handy Dandy Little Giant Sonic Repulsor Pistol. Guaranteed to play havoc with your opponent's emotions— or put a severe dent in a solid wall—at distances of up to six feet."

"Six feet?" Bruce repeated. "That's not much range."

Jesse's grin sagged a bit. "Well, it's only a prototype, but look—" He held up the repulsor for Bruce's inspection. "Remember our discussion of the range-to-power ratio?"

Bruce nodded, taking the dubious weapon and turning it in his hands. "Something about a generator the size of a fridge, barrel the length of a surfboard?"

"This uses nicads."

"Nicad batteries?" Bruce repeated in disbelief.

"*Lots* of nicads," Jesse said, grimacing. "One pack for every three uses . . . maybe four at a stretch. But I'm working on that."

"Cool. This the only one you've got?"

"No, there's another one. In case I screw this one up."

Bruce ran his thumb along the sleek metallic surface. He grinned. "One nice thing about owning the company—you don't have to ask to borrow things."

"*You've reached the office of Grey Berwald. I'm working to a hot deadline right now and can't take time to chat. Please leave your number and a message at the tone.*"

She left yet another message, this time letting her worry and exasperation filter into her voice. "Grey, it's Maggie. *Please* call me back. I've . . . I've got some news from the front." *Liar.* The police weren't telling her anything at this point. But she'd do whatever it took to get him to engage with her again. "And I'm . . . I'm seeing Bruce Wayne tonight. I don't suppose I could hope you're the least little bit jealous. Anyway, please, *please* call me."

She hung up and glanced at the clock for the gazillionth time that afternoon. Bruce Wayne would be there to pick her up in an hour.

He *was* jealous, Grey reflected, listening to Maggie's message. The urge to pick up the receiver and talk to her was strong, but he didn't dare. Not now.

Not with the Monster in the house.

"Your girlfriend?"

Grey spun to find Jonathan Crane standing in the door of his library/office, a sheaf of newspaper clippings in one slender hand.

"*Ex*-girlfriend," he lied. "She just won't give up."

Crane canted his head. "Some men seem to have it all—talent, wealth, good looks, a surfeit of women." He stepped fully into the room. "The couple who work for you—they'll be up to prepare supper, correct?"

"If you need me to, I can send them away—"

"Good Lord, no. Franco is an exquisite chef. In fact, after dinner I'd like you to invite them down into the gallery. I thought a spot of storytelling might be just the thing."

Grey's heart kicked hard, then raced. "You're thinking about experimenting on them, aren't you? No. I can't let you do that."

"And why not? They're available at short notice; they trust you. What could be the problem?"

"They're my employees. They've been with me for years."

"Yes, and . . . ?"

When Grey found himself at a loss for words, Crane added, "Grey, I value your opinion. You've become, after all, somewhat of a mentor to me."

Grey let out a bark of laughter. "You're kidding."

The limpid eyes went dark and hooded for a moment, and the effect was like having alcohol poured down his spine. "I assure you, I never 'kid.' The reason is clear and spelled out in these newspaper accounts Ulysses has brought me. Bizarre behavior, freak accidents, and the confiscation of your books." Crane smiled, and somehow the dreamy quality of it was ten times more chilling than the look he'd given Grey a moment ago. "Grey, Grey, as much as it costs my ego to admit it, I am a mere technician; *you* are an artist. The experiments I propose will only confirm what I already know in my heart. My toxin didn't *trigger* the fear response in these people; the horrific scenarios in your novel did that. My toxin merely *amplifies* the effect. You bring the real power to this partnership. And so I will defer to you in the matter of selecting subjects. But I would like to know why we shouldn't use the resources at hand."

Grey felt as if every one of his internal organs had turned to stone. Cold, hard, heavy, stone. He took a deep breath, knowing that his next words would save or doom two innocent people, and said, "Everybody knows they work for me. If their friends and family don't hear from them, this is the first place they'll look. Franco and Natalie aren't stupid, and they're not hermits. They know something's up with my books; they know I'm . . . not myself. Better I just send 'em on vacation. They've been planning to visit his family in Rio for Christmas. I'll just send them off a bit early. I'm sure we can make alternative arrangements for meals."

Crane smiled. "Right you are. You see, you truly are the brains of this operation."

The wave of relief that washed over him felt almost palpable as he realized Franco and Natalie would be allowed safe passage. "I don't feel like the brains. I don't even know what 'this operation' *is* or what it's about."

"About? It's *always* been about control, dear friend. Control through fear."

"Control of what? Gotham City? The nation? The world?"

Crane's smile deepened into something that was both sly and child-like. "Oh, better than any of those," he murmured.

Better than controlling the world? Grey wondered. What—controlling the cosmos? He didn't ask that; instead he said, "You meant for all this to happen then, didn't you? It really isn't some sort of freakish accident. The reaction to the books, I mean. You meant for it to get out of hand."

"Out of hand? Yes, I suppose you could say I . . . raised the stakes a bit."

"I only meant for the toxin to give people a—a little extra . . ."

"Chill?"

Grey nodded. "Yeah. A chill." Even as he spoke, the true monstrousness of what he'd gotten involved in was breaking through the clouds for him. "A delicious tickle of dread, the frisson that would push my sales back to where they needed to be." He was having trouble keeping his voice level. "I didn't mean for them to experience psychotic breaks!"

Crane laughed, and again it was the innocuousness of the sound—not a madman's insane cackle, but merely a pleasant peal of amusement—that made the horror of the situation so much worse. "No, but I *did*. Now, how about you call that marvelous chef of yours about dinner? Then I've got something downstairs I want to show you."

He started for the door, clutching his sheaf of clippings to his heart, then paused to look back at Grey. "By the way, I'd prefer you not place any calls while I'm here. In fact, I think it would be a good idea if you were to stay close to home for a time. Very close to home. It's not safe out there." He glanced from side to side with seriocomic exaggeration, then lowered his voice to a stage whisper. "The Bat's about, you know."

He slipped around the door frame and was gone, leaving Grey to wish fervently that the Bat really was about.

Entering through the grand front hall of Wayne Manor, Maggie could only reflect on the fact that it looked even grander and more impressive without several hundred party guests clogging it.

"Do you ever get lost in this place?" she asked her host.

Bruce paused to scan his surroundings. "Nope. But then, I've lived here since I was born—mostly—so it's sort of mapped into my brain."

"Yeah, well, I'd need a GPS system just to find my way to the bathroom."

"I've got one you can borrow, if you want," he told her, taking her arm and leading her to a surprisingly cozy dining room, "but I make a pretty decent Sherpa."

*Cozy,* Maggie reflected, was not always synonymous with *small.* The room boasted a table for six and a seating group of four chairs and two ottomans, bracketed on either end by matching red marble fireplaces with mantels of bird's-eye maple. Alfred was in the throes of setting the table, so Bruce seated Maggie in an elegant chair before one of the two cheerfully crackling fires. The scene couldn't help but remind her of her evening with Grey, although as far as movie influences went, this fireplace was more out of *Wuthering Heights.*

"What is it with celebrity bachelors and their big fireplaces?" she asked.

She surprised Bruce into laughter. "What?"

"Grey Berwald has a big old fireplace in just about every room in his house, though none as impressive as the one in his front parlor. He said it was an exact replica of the one in *Son of Frankenstein.*"

"Seriously?"

"Yeah. He had another one just like it in his bedroom. Which I didn't see," she added, when his eyebrows rose.

"So what's the rest of his place like? He collect movie memorabilia or something?"

She accepted the glass of red wine he offered, pleased that he was making her job so easy. "Or something. You should see his basement. A real chamber of horrors. Literally. Everything from Poe to the Spanish Inquisition. Wild."

"Wow. Imagine that. I never would have guessed."

She sipped her wine, peering at her host over the rim of the glass. "I take it you've seen a different side of our man Grey."

"Apparently. Plays racquetball pretty well. Takes care of himself. Not the geeky type. Into causes."

"Causes?"

"Kids' charities. Literacy. That sort of thing. What do you see in him?" he asked suddenly, surprising her.

"He's funny. Nice. Gentle."

"And collects implements of torture."

"Okay. So he's a paradox."

"Sounds like he's bipolar to me."

She looked at him sharply. "You being catty, or you know something?"

He returned the look. "Neither. He just seems . . . troubled."

*I'm surprised you noticed,* Maggie thought. Aloud she said, "I've seen that, too. Any idea what the deal is?"

"Honestly? I thought it was you, at first. I still think it's you. At least in part."

She bristled. "Look, Wayne—"

He held up a hand. "I'm not blaming. And please, call me Bruce. No one's called me Wayne since my college English professor. It was not a term of affection. I'll stop being flippant, okay?" He paused to sip his wine, then said, "Something happened the other day—something about his books being confiscated by the Gotham police and the FBI, who apparently, according to Grey, thought the publisher had 'done something' to them."

"Yeah. Yeah, I know. They were . . ." She frowned. "I'm not sure I should be telling you this."

He set his wineglass down on the table next to his chair. "Maggie, I own WayneTech. You can take me for a complete lint-brain if you like, but I know what my R-and-D team is working on. And I know it's pretty serious. They've been analyzing the substance on the books, helping the police ferret it out, trying to construct a vaccine or, at least, an antidote. The night of the party, you were ready to blame Grey's storytelling for a near disaster. Do you think *he's* responsible for the toxin on his books?"

Thankfully, she didn't have to answer. Alfred the butler announced that dinner was served. They picked up their drinks and moved to the table. Maggie waited for Bruce to reprise the dreaded Question, but he didn't. She allowed herself to relax.

"Have you read *Fear Itself*?" she asked a few bites into her salad.

"Uh, yeah, I have actually. I had a pre-release copy." He made a wry face. "I assume it was clean. Or maybe I'm just too dense to be scared by anything."

She ignored the self-deprecatory comment, considering how much of her own involvement she wanted to reveal. "I . . . um . . . I had a contaminated copy in my possession for a while. It was pretty freaky."

He stopped eating and looked at her. "How so? I mean, the police seem to think just *touching* it might have an effect. Is that what you experienced?"

She nodded, relieved to be talking about it. "I've had some time to think about it now, and I'd swear the effect escalated. Touching it made me feel . . . creepy. Tingly. Like I had an itch I couldn't scratch. Like I wanted to wriggle out of my skin. Then I made the mistake of reading some of it . . ." She shook her head. "I saw things . . .

scenes that weren't in the book, but were *like* what was in the book."

"You mean like the train driver and the tunnel. You projected something from the story onto reality."

"Something like that. But even after I put the book down I found myself almost hallucinating. Sounds, shadows that weren't there . . ." *Except for that big bat-shaped one.* "I imagined the book was trying to escape from my desk drawer. Isn't that a hoot?"

Bruce blinked at her. "No."

"No. I didn't think so, either, at the time. After the fact . . ." She put down her salad fork, stared hard at the wine in her glass—noting the way shadows swam through it, cast by fire and candlelight. "People have died because of this . . . thing. The police told me that one poor kid got hold of the toxin in its pure form, and it killed him outright. Literally scared him to death."

Bruce reached across the table and put a hand over hers. "I don't believe Grey could have meant for something like that to happen, do you? Besides, the police seem to be laying it all at the Scarecrow's door. Are you really afraid Grey's involved in this?"

The Question, again.

She looked up and met his eyes. Hazel. Gunmetal blue just now because of the blue-gray sweater he was wearing. There was concern in them. Honest concern, she thought, but then how good a judge of character was she, really?

She nodded.

"Why?"

"I saw him last night at his house. He was a wreck. It might have been the impending collapse of his career, but he said some things. Defensive things. 'I only ever wanted to engage people,' he said. Then he started talking about choices, about karma. 'As ye sow, so shall ye reap.' "

Bruce frowned. "As if the books being impounded was his karma, you mean?"

She nodded again.

"Maggie, that doesn't necessarily mean he's guilty of anything. Maybe he feels responsible because his books became a weapon in someone else's arsenal. Artistic responsibility—isn't that what you wanted from him?"

She leapt at the idea, accepted it gratefully. It made sense. Alfred reentered the room just then with their main course and, suddenly ravenous, she accepted that gratefully, as well.

20

Dr. Crane's lab equipment fit so flawlessly into the Frankenstein room that it took Grey several moments to spot it. Only after he recognized the more modern centrifuges and computer terminals did he realize that what lurked behind a newly installed, outsized velvet curtain was a clean room.

"That's real," he murmured.

"Oh, yes, sir. It's real enough." Ulysses Cutter moved past him through the doorway, carrying a tray of vials.

Grey followed him. "Where's Doctor Crane?"

Cutter's elbows flapped wildly for a moment, making the vials tinkle like wind chimes. He set the tray down and glanced back at Grey over one bony shoulder. "Don't know."

"He's . . . he's not going through with his experiments, is he?"

The elbows continued to flap. "No. Field studies, he calls them."

*Field studies?* "You mean, studies somewhere else? Not at the house?"

"No, not at the house."

"Then what's going on in the other rooms?" Grey could hear the scrape and shuffle of activity even from here, and knew that behind those new heavy-duty metal doors with their high-tech locks, Crane's stealthy hired workmen were doing *something* to his exhibits.

The whites of Ulysses Cutter's eyes showed, wild, around the irises. He shook his head.

"You don't know? Or you're not going to tell?" Grey asked, anger warring with fear in his breast.

"Don't wanna know. Neither do you."

"It's *my house*, dammit!" Grey said.

Cutter gave him a disconcertingly shrewd look. "*Nothing's* yours with him around. Not your house. Not your life. Nothing."

"What do you mean by 'field studies'?" Grey asked, trying to skate back to thicker ice. "What sort of field studies?"

"Your words; his . . . medicine."

"But the police have confiscated every copy of *Fear Itself* they found."

Cutter gave him a look. "You wrote lots of books, Mr. Berwald. Lots of books." Elbows finally stilled, he picked up his tray of vials and headed for the clean room.

Grey stood and stared at his back, trying to think, desperate to have a clever moment. Or a brave one. He thought about trying to gain admittance to one of those locked rooms. Of trying to get a message to the Gotham police about what Crane was planning. Crane seemed to come and go at will. His workers did likewise, working odd hours, all but invisible even to the owner of the house. Cutter didn't know where his master went when he wasn't around, like now. Or at least he claimed not to know.

Maybe now was the time.

Grey turned and headed back upstairs. He'd send e-mail, that's what he'd do. He'd send e-mail to the police, to Maggie, to the *Gotham Gazette*. And he'd call. Surely his calls would get out.

Upstairs in his office he went immediately to the phone and picked up the receiver. There was no dial tone.

Okay, his cell phone then. He'd left it recharging in the top drawer of his desk.

He opened the drawer. The charger was still there; the phone was gone. *Surprise.*

E-mail then. He sat down at his computer, opened his e-mail program, and was greeted with a dozen SERVER NOT ACCESSIBLE messages. He glanced at the signal meter in the system menu bar. There was no signal.

He gritted his teeth. The car, then. He'd climb in; drive away. But somehow he knew, before he even looked, that he wouldn't be able to find his keys.

He paced the library as darkness came on, trying to make his brain work. Ironic, he thought, that in the grip of fictional terrors he could spin wild scenarios, hatch devious plots, navigate labyrinthine thought processes. In the grip of real terror, he couldn't even plot how to escape from his own house. He stopped his pacing at one of the tall windows that looked out over the broad rear lawn and topiary gardens. It was dark enough now to escape. And escape he must.

The kitchen, he decided—he would go out through the kitchen's side door, slip into the gardens, and make his way down to the road. Or maybe he could stow away in one of the nondescript "company" vehicles Crane's worker bees had parked about the neighborhood.

He went upstairs to his room and changed into black jeans, a black turtleneck sweater, and a black leather jacket. He quickly discovered the jacket creaked when

he moved, and discarded it in favor of a thick black
hooded sweatshirt. He stuffed black gloves into the
sweater's pockets and slipped downstairs, hands in the
pockets of his jeans. He strolled casually into the kitchen,
waiting until the door swung shut behind him to pull
out his gloves.

A soft sound filtered through the door from the breakfast room. Grey stuck the gloves back into his pocket,
opened the fridge, and pretended to forage for food. He
pulled out a jar of Spanish olives and popped a few into
his mouth, chewing slowly and listening.

Nothing.

Heaving a sigh of relief, he put the jar back and started
to close the refrigerator door.

Jonathan Crane stood just on the other side, watching
him with pale, bottomless eyes. Except that it wasn't
Crane, not exactly. What stood before Grey Berwald
was an apparition. Crane wore a pair of ill-fitting dark
brown dungarees and an orange–and-black-plaid shirt.
From the cuffs of the pants and the sleeves and collar of
the shirt, tufts of straw protruded. His face was covered
by a burlap bag, with a poorly stitched gash for the
mouth, and two eyeholes. The latter had not been cut—
they had been burned through the burlap, as if by a hot
poker; Grey could see blackened threads, curling like
lashes, about the edges of the holes, and Crane's eyes
judging him from within. A large, floppy straw hat completed the grotesque ensemble.

It should have looked ridiculous, absurd. It didn't. It
was terrifying.

Grey nearly shrieked aloud. He shoved the refrigerator door hard enough to bounce it half open again, its
tiny bulb casting a sharp, triangular shard of light onto
the floor.

"I was afraid you'd gone out," the Scarecrow said softly.

"N-no." Grey cleared his throat, steadied his voice. "I was just hungry."

"I'm hungry, too, my friend. Hungry for knowledge you possess. I have read several of your books now, Grey, and I have come to the conclusion that you are a master of terror. I want to learn how to do what you do: how to terrify with words and images alone, how to conjure demons with no tools but skill and imagination. You must take me as a disciple, a student, an apprentice. You must teach me." His eyes glittered in the shadows of the mask.

Like ice cubes, Grey thought. In some distant corner of his mind, the Writer sat up and took in the scene: the darkened kitchen, the two men facing off—one looming over the other with vulture-like attentiveness, the other gazing up in abject fear, a tableau that would conjure demons hovering in the air between them.

It was a very good scene, he thought, analytically. He wished he'd written it.

Maggie Tollyer had the yips. Or so Jesse Rosen would have said. Batman watched her from the fire escape outside her kitchen, from which vantage point he could see almost the entire trail of her pacing—kitchen to living room to office and back again.

She stopped several times to place a phone call—or attempt to place a call; the speed with which she hung up indicated she was getting a message machine or a busy signal. She was calling Grey Berwald's number each time, her fingers tracing a pattern she could probably execute by now in her sleep.

She stopped twice to pick up her jacket from the sofa.

Once she started to put it on, then raked her cropped hair into wild disarray, tore the jacket off, flung it back to the sofa, and resumed pacing.

Batman thought about slipping into her apartment and confronting her, telling her to back off, not to concern herself with Berwald, who was almost certainly hiding out from the publicity surrounding the sudden disappearance of his books from stores across the nation. But that, he was fairly certain, would have the perversely opposite effect of causing Maggie Tollyer to throw herself smack into the middle of things.

Which he would like to avoid, if possible.

Over dinner, she had revealed deep concern that she hadn't been able to reach the writer throughout the day. Bruce Wayne had consoled her with the palliative theory that Berwald was merely lying low, trying—as Grey, himself, had told her—to find a way out of his current difficulties.

"But what if he can't find a way out?" she'd asked him. "He's not a man who asks for help easily. And even though he says he's not the type for self-immolation . . . what if he doesn't see any light at the end of the tunnel?"

He'd soothed her with the reminder that Grey was a sensible guy; a pragmatist. And that he must also be resilient to have risen to such heights in the literary world.

"You don't get to where he is without a very thick skin, Maggie," Bruce had told her.

"But you're worried, too," she charged him. "Aren't you?"

And he'd had to admit that he was. Which was how Maggie had extracted from him a promise to "look in on" the writer. To use Bruce Wayne's considerable clout to find out what was going on at Nightfall Manor.

He had every intention of doing that, but not until

he'd assured himself that Maggie Tollyer was safely
down for the count. And it was not Bruce Wayne's clout
he'd be depending on.

Already, Batman had gotten James Gordon to check
Berwald's recent credit card activity, which had netted
the news that, earlier this evening, he had purchased two
airline tickets for a red-eye flight from Gotham City to
Rio de Janeiro. All phone messages were now being intercepted by a professional voice-mail service. Calls to
the residence of the chef and housekeeper were similarly
intercepted. The staff at the publishing house knew
nothing; indeed, they hadn't yet decided how to respond
to the situation.

There was every indication that Grey Berwald had left
the country to get away from it all.

Maggie had stopped pacing and stood in the middle
of her kitchen, staring at the black-and-white tile floor.
She raised her eyes to the kitchen window momentarily,
seeming to gaze directly at her watcher. She couldn't see
him, of course, but the expression on her face was so
bleak that he thought for a split second of revealing himself.

The moment passed, though, and she turned, crossed
the kitchen, flipped off the light, and vanished into her
bedroom. Slipping across the roof, Batman stationed
himself at her bedroom window to make sure she was
really bound for sleep. At last, when she emerged from
her bathroom clad in her plaid flannel pajamas, he left,
abandoning her to dreams that he had little hope would
be pleasant.

Berwald's house was dark. Which meant nothing,
given that it was the middle of the night. The Mercedes
was in its usual spot in the parking area just off the curv-

ing driveway. If Berwald had gone to the airport—*with what companion?*—he'd taken a cab or an airport limo.

Batman circled the house, listening with more than his own senses. There was something going on in the basement—a rhythmic cadence not unlike the ticking of a large clock, regular, continuous. Because "The Pit and the Pendulum" was one of the prize exhibits, this wasn't surprising.

Scanning the back of the house through infrared lenses, he noted that some masonry work had been done along the foundation. He was about to take a closer look when he saw the fading heat signature of footsteps cutting across the garden at the back of the house, and entering through the breakfast room.

Someone was home after all. He was considering employing his lock-picking talents when he caught the tiniest movement in a second-floor window. Firelight, he thought, flickering along the edge of a drawn curtain.

Soundlessly moving from grass to pergola to balcony, he alit next to a set of French doors that gave onto the firelit room. Once there, he could see what was hidden from below by the thick growth of star jasmine on the balcony railing: firelight spilled across hardwood and carpet, licking at the sock-clad toes of a man lounging in an elegant, overstuffed chair.

The cozy first impression of the writer's condition was quickly exploded. There was a half-empty brandy bottle on the side table, and a large snifter dangled from his fingers. And although he was dressed for the outdoors in a black hooded sweatshirt—possibly having just returned from a nocturnal stroll—he was clearly in no condition now to go anywhere.

As Batman watched, Berwald's eyes drifted closed and

the brandy snifter clattered to the side table, remaining miraculously upright.

He had not flown to Rio, after all. For some reason he had elected instead to stay in Gotham and drown his troubles in fine liquor. Any cynical thoughts Batman had were tempered by the knowledge that different men hid from tragedy and guilt in different ways. In the final analysis it all amounted to the same thing—suppression and concealment.

As he slipped away into the night, Batman wondered if Grey Berwald would eventually step from concealment, accept whatever shame he truly owned, and take action.

## 21

"It's Masterson. Do we know who used the airline tickets Berwald bought?"

"A moment." Captain Gordon moved to close his office door, then returned to his desk to pick up the phone, wondering for the thousandth time what the voice of the man beneath the cowl really sounded like. "You there?"

"Yes."

Gordon scratched the bridge of his nose. "Natalie and Franco Guerra. His housekeeper and chef. It doesn't look as if Berwald ever intended to use them himself. Why do we care?"

"Because Maggie Tollyer does. Every time she's talked to Berwald since the subway incident, she's come away with the impression that he's nervous, guilty, hiding something. She's a journalist; I'd at least consider trusting her instincts."

"Hiding what? The toxin is the Scarecrow's work."

"Yes, but he chose to use it on Berwald's book. I have to wonder why."

"What are you thinking?"

"That maybe you should reestablish surveillance of Berwald's house."

Gordon exhaled gustily. "Don't have the resources. Between the book sweep and the manhunt, we're pretty tapped out. And unfortunately, the more mundane criminals just can't be persuaded to take a vacation until such time as we've closed this case."

"FBI?"

"You suggesting I *invite* them to dabble in local matters? Trust me, that's a recipe for chaos. The last time I had to 'work with' the FBI—"

"I remember," Batman said; then, "So he sent his household staff out of the country."

"Yeah. Turns out the husband, Franco, has family in Rio. So what are we worried about with Berwald, exactly?"

"He seems depressed. Ms. Tollyer is concerned for his well-being. Can't say I blame her."

"I can increase the patrol rotation in Blackthorne," Gordon offered. "Make sure they go past his place. What should I have them look for?"

"Anything out of the ordinary, but especially around sunset, a lack of activity—no lights going on, no smoke from the chimneys, that sort of thing—could be meaningful. Anything at your end?"

"Ah . . . No. No, I'm afraid not. The good news is, we've swept every bookstore—used and new—in Gotham and the 'burbs, and have started doing a blanket search of the warehouse district. All the bookstores are clean now, and we've gotten a massive response to the recall. Thousands of copies of the book have been turned in. And that's just in Gotham. The FBI reports good compliance nationwide." Gordon allowed himself a smile. "The *really* good news is that, thanks to our friends at WayneTech, the immediate danger is past. Now we just need to find the Scarecrow and clean up his mess."

" 'Just'?" Batman repeated.

Gordon's smile slipped toward the rueful. "Okay, that came out sounding pretty cocky, didn't it? I'm not nearly so sanguine. Trying to stay positive, that's all."

"As you should. We'll find Crane. He may be lying low now, but eventually he'll overreach. And when he does, we'll get him."

Gordon rang off, feeling vaguely unsettled. When Jonathan Crane overreached, the consequences were usually dire.


"The key is understanding different varieties of fear," Grey Berwald said to his class of one. He was exhausted, hungover, and depressed, but the material was practically written on the inside of his skull. He could teach horror writing in a coma.

He moved to the whiteboard fastened to the wall at one end of his desk, picked up a marker, and made a list.

1. Fear of the known.
2. Fear of the unknown.
3. Sudden fear/panic.
4. Gradually compounded fear/suspense.

He turned back to his student. "Fear of the known is limited, although it can be devastating when compounded. You know what's going to happen to you and you react to that. The shark is swimming ever nearer, the ax murderer is behind one of the doors you have to creep past, et cetera."

"Delightful," said Crane. "We're talking about heart-pounding, mind-numbing terror, yes?"

"Yes, but please note—there's a limit to the effectiveness of this. The moment your reader's—or subject's—mind grasps the threat, it begins to work at dealing with it. It circles the wagons, which can result in rage taking over—*blam!* the book hits the wall—or with a calculated response to the threat—'Oh, I'd just do this or that'—or with quiet resignation."

Crane frowned. "That won't do. You want to induce panic, then, correct?"

"Well, panic is great, but again, it's a one-note response. *Boo!* It happens and it's over. And you can't perpetuate it. Not for any length of time."

"But it could incapacitate the subject, yes? The way it did that woman in the subway train. It might possibly kill someone, mightn't it?"

"Die of fright? Heart attack?" Grey considered that. "Yes, I suppose, if the subject's constitution was weak."

Crane leaned forward, elbows on his bony knees. He'd abandoned his costume—or as he referred to it, his "vestments"—and was clad now in a simple pair of slacks and a sweater, for which Grey was devoutly thankful; the entire "classroom" setting was surreal enough as it was. "What would scare a *strong* subject to death?"

"Well, that's where you get into the other varieties of fear." He circled them on the board. "Fear of the unknown and compound fear. You don't know what's going to happen. You just know it's going to be horrible. *But* you don't know how horrible, so your mind . . ." He took a deep breath, feeling around inside his own fragile psyche. "Your mind fills in the blanks from your own personal stable of demons. We're our own worst enemies when it comes to this stuff. We can manufacture horrors for ourselves much more effectively than anyone else can do it for us. And *that*," he said, punctuating his words with a stab at the whiteboard, "is where the writer comes in."

Crane looked as if he was having an epiphany; his

pale face glowed with rapturous delight. "And what does the writer do?"

"He hints. He suggests. He whispers dark little ideas into the reader's ear. He plants a seed of dread. 'What's that?' the reader asks. But the writer doesn't answer right away. He whispers some more. 'No,' the reader thinks, 'it can't be *that*.' But the writer never speaks aloud. He murmurs and shows bits and pieces of horrific landscapes or portraits, and he *never* lets the reader see the entire image. Misdirection, glimpses of the unknown, but *never* the whole landscape."

"Until the last second, of course."

Grey shook his head. "Not even then. Oh, well, some writers do. But I think the best know that if you show all your cards—even at the last moment—you'll disappoint the reader. You have to hold something back. You have to finish the story without telling the reader everything you know. Personally, I think that's the secret of a successful career in writing horror: you never reveal all, so people follow you in the hope of getting a fuller glimpse of what you're hiding."

"And what are *you* hiding, Grey Berwald?"

The question was so unexpected that he was surprised into answering it. "I . . . don't know. I'm not sure any of us ever knows."

Crane seemed to like that answer well enough, and happily threw himself into learning techniques for eliciting the various types of fear.

Around midday, they knocked off for lunch. Crane had found among his stealthy minions one capable of preparing a more-than-adequate meal. Grey ate, telling himself that he was still looking for a way to escape, and therefore needed to stay healthy and sharp.

Class resumed in the early afternoon, with Crane in

his front-row seat and the ubiquitous Ulysses slipping in and out, occasionally hovering to listen.

That evening after dinner, Crane ushered Grey downstairs. The door to one of his special chambers, "The Pit and the Pendulum," was now open. Crane led him to the door, burbling cheerfully like the host of one of those home design shows preparing to reveal a room makeover to the lucky homeowner.

The differences in the room were subtle at first glance; he heard them rather than saw them. The pendulum, mounted on an electrically powered gear, had always swung to and fro like that, but it had never made that *sound*. What had been a high-pitched *swish* was now deep-throated and heavy, and the bed frame—which was now a sturdy edifice of thick, polished beams—creaked ponderously.

His eyes followed the progress of the blade—gleaming, solid, knife-sharp—it was sinking lower with each pass. The hollow aluminum one he'd had installed had merely arced harmlessly in place.

He found his voice. "Is this by way of extra credit for the writing course, Dr. Crane?"

"Oh, hardly *that*," Crane simpered. "You've given these rooms a wonderful start, Grey. I stand in awe of your vision. I hope you won't mind that I took it upon myself to finish them. Think of it as an apple for the teacher."

"You've . . . finished all of them?" "Mask of the Red Death," "Cask of Amontillado," the Mummy's Tomb, Carfax Abbey—his mind shied violently away from imagining what "finished" meant in this context.

"Well, all but one. You see, I wanted to present you with something truly special. Something personal and appropriate. So I chose one of your own tales for the last room." He pointed to the farthest door on the left—the door that had opened into the Gill-Man's grotto. "It's not quite complete, but very soon. And then I'll show you. So until then—" He smiled and raised a warning finger. "—no peeking."

"No," Grey murmured. "No peeking."

Four varieties of fear—he had never expected to experience all of them, simultaneously.

"Coffee, sir?"

Bruce Wayne stretched, realizing as he did that Alfred had appeared next to his workstation as silently as—well, as silently as Batman—and that he had been sitting in the same position for far too long. It had been a quiet day on all fronts, like the lull before a squall, and he was impatient, edgy, and too frustrated to sleep.

"That would be that deep amber liquid you keep plying me with?"

"Yes, sir. Only I would have said it was closer to brown garnet."

"I'll take a pot or two."

Alfred poured; Bruce inhaled as the aroma invaded his nostrils. "Ah, black gold."

"I thought *black gold* was oil, sir," Alfred said, offering him a tall, insulated cup.

He sipped. "No, definitely coffee."

"And what are we poring over so late into the night, Master Bruce?"

Bruce ignored the hint of censure in the question. " 'We' are poring over chemical analyses, accident accounts, a coroner's report, anecdotal evidence, and personal observation."

Alfred lowered himself slowly into the chair next to Bruce. "To what end?"

"A greater understanding of what we're dealing with and why we're having to deal with it." He sat back, closed his eyes, and let the steam from his cup massage his face. "Same substance; different permutations. The train driver collapses in abject fear; Maggie feels as if she's being drawn into a nightmare little by little—first edgy, then frightened, then paranoid. I . . . I was just plain scared. Flashback scared. Like I was eight years old again and lying . . . at the mouth of this cave."

He glanced around the cavern, pausing to listen to the cascade of water somewhere below. The bats flapped and chattered—a whispered cacophony that he now found perversely comforting.

"Others react just like the train driver," he went on. "A cabbie, a couple of guys on treadmills at a health club, a kid in a bookstore. But at Gotham U, over a hundred exposures at a greater concentration cause nothing more serious than a latte binge."

"While on the other side of town," Alfred murmured, "a young gang member dies of overexposure."

"But was it that simple?" Bruce opened his eyes and sat up straighter in his chair. "He took it orally, but, according to Cutter, so did a girl in the library. Yes, the concentration was greater, but this guy didn't just twitch to death. Witnesses said he was scared—terrified—of someone named Butcher or someone who *was* a butcher. And when the police did a little more poking around down there, they verified that the kid's stepdad was a butcher."

"And so?"

"And so . . ." *Come on,* he told himself. *It's right there. It's staring you in the face.* "And so, I don't think the difference is in the delivery method, which is what I proposed to Jim Gordon. I think the difference is . . . context."

"Context, Master Bruce?"

Bruce rocked forward in the chair and set his coffee mug down on the workbench. "See if this makes sense to you. The effects of the toxin depend upon the context in which it's ingested or absorbed. The train driver absorbed it in context with a particular passage in Berwald's novel *Fear Itself* that overlapped her reality."

"The tunnel."

"Right. Maggie was exposed to the toxin *before* she had a context for the effects. She was edgy, creeped out; *then* she read a passage in the book and connected it to a disturbing reality of her own."

"Which was?"

"Long story. *I* got hit with toxin and context simultaneously. I touched the book and read the passage about the tunnels, which, for me, was like a trip in a time machine." Bruce stood, feeling the need for action, the edgy desire to do *something,* but not knowing what.

"Here's the point, Alfred: the college kids never received a context. They were exposed to the toxin, but the psychological landscape was featureless and barren. So no terror. Unless you count fear of studying."

"And the boy who died?" Alfred asked.

"El Pájaro apparently provided his own context, as well. Something based on a childhood fear of his stepfather."

"But what caused it to surface at that precise moment?"

"I'm only theorizing here, but there is a connotative similarity between *butcher* and *cutter.*"

"My word," Alfred murmured. "I believe you may have something there. And all of this leads to . . . ?"

Bruce moved to the railing of the upper level, which afforded a stunning view of the far reaches of the cavern. Below, the Batmobile gleamed under its stark illumination, while above, the vaulted ceiling was in constant, fluttering motion. As he watched, a flash of red stabbed the night for a fraction of a second, indicating that the laser grid and fan system installed high overhead were doing their jobs. Given the huge population of bats and their penchant for treating the cave floor as a lavatory, the environment below would be much less pleasant without said equipment.

"Motive, maybe? Crane once created a neurotoxin that caused the brain to fear whatever was put in front of it. This one seems far more selective. It's not an agonist, it's a *catalyst*—it doesn't *cause* the effect, it only triggers it. Like an accelerant in an arson."

"Not deadly, unless combined with fire," mused Alfred. "And then quite devastating indeed."

"Yes. Quite."

"But that's good news, isn't it, sir? For the most part any toxin he releases will lie dormant and ineffective."

Bruce turned to face his older companion, leaning against the railing. "Until someone lights a 'match.' This stuff turns everyday objects into a . . . a psychic minefield. He could bury it just about anywhere and it would surface randomly as people came in contextual contact with it. Sure, it's hit or miss, but when it hits . . ."

"But you can detect it," Alfred objected.

"Yes. But WayneTech will have to find a much more efficient way of—"

The Batphone erupted just then, startling both men. Bruce glanced at his watch as he moved to answer it. It was late, even for Captain Gordon, which did not bode well.

"We've got a hostage situation," Gordon said, the moment Batman identified himself. "Gotham Book Emporium."

A frisson of dread coursed up Bruce Wayne's spine. "Gotham Book Emporium . . . that's a weird place to hole up with hostages."

"Not when the hostages are already there for the taking. The store was hosting a special book event tonight." Gordon uttered a joyless bark of laughter. "They called it Midnight Madness."

"Do you think this is connected to—"

"Oh, yeah. The hostage taker insists we call him Mr. Nightfall."

22

The hostage situation lasted for three hours and re-
solved itself when the toxin wore off, leaving "Mr.
Nightfall" disoriented and confused about why he should
have held three other book enthusiasts at sword point.
The thirty-three-year-old man was remanded to the care
of Gotham University Hospital's foremost neurology
specialist, and removed immediately to a clinical environment.

The manager of the emporium swore that never
again would a historical display of any type contain
actual weapons; the samurai mannequins were dis-
armed forthwith, as was the life-sized King Arthur behind the fantasy section's end cap. The patrons were
checked by EMTs, soothed with gift certificates, and
sent home.

Which left a crime scene team, an exhausted Captain
Gordon, and a wired Jesse Rosen to mull over the evidence. There wasn't much to mull. Jesse had no more
fired up his Sniffer than it started pinging, leading them
right to the paperback novel the perp had dropped just
inside the door of the office in which he'd holed up with
his hostages.

Gordon used a gloved hand to pop it into a special

airtight evidence bag, holding it up so Jesse could read the cover.

"*Mr. Nightfall,*" the tech read. "Berwald's first novel?"

"Check the rest of the store." Captain Gordon gestured at the Sniffer in Jesse's hands. It looked, he thought, like the old press his mom had used to make grilled cheese sandwiches, only with a high-tech, computerized handle.

Jesse took the little machine out into the emporium's cavernous main room. Gordon followed and wasn't much surprised when the accelerated pinging led them to a shelf that was almost entirely dedicated to the work of Grey Berwald.

Jesse turned to look at the detective captain, more sober than Gordon had ever seen the kid. "This was the first store we swept, Captain. It was clean. Two days ago, it was clean."

"Yeah. I know." Gordon pushed his glasses up his nose, then rubbed the back of his neck. "A special encore performance, I guess. I'll have our boys bag and box this stuff. Sweep the rest of the store . . . just in case. I'll be . . . out in the alley. Use my cell number if you need me."

Jesse frowned. "What's out in the alley?"

"Clarity, I hope."

Beneath the starless, moonless sky, the service alley behind the Gotham Book Emporium was darker than the inside of a patrolman's cap. This didn't hinder Batman from seeing James Gordon slip out through the emergency exit to lean wearily against the iron railing.

"What are we looking at?"

The detective didn't so much as glance down the concrete steps into the pool of darkness Batman inhabited.

"What I was afraid of—the Scarecrow has struck again. This time he pumped Berwald's *first* novel full of the toxin. We're going to have to backtrack, start the sweep all over again, close down the same businesses we closed down before, recall more books."

He glanced over now, finding Batman in his shadow. "What's the endgame?" he asked. "Are we going to have to confiscate every Berwald book in print? Then what? Crane doses some other writer's stuff? We confiscate every horror novel in Gotham? Then what—he moves on to fantasy? This could conceivably ruin the publishing industry, not to mention a host of genre writers. This may not end with Grey Berwald."

"What happened to keeping it positive?" Batman asked. If Gordon was grim now, wait until he added *his* ruminations to the equation.

The detective just looked at him. "You know, I've been thinking about taking up smoking. Cigars maybe, or a pipe. I need to develop a habit. Something nice and mindless and distasteful. Something I can promise myself I'll give up after this case." He straightened, facing Batman directly. "You're about to tell me something I don't want to hear, aren't you?"

"Chances are good."

Gordon made a face that might have been either a grimace or a smile. "Bring it on."

The phone was ringing. The sound, like a rogue current, was pulling Maggie closer and closer to consciousness.

*Damn.*

She reached for the receiver, finally fumbling it from the stand. She rolled over on her back and brought the receiver to her ear. "It's three AM," she told the open line.

"Maggie."

The single, emotionally charged word was delivered in a man's voice. Maggie sat bolt-upright, suddenly and tinglingly awake.

"Grey? Grey, what—"

"Oh, hell, Maggie . . . ," he said. The receiver clicked, followed by a dial tone.

Maggie sat stunned for a moment, gathering her thoughts. They fled every which way, foiling her best efforts to herd them into some coherent order. She gave up, threw herself out of bed, and tore jeans and a sweater out of her dresser.

Five minutes later she was on her way to Nightfall Manor.

The urge to go home and sleep was powerful. The urge to prod some hidden truths out of Grey Berwald was more so. A middle-of-the-night visit from Batman might just loosen the writer's tongue. Batman could no longer credit the idea that Berwald's connection to the toxin on his books was coincidental.

Sure, it could be a case of Jonathan Crane's purely random fixation on the work of a particular writer, but there was still the matter of Dr. Crane's privately documented observer—an oversight for which James Gordon was ready to toss both Roderick MacMillan and Fenton Avery into Blackgate for obstruction. And someone had to have financed Crane's little experiments. Someone with lots of money.

As soon as the banks opened, the movement of funds into and out of Grey Berwald's accounts would be revealed to a sleep-deprived Captain Gordon.

Batman didn't keep banker's hours.

He reached Nightfall Manor quickly in the predawn dearth of traffic. He defeated the electronic gate at the entrance to the exclusive neighborhood with a simple electromagnetic pulse and brought the Batmobile all the way to the property's street-side fence, parking beneath the drooping forsythia.

He slipped into the topiary garden at the side of the house, pausing when his progress allowed him a clear sight line across the front of the property. What he saw changed his agenda rather drastically: Maggie Tollyer's old Beemer was parked next to Berwald's Mercedes, steam still rising from the engine block.

Batman took a deep breath, quelled the urge to growl or swear, and darted into the shadow of the house.

Maggie and Grey faced off across the silk runner in the entry hall, both trembling.

She had thrown her arms around him when she'd first shot through the front door. Protectively, he thought. As if she could shield him from the sheer, mad evil in his house.

He hadn't seen Crane for hours, but that meant nothing in the scheme of things. The doctor came and went as he pleased, counting on his inconstancy to keep Grey from seriously considering escape. He could be sleeping—presumably he had to sleep sometime—or he could be . . . lurking. The thought of him witnessing Maggie's arrival reduced Grey to cold panic.

"Get out," he said tersely. "You don't belong here."

She blinked at him, then set her jaw. He recognized that look. It told him he'd said exactly the wrong thing.

"I'm not going anywhere until you tell me what's going on."

"You came out here in the middle of the night to ask me that?" he asked, incredulously. "You *know* what's going on. A whole lot of nothing—that's what's going on. My publisher hasn't even contacted me since . . . since all this came down. I told you I'd call if I—"

"You *did* call! That's why I'm here."

Grey felt as if his lungs had forgotten how to pump air. "What are you talking about? When?"

"Less than half an hour ago. You called me and just— just said my name, then hung up. Don't tell me you don't remember." She took a step closer. "Are you drunk?"

He shook his head. "No, not drunk. Terrified." He grasped her arm, pushing her back toward the door. "You need to get out of here, Maggie. Get out of this house. Now."

She struggled to pull her arm away. "Why? What's wrong? Why did you call me?"

Grey swallowed the sick moan that rose in the back of his throat. "I *didn't* call you, Maggie. It was my voice, but I didn't place the call."

"What sort of double talk is that? You *are* drunk!" She wrenched her arm away and darted around him, heading toward the parlor. "I'm going to make you a big pot of black coffee, and then you're going to talk to me."

He lunged after her. "I didn't call you, Maggie. I don't want you here."

He'd drag her to the door, he decided. He'd throw her out and lock the door after her.

"Oh, right. You didn't call me," she snapped over her shoulder. "It was your evil twin, *Beige* Berwald."

"No, actually, it was me."

Grey froze in place, staring at the man standing in the open doorway to his subterranean gallery. He was vaguely aware that Maggie had stopped, too, tantalizingly within reach.

She took a step backward, practically into his arms, and set her hands on her hips. "And just who the hell are you?"

Crane laughed delightedly and made a sweeping gesture toward the stairwell. "Why don't we go downstairs where it's more comfortable, and I'll tell you everything you want to know. And more."

Batman chose the fragile, mullioned doors of the solarium for a point of entry and was relieved to discover that the security system worked just as it had previously. The "secret" door to the basement gallery did not. It had locked itself behind Crane and his two captives.

Or, Batman wondered grimly as he inspected the lock, was he dealing with an accomplice and one captive? He paused long enough to press a contact microphone the size of a ladybug to the wall above the door, hoping, but not expecting, to catch snatches of conversation. He need not have worried; the conversation taking place below was not a quiet one.

As he extracted a thin wafer of transparent aluminum from his belt kit, he heard Grey's impassioned argument for Maggie Tollyer's immediate release. To the writer's credit, he was not so unimaginative as to couch it in precisely those terms.

"She's a traitor, Doctor," he told Crane as Batman slipped the thin but stiff wafer of transparent aluminum into the almost invisible breach between door and door frame. "She's done nothing but vilify me for my work. Making me out to be some sort of monster. Send her away. She doesn't deserve to see what you've been doing here."

As Maggie exclaimed heatedly that she'd done no such thing—and what was the so-called doctor doing here anyway—Batman slid the aluminum "card" down toward the locking mechanism.

"What *we've* done, Grey," Crane cut across Maggie's protests. "This is ultimately your domain—the fruits of your inspiration and imagination. And while I agree that this woman is a philistine—how could I not?—I think her very unworthiness warrants her being brought to an appreciation of the art of terror." His voice was becoming softer as he moved away from the microphone down the length of the hall.

In Batman's hands the sliver of aluminum stopped against the obstructing dead bolt. He quickly extracted a length of what looked like steel wire from his kit. Pulling it into a C-shape, he applied a tiny jolt of electricity from his glove. The wire stiffened. He slipped it through the seam just above the dead bolt, sliding the curving end of the C carefully downward.

"I ask again," said Maggie, her voice distant. "Who are you?"

"I am Jonathan Crane, PhD."

"Crane?" He could hear the sharpness of fear in Maggie's voice. "Not . . ." There was a moment of silence, then she said "the Scarecrow" so softly the microphone barely registered the sound.

Batman caught the bottom end of the wire, effectively lashing the dead bolt, then whisked the aluminum card back into his kit. He palmed a small box that looked like a miniature remote control. On its black, insulated face was a single slider set into a two-inch-long slot. He deftly plugged the two ends of the wire into the top of the device and pushed the slider to the end of the slot. The visible part of the wire began to glow red.

"Please, Ms. Tollyer," the doctor said gently, "indulge me. I think you'll both find this an interesting study in the art of terror."

There was a loud *snick,* as of a door opening, and Crane said, "This is for you, Grey. Your special room. Tonight we'll both see if your star pupil passes the test."

"What's he talking about?" Maggie asked. "What test?"

"Look, Doctor Crane," said Berwald, panic quivering in his voice. "She'll never learn to appreciate any of this. Get her out of here."

"Oh, she'll be gone very shortly, Grey. And what an exit she'll make!"

There was a classic groan of metal on metal, then silence.

Batman glanced down at the wire. It was now white-hot. He tugged it gently toward him.

The darkness was complete, and had a heavy, sodden quality to it. Maggie imagined for a moment that she could breathe no better than she could see. She gasped, drew damp air into her lungs, and tried to orient herself.

Crane was behind her, as was the door. Grey was on her right, his hand clutching her upper arm. She strained to hear sounds above their breathing.

Somewhere ahead of them in the absolute darkness, water dripped musically. But wait—it couldn't be that far ahead. The walls of these underground rooms extended only about twenty feet or so. They were big rooms, but not *that* big.

A moist, earthy breeze fanned her face, like the exhalation of a mountain cave. She squinted into the darkness, trying to make stalactites appear.

She heard Grey swallow. Then he said, "What is this, Doctor? Where are we?"

"Have I failed to do this landscape justice? Here, let me cycle the exhibit on."

The darkness was softened by a strange, pallid luminescence that seemed to emanate from the moss on the dank, glistening walls. The soundscape changed as well—a new sound joining the subtle chorus. A soft mechanical hum like . . . electricity. Almost immediately she felt it, too, dancing across the surface of her face, tickling her nose, making every last hair on her body stand on end. And farther away than even the dripping came a rushing as of surf, but . . .

"Oh, my God," Grey whispered. "The tunnels. You don't . . . you can't have *trains* down here."

Crane's laughter was child-like in its exuberance. "How delightful! Did you really think—? What an imagination you have. But then, we knew that. No, Grey. No trains. But everything else is here."

It was merely the suggestion, she told herself as Crane pressed her forward, that Grey's shapeless, unknown creatures lived in this make-believe world that made her imagine movement at the extreme edges of her senses. Made her feel as if something unseen displaced the palpable darkness.

"A bit more light, Ulysses," Crane said to the anonymous darkness.

Ahead, on their left, a dim, crimson spot of light illuminated a wall and the narrow walkway below it. With Crane herding her, she edged out and along the walkway, one hand on the uneven concrete wall.

Something metallic glittered in the wall at about

shoulder height. She had just realized what it was when Crane shoved her smartly forward. Before she could do more than utter an incoherent bleat of fear, she was spread-eagled against the slimy wall, both her wrists imprisoned in steel manacles. She tested them, pulling outward, and found that there was about two feet of play in the chains that connected them to the wall.

Grey surged forward at Crane, looking like a demon in the stygian red glow. His right foot slipped from the narrow concrete walkway, and he fell to his knees against the wall.

"Mind the third rail," said Crane as if he were warning a guest not to trip over the carpet. "It's fully as lethal as the real ones in Gotham's superlative subway system."

The writer jerked his gaze downward into the railbed. Maggie saw it before he did— the toe of his left boot was mere inches from the deadly power source. He pulled himself upright, trembling.

The two feet of play in her chains, Maggie realized, was just enough to get her electrocuted.

"Grey . . ." A dry whisper was all she could manage. "I'm okay. I'm not afraid. This guy's a fake. All his tricks are fake. Don't flip out on my account, okay? I'm not afraid," she repeated, knowing the words for a lie. "He can dose me with his fear factor if he wants to. The cops have the antidote now."

Also a lie. She had no idea if the police had an antidote. But maybe if Crane thought they did . . .

The madman laughed softly. "Stubborn, isn't she? That will change. All other emotions must, in the end, bow to fear. What is it you said, Grey? 'Terror is a most excellent emotion.' It's more than that, you know. It's the king of emotions. It holds dominion over all the rest—over love, over pride, over hope. It defines us, acutely and abjectly. Observe."

He turned then, pressing Grey back away from the third rail. "Ulysses," he said, "light the doorway." He started back as he spoke, pushing the writer before him.

A pale blue glow haloed the exit. Maggie stared at it, willing herself to remember location and distance.

The two men reached the door; it opened, flooding the long, narrow space with firelight from the braziers and torches that had been installed in the gallery. She turned her head swiftly to her left, peering into the depths of the chamber. What she saw could not be real. In that brief illumination, the chamber seemed to go on forever.

His mind was racing. Looking for a place to hide and finding none. He had often had to imagine what his characters would do if someone they cared about was threatened with the dangers he had so cavalierly invented.

*If it were me, what would I do?* God, how often had he asked himself that question? And now that it *was* him and the danger was real, he had nothing.

*Dammit. That's not acceptable,* he told himself. *Okay . . . first rule of the road: understand what you're up against.*

He almost giggled with the sheer insanity of it, but swallowed the preposterous urge and asked, "So how does it work, Doctor?"

Crane had moved ahead of him down the gallery and unlocked the door to Frankenstein's lab. He gestured Grey to enter.

"A perfect pairing of your art and my science," he

said cheerfully. "As our damsel in distress will soon discover."

Grey entered the lab, his attention drawn immediately to Ulysses, who sat before a bank of video displays that hadn't been there twenty-four hours ago. Crane, he mused, had certainly used his ten-million-dollar fee well.

The door fell heavily shut behind him. The doctor's assistant—not hunchbacked, but handicapped nonetheless—came quickly to his feet.

"But just *how* perfect is for you to decide," Crane continued, offering Grey the seat his gofer had vacated.

He tilted his head to one side and fixed the writer with a hopeful look. "I guess this is somewhat of a final exam, isn't it? And I believe I shall acquit myself well. I've learned a lot from you." He held up a spidery finger. "First, the context for terror. The venue—inspired by your work—provides that. Terror of the unknown. Ms. Tollyer may suspect, but doesn't really *know,* what's in that chamber with her. Second, suspense. Doom—again, inspired by your work—approaches in deliciously slow slithers. But there is also heart-pounding panic, because if, in attempting to escape the unknown, Ms. Tollyer strays too near the edge of the ledge—" He paused to smile at the internal rhyme. "—she will fall and connect with a fatal jolt of electricity. She knows this, of course. What she *doesn't* know is which form of annihilation she will ultimately choose—the devil she knows, or the devil she doesn't."

He folded himself into a chair next to Grey at the display console. "Well, what do you think?"

"And what . . ." Grey cleared his constricted throat. "What have *you* brought to the partnership, Doctor?"

"Why, the toxin, of course. And the Unknown, which I've drawn from your inspired work. It consists of two amorphous 'amoeboids,' as I believed you named them, formed of a highly malleable silicone gel—I believe the toymakers call it 'goop'—each about the size of a large Saint Bernard. I've made some modifications to the cohesion factor, of course. At the core of each is a self-motivating robot that responds to heat and movement—though they can also be remotely controlled individually from this console. Coating the surface of each . . ." He paused, as if savoring the thought, then continued, "is a semi-liquid suspension containing a small amount of bioluminescence and a large amount of my neurotoxin. When these—*your*—creatures interact with Ms. Tollyer, they will deliver a double whammy—a one–two punch, as it were—of both terror and terror enhancer. Unless, of course, she opts for *certain* death."

Grey raised his eyes to the monitor labeled FEAR IT-SELF. "Then they can't kill her." He tried to make his voice sound disappointed instead of hopeful.

"Oh, certainly they can. Either one of them can suffocate or crush her quite readily . . . if they have to. But somehow, I doubt it will come to that. I think our Maggie will choose the devil she knows." Crane followed Grey's gaze to the monitor. "Look—here they come."

The background noise, which Grey had just realized was Maggie's muttered swearing, gained volume and changed character. And he knew why, for he could see what she saw from her vantage point, just above the tracks. Deep down in the impossible distance, the faintest rippling, green light stirred. The soundscape of the place had also altered: in addition to the hum of the tracks and the drip of water, and Maggie's too-rapid breathing, the room microphones picked up the soft, gelatinous sound of movement.

Grey felt a scream rising in his throat. He looked

wildly around for Ulysses and found him perched about five feet away, on a stool near one of the centrifuges, between Grey and the door. In the instant their eyes met, Ulysses shook his head very slightly.

A threat, Grey wondered, or a caution?

He turned back to Crane. "Why? Why are you doing this to Maggie?"

Crane's dark, silken brows rose. "Maggie, is it? I thought you disliked her."

"I was lying to . . . to myself, mostly. I care for her, Doctor. I don't want her to die or to be terrified out of her mind. This is . . . this is scaring *me*. You don't want to scare me, do you? Your mentor? Your . . . partner?" He tried to smile, but it slipped away before he got it in place.

Crane frowned. "Well, now I have to admit, this does put a new wrinkle in things. But I really can't change my plans now, dear boy."

Panic, cold and rigid, wrapped itself around Grey Berwald's heart. "Why not? For God's sake, Doctor Crane—Jonathan! I don't understand. What have you got against me? I paid you a lot of money for that toxin; I-I gave you a means of escape. I've mentored you. Why are you doing this to me?"

"The world doesn't revolve around you, Grey. Yes, you're my mentor, and—yes—you did facilitate my escape from Arkham, albeit unintentionally. But this has never been about you." His gaze moved to another of the monitors, and he smiled a slow, crooked smile. "This is about something . . . *someone* else."

From the corner of his eye Grey saw Ulysses Cutter rise slowly from his stool, his own gaze locked on the monitor.

"Ulysses," said Crane softly. "We have company."

Grey glanced up at the monitor labeled GALLERY and gasped as a solid pool of black rushed across the broad hall to the door of the lab. He jumped half out of his skin when the door rattled on its solid steel hinges, and jumped the rest of the way when Maggie screamed.

Crane turned toward another door, almost hidden in the darkness. "It's all turning out quite well," he said cheerfully. "If you'll excuse me, I think I'll dress for the occasion."

23

Batman noticed, as he bolted across the gallery, that the displays were subtly different, beginning with the lighting. In lieu of the track lighting that had run on gracefully curved metal frames, the wall had sprouted ensconced torches, while from the high ceiling hung a row of wrought-iron pendants sporting braziers full of flame. Over the very center of the long room was a massive chandelier worthy of the *Phantom of the Opera*.

As he reached the laboratory door, other differences literally came to light. The blade on Dr. Guillotine's infernal machine gleamed as if burnished, clearly no longer composed of anodized aluminum. The flames leaping about Jeanne d'Arc's feet were no longer merely air-blown tubes of red and orange silk—they were real.

He was certain other anomalies could be found if he had time to look for them. He didn't; the locked door to the lab refused to give, and he was just reaching for his lock kit when a faint scream sounded in bizarre stereo. It came at once from behind this locked door and from the door at the end of the gallery—the one he was certain now hid the "special room" Crane had been blathering about.

The echo from behind the door of the lab didn't

confuse him. Maggie Tollyer was behind Door Number Two.

His swift passage down the center of the gallery left him with the unsettling feeling of being watched. A feeling that made him turn his head as he reached and grasped the door handle.

At first he saw nothing; then he realized that the executioner standing by his guillotine had changed position. His head had turned to follow Batman's progress down the length of the hall. The two empty eyeholes in the black cowl were fixed on him.

Skin crawling, galvanized by Maggie's screams, he bent to the lock. In mere seconds it surrendered—*perhaps too easily?*—and he slipped into the chamber.

He activated his night vision immediately and was rewarded, if one could call it that, with the sight of Maggie futilely tugging her chains, while beyond her, four or five yards away at best, two huge, faintly luminous shapes rippled toward her, making wet, sucking sounds as they parted the moist air with their passage. He recognized them from Grey's novel: amoeboids, enormous, gelatinous mutations of bacteria, brewed in the toxic chemical soup that had gathered over decades in the lower portions of the Gotham subway system. At first he was taken aback, but then the HUD readout over his left eye glimmered. The magnetometer circuit built into his belt buckle was registering a steady power source within each one.

Not mutants. Machines. But no doubt just as deadly.

"Who is it?" Maggie gasped. Her voice, raw from screaming, trembled. "Who are you?"

"Batman."

"Well, for God's sake don't just *stand* there! Get me out of here!"

He stepped lightly onto the concrete walkway and moved toward her, noting how easy it would be to go over the edge onto the ersatz third rail. His heads-up display told him it was live. He reached her in moments, gave the approaching "creatures" a glance, then looked to the manacles.

These were not garden-variety shackles. They had no visible locking mechanism whatsoever.

It took several seconds and a concentrated beam of white light to find the tiniest of seams in each band. The loop cutter was out of the question. It reached temperatures so extreme, it would incinerate Maggie's flesh. He opted for the only alternative—the laser glass cutter.

"I'm going to have to cut these," he told Maggie, wondering at what point Crane would intervene.

As if on cue, the Scarecrow's disembodied voice spoke, coming from everywhere at once. "Happy Doomsday, Batman! By now you've had a little time to admire my work. What do you think?"

"I think," Batman said, not taking his attention from the delicate tool he'd removed from his belt, "it lacks visual impact."

"Perhaps. But it does possess impact of a different kind."

The chamber was suddenly filled with a growing rumble, then began to shudder like a fever victim, the floor reeling drunkenly.

"What do you think of my version of the Great Gotham Quake?" Crane asked. "I borrowed the technology from a movie studio's amusement park in Hollywood."

Batman reached out to anchor himself on the chains that connected Maggie's manacles to the wall, but he got no more than a fingerhold before the tunnel gave a vicious jolt. He pitched over backward, directly onto the third rail.

Grey staggered up from his chair, wincing at the bright shower of sparks that erupted across the monitor screen, followed by curls of smoke.

Crane, clad once more in his "vestments," laughed delightedly. "How are the mighty fallen."

"Is he dead?"

"Probably not," the Scarecrow said. "I'm sure that outfit of his can protect him against even voltage that high. But he's certainly stunned, and no more able to move than our fair damsel." He palmed a control on the panel below the bank of monitors, and the rumbling in the *Fear* chamber subsided.

Which meant that Grey could hear Maggie's renewed screams. He started for the lab door.

"It's locked," said the Scarecrow, not taking his eyes from the monitors. "Remotely controlled. Sorry, Grey. I can't allow you to save your lady friend. She is part of my master's thesis, you might say. Her presence will make this terror far more . . . piquant . . . to my old friend Batman."

Grey stopped, his hand on the door handle. "*He* was the target. All the time, *Batman* was the target."

"Of course."

"Controlling Batman—through fear—that was the thing you were talking about the other night. Better than controlling the world, you said."

The Scarecrow turned and fixed Grey with pale, mad eyes. "Yes. That was the thing." He returned his attention to the monitor.

Grey watched, helpless, as Batman heaved himself painfully back up onto the narrow curbing, rolled against the wall, and lay still. His suit smoked from his collision with the rail.

Stifling a moan, Grey tried the door, yanking the steel handle downward with all his strength. Nothing. With a snarl of rage and fear, he wheeled back toward the Scarecrow, who was transfixed by the scene in the monitor.

And there was Ulysses, sitting on his stool at a workbench near the center of the room, silent and watchful. What would he do if Grey attacked his boss?

Their eyes met—an act that seemed to send Ulysses into a series of wild, two-armed salutes. As Grey watched, hope guttering, the seizure carried the other man off his stool and onto the floor. The Scarecrow seemed not even to notice.

The lab door issued a solid *click,* and the handle moved delicately beneath Grey's hand. His gaze on the spasming Ulysses, Grey opened the door and slipped out into the gallery.

He was clear of the third rail, the surface of his suit still discharging electrostatic energy, when he heard the door behind him open and close.

Crane? Cutter? It hardly mattered. He couldn't move, and Crane's amoebic creatures were edging ever nearer along the walkway, leaving a damp trail of glowing luminescence in their wake. Already they were approaching a shallow turnout that was a mere two yards from where Maggie was pinned to the wall. The sound of their passage made his skin crawl.

He saw four of them now, and two Maggies, all blurred. His arms and legs felt as if he'd just been pulled out of an ice bath. Hearing sounds of stealthy approach behind him, he tried again to move, but could not.

Nor could he respond to Maggie's terror. "Damn you, Crane. Y-you *coward*," she snarled. "I'm scared already. Okay? I admit it. I'm scared!" Her voice cut off in a gasp for breath, and she turned her face toward the approaching menace.

Crane laughed, the sound echoing via speakers throughout the tunnel room. The robotic creatures, Batman noticed, hesitated momentarily at the new sound before moving forward again.

"Can you move?" Grey Berwald's whisper sounded directly in his ear. The writer had crawled up beside him, hidden, as was Batman, in the tunnel shadows.

"No." He forced the single word out—also in a whisper. "A moment." He took two deep breaths, reached into his past, into inner reserves developed through years of self-discipline. He got his hand wrapped around the laser cutter, pulled it out where Grey, stooped above him, would be able to see it, then tried again to speak. "M-Maggie! Fight it! Fight the chains! Fight!"

She turned her head to look at him, then did exactly as asked. Growling, spitting, screaming, she rattled the chains and tried to slip her hands from them.

Beneath the cover of her struggle, Batman turned his face up to Grey's and activated the cutter briefly. "Laser cutter," he murmured. "For the shackles. Take it." He pressed the little instrument into the writer's quaking fingers. "Get her out."

"But Crane . . . There're night filters on the cameras. And th-the monsters . . ."

"Diversion."

The writer nodded. "Yeah. Uh, they sense heat and movement."

*And sound,* Batman thought. "My belt," he told Grey. "The silver nodules. Flash bombs. Take two. Twist the halves . . . opposite directions. Throw them into that turnout."

Berwald was already scrabbling for the little silver spheres. He slipped two from the belt and stood. Batman watched as the writer stepped over him and moved toward the struggling Maggie and Crane's shapeless monsters.

He concentrated on reclaiming his body then. On breathing, moving, rising. He had gotten to his knees when the flash bomb went off in the recess ahead. The tunnel was flooded with sudden white light and heat. The protective lenses in his cowl responded immediately, but he knew the cameras would be momentarily blind. He pushed himself up and forward, noticing as he did that the creatures were eddying just on the other side of the turnout.

As he reached Maggie and Berwald, a cry of pure rage reverberated throughout the tunnel.

"Oh, God," Berwald said, then, "One hand's free. Can you—"

In answer, Batman retrieved the laser cutter and went to work on the second shackle.

"I still have one of those bombs," Berwald said. "If he comes in through the door—"

"Not his style. Crane maintains . . . distance."

"Then what—?"

"He'll let them finish us off." Batman nodded toward the amoeboids. They'd begun to move again, purposefully, not toward where the flash had gone off, but toward the three people clustered on the walkway.

"What have you *done*?" Crane screamed. "Damn you, Batman! What was that?"

The amoeboids were nearing the center of the alcove, their rippling luminescence clearly visible in the dark.

"Sonofabitch," Berwald said, and moved straight for them.

"Grey!" Maggie reached for him with her free hand, then yelped in pain as the laser bit into her shackled wrist.

Batman steadied her. "Hold still."

Grey disappeared momentarily around the lip of the turnout. He came back into view a moment later at the center rear of the recess. He had a little silver sphere in one hand.

Batman gave his entire attention to the shackle. He was having to slice back and forth across the narrow width of the band, alternating between the top and bottom, working toward the middle.

*One more pass,* he thought as the metal began to give. He wondered why Crane had not activated the quake mechanism again. Most likely it took time for it to reset itself.

There was a flurry of movement from the turnout, and Grey shouted incoherently. The next second another flash bomb went off. Maggie swore and winced as the laser nicked her a second time . . . and the cuff around her wrist sprang open.

Batman turned toward the alcove. He saw at a glance that Grey had blinded himself with the flash bomb. He was pressed against the curving wall, one arm flung over his eyes, while the fear-coated monsters, seemingly unaffected by the blast, embarked on a new tactic. They ignored Grey and advanced on Batman and Maggie with increased speed.

Clearly, they were no longer on autopilot.

Batman pushed Maggie behind him. "Make your way to the door. Keep to the wall," he told her. Then he drew Jesse Rosen's sonic pistol from a clip on his belt. Hell of a time for a field test, he thought, then aimed and fired at the two amorphous globs. The gun emitted a penetrating *thud,* as if a giant's fist had pounded the still air.

The lead creature, just slithering onto the walkway, compressed as if the fist had flattened it. The second reared up, then pitched over onto the tracks. A Roman candle of sparks fountained into the gloom, illuminating the area in fitful, lurid light. The smell of burning silicone filled the air, oppressive and acrid.

In the shower of sparks, Batman saw Grey Berwald pull himself to his feet and stumble toward him. He was about to shout a warning when Berwald saw the dormant creature lying across his escape route. He stopped in confusion, blinking at Batman in the waning light of the second creature's demise.

He backed away from the bloated silicone carcass and squatted down behind it. "It's too big. I can't get around it without touching it or the rail. Look, I can wait. Just . . . get Maggie out of here."

Batman weighed the situation quickly. Deprived of his killer robots, the Scarecrow would be either turning to some deadly alternative, or escaping. Either way, he had to be stopped.

"Out." He grasped Maggie by the shoulders, turned her about, and guided her toward the door.

"You can't leave him—"

"I can't let Crane escape. The robots are down. He can't use them anymore."

The Scarecrow leapt from his chair, shoving it backward on its rollers to collide with a workbench. He'd lost control of the room. *Lost control.*

"I'm s-s-sorry, sir."

He gave Ulysses only a splinter of his attention, noticing peripherally that the other man was still crouched on the floor where Grey Berwald must have left him. He was rubbing one arm.

"You're a weak man, Ulysses. A weak intellect. But I . . . I *will* win this contest!"

He turned his gaze to a different monitor, one that now showed the door of the *Fear* chamber opening, and that annoying woman being shoved out through it. Batman was right behind her, looking infuriatingly unruffled.

Well. He would deal with that. He'd not yet exhausted his repertoire.

"Doctor," Ulysses said softly from behind him. "Doctor, we should go. He'll come for you."

"Let him," the Scarecrow said. There was a row of sliders on the control panel below the monitors. He grasped one and shoved it forward violently.

Batman made a swift survey of the gallery. It was quiet but for the snap of flame from brazier and torch. To his right, past a diorama of the death of Anne Boleyn, he saw that the door of Frankenstein's lab was still closed. He was reluctant to leave Maggie out here, but getting her to safety would take too much time. He'd activated his transponder as soon as he'd realized Crane was here. Even at that, it could be some minutes before the police arrived. Plenty of time for—

He saw the sudden movement from the tail of his eye—the abrupt, arcing swing of the headsman's ax. He dropped, bearing Maggie with him to the floor. The ax cut the air just above their heads and struck the door behind them with a sound like the peal of a gong.

Maggie screamed.

Not waiting for the ax-wielding automaton to recoil,

Batman wrapped Maggie in his arms and rolled out into the center of the room. As he did, he looked around for an escape route and for potential dangers. The dangers were far more evident. On the opposite side of the *Fear* chamber at the end of the hall, a troop of pygmies with blowguns and a knife thrower had been incorporated into Mr. Dark's Pandemonium Carnival. Even as Batman rolled back up to a crouch, the pygmies lifted their weapons to their lips. He doubted the darts would penetrate his suit, but Maggie . . .

He turned his head. Across the gallery, roughly thirty feet away toward the stairs, Houdini's trunk hung from its chain over a pool of what, judging by its color and viscosity, was not water.

"Ever do a cannonball into a pool?" he murmured in Maggie's ear.

"What?"

He wrapped his arms around her waist. "Make a cannonball."

She did, pulling her head down and tucking her knees up under her chin.

Turning his back to Mr. Dark and his lethal pygmies, Batman stood. Then, holding Maggie in front of him, he raced down the gallery, feeling the collision of pygmy darts with his trailing cape and the back of his cowl.

Five feet from the trunk, he dropped to one knee and sent a pulse of electricity to his cape. It stiffened, and a shower of spent darts hit the floor. Batman drew the sonic pistol again and fired at the trunk.

"What are you—?"

The trunk slammed against the rear wall of the exhibit, taking a chunk out of the ersatz pier from which it hung. As it swung forward again, Batman pulled out a Batarang and spun it at the chain. It connected with a shower of sparks, and the trunk shifted downward as the link gave—but didn't part.

*Damn.* He pulled out a second bat-shaped weapon and waited, mentally counting the seconds during which his distended cape took several palpable hits. The knife throwers had entered the fray, while across the hall Jeanne d'Arc's tormentor was dipping a torch into her consuming flames.

He flung the Batarang. It struck the chain in the same spot as its twin. The chain groaned delicately, then broke. The trunk, torn from its tether at the outer end of its arc, dropped to the edge of the tank, teetered for a second, then crashed noisily to the floor, standing on one end.

The lid fell open, and the Houdini mannequin tumbled out, looking like a corpse caught in the grip of sudden rigor mortis.

"Get in."

"You've got to be—"

"I'm not. Get in!" Batman rose to literally cover Maggie as she crawled the last several feet to the metal box, aware that the knife throwers had depleted their ammunition. Jeanne's executioner, however, was just winding up for a throw.

*"In!"* he roared, simultaneously flinging the cape over his head and hitting it with another minute charge of electricity.

Maggie dove forward into the box. Batman shoved the door shut behind her as fire rained down on them from several directions at once. Mr. Dark, it seemed, now also employed flame swallowers.

"Stay down," he told her and charged into the hail of fire, making for the lab. The torches hit and bounced harmlessly away to gutter out.

He had reached the door when he heard the scream. Raw and guttural, it came from the *Fear* chamber, its tinny effigy echoing from within the lab. He swung back toward the Houdini trunk. The lid was even now swinging open again.

"Maggie! No!"

Her terrified eyes peered at him through the grille on the lid.

"Don't move."

Whether he could trust her to obey or not, he knew that he must concentrate on Jonathan Crane. Rescuing Maggie again would only allow the Scarecrow an opportunity for escape. He turned back to the lab and was surprised to find that the door was unlocked.

He took a deep breath and slipped into the room.

24

Grey heard nothing from the gallery after Maggie's initial shriek, followed by something heavy impacting the metal door. He tried to relax, to tell himself that no news was good news.

He relaxed so well that he quite nearly fell asleep. Funny, that—how tiring fear was. It sapped the strength and stole the will.

*Enough of that,* he thought, and hauled himself to his feet.

He moved to where the defunct monster lay, half draped over the edge of the walkway. Theoretically, it should be a piece of cake to tip it over onto the rails. Not that that was a particularly savory idea. The air still reeked of melted silicone and machine oil after the demise of the other one.

He momentarily considered taking a running jump over it, but gave that up as a bad plan. Instead, because he wanted to do *something*, he pulled off his sweatshirt, wrapped it around his hands, and tried to shove the glowing, corpulent mass over the edge.

It was heavier than he'd expected. He psyched himself up and tried again, leaning into the push. He was rewarded when the thing finally moved. Not much, but enough to suggest he was on the right track. He smiled at his own pun.

He was prepping for another herculean effort when he realized the damn thing was *still* moving—was trembling. He sat back on his haunches and watched the rippling glow. Residual energy? Like that last little spurt of life from a windup toy?

It lurched *toward* him.

He fell backward, sitting hard on the cold, wet cement of the turnout. It lurched again, its ragged, fleshy folds touching his foot. He rolled away from it and scrambled to his feet, tossing the sweatshirt away beyond it, hoping it would follow the movement.

It didn't. It came for him, undulating, pulsating. He turned and tried to run, but the thing behind him was the only real illumination in the room and he couldn't see where he was going. He collided with the curving far wall of the recess, headfirst. In the flash of light from that impact, he saw nothing, but he felt *it* ride up and over his legs, crushing them.

He put his hands out to shove it away and screamed. The amoeboid's surface was cold and clammy, but far worse was the kaleidoscope of horrific images the touch of it unleashed in his mind. Grey Berwald remembered, too late, that the silicone skin had been tainted with the Scarecrow's vile concoction.

He screamed again as every fear, every nightmare, every horrific vision he'd had and put to work for him over the course of his career came back to him. All the demons he thought he'd exorcised, all the unsettled ghosts he'd laid to rest, all the bogeymen he'd chased back into their closets—all of them were there, now. Waiting.

For him.

\*    \*    \*

"My, but you *are* hard to kill." The Scarecrow stood in the center of the lab, hands folded at his waist.

Poised just inside the door, Batman took in the room at a glance. There were neither knife throwers nor pygmies, but that hardly meant the place was without peril. For one thing, Cutter—still a question as to where his loyalties lay—stood not five feet from the spindly apparition that was his boss, rubbing his left arm.

"Perseverance," Batman said, "is a virtue. I don't suppose you're ready to surrender."

The Scarecrow laughed softly. "Hear that, Ulysses? He thinks he's got us. He's wrong, of course. Dear Batman, you didn't suppose that I'd allow myself to be cornered someplace that wasn't defensible?"

Cutter, his mouth drawn into a grim line, was glancing about at the walls, which for the most part were covered with floor-to-ceiling metal shelves, all lined with—

The Scarecrow grinned. Then he began to sing, "Two thousand bottles of fear on the walls—two thousand bottles of fear. You knock some down . . ." He unfolded his hands, revealing a remote-control device, then aimed it at the shelves nearest Batman. "And slosh 'em around . . ."

"You'll slosh it around on yourselves, too."

"Oh, but unlike you, *we* are immune." He punched a button.

Above and to the left of the door, a shelf tilted sharply forward, the row of bottles it supported spilling their contents in a toxic cascade to the floor. Batman had no choice but to leap away to his right.

The Scarecrow laughed. "Heads up!" he crowed and punched another button. Batman heard the metallic *click* above his head and dove forward, narrowly avoiding the shower of neurotoxin that rained down from a shelf above the door.

He somersaulted and rolled to his feet, spinning toward the cackling tatterdemalion. But Cutter had grasped his mentor's arm and was dragging him toward the door.

"I'm not done!" the Scarecrow objected. "I'm just getting started!" He aimed the remote toward the back of the room and activated something there.

Batman kept his eyes on the Scarecrow but heard the sudden thrum of electrical power from behind him.

And he heard sirens.

So did Cutter. "No time, Doctor," he said. "Gotta go."

The Scarecrow frowned, listening.

"Impressive," Batman said, watching the dread stain spread across the floor toward him. "You seem to have thought of everything."

His adversary seemed to forget the sirens and smiled. "I did, didn't I? Did you know there's enough fear toxin in this basement to flood it to a depth of two inches? Well, you do now, obviously."

"How did you do it? How did you manage all of this?"

The Scarecrow could never resist the urge to gloat. "Your novelist friend set it all in motion. He needed—or thought he needed—a little extra kick to make his new book a bestseller. He didn't, of course, but when, in the course of his research, he found note of my work in the area of neurotoxins, he . . . arranged an interview with me at Arkham. A private interview. We struck a deal: his books got that little extra something, and I got a little extra money with which to conduct my research and arrange for my escape."

"A little money?"

"Oh, all right. A *lot* of money. Ten million, to be exact. But somewhere along the way I realized that this toxin wasn't turning out to be quite what I expected."

"Yes, I know. It's not an agonist, it's an accelerant."

The straw man managed to look surprised behind the burlap mask. "You surprise me, Batman. I'd no idea you were conversant with my field. But I digress. And you are playing for time." He grinned. "I may be crazy, but I'm far from stupid."

Batman darted forward, but the Scarecrow, already edging toward the door, wielded the remote again, bringing another volley of toxic rain down from the shelves. In the glistening and growing wet stain Batman could see that, behind him, streamers of electricity were arcing back and forth between two tall metal poles . . . moving lower with each arc.

"Must run," the Scarecrow said, bolting past Cutter to the door, the soles of his shoes squelching in the growing toxic puddle. He disappeared, then popped his head back into the room, making Cutter jump. "I hope you find this an enlightening experience." He gave the remote a rapid series of punches, and shelf after shelf tilted its cargo onto the floor.

The Scarecrow favored his nemesis with a final, beaming smile, then disappeared. Cutter hesitated for a moment, then bolted out of the room, hot on his employer's heels.

Just outside the door of his lab, Jonathan Crane pulled off his mask. Though he would never admit it, after enough exertion to raise a sweat the damn thing tended to itch unbearably. Then he hesitated. The trunk containing that annoying journalist was lying on the floor, the lid partly open. He took a step toward it, of half a mind to finish her. But the sirens were growing louder, and some had stopped, which could mean only one thing. Besides, Ulysses had caught him up and was pressing him to flee.

"This way, Doctor," he said. "You'll be safe this way." He took the other's arm and dragged him across the gallery toward the first of Grey Berwald's special rooms.

Dear, loyal Ulysses. He wasn't a bright man, and the Tourette's was so bad at times, Crane felt that he must either discover a cure or put the poor man out of his misery.

*Now, now, Doctor,* he told himself. *That would hardly be fair. Cook or get out of the kitchen. That's what they say.*

"How would you like me to cure you, Ulysses?" he asked as his companion opened the door to the room and urged him inside. It was the "Cask of Amontillado" room, of course. A fitting egress, since it was the way he had entered Nightfall Manor in the first place.

Ulysses was intent on getting the cell door open. "Cure me? Of what?"

"Of your Tourette's, of course."

The cell door swung to with an ear-rending groan. Ulysses turned to stare at him, his right cheek twitching. "But you've already done so much, sir. You helped me kick crack, and alcohol . . ."

Crane entered the cell, making a dismissive gesture. "A mere exercise. I believe—no, I *know* I can do much more for you."

Ulysses's eyes glistened with sudden tears. "I . . . that would be . . . a miracle, Doctor."

Gratifying, those tears. Crane smiled. "Yes, it would

be, wouldn't it?" He crossed the cell and pulled himself up into the small hole high in the rear wall, easily dislocating his shoulders, and then his hips, to gain access.

Miracles, indeed. Even this freakish ability—so normal to him—of being able to contort and twist and adjust his lanky body to fit through such a tiny aperture seemed miraculous to someone as credulous as Ulysses Simon Cutter. Crane flowed like oil into the cramped space behind the partial wall, then pulled himself together—he'd always gotten a chuckle out of that expression—and placed a hand on the wall of the outer foundation. He frowned then, turning back to peer at Ulysses through the entrance hole.

"Ulysses, the wall is solid. How am I to escape?"

The other man blinked, twitched, and raked a hand through his hair. "No worries, Doctor. They won't look for you here. I'll come back for you."

Crane nodded, waved him away, and settled down on the floor to wait.

He had no real concern about absorbing the toxin through the soles of his boots, but contact between liquid and electricity concerned Batman a great deal. His suit had already absorbed and rerouted a significant charge tonight. He wasn't sure of its ability to handle another so soon.

From his rapidly dwindling patch of dry floor, he sent a swift glance to the metal shelving above the chamber door, then followed it with a line of monofilament from the T-gun. He took three steps backward, drawing close enough to the arcs of electricity that he could feel static dancing on the exposed skin of his face.

Four running steps and a leap carried him up toward the shelving over the door, the monofilament line swiftly taking up its slack. His feet had no sooner left the ground then one of the arcs grounded itself on the drenched tile. There was a brilliant flash of light, a sound like a gigantic bug zapper, and the sensation of being hammered from behind by an air bag.

Batman hit the shelving above the door with enough force to nearly collapse it. Grasping the groaning metal, he reached down a foot to catch the handle, wrenched open the door, and flung himself out, feetfirst.

Behind him, Frankenstein's laboratory exploded in flame and heat, and the metal door slammed irrevocably shut.

He landed upright, caught his balance, and found himself face-to-face with Ulysses Cutter. Crane was nowhere in sight.

The two men stood immobile for a long measure as a sound like the popping of a hundred balloons issued from the lab Batman had just exited.

*Well, Mr. Cutter, what side will you come down on?*

As if he'd heard the unasked question, Cutter turned his head and looked over his shoulder at the door of the "Amontillado" room. It was very slightly ajar.

*A trap?*

Cutter turned back to Batman, his face bleak. The dried tracks of tears marred his furrowed cheeks. "He was good to me," he whispered, "but that doesn't make him good."

"You lied to me," Batman said.

Cutter frowned, and shook his head. "No, sir. Never."

"You said you didn't know where Crane was, but you must have known he was at Arkham."

"You asked me if I knew where he was *then*," Cutter said simply. "You didn't ask me if I knew where he'd *been*."

The decision to trust wasn't easy, but Batman made it. As he moved across the gallery, he heard Cutter say, "I'll check on the woman."

The "Amontillado" chamber was quiet—but on the fringes of his hearing Batman caught the sounds of the police presence outside and above. He crossed to the cell where the Montresor mannequin knelt, perpetually troweling mortar onto the same brick, and opened the barred iron door. It groaned loudly. Cursing Berwald's penchant for authenticity, he fell back from the door, drawing the sonic pistol.

He was quick, but Crane was both quick and hyper-limber. Before Batman could take aim at the wall, the Scarecrow had corkscrewed his head and one arm through the aperture, the remote device clutched in his elongated fingers.

Batman didn't wait to find out what the device triggered. He fired. His gun's sound wave struck the brick wall with an audible *thud*. It buckled inward, slipping just enough to make Crane drop the remote. Eerily fast, the doctor scooped the device out of the air and pinned it to the teetering wall with the flat of his hand. His fingers flexed, cradling it.

Three shots on a charge, Jesse had said. Three shots for sure; an outside chance of four. With nothing to lose, Batman aimed at the wall just below Crane's contorted body and fired.

For a heartbeat, nothing happened. Then the gun gave up a weird double *thud*. Crane's dangling hand spasmed and he dropped the remote. He dove after it, stretching as if his ligaments were made of rubber. He was half out of the aperture when the beleaguered wall trembled as if in the grip of an earthquake and collapsed.

When the dust settled, Crane lay still on the floor of the cell, the lower half of his body only partly visible in the rubble. Batman rolled to his feet and moved to lay the tips of two gloved fingers against the madman's neck. Through the sensors in the tips, he could feel a faint pulse.

Alive, but unconscious.

Batman drew a set of thin handcuffs from his belt. He was fastening them around Crane's wrists when he heard shouting in the gallery beyond the door. Someone was yelling "Batman!" over and over again.

He finished securing Crane and slipped out into the gallery. A wild-eyed Cutter was standing just outside the *Fear* chamber, the door flung wide open. Seeing Batman, he flailed his right arm as if waving in a base runner.

"The girl! The girl! I can't get her to leave. Please— the fire—it's spreading! You gotta get her to leave!" He pulled a torch from the wall and dove back into the chamber, Batman following.

He found Maggie in the alcove on her knees beside Grey Berwald.

No, beside Grey Berwald's body, he corrected grimly, when the fitful light of Cutter's torch illuminated the scene. The writer was quite obviously dead, his eyes staring sightlessly at the low, curving ceiling of the shallow alcove, his skin gleaming damply with bioluminescence, his torso still half covered by the still mound of deadly silicone that had suffocated him.

*Because I assumed it was dormant and safe.*

He shook himself, realizing that the room was quite warm. Cutter was right—the fire had apparently spread from the lab to the intervening room.

He knelt beside Maggie, put a hand on her shoulder.

"We shouldn't have left him," she said without looking at him.

*No. We shouldn't have.* "Maggie, the house is on fire. We need to go."

Now she looked at him, her eyes haunted. "Are we going to leave him again?"

"No." He beckoned Cutter to help Maggie to her feet, then kicked the tunnel creature away and lifted Berwald's lifeless body.

Maggie let herself be drawn along by the man she thought of as Twitch. She had probably, she realized in some detached corner of her mind, never been so docile in her entire life. They had just stepped through the door into the gallery when two things happened at once: the first Kevlar-clad policemen reached the bottom of the spiral stair, and a sound like a sonic boom shook Frankenstein's lab. The door blew out, flipped end-over-end, and landed in the center of the gallery. A gout of flame boiled out of the open lab, momentarily obscuring the SWAT team from view.

Maggie's throat, already painful and tight, closed almost to choking. Those stairs were the only way out of here. If the fire spread to the gallery . . . already flames were licking around the doorjamb.

Batman pressed her forward toward the police, now recovering from the blast of heat. She felt him at her back until they were almost level with the lab door. Unexpectedly, he spoke, his voice a low growl in her ear. "Keep moving, steadily, with your hands up."

"Freeze!" she heard one of the policemen shout. Which she did, but the lab chose that moment to exhale again, and all freezing was off. The police scrambled forward, guns drawn, took her and Cutter into hasty custody, and hustled them toward the stairs. Confused, she turned back to see what had become of Batman.

What she saw was the huge *Phantom of the Opera* chandelier lurch suddenly before it came crashing down from the ceiling. A moment later the entire gallery was on fire. Then Maggie felt herself being drawn upward, her feet never touching the stair treads as angels in black Kevlar pulled her up from Hell.

Captain Gordon lifted his glasses and wiped the film of soot from his cheeks and nose. He leaned against a GCFD fire truck, watching as the firefighters retracted their hoses and locked down the operation. It was dawn, and all that was left of Nightfall Manor was the rear corner of the west wing. The rest of the house had collapsed into the basement, filling it with superheated rubble.

The sun rose behind the ruin, throwing it into stark silhouette, its rays gleaming, rose red, through the blown-out windows. Curls of smoke ascended from the rubble like spirits being lifted into heaven.

It looked haunted, he thought. Which was more or less how he felt. He hadn't seen Batman since he and his SWAT team had rescued Maggie Tollyer and Ulysses Cutter from the burning building.

"Captain?" The fire chief had rounded the nose of the truck and was pulling off his hard hat and goggles. "Fire's out. The place is pretty much a loss. Gonna be hell for your forensics guys."

Gordon nodded. "When will it be safe for them to go in?"

The fire chief shook his head. "Go in? Go into what,

Cap? There's no 'there' there. I'd say three days to a week to let it cool off, then bring in the backhoes."

"There may be . . . bodies in there," Gordon said. "You telling me I have to wait three days to recover them?"

"I'm telling you that you *should*. But you'll do what you'll do." He sketched a salute at the detective and moved off.

*Three days.*

Gordon caught sight of Jesse Rosen, Sniffer in hand, making his way around the outside of the hazard-taped perimeter, his attention on the illuminated readout of the instrument. Gordon crossed the ruined lawn to the tech's side.

"What are you getting?" he asked.

Jesse glanced at him briefly, then went back to his readings. "Nothing. Apparently the extreme heat changed the chemical composition of the neurotoxin. Wouldn't hurt to keep an eye on your SWAT team and hostages, though."

"You anywhere close to an antidote—just in case?"

"Somewhere close," Jesse said. "Lucius figures about a week before we can start doing lab tests." He hesitated, then said, "One of the SWAT guys said something about seeing Batman in there just before the place went up. D'you think he got out?"

"Don't know."

"D'you care?"

Gordon met his eyes. "Yeah. Yeah, I do care."

He heard someone calling his name just then, from the direction of the emergency vehicles still left on the scene. One had already transported Maggie Tollyer and Ulysses Cutter to the university hospital. He left the tech to his air scans and headed back the way he'd come, skirting the rear of the fire truck.

"Gordon."

The voice came from so close by, he nearly teleported sideways three feet. Batman, his black suit looking much the worse for wear, hunkered in the rear of the fire truck between two large equipment lockers.

"Damn, you're alive!" The words popped out of his mouth before he could stop them.

Startlingly, Batman's teeth flashed white in his sooty face. "Was that a disappointed *damn* or a relieved *damn*?"

"Relieved. It was going to be three days before I could get to your body." He gestured toward the EMT vans with his head. "I've been summoned—"

"To verify that that's Grey Berwald's body they just found in their ambulance. It is. He was the Scarecrow's last victim."

"Then Crane didn't get out?"

"I was actually about to ask you that. You didn't—"

Gordon shook his head. "We had to grab the hostages and bug out when the lab blew and took the front parlor with it. The whole place came apart after that. You think Crane's dead?"

Batman hesitated before answering, seeming to go inside himself for a moment. "I left him trussed up and cuffed to a piece of ironwork. The lower part of his body was trapped beneath a fall of bricks. I . . . doubt he got out. Hopefully, he never regained consciousness."

Gordon studied the cowled face for a moment, then said, "It wasn't as if you had much choice."

"I suppose I could have left Berwald's body and gone after Crane . . ."

"Could you, really? Cutter said he was in the room directly across the hall from the lab."

Batman grimaced. "Saved by logistics." He jerked his head toward the EMTs. "You're being paged."

"You going to tell me what happened, and why?"

"Tonight . . . maybe."

"You can just call."

"I'll come. It's important."

Gordon nodded and continued on to the ambulance that held Grey Berwald's body.

# EPILOGUE

"A lovely service," said Alfred, closing the driver's door of the Bentley. "Very fitting—the readings from his favorite authors."

He glanced up into the rearview mirror, catching the pensive look on Bruce Wayne's face as he settled into the backseat next to Maggie Tollyer.

"Yes, fitting." Bruce smiled, a bit wanly, Alfred thought. "I bet that was the first time a selection from a horror novel's ever been read at a funeral."

Maggie's smile was a bit brighter. " 'Even larks and katydids are supposed, by some, to dream,' " she quoted softly from Shirley Jackson's *The Haunting of Hill House*. Then, "He wasn't a bad man. Not even a greedy man, except maybe greedy for approval. What was it he said? He just wanted people to say 'wow' a lot. I just wish he'd realized they'd do that without Crane's help."

"From everything I've read, Crane was a master manipulator," said Bruce. "And Grey actually interviewed him at Arkham. I imagine Crane read Grey's insecurities right through the bulletproof glass, and figured out how best to exploit them. Just the way he exploited Ulysses Cutter."

"What happened to old Twitch?" Maggie asked, tilting her head back and closing her eyes.

She looked vulnerable, child-like, and Alfred did not even try to curb his impulse to take her back to Wayne Manor and cook her lobster bisque. "Actually, miss, Mr. Cutter is to be outplaced in a special work-service program. He will be putting his unusual collection of talents to use at WayneTech."

She aimed a startled glance at Bruce, who shrugged.

"I gave him a job. Turns out he's got an affinity for programming. He's self-taught and takes an unusual approach to it, but he's quite good at debugging computer code."

She shook her head. "You . . . puzzle me, Bruce. It's like . . . like you're two different people."

Alfred, stifling amusement, glanced up into the rearview mirror and met answering humor in his employer's eyes.

"At *least* that many," Bruce said. "I'm told I'm a real pain in the ass that way—you never know which Bruce Wayne you're going to get."

"Sounds unsettling," Maggie said.

"Tell you what—you pick the personality you like, that's the one I'll stick with."

Maggie smiled, lighting up all the way to her weary eyes. "This one's pretty nice."

Alfred was as pleased with the tenor of the conversation as he was with the direction it was taking. "Master Bruce, I assume you still wish to return to Wayne Manor for an early repast before I drive Ms. Tollyer home."

The amusement in Bruce Wayne's eyes deepened, possibly because he'd made no such plans—Alfred had just made them up.

"You assume correctly, Alfred. And I'll drive Maggie home myself. That is—" He turned to look at the young woman. "—if she's agreeable."

"I'd like that, thanks. Being alone right now isn't particularly appetizing."

"Then I shall hope," Alfred said, "that my lobster bisque and fillet of salmon will be."

He turned his attention to the road, listening with half an ear to the conversation behind him. In his social set, it wasn't often that Bruce Wayne connected with a woman who was both intelligent and goodhearted. Intelligence was often coupled with cunning and acquisitiveness. And beauty was a veneer that often masked vanity and selfishness.

"You know," said Maggie as they turned into the long, wooded drive of Wayne Manor, "someone still owes me a roller-coaster ride and a day at Six Flags Over Gotham."

"Really?" Bruce glanced up at their driver. "Alfred, did you promise Maggie a roller-coaster ride?"

"Oh, not I, sir. You know me. I prefer the sedentary life. I avoid excitement at all costs."

Bruce sighed. "Then I suppose it must have been one of my other personalities. Never fear, Maggie-the-Cat, I intend to honor his commitment. It may be one of the smarter things he's done lately." He hesitated a moment then said, more solemnly, "Do you mind if I call you that—Maggie-the-Cat? It . . . suits you."

She canted her head to one side, considering it. "Mind? No, I'd like that. Every time you call me that, I'll think of Grey."

The car swept into the circle before the house, Alfred bringing it to a smooth stop before the front steps.

"Oh, I didn't tell you," Maggie said as he opened the passenger's door and handed her out. "I got a new job. With the *Gotham Gazette*. I applied for an editorial position they had open, but they assigned me—you're gonna love this—to the police blotter." She smiled brightly at Alfred and Bruce as she mounted the marble steps. "You're looking at the *Gazette*'s newest crime-beat reporter. Looks like I'm going to have to keep even closer tabs on Batman from now on."

Moving ahead of them up the grand staircase, she didn't see the look the two men exchanged . . . though she did turn back when Bruce laughed and Alfred emitted an amused cough.

"What?" she said. "What'd I say that was so funny?"

Bruce waved a hand dismissively. "Oh, Batman. Sneaky guy in tights. I'm telling you—he's got serious issues."

"Okay," Maggie said, "you can put this personality back where you got it."

"Yes, ma'am." He saluted, sharing another look with Alfred, then escorted Maggie-the-Cat through the doors of Wayne Manor.

Alfred stopped in the huge foyer, watching Master Bruce accompany their guest toward the upstairs parlor. A brisk breeze slipped beneath the double doors behind him, bringing with it a slight chill. Autumn was sliding into winter; the first big snow was predicted for the beginning of the week.

The world turned on its axis, and the seasons changed. Though one could always hope, Alfred knew that there was little chance of anything lasting between Ms. Tollyer and his employer. They were far too much alike, in far too many ways, not the least of which was the dedication each had to their respective callings—which were also more similar than Maggie, at least, could imagine.

Alfred sighed. It would be wonderful if Master Bruce were to find someone he could share that secret darkness with. Perhaps, someday, he would find the right person.

It might not even be a romantic relationship with a woman; for a short time over the last few weeks, he had thought the friendship with Grey Berwald might have provided Bruce with just such a confidant. He, Alfred, would not be around forever, after all, and, while the connection between Master Bruce and Captain Gordon looked promising, there was still that distance, that mystery, that had to be maintained.

He shrugged, and smiled a slight, sad smile. Ah, well. Things would sort themselves out, as they always did. If Master Bruce was meant to have someone to help him shoulder the burden of that most private part of himself, then it would eventually come to pass.

In the meantime, best he begin thawing the seafood.

As he started for the kitchen, Alfred made a mental note to look into clearing Master Bruce's schedule so that he could escort the lovely Ms. Tollyer to the amusement park she had mentioned. Or if the weather proved too inclement, he had heard that the circus was in town. The thought made the butler's eyes light up. He'd always loved the circus, especially the high-wire and flying trapeze acts. He'd heard that this circus had a particularly good troupe of such daredevils.

Alfred remembered a quote by the late Sister Corita Kent, which he'd always liked: "Damn everything but the circus." Indeed, he thought, and especially roller coasters. He decided that, come what might, he would make sure that Master Bruce and Maggie Tollyer went to the circus.

It would, no doubt, be a night to remember.